CHAPTER I - SHIPW[...]

Once only, in the occasional travelling of thirty years, [...] luggage; and that loss occurred, not under the haphazard, [...] of English, or the elaborate misrule of Continental journeys, but through the absolute perfection and democratic despotism of the American system. I had to give up a visit to the scenery of Cooper's best Indian novels—no slight sacrifice—and hasten at once to New York to repair the loss. This incident brought me, on an evening near the middle of September 1874, on board a river steamboat starting from Albany, the capital of the State, for the Empire City. The banks of the lower Hudson are as well worth seeing as those of the Rhine itself, but even America has not yet devised means of lighting them up at night, and consequently I had no amusement but such as I could find in the conversation of my fellow-travellers. With one of these, whose abstinence from personal questions led me to take him for an Englishman, I spoke of my visit to Niagara—the one wonder of the world that answers its warranty—and to Montreal. As I spoke of the strong and general Canadian feeling of loyalty to the English Crown and connection, a Yankee bystander observed—

"Wal, stranger, I reckon we could take 'em if we wanted tu!"

"Yes," I replied, "if you think them worth the price. But if you do, you rate them even more highly than they rate themselves; and English colonists are not much behind the citizens of the model Republic in honest self-esteem."

"Wal," he said, "how much du yew calc'late we shall hev to pay?"

"Not more, perhaps, than you can afford; only California, and every Atlantic seaport from Portland to Galveston."

"Reckon yew may be about right, stranger," he said, falling back with tolerable good-humour; and, to do them justice, the bystanders seemed to think the retort no worse than the provocation deserved.

"I am sorry," said my friend, "you should have fallen in with so unpleasant a specimen of the character your countrymen ascribe with too much reason to Americans. I have been long in England, and never met with such discourtesy from any one who recognised me as an American."

After this our conversation became less reserved; and I found that I was conversing with one of the most renowned officers of irregular cavalry in the late Confederate service—a service which, in the efficiency, brilliancy, and daring of that especial arm, has never been surpassed since Maharbal's African Light Horse were recognised by friends and foes as the finest corps in the small splendid army of Hannibal.

Colonel A—— (the reader will learn why I give neither his name nor real rank) spoke with some bitterness of the inquisitiveness which rendered it impossible, he said, to trust an American with a secret, and very difficult to keep one without lying. We were presently joined by Major B——, who had been employed during the war in the conduct of many critical communications, and had shown great ingenuity in devising and unravelling ciphers. On this subject a somewhat protracted discussion arose. I inclined to the doctrine of Poe, that no cipher can be devised which cannot be detected by an experienced hand; my friends indicated simple methods of defeating the processes on which decipherers rely.

"Poe's theory," said the Major, "depends upon the frequent recurrence of certain letters, syllables, and brief words in any given language; for instance, of e's and t's, tion and ed, a, and, and the in English. Now it is perfectly easy to introduce abbreviations for each of the common short words and terminations, and equally easy to baffle the decipherer's reliance thereon by inserting meaningless symbols to separate the words; by employing two signs for a common letter, or so arranging your cipher that no one shall without extreme difficulty know which marks stand for single and which for several combined letters, where one letter ends and another begins."

After some debate, Colonel A—— wrote down and handed me two lines in a cipher whose character at once struck me as very remarkable.

"I grant," said I, "that these hieroglyphics might well puzzle a more practised decipherer than myself. Still, I can point out even here a clue which might help detection. There occur, even in these two lines, three or four symbols which, from their size and complication, are evidently abbreviations. Again, the distinct forms are very few, and have obviously been made to serve for different letters by some slight alterations devised upon a fixed rule. In a word, the cipher has been constructed upon a general principle; and though it may take a long time to find out what that principle is, it affords a clue which, carefully followed out, will probably lead to detection."

"You have perceived," said Colonel A——, "a fact which it took me very long to discover. I have not deciphered all the more difficult passages of the manuscript from which I took this example; but I have ascertained the meaning of all its simple characters, and your inference is certainly correct."

Here he stopped abruptly, as if he thought he had said too much, and the subject dropped.

We reached New York early in the morning and separated, having arranged to visit that afternoon a celebrated "spiritual" medium who was then giving séances in the Empire City, and of whom my friend had heard and repeated to me several more or less marvellous stories. Our visit, however, was unsatisfactory; and as we came away Colonel A—— said—

"Well, I suppose this experience confirms you in your disbelief?"

"No," said I. "My first visits have generally been failures, and I have more than once been told that my own temperament is most unfavourable to the success of a seance. Nevertheless, I have in some cases witnessed marvels perfectly inexplicable by known natural laws; and I have heard and read of others attested by evidence I certainly cannot consider inferior to my own."

"Why," he said, "I thought from your conversation last night you were a complete disbeliever."

"I believe," answered I, "in very little of what I have seen. But that little is quite sufficient to dispose of the theory of pure imposture. On the other hand, there is nothing spiritual and nothing very human in the pranks

played by or in the presence of the mediums. They remind one more of the feats of traditional goblins; mischievous, noisy, untrustworthy; insensible to ridicule, apparently delighting to make fools of men, and perfectly indifferent to having the tables turned upon themselves."

"But do you believe in goblins?"

"No," I replied; "no more than in table-turning ghosts, and less than in apparitions. I am not bound to find either sceptics or spiritualists in plausible explanations. But when they insist on an alternative to their respective theories, I suggest Puck as at least equally credible with Satan, Shakespeare, or the parrot-cry of imposture. It is the very extravagance of illogical temper to call on me to furnish an explanation because I say 'we know far too little of the thing itself to guess at its causes;' but of the current guesses, imposture seems inconsistent with the evidence, and

'spiritual agency' with the character of the phenomena."

"That," replied Colonel A——, "sounds common sense, and sounds even more commonplace. And yet, no one seems really to draw a strong, clear line between non-belief and disbelief. And you are the first and only man I ever met who hesitates to affirm the impossibility of that which seems to him wildly improbable, contrary at once to received opinion and to his own experience, and contrary, moreover, to all known natural laws, and all inferences hitherto drawn from them. Your men of science dogmatise like divines, not only on things they have not seen, but on things they refuse to see; and your divines are half of them afraid of Satan, and the other half of science."

"The men of science have," I replied, "like every other class, their especial bias, their peculiar professional temptation. The anti-religious bigotry of Positivists is quite as bitter and irrational as the theological bigotry of religious fanatics. At present the two powers countervail and balance each other. But, as three hundred years ago I should certainly have been burnt for a heretic, so fifty or a hundred years hence, could I live so long, I should be in equal apprehension of being burnt by some successor of Mr.

Congreve, Mr. Harrison, or Professor Huxley, for presuming to believe in Providential government."

"The intolerance of incredulity," returned Colonel A——, "is a sore subject with me. I once witnessed a phenomenon which was to me quite as extraordinary as any of the 'spiritual' performances. I have at this moment in my possession apparently irresistible evidence of the reality of what then took place; and I am sure that there exists at a point on the earth's surface, which unluckily I cannot define, strong corroborative proof of my story.

Nevertheless, the first persons who heard it utterly ridiculed it, and were disposed to treat me either as a madman, or at best as an audacious trespasser on that privilege of lying which belonged to them as mariners. I told it afterwards to three gentlemen of station, character, and intelligence, every one of whom had known me as soldier, and I hope as gentleman, for years; and in each case the result was a duel, which has silenced those who imputed to me an unworthy and purposeless falsehood, but has left a heavy burden on my conscience, and has prevented me ever since from repeating what I know to be true and believe to be of greater interest, and in some sense of greater importance, than any scientific discovery of the last century. Since the last occasion on which I told it seven years have elapsed, and I never have met any one but yourself to whom I have thought it possible to disclose it."

"I have," I answered, "an intense interest in all occult phenomena; believing in regard to alleged magic, as the scientists say of practical science, that every one branch of such knowledge throws light on others; and if there be nothing in your story which it is personally painful to relate, you need not be silenced by any apprehension of discourteous criticism on my part."

"I assure you," he said, "I have no such wish now to tell the story as I had at first. It is now associated with the most painful incident of my life, and I have lost altogether that natural desire for sympathy and human interest in a matter deeply interesting to myself, which, like every one else, I felt at first, and which is, I suppose, the motive that prompts us all to relate often and early any occurrence that has keenly affected us, in whatever manner.

But I think that I have no right to suppress so remarkable a fact, if by telling it I can place it effectually on record for the benefit of men sensible enough to believe that it may have occurred, especially since somewhere in the

world there must yet exist proof that it did occur. If you will come to my rooms in —— Street tomorrow, Number 999, I will not promise, but I think that I shall have made up my mind to tell you what I have to tell, and to place in your hands that portion of the evidence which is still at my command—evidence that has a significance of its own, to which my experience is merely episodical."

I spent that evening with the family of a friend, one of several former officers of the Confederacy, whose friendship is the one permanent and valuable result of my American tour. I mentioned the Colonel's name, and my friend, the head of the family, having served with him through the Virginian campaigns, expressed the highest confidence in his character, the highest opinion of his honour and veracity; but spoke with bitter regret and pain of the duels in which he had been engaged, especially of one which had been fatal; remarking that the motive in each instance remained unknown even to the seconds. "I am sure," he said "that they were not, could not have been, fought for the one cause that would justify them and explain the secrecy of the quarrel—some question involving female honour or reputation. I can hardly conceive that any one of his adversaries could have called in question in any way the personal loyalty of Colonel A——; and, as you remarked of General M——, it is too absurd for a man who had faced over and over again the fire of a whole brigade, who had led charges against fourfold numbers, to prove his personal courage with sword or pistol, or to think that any one would have doubted either his spirit or his nerve had he refused to fight, whatever the provocation. Moreover, in each case he was the challenger."

"Then these duels have injured him in Southern opinion, and have probably tended to isolate him from society?"

"No," he replied. "Deeply as they were regretted and disapproved, his services during the war were so brilliant, and his personal character stands so high, that nothing could have induced his fellow-soldiers to put any social stigma upon him. To me he must know that he would be most welcome. Yet, though we have lived in the same city for five years, I have only encountered him three or four times in the street, and then he has

passed with the fewest possible words, and has neither given me his address nor accepted my urgent invitations to visit us here. I think that there is something in the story of those duels that will never be known, certainly something that has never been guessed yet. And I think that either the circumstances in which they must have had their origin, or the duels themselves, have so weighed upon his spirits, perhaps upon his conscience, that he has chosen to avoid his former friends, most of them also the friends of his antagonists. Though the war ruined him as utterly as any of the thousands of Southern gentlemen whom it has reduced from wealth to absolute poverty, he has refused every employment which would bring him before the public eye."

"Is there," I asked, "any point of honour on which you could suppose him to be so exceptionally sensitive that he would think it necessary to take the life of a man who touched him on that point, though afterwards his regret, if not repentance, might be keen enough to crush his spirit or break his heart?"

The General paused for a moment, and his son then interposed—

"I have heard it said that Colonel A—— was in general the least quarrelsome of Confederate officers; but that on more than one occasion, where his statement upon some point of fact had been challenged by a comrade, who did not intend to question his veracity but simply the accuracy of his observation, their brother officers had much trouble in preventing a serious difficulty."

The next day I called as agreed upon my new-found friend, and with some reluctance he commenced his story.

"During the last campaign, in February 1865, I was sent by General Lee with despatches for Kirby Smith, then commanding beyond the Mississippi. I was unable to return before the surrender, and, for reasons into which I need not enter, I believed myself to be marked out by the Federal Government for vengeance. If I had remained within their reach, I might have shared the fate of Wirz and other victims of calumnies which, once put in circulation during the war, their official authors dared not

retract at its close. Now I and others, who, if captured in 1865, might probably have been hanged, are neither molested nor even suspected of any other offence than that of fighting, as our opponents fought, for the State to which our allegiance was due. However, I thought it necessary to escape before the final surrender of our forces beyond the Mississippi. I made my way to Mexico, and, like one or two Southern officers of greater distinction than myself, entered the service of the Emperor Maximilian, not as mere soldiers of fortune, but because, knowing better than any but her Southern neighbours knew it the miserable anarchy of Mexico under the Republic, we regarded conquest as the one chance of regeneration for that country, and the Emperor Maximilian as a hero who had devoted himself to a task heroic at once in its danger and difficulty—the restoration of a people with whom his house had a certain historical connection to a place among the nations of the civilised world. After his fall, I should certainly have been shot had I been caught by the Juarists in pursuit of me. I gained the Pacific coast, and got on board an English vessel, whose captain—

loading for San Francisco—generously weighed anchor and sailed with but half a cargo to give me a chance of safety. He transferred me a few days afterwards to a Dutch vessel bound for Brisbane, for at that time I thought of settling in Queensland. The crew was weak-handed, and consisted chiefly of Lascars, Malays, and two or three European desperadoes of all languages and of no country. Her master was barely competent to the ordinary duties of his command; and it was no surprise to me when the first storm that we encountered drove us completely out of our course, nor was I much astonished that the captain was for some days, partly from fright and partly from drink, incapable of using his sextant to ascertain the position of the ship. One night we were awakened by a tremendous shock; and, to spare you the details of a shipwreck, which have nothing to do with my story, we found ourselves when day broke fast on a coral reef, about a mile from an island of no great size, and out of sight of all other land. The sextant having been broken to pieces, I had no means of ascertaining the position of this island, nor do I now know anything of it except that it lay, in the month of August, within the region of the southeast trade winds. We pulled on shore, but, after exploring the island, it was found to yield

nothing attractive to seamen except cocoa-nuts, with which our crew had soon supplied themselves as largely as they wished, and fish, which were abundant and easily caught, and of which they were soon tired. The captain, therefore, when he had recovered his sobriety and his courage, had no great difficulty in inducing them to return to the ship, and endeavour either to get her off or construct from her timbers a raft which, following the course of the winds, might, it was thought, bring them into the track of vessels. This would take some time, and I meanwhile was allowed to remain (my own wish) on terra firma; the noise, dirt, and foul smells of the vessel being, especially in that climate, intolerable.

"About ten o'clock in the morning of the 25th August 1867, I was lying towards the southern end of the island, on a little hillock tolerably clear of trees, and facing a sort of glade or avenue, covered only with brush and young trees, which allowed me to see the sky within perhaps twenty degrees of the horizon. Suddenly, looking up, I saw what appeared at first like a brilliant star considerably higher than the sun. It increased in size with amazing rapidity, till, in a very few seconds after its first appearance, it had a very perceptible disc. For an instant it obscured the sun. In another moment a tremendous shock temporarily deprived me of my senses, and I think that more than an hour had elapsed before I recovered them. Sitting up, somewhat confused, and looking around me, I became aware that some strange accident had occurred. In every direction I saw such traces of havoc as I had witnessed more than once when a Confederate force holding an impenetrable woodland had been shelled at random for some hours with the largest guns that the enemy could bring into the field. Trees were torn and broken, branches scattered in all directions, fragments of stone, earth, and coral rock flung all around. Particularly I remember that a piece of metal of considerable size had cut off the tops of two or three trees, and fixed itself at last on what was now the summit of one about a third of whose length had been broken off and lay on the ground. I soon perceived that this miraculous bombardment had proceeded from a point to the north-eastward, the direction in which at that season and hour the sun was visible. Proceeding thitherward, the evidences of destruction became every minute more marked, I might say more universal. Trees had been thrown

down, torn up by the roots, hurled against one another; rocks broken and flung to great distances, some even thrown up in the air, and so reversed in falling that, while again half buried in the soil, they exposed what had been their undermost surface. In a word, before I had gone two miles I saw that the island had sustained a shock which might have been that of an earthquake, which certainly equalled that of the most violent Central American earthquakes in severity, but which had none of the special peculiarities of that kind of natural convulsion. Presently I came upon fragments of a shining pale yellow metal, generally small, but in one or two cases of remarkable size and shape, apparently torn from some sheet of great thickness. In one case I found embedded between two such jagged fragments a piece of remarkably hard impenetrable cement. At last I came to a point from which through the destruction of the trees the sea was visible in the direction in which the ship had lain; but the ship, as in a few moments I satisfied myself, had utterly disappeared. Reaching the beach, I found that the shock had driven the sea far up upon the land; fishes lying fifty yards inland, and everything drenched in salt water. At last, guided by the signs of ever-increasing devastation, I reached the point whence the mischief had proceeded. I can give no idea in words of what I there found.

The earth had been torn open, rooted up as if by a gigantic explosion. In some places sharp-pointed fragments of the coral rock, which at a depth of several feet formed the bed of the island, were discernible far below the actual surface. At others, the surface itself was raised several feet by dèbris of every kind. What I may call the crater—though it was no actual hole, but rather a cavity torn and then filled up by falling fragments—was two or three hundred feet in circumference; and in this space I found considerable masses of the same metallic substance, attached generally to pieces of the cement. After examining and puzzling myself over this strange scene for some time, my next care was to seek traces of the ship and of her crew; and before long I saw just outside the coral reef what had been her bowsprit, and presently, floating on the sea, one of her masts, with the sail attached.

There could be little doubt that the shock had extended to her, had driven her off the reef where she had been fixed into the deep water outside, where she must have sunk immediately, and had broken her spars. No

traces of her crew were to be seen. They had probably been stunned at the same time that they were thrown into deep water; and before I came in sight of the point where she had perished, whatever animal bodies were to be found must have been devoured by the sharks, which abounded in that neighbourhood. Dismay, perplexity, and horror prevented my doing anything to solve my doubts or relieve my astonishment before the sun went down; and during the night my sleep was broken by snatches of horrible dreams and intervals of waking, during which I marvelled over what I had seen, scarcely crediting my memory or my senses. In the morning, I went back to the crater, and with some tools that had been left on shore contrived to dig somewhat deeply among the debris with which it was filled. I found very little that could enlighten me except pieces of glass, of various metals, of wood, some of which seemed apparently to have been portions of furniture; and one damaged but still entire relic, which I preserved and brought away with me."

Here the Colonel removed a newspaper which had covered a portion of his table, and showed me a metallic case beaten out of all shape, but apparently of what had been a silvery colour, very little rusted, though much soiled. This he opened, and I saw at once that it was of enormous thickness and solidity, to which and to favouring circumstances it owed its preservation in the general ruin he described. That it had undergone some severe and violent shock there could be no question. Beside the box lay a less damaged though still seriously injured object, in which I recognised the resemblance of a book of considerable thickness, and bound in metal like that of the case. This I afterwards ascertained beyond doubt to be a metalloid alloy whereof the principal ingredient was aluminium, or some substance so closely resembling it as not to be distinguishable from it by simple chemical tests. A friend to whom I submitted a small portion broken off from the rest expressed no doubt that it was a kind of aluminium bronze, but inclined to believe that it contained no inconsiderable proportion of a metal with which chemists are as yet imperfectly acquainted; perhaps, he said, silicon; certainly something which had given to the alloy a hardness and tenacity unknown to any familiar metallurgical compound.

"This," said my friend, opening the volume, "is a manuscript which was contained in this case when I took it from among the debris of the crater. I should have told you that I found there what I believed to be fragments of human flesh and bone, but so crushed and mangled that I could form no positive conclusion. My next care was to escape from the island, which I felt sure lay far from the ordinary course of merchant vessels. A boat which had brought me ashore—the smaller of the two belonging to the ship—had fortunately been left on the end of the island furthest from that on which the vessel had been driven, and had, owing to its remoteness, though damaged, not been fatally injured by the shock. I repaired this, made and fixed a mast, and with no little difficulty contrived to manufacture a sort of sail from strips of bark woven together. Knowing that, even if I could sustain life on the island, life under such circumstances would not be worth having, I was perfectly willing to embark upon a voyage in which I was well aware the chances of death were at least as five to one. I caught and contrived to smoke a quantity of fish sufficient to last me for a fortnight, and filled a small cask with brackish but still drinkable water. In this vessel, thus stored, I embarked about a fortnight after the day of the mysterious shock. On the second evening of my voyage I was caught by a gale which compelled me to lower the sail, and before which I was driven for three days and nights, in what direction I can hardly guess. On the fourth morning the wind had fallen, and by noon it was a perfect calm. I need not describe what has been described by so many shipwrecked sailors,—the sufferings of a solitary voyager in an open boat under a tropical sun. The storm had supplied me with water more than enough; so that I was spared that arch-torture of thirst which seems, in the memory of such sufferers, to absorb all others. Towards evening a slight breeze sprang up, and by morning I came in sight of a vessel, which I contrived to board.

Her crew, however, and even her captain, utterly discredited such part of my strange story as I told them. On that point, however, I will say no more than this: I will place this manuscript in your hands. I will give you the key to such of its ciphers as I have been able to make out. The language, I believe, for I am no scholar, is Latin of a mediæval type; but there are words which, if I rightly decipher them, are not Latin, and hardly seem to

belong to any known language; most of them, I fancy, quasi-scientific terms, invented to describe various technical devices unknown to the world when the manuscript was written. I only make it a condition that you shall not publish the story during my life; that if you show the manuscript or mention the tale in confidence to any one, you will strictly keep my secret; and that if after my death, of which you shall be advised, you do publish it, you will afford no clue by which the donor could be confidently identified."

"I promise," said I. "But I should like to ask you one question. What do you conceive to have been the cause of the extraordinary shock you felt and of the havoc you witnessed? What, in short, the nature of the occurrence and the origin of the manuscript you entrust to my care?"

"Why need you ask me?" he returned. "You are as capable as myself of drawing a deduction from what I have told you, and I have told you everything, I believe, that could assist you. The manuscript will tell the rest."

"But," said I, "an actual eye-witness often receives from a number of little facts which he cannot remember, which are perhaps too minute to have been actually and individually noted by him, an impression which is more likely to be correct than any that could be formed by a stranger on the fullest cross-questioning, on the closest examination of what remains in the witness's memory. I should like to hear, before opening the manuscript, what you believe to have been its origin.

"I can only say," he answered, "that what must be inferred from the manuscript is what I had inferred before I opened it. That same explanation was the only one that ever occurred to me, even in the first night. It then seemed to me utterly incredible, but it is still the only conceivable explanation that my mind can suggest."

"Did you," asked I, "connect the shock and the relics, which I presume you know were not on the island before the shock, with the meteor and the strange obscuration of the sun?"

"I certainly did," he said. "Having done so, there could be but one conclusion as to the quarter from which the shock was received."

The examination and transcription of the manuscript, with all the help afforded me by my friend's previous efforts, was the work of several years.

There is, as the reader will see, more than one hiatus valde deflendus, as the scholiasts have it, and there are passages in which, whether from the illegibility of the manuscript or the employment of technical terms unknown to me, I cannot be certain of the correctness of my translation.

Such, however, as it is, I give it to the world, having fulfilled, I believe, every one of the conditions imposed upon me by my late and deeply regretted friend.

The character of the manuscript is very curious, and its translation was exceedingly difficult. The material on which it is written resembles nothing used for such purposes on Earth. It is more like a very fine linen or silken web, but it is far closer in texture, and has never been woven in any kind of loom at all like those employed in any manufacture known to history or archaeology. The letters, or more properly symbols, are minute, but executed with extraordinary clearness. I should fancy that something more like a pencil than a pen, but with a finer point than that of the finest pencil, was employed in the writing. Contractions and combinations are not merely frequent, but almost universal. There is scarcely an instance in which five consecutive letters are separately written, and there is no single line in which half a dozen contractions, often including from four to ten letters, do not occur. The pages are of the size of an ordinary duodecimo, but contain some fifty lines per page, and perhaps one hundred and fifty letters in each line. What were probably the first half dozen pages have been utterly destroyed, and the next half dozen are so mashed, tattered, and defaced, that only a few sentences here and there are legible. I have contrived, however, to combine these into what I believe to be a substantially correct representation of the author's meaning. The Latin is of a monastic—sometimes almost canine—quality, with many words which are not Latin at all. For the rest, though here and there pages are illegible, and though some symbols, especially those representing numbers or

chemical compounds, are absolutely undecipherable, it has been possible to effect what I hope will be found a clear and coherent translation. I have condensed the narrative but have not altered or suppressed a line for fear of offending those who must be unreasonable, indeed, if they lay the offence to my charge.

One word more. It is possible, if not likely, that some of those friends of the narrator, for whom the account was evidently written, may still be living, and that these pages may meet their eyes. If so, they may be able to solve the few problems that have entirely baffled me, and to explain, if they so choose, the secrets to which, intentionally or through the destruction of its introductory portion, the manuscript affords no clue.

I must add that these volumes contain only the first section of the MS.

record. The rest, relating the incidents of a second voyage and describing another world, remains in my hands; and, should this part of the work excite general attention, the conclusion will, by myself or by my executors, be given to the public. Otherwise, on my death, it will be placed in the library of some national or scientific institution.

CHAPTER II - OUTWARD BOUND.

… For obvious reasons, those who possessed the secret of the Apergy had never dreamed of applying it in the manner I proposed. It had seemed to them little more than a curious secret of nature, perhaps hardly so much, since the existence of a repulsive force in the atomic sphere had been long suspected and of late certainly ascertained, and its preponderance is held to be the characteristic of the gaseous as distinguished from the liquid or solid state of matter. Till lately, no means of generating or collecting this force in large quantity had been found. The progress of electrical science had solved this difficulty; and when the secret was communicated to me, it possessed a value which had never before belonged to it.

Ever since, in childhood, I learnt that the planets were worlds, a visit to one or more of the nearest of them had been my favourite day-dream.

Treasuring every hint afforded by science or fancy that bore upon the subject, I felt confident that such a voyage would be one day achieved.

Helped by one or two really ingenious romances on this theme, I had dreamed out my dream, realised every difficulty, ascertained every factor in the problem. I had satisfied myself that only one thing needful was as yet wholly beyond the reach and even the proximate hopes of science.

Human invention could furnish as yet no motive power that could fulfil the main requirement of the problem—uniform or constantly increasing motion in vacuo—motion through a region affording no resisting medium.

This must be a repulsive energy capable of acting through an utter void.

Man, animals, birds, fishes move by repulsion applied at every moment. In air or water, paddles, oars, sails, fins, wings act by repulsion exerted on the fluid element in which they work. But in space there is no such resisting element on which repulsion can operate. I needed a repulsion which would act like gravitation through an indefinite distance and in a void—act upon a remote fulcrum, such as might be the Earth in a voyage to the Moon, or the Sun in a more distant journey. As soon, then, as the character of the apergic force was made known to me, its application to this purpose seized on my mind. Experiment had proved it possible, by the method described at the commencement of this record, to generate and collect it in amounts

practically unlimited. The other hindrances to a voyage through space were trivial in comparison with that thus overcome; there were difficulties to be surmounted, not absent or deficient powers in nature to be discovered. The chief of these, of course, concerned the conveyance of air sufficient for the needs of the traveller during the period of his journey. The construction of an air-tight vessel was easy enough; but however large the body of air conveyed, even though its oxygen should not be exhausted, the carbonic acid given out by breathing would very soon so contaminate the whole that life would be impossible. To eliminate this element it would only be necessary to carry a certain quantity of lime-water, easily calculated, and by means of a fan or similar instrument to drive the whole of the air periodically through the vessel containing it. The lime in solution combining with the noxious gas would show by the turbid whiteness of the water the absorption of the carbonic acid and formation of carbonate of lime. But if the carbonic acid gas were merely to be removed, it is obvious that the oxygen of the air, which forms a part of that gas, would be constantly diminished and ultimately exhausted; and the effect of highly oxygenated air upon the circulation is notoriously too great to allow of any considerable increase at the outset in the proportion of this element. I might carry a fresh supply of oxygen, available at need, in some solid combination like chlorate of potash; but the electricity employed for the generation of the apergy might be also applied to the decomposition of carbonic acid and the restoration of its oxygen to the atmosphere.

But the vessel had to be steered as well as propelled; and in order to accomplish this it would be necessary to command the direction of the apergy at pleasure. My means of doing this depended on two of the best-established peculiarities of this strange force: its rectilinear direction and its conductibility. We found that it acts through air or in a vacuum in a single straight line, without deflection, and seemingly without diminution. Most solids, and especially metals, according to their electric condition, are more or less impervious to it—antapergic. Its power of penetration diminishes under a very obscure law, but so rapidly that no conceivable strength of current would affect an object protected by an intervening sheet half an inch in thickness. On the other hand, it prefers to all other lines the axis of a

conductive bar, such as may be formed of [undecipherable] in an antapergic sheath. However such bar may be curved, bent, or divided, the current will fill and follow it, and pursue indefinitely, without divergence, diffusion, or loss, the direction in which it emerges. Therefore, by collecting the current from the generator in a vessel cased with antapergic material, and leaving no other aperture, its entire volume might be sent into a conductor. By cutting across this conductor, and causing the further part to rotate upon the nearer, I could divert the current through any required angle. Thus I could turn the repulsion upon the resistant body (sun or planet), and so propel the vessel in any direction I pleased.

I had determined that my first attempt should be a visit to Mars. The Moon is a far less interesting body, since, on the hemisphere turned towards the Earth, the absence of an atmosphere and of water ensures the absence of any such life as is known to us—probably of any life that could be discerned by our senses—and would prevent landing; while nearly all the soundest astronomers agree in believing, on apparently sufficient grounds, that even the opposite hemisphere [of which small portions are from time to time rendered visible by the libration, though greatly foreshortened and consequently somewhat imperfectly seen] is equally devoid of the two primary necessaries of animal and vegetable life. That Mars has seas, clouds, and an atmosphere was generally admitted, and I held it to be beyond question. Of Venus, owing to her extraordinary brilliancy, to the fact that when nearest to the Earth a very small portion of her lighted surface is visible to us, and above all to her dense cloud-envelope, very little was known; and though I cherished the intention to visit her even more earnestly than my resolve to reach the probably less attractive planet Mars, I determined to begin with that voyage of which the conditions and the probable result were most obvious and certain. I preferred, moreover, in the first instance, to employ the apergy as a propelling rather than as a resisting force. Now, after passing beyond the immediate sphere of the Earth's attraction, it is plain that in going towards Mars I should be departing from the Sun, relying upon the apergy to overcome his attraction; whereas in seeking to attain Venus I should be approaching the Sun, relying for my main motive power upon that tremendous attraction,

and employing the apergy only to moderate the rate of movement and control its direction. The latter appeared to me the more delicate, difficult, and perhaps dangerous task of the two; and I resolved to defer it until after I had acquired some practical experience and dexterity in the control of my machinery.

It was expedient, of course, to make my vessel as light as possible, and, at the same time, as large as considerations of weight would admit. But it was of paramount importance to have walls of great thickness, in order to prevent the penetration of the outer cold of space, or rather the outward passage into that intense cold of the heat generated within the vessel itself, as well as to resist the tremendous outward pressure of the air inside.

Partly for these reasons, and partly because its electric character makes it especially capable of being rendered at will pervious or impervious to the apergic current, I resolved to make the outer and inner walls of an alloy of

…, while the space between should be filled up with a mass of concrete or cement, in its nature less penetrable to heat than any other substance which Nature has furnished or the wit of man constructed from her materials. The materials of this cement and their proportions were as follows.

Briefly, having determined to take advantage of the approaching opposition of Mars in MDCCCXX … , I had my vessel constructed with walls three feet thick, of which the outer six and the inner three inches were formed of the metalloid. In shape my Astronaut somewhat resembled the form of an antique Dutch East-Indiaman, being widest and longest in a plane equidistant from floor and ceiling, the sides and ends sloping outwards from the floor and again inwards towards the roof. The deck and keel, however, were absolutely flat, and each one hundred feet in length and fifty in breadth, the height of the vessel being about twenty feet. In the centre of the floor and in that of the roof respectively I placed a large lens of crystal, intended to act as a window in the first instance, the lower to admit the rays of the Sun, while through the upper I should discern the star towards which I was steering. The floor, being much heavier than the rest of the vessel, would naturally be turned downwards; that is, during the greater part of the voyage towards the Sun. I placed a similar lens in the

centre of each of the four sides, with two plane windows of the same material, one in the upper, the other in the lower half of the wall, to enable me to discern any object in whatever direction. The crystal in question consisted of ..., which, as those who manufactured it for me are aware, admits of being cast with a perfection and equality of structure throughout unattainable with ordinary glass, and wrought to a certainty and accuracy of curvature which the most patient and laborious polishing can hardly give to the lenses even of moderate-sized telescopes, whether made of glass or metal, and is singularly impervious to heat. I had so calculated the curvature that several eye-pieces of different magnifying powers which I carried with me might be adapted equally to any of the window lenses, and throw a perfect image, magnified by 100, 1000, or 5000, upon mirrors properly placed.

I carpeted the floor with several alternate layers of cork and cloth. At one end I placed my couch, table, bookshelves, and other necessary furniture, with all the stores needed for my voyage, and with a further weight sufficient to preserve equilibrium. At the other I made a garden with soil three feet deep and five feet in width, divided into two parts so as to permit access to the windows. I filled each garden closely with shrubs and flowering plants of the greatest possible variety, partly to absorb animal waste, partly in the hope of naturalising them elsewhere. Covering both with wire netting extending from the roof to the floor, I filled the cages thus formed with a variety of birds. In the centre of the vessel was the machinery, occupying altogether a space of about thirty feet by twenty. The larger portion of this area was, of course, taken up by the generator, above which was the receptacle of the apergy. From this descended right through the floor a conducting bar in an antapergic sheath, so divided that without separating it from the upper portion the lower might revolve in any direction through an angle of twenty minutes (20'). This, of course, was intended to direct the stream of the repulsive force against the Sun. The angle might have been extended to thirty minutes, but that I deemed it inexpedient to rely upon a force, directed against the outer portions of the Sun's disc, believing that these are occupied by matter of density so small that it might afford no sufficient base, so to speak, for the repulsive action.

It was obviously necessary also to repel or counteract the attraction of any body which might come near me during the voyage. Again, in getting free from the Earth's influence, I must be able to steer in any direction and at any angle to the surface. For this purpose I placed five smaller bars, passing through the roof and four sides, connected, like the main conductor, with the receptacle or apergion, but so that they could revolve through a much larger angle, and could at any moment be detached and insulated. My steering apparatus consisted of a table in which were three large circles. The midmost and left hand of these were occupied by accurately polished plane mirrors. The central circle, or metacompass, was divided by three hundred and sixty fine lines, radiating from the centre to the circumference, marking as many different directions, each deviating by one degree of arc from the next. This mirror was to receive through the lens in the roof the image of the star towards which I was steering. While this remained stationary in the centre all was well. When it moved along any one of the lines, the vessel was obviously deviating from her course in the opposite direction; and, to recover the right course, the repellent force must be caused to drive her in the direction in which the image had moved. To accomplish this, a helm was attached to the lower division of the main conductor, by which the latter could be made to move at will in any direction within the limit of its rotation. Controlling this helm was, in the open or steering circle on the right hand, a small knob to be moved exactly parallel to the deviation of the star in the mirror of the metacompass. The left-hand circle, or discometer, was divided by nineteen hundred and twenty concentric circles, equidistant from each other. The outermost, about twice as far from the centre as from the external edge of the mirror, was exactly equal to the Sun's circumference when presenting the largest disc he ever shows to an observer on Earth. Each inner circle corresponded to a diameter reduced by one second. By means of a vernier or eye-piece, the diameter of the Sun could be read off the discometer, and from his diameter my distance could be accurately calculated. On the further side of the machinery was a chamber for the decomposition of the carbonic acid, through which the air was driven by a fan. This fan itself was worked by a horizontal wheel with two projecting squares of antapergic metal, against

each of which, as it reached a certain point, a very small stream of repulsive force was directed from the apergion, keeping the wheel in constant and rapid motion. I had, of course, supplied myself with an ample store of compressed vegetables, preserved meats, milk, tea, coffee, &c., and a supply of water sufficient to last for double the period which the voyage was expected to occupy; also a well-furnished tool-chest (with wires, tubes,

&c.). One of the lower windows was made just large enough to admit my person, and after entering I had to close it and fix it in its place firmly with cement, which, when I wished to quit the vessel, would have again to be removed.

Of course some months were occupied in the manufacture of the different portions of the vessel and her machinery, and sometime more in their combination; so that when, at the end of July, I was ready to start, the opposition was rapidly approaching. In the course of some fifty days the Earth, moving in her orbit at a rate of about eleven hundred miles per minute, would overtake Mars; that is to say, would pass between him and the Sun. In starting from the Earth I should share this motion; I too should go eleven hundred miles a minute in the same direction; but as I should travel along an orbit constantly widening, the Earth would leave me behind. The apergy had to make up for this, as well as to carry me some forty millions of miles in a direction at right angles to the former—right outward towards the orbit of Mars. Again, I should share the motion of that particular spot of the Earth's surface from which I rose around her axis, a motion varying with the latitude, greatest at the equator, nothing at the pole. This would whirl me round and round the Earth at the rate of a thousand miles an hour; of this I must, of course, get rid as soon as possible. And when I should be rid of it, I meant to start at first right upward; that is, straight away from the Sun and in the plane of the ecliptic, which is not very different from that in which Mars also moves. Therefore I should begin my effective ascent from a point of the Earth as far as possible from the Sun; that is, on the midnight meridian.

For the same reason which led me to start so long before the date of the opposition, I resolved, having regard to the action of the Earth's rotation on

her axis, to start some hours before midnight. Taking leave, then, of the two friends who had thus far assisted me, I entered the Astronaut on the 1st August, about 4.30 P.M. After sealing up the entrance-window, and ascertaining carefully that everything was in order—a task which occupied me about an hour—I set the generator to work; and when I had ascertained that the apergion was full, and that the force was supplied at the required rate, I directed the whole at first into the main conductor. After doing this I turned towards the lower window on the west—or, as it was then, the right-hand side—and was in time to catch sight of the trees on the hills, some half mile off and about two hundred feet above the level of my starting-point. I should have said that I had considerably compressed my atmosphere and increased the proportion of oxygen by about ten per cent., and also carried with me the means of reproducing the whole amount of the latter in case of need. Among my instruments was a pressure-gauge, so minutely divided that, with a movable vernier of the same power as the fixed ones employed to read the glass circles, I could discover the slightest escape of air in a very few seconds. The pressure-gauge, however, remained immovable. Going close to the window and looking out, I saw the Earth falling from me so fast that, within five minutes after my departure, objects like trees and even houses had become almost indistinguishable to the naked eye. I had half expected to hear the whistling of the air as the vessel rushed upward, but nothing of the kind was perceptible through her dense walls. It was strange to observe the rapid rise of the sun from the westward. Still more remarkable, on turning to the upper window, was the rapidly blackening aspect of the sky.

Suddenly everything disappeared except a brilliant rainbow at some little distance—or perhaps I should rather have said a halo of more than ordinary rainbow brilliancy, since it occupied, not like the rainbows seen from below, something less than half, but nearly two-thirds of a circle. I was, of course, aware that I was passing through a cloud, and one of very unusual thickness. In a few seconds, however, I was looking down upon its upper surface, reflecting from a thousand broken masses of vapour at different levels, from cavities and hillocks of mist, the light of the sun; white beams mixed with innumerable rays of all colours in a confusion, of

indescribable brilliancy. I presume that the total obscuration of everything outside the cloud during my passage through it was due to its extent and not to its density, since at that height it could not have been otherwise than exceedingly light and diffuse. Looking upward through the eastern window, I could now discern a number of brighter stars, and at nearly every moment fresh ones came into view on a constantly darkening background. Looking downward to the west, where alone the entire landscape lay in daylight, I presently discerned the outline of shore and sea extending over a semicircle whose radius much exceeded five hundred miles, implying that I was about thirty-five miles from the sea-level. Even at this height the extent of my survey was so great in comparison to my elevation, that a line drawn from the vessel to the horizon was, though very roughly, almost parallel to the surface; and the horizon therefore seemed to be not very far from my own level, while the point below me, of course, appeared at a vast distance. The appearance of the surface, therefore, was as if the horizon had been, say, some thirty miles higher than the centre of the semicircle bounding my view, and the area included in my prospect had the form of a saucer or shallow bowl. But since the diameter of the visible surface increases only as the square root of the height, this appearance became less and less perceptible as I rose higher. It had taken me twenty minutes to attain the elevation of thirty-five miles; but my speed was, of course, constantly increasing, very much as the speed of an object falling to the Earth from a great height increases; and before ten more minutes had elapsed, I found myself surrounded by a blackness nearly absolute, except in the direction of the Sun,—which was still well above the sea—and immediately round the terrestrial horizon, on which rested a ring of sunlit azure sky, broken here and there by clouds. In every other direction I seemed to be looking not merely upon a black or almost black sky, but into close surrounding darkness. Amid this darkness, however, were visible innumerable points of light, more or less brilliant—

the stars—which no longer seemed to be spangled over the surface of a distant vault, but rather scattered immediately about me, nearer or farther to the instinctive apprehension of the eye as they were brighter or fainter.

Scintillation there was none, except in the immediate vicinity of the eastern

horizon, where I still saw them through a dense atmosphere. In short, before thirty minutes had elapsed since the start, I was satisfied that I had passed entirely out of the atmosphere, and had entered into the vacancy of space—if such a thing as vacant space there be.

At this point I had to cut off the greater part of the apergy and check my speed, for reasons that will be presently apparent. I had started in daylight in order that during the first hundred miles of my ascent I might have a clear view of the Earth's surface. Not only did I wish to enjoy the spectacle, but as I had to direct my course by terrestrial landmarks, it was necessary that I should be able to see these so as to determine the rate and direction of the Astronaut's motion, and discern the first symptoms of any possible danger. But obviously, since my course lay generally in the plane of the ecliptic, and for the present at least nearly in the line joining the centres of the Earth and Sun, it was desirable that my real journey into space should commence in the plane of the midnight meridian; that is, from above the part of the Earth's surface immediately opposite the Sun. I had to reach this line, and having reached it, to remain for some time above it. To do both, I must attain it, if possible, at the same moment at which I secured a westward impulse just sufficient to counterbalance the eastward impulse derived from the rotation of the Earth;—that is, in the latitude from which I started, a thousand miles an hour. I had calculated that while directing through the main bar a current of apergy sufficient to keep the Astronaut at a fixed elevation, I could easily spare for the eastward conductor sufficient force to create in the space of one hour the impulse required, but that in the course of that hour the gradually increasing apergic force would drive me 500 miles westward. Now in six hours the Earth's rotation would carry an object close to its surface through an angle of 90°; that is, from the sunset to the midnight meridian. But the greater the elevation of the object the wider its orbit round the Earth's centre, and the longer each degree; so that moving eastward only a thousand miles an hour, I should constantly lag behind a point on the Earth's surface, and should not reach the midnight meridian till somewhat later. I had, moreover, to lose 500 miles of the eastward drift during the last hour in which I should be subject to it, through the action of the apergic force above-mentioned. Now, an

elevation of 330 miles would give the Astronaut an orbit on which 90°

would represent 6500 miles. In seven hours I should be carried along that orbit 7000 miles eastward by the impulse my Astronaut had received from the Earth, and driven back 500 miles by the apergy; so that at 1 A.M. by my chronometer I should be exactly in the plane of the midnight meridian, or 6500 miles east of my starting-point in space, provided that I put the eastward apergic current in action exactly at 12 P.M. by the chronometer.

At 1 A.M. also I should have generated a westward impulse of 1000 miles an hour. This, once created, would continue to exist though the force that created it were cut off, and would exactly counterbalance the opposite rotation impulse derived from the Earth; so that thenceforward I should be entirely free from the influence of the latter, though still sharing that motion of the Earth through space at the rate of nearly nineteen miles per second, which would carry me towards the line joining at the moment of opposition her centre with that of Mars.

All went as I had calculated. I contrived to arrest the Astronaut's motion at the required elevation just about the moment of sunset on the region of the Earth immediately underneath. At 12 P.M., or 24h by the chronometer, I directed a current of the requisite strength into the eastward conductor, which I had previously pointed to the Earth's surface, but a little short of the extreme terrestrial horizon, as I calculated it. At 1 A.M. I found myself, judging by the stars, exactly where I wished to be, and nearly stationary as regarded the Earth. I instantly arrested the eastward current, detaching that conductor from the apergion; and, directing the whole force of the current into the downward conductor, I had the pleasure of seeing that, after a very little adjustment of the helm, the stars remained stationary in the mirror of the metacompass, showing that I had escaped from the influence of the Earth's rotation. It was of course impossible to measure the distance traversed during the invisibility of the Earth, but I reckoned that I had made above 500 miles between 1h. and 2h. A.M., and that at 4h. I was not less than 4800 miles from the surface. With this inference the indication of my barycrite substantially agreed. The latter instrument consisted of a spring whose deflection by a given weight upon the equator had been very carefully tested. Gravity diminishing as the square of the distance from the

centre, it was obvious that at about 8000 miles—or 4000 above the Earth's surface—this spring would be deflected only one quarter as much by a given weight as on Earth: at 16,000 miles from the surface, or 20,000 from the centre, one-twenty-fifth as much, and so on. I had graduated the scale accordingly, and it indicated at present a distance somewhat less than 9000 miles from the centre. Having adjusted the helm and set the alarum to wake me in six hours, I lay down upon my bed.

The anxiety and peril of my position had disturbed me very little whilst I was actively engaged either in steering and manipulating my machinery, or in looking upon the marvellous and novel spectacles presented to my eyes; but it now oppressed me in my sleep, and caused me frequently to wake from dreams of a hideous character. Two or three times, on such awaking, I went to examine the metacompass, and on one occasion found it necessary slightly to readjust the helm; the stars by which I steered having moved some second or two to the right of their proper position.

On rising, I completed the circuit which filled my vessel with brilliant light emitted from an electric lamp at the upper part of the stern, and reflected by the polished metallic walls. I then proceeded to get my breakfast, for which, as I had tasted nothing since some hours before the start, I had a hearty appetite. I had anticipated some trouble from the diminished action of gravity, doubting whether the boiling-point at this immense height above the Earth might not be affected; but I found that this depends upon the pressure of the atmosphere alone, and that this pressure was in nowise affected by the absence of gravity. My atmosphere being somewhat denser than that of the Earth, the boiling-point was not 100°, but 101° Cent. The temperature of the interior of the vessel, taken at a point equidistant from the stove and from the walls, was about 5° C.; unpleasantly cool, but still, with the help of a greatcoat, not inconveniently so. I found it absolutely impossible to measure by means of the thermometers I had placed outside the windows the cold of space; but that it falls far short of the extreme supposed by some writers, I confidently believe. It is, however, cold enough to freeze mercury, and to reduce every other substance employed as a test of atmospheric or laboratory temperatures to a solidity which

admits of no further contraction. I had filled one outside thermometer with spirit, but this was broken before I looked at it; and in another, whose bulb unfortunately was blackened, and which was filled with carbonic acid gas, an apparent vacuum had been created. Was it that the gas had been frozen, and had sunk into the lower part of the bulb, where it would, of course, be invisible? When I had completed my meal and smoked the very small cigar which alone a prudent consideration for the state of the atmosphere would allow me, the chronometer showed 10 A.M. It was not surprising that by this time weight had become almost non-existent. My twelve stone had dwindled to the weight of a small fowl, and hooking my little finger into the loop of a string hung from a peg fixed near the top of the stern wall, I found myself able thus to support my weight without any sense of fatigue for a quarter of an hour or more; in fact, I felt during that time absolutely no sense of muscular weariness. This state of things entailed only one inconvenience. Nothing had any stability; so that the slightest push or jerk would upset everything that was not fixed. However, I had so far anticipated this that nothing of any material consequence was unfixed, and except that a touch with my spoon upset the egg-cup and egg on which I was about to breakfast, and that this, falling against a breakfast cup full of coffee, overturned that, I was not incommoded. I managed to save the greater part of the beverage, since, the atmospheric pressure being the same though the weight was so changed, lead, and still more china or liquid, fell in the Astronaut as slowly as feathers in the immediate vicinity of the Earth. Still it was a novel experience to find myself able to lean in any direction, and rest in almost any posture, with but the slightest support for the body's centre of gravity; and further to find on experiment that it was possible to remain for a couple of hours with my heels above my head, in the favourite position of a Yankee's lower limbs, without any perceptible congestion of blood or confusion of brain.

I was occupied all day with abstract calculations; and knowing that for some time I could see nothing of the Earth—her dark side being opposite me and wholly obscuring the Sun, while I was as yet far from having entered within the sphere where any novel celestial phenomena might be expected—I only gave an occasional glance at the discometer and metacompass, suppressing of course the electric glare within my vessel, till I awoke from a short siesta about 19h. (7 P.M.) The Earth at this time occupied on the sphere of view a space—defined at first only by the absence of stars—about thirty times greater than the disc of the Moon as seen through a tube; but, being dark, scarcely seemed larger to the eye than the full Moon when on the horizon. But a new method of defining its disc was presently afforded me. I was, in fact, when looking through the lower window, in the same position as regards the Earth as would be an inhabitant of the lunar hemisphere turned towards her, having no external atmosphere interposed between us, but being at about two-thirds of the lunar distance. And as, during an eclipse, the Lunarian would see round the Earth a halo created by the refraction of the Sun's rays in the terrestrial atmosphere—a halo bright enough on most occasions so to illuminate the Moon as to render her visible to us—so to my eyes the Earth was surrounded by a halo somewhat resembling the solar corona as seen in eclipses, if not nearly so brilliant, but, unlike the solar corona, coloured, with a preponderance of red so decided as fully to account for the peculiar hue of the eclipsed Moon. To paint this, unless means of painting light—

the one great deficiency which is still the opprobrium of human art—were discovered, would task to the uttermost the powers of the ablest artist, and at best he could give but a very imperfect notion of it. To describe it so that its beauty, brilliancy, and wondrous nature shall be in the slightest degree appreciated by my readers would require a command of words such as no poet since Homer—nay, not Homer himself—possessed. What was strange, and can perhaps be rendered intelligible, was the variation, or, to use a phrase more suggestive and more natural, if not more accurate, the extreme mobility of the hues of this earthly corona. There were none of the efflorescences, if one may so term them, which are so generally visible at four cardinal points of its solar prototype. The outer portion of the band faded very rapidly into the darkness of space; but the edge, though absolutely undefined, was perfectly even. But on the generally rainbow-tinted ground suffused with red—which perhaps might best be described by calling it a rainbow seen on a background of brilliant crimson—there were here and there blotches of black or of lighter or darker grey, caused

apparently by vast expanses of cloud, more or less dense. Round the edges of each of these were little irregular rainbow-coloured halos of their own interrupting and variegating the continuous bands of the corona; while throughout all was discernible a perpetual variability, like the flashing or shooting of colour in the opal, the mother-of-pearl, or similarly tinted translucent substances when exposed to the irregular play of bright light—

only that in this case the tints were incomparably more brilliant, the change more striking, if not more rapid. I could not say that at any particular moment any point or part of the surface presented this or that definite hue; and yet the general character of the rainbow, suffused with or backed by crimson, was constant and unmistakable. The light sent through the window was too dim and too imperfectly diffused within my vessel to be serviceable, but for some time I put out the electric lamp in order that its diffused light should not impair my view of this exquisite spectacle. As thrown, after several reflections, upon the mirror destined afterwards to measure the image of the solar disc, the apparition of the halo was of course much less bright, and its outer boundary ill defined for accurate measurement. The inner edge, where the light was bounded by the black disc of the Earth, shaded off much more quickly from dark reddish purple into absolute blackness.

And now a surprise, the first I had encountered, awaited me. I registered the gravity as shown by the barycrite; and, extinguishing the electric lamp, measured repeatedly the semi-diameter of the Earth and of the halo around her upon the discometer, the inner edge of the latter affording the measurement of the black disc, which of itself, of course, cast no reflection.

I saw at once that there was a signal difference in the two indications, and proceeded carefully to revise the earth-measurements. On the average of thirteen measures the halo was about 87", or nearly 1-1/2' in breadth, the disc, allowing for the twilight round its edge or limb, about 2° 50'. If the refracting atmosphere were some 65 miles in depth, these proportions were correct. Relighting the lamp, I worked out severally on paper the results indicated by the two instruments. The discometer gave a distance, roughly speaking, of 40 terrestrial radii, or 160,000 miles. The barycrite should have shown a gravity, due to the Earth's attraction, not 40 but 1600 times less

than that prevailing on the Earth's surface; or, to put it in a less accurate form, a weight of 100 lbs. should have weighed an ounce. It did weigh two ounces, the gravity being not one 1600th but one 800th of terrestrial gravity, or just double what, I expected. I puzzled myself over this matter longer, probably, than the intelligent reader will do: the explanation being obvious, like that of many puzzles that bewilder our minds intensely, only to humiliate us proportionately when the solution is found—a solution as simple as that of Columbus's egg-riddle. At length, finding that the lunar angle—the apparent position of the Moon—confirmed the reading of the discometer, giving the same apogaic distance or elevation, I supposed that the barycrite must be out of order or subject to some unsuspected law of which future observations might afford evidence and explanation, and turned to other subjects of interest.

Looking through the upper window on the left, I was struck by the rapid enlargement of a star which, when I first noticed it, might be of the third magnitude, but which in less than a minute attained the first, and in a minute more was as large as the planet Jupiter when seen with a magnifying power of one hundred diameters.

Its disc, however, had no continuous outline; and as it approached I perceived that it was an irregular mass of whose size I could form not even a conjectural estimate, since its distance must be absolutely uncertain. Its brilliancy grew fainter in proportion to the enlargement as it approached, proving that its light was reflected; and as it passed me, apparently in the direction of the earth, I had a sufficiently distinct view of it to know that it was a mainly metallic mass, certainly of some size, perhaps four, perhaps twenty feet in diameter, and apparently composed chiefly of iron; showing a more or less blistered surface, but with angles sharper and faces more regularly defined than most of those which have been found upon the earth's surface—as if the shape of the latter might be due in part to the conflagration they undergo in passing at such tremendous speed through the atmosphere, or, in an opposite sense, to the fractures caused by the shock of their falling. Though I made no attempt to count the innumerable stars in the midst of which I appeared to float, I was convinced that their

number was infinitely greater than that visible to the naked eye on the brightest night. I remembered how greatly the inexperienced eye exaggerates the number of stars visible from the Earth, since poets, and even olden observers, liken their number to that of the sands on the seashore; whereas the patient work of map and catalogue makers has shown that there are but a few thousands visible in the whole heavens to the keenest unaided sight. I suppose that I saw a hundred times that number. In one word, the sphere of darkness in which I floated seemed to be filled with points of light, while the absolute blackness that surrounded them, the absence of the slightest radiation, or illumination of space at large, was strange beyond expression to an eye accustomed to that diffusion of light which is produced by the atmosphere. I may mention here that the recognition of the constellations was at first exceedingly difficult. On Earth we see so few stars in any given portion of the heavens, that one recognises without an effort the figure marked out by a small number of the brightest amongst them; while in my position the multitude was so great that only patient and repeated effort enabled me to separate from the rest those peculiarly brilliant luminaries by which we are accustomed to define such constellations as Orion or the Bear, to say nothing of those minor or more arbitrarily drawn figures which contain few stars of the second magnitude. The eye had no instinctive sense of distance; any star might have been within a stone's throw. I need hardly observe that, while on one hand the motion of the vessel was absolutely imperceptible, there was, on the other, no change of position among the stars which could enable me to verify the fact that I was moving, much less suggest it to the senses. The direction of every recognisable star was the same as on Earth, as it appears the same from the two extremities of the Earth's orbit, 19 millions of miles apart. Looking from any one window, I could see no greater space of the heavens than in looking through a similar aperture on Earth. What was novel and interesting in my stellar prospect was, not merely that I could see those stars north and south which are never visible from the same point on Earth, except in the immediate neighbourhood of the Equator; but that, save on the small space concealed by the Earth's disc, I could, by moving from window to window, survey

the entire heavens, looking at one minute upon the stars surrounding the vernal, and at another, by changing my position, upon those in the neighbourhood of the autumnal equinox. By little more than a turn of my head I could see in one direction Polaris (alpha Ursæ Minoris) with the Great Bear, and in another the Southern Cross, the Ship, and the Centaur.

About 23h. 30m., near the close of the first day, I again inspected the barycrite. It showed 1/1100 of terrestrial gravity, an incredibly small change from the 1/800 recorded at 19h., since it implied a progress proportionate only to the square root of the difference. The observation indicated, if the instrument could be trusted, an advance of only 18,000

miles. It was impossible that the Astronaut had not by this time attained a very much greater speed than 4000 miles an hour, and a greater distance from the Earth than 33 terrestrial radii, or 132,000 miles. Moreover, the barycrite itself had given at 19h. a distance of 28-1/2 radii, and a speed far greater than that which upon its showing had since been maintained.

Extinguishing the lamp, I found that the Earth's diameter on the discometer measured 2° 3' 52" (?). This represented a gain of some 90,000 miles; much more approximate to that which, judging by calculation, I ought to have accomplished during the last four hours and a half, if my speed approached to that I had estimated. I inspected the cratometer, which indicated a force as great as that with which I had started,—a force which should by this time have given me a speed of at least 22,000 miles an hour.

At last the solution of the problem flashed upon me, suggested by the very extravagance of the contradictions. Not only did the barycrite contradict the discometer and the reckoning but it contradicted itself; since it was impossible that under one continuous impulsation I should have traversed 28-1/2 radii of the Earth in the first eighteen hours and no more than 4-1/2

in the next four and a half hours. In truth, the barycrite was effected by two separate attractions,—that of the Earth and that of the Sun, as yet operating almost exactly in the same direction. At first the attraction of the former was so great that that of the Sun was no more perceived than upon the Earth's surface. But as I rose, and the Earth's attraction diminished in proportion to the square of the distance from her centre—which was doubled at 8000 miles, quadrupled at 16,000, and so on—the Sun's

attraction, which was not perceptibly affected by differences so small in proportion to his vast distance of 95,000,000 miles, became a more and more important element in the total gravity. If, as I calculated, I had by 19h.

attained a distance from the earth of 160,000 miles, the attractions of Earth and Sun were by that time pretty nearly equal; and hence the phenomenon which had so puzzled me, that the gravitation, as indicated by the barycrite, was exactly double that which, bearing in mind the Earth's attraction alone, I had calculated. From this point forward the Sun's attraction was the factor which mainly caused such weight as still existed; a change of position which, doubling my distance from the Earth, reduced her influence to one-fourth, not perceptibly affecting that of a body four hundred times more remote. A short calculation showed that, this fact borne in mind, the indication of the barycrite substantially agreed with that of the discometer, and that I was in fact very nearly where I supposed, that is, a little farther than the Moon's farthest distance from the Earth. It did not follow that I had crossed the orbit of the Moon; and if I had, she was at that time too far off to exercise a serious influence on my course. I adjusted the helm and betook myself to rest, the second day of my journey having already commenced.

CHAPTER III - THE UNTRAVELLED DEEP.

Rising at 5h., I observed a drooping in the leaves of my garden, and especially of the larger shrubs and plants, for which I was not wholly unprepared, but which might entail some inconvenience if, failing altogether, they should cease to absorb the gases generated from buried waste, to consume which they had been planted. Besides this, I should, of course, lose the opportunity of transplanting them to Mars, though I had more hope of acclimatising seedlings raised from the seed I carried with me than plants which had actually begun their life on the surface of the Earth. The failure I ascribed naturally to the known connection between the action of gravity and the circulation of the sap; though, as I had experienced no analogous inconvenience in my own person, I had hoped that this would not seriously affect vegetation. I was afraid to try the effect of more liberal watering, the more so that already the congelation of moisture upon the glasses from the internal air, dry as the latter had been kept, was a sensible annoyance—an annoyance which would have become an insuperable trouble had I not taken so much pains, by directing the thermic currents upon the walls, to keep the internal temperature, in so far as comfort would permit—it had now fallen to 4° C.—as near as possible to that of the inner surface of the walls and windows. A careful use of the thermometer indicated that the metallic surface of the former was now nearly zero C., or 32° F. The inner surface of the windows was somewhat colder, showing that the crystal was more pervious to heat than the walls, with their greater thickness, their outer and inner lining of metal, and massive interior of concrete. I directed a current from the thermogene upon either division of the garden, hoping thus to protect the plants from whatever injury they might receive from the cold. Somewhat later, perceiving that the drooping still continued, I resolved upon another experiment, and arranging an apparatus of copper wire beneath the soil, so as to bring the extremities in immediate contact with their roots, I directed through these wires a prolonged feeble current of electricity; by which, as I had hoped rather than expected, the plants were after a time materially benefited, and to which I believe I owed it that they had not all perished long before the termination of my voyage.

It would be mere waste of space and time were I to attempt anything like a journal of the weeks I spent in the solitude of this artificial planet. As matter of course, the monotony of a voyage through space is in general greater than that of a voyage across an ocean like the Atlantic, where no islands and few ships are to be encountered. It was necessary to be very frequently, if not constantly, on the look-out for possible incidents of interest in a journey so utterly novel through regions which the telescope can but imperfectly explore. It was difficult, therefore, to sit down to a book, or even to pursue any necessary occupation unconnected with the actual conduct of the vessel, with uninterrupted attention. My eyes, the only sense organs I could employ, were constantly on the alert; but, of course, by far the greater portion of my time passed without a single new object or occasion of remark. That a journey so utterly without precedent or parallel, in which so little could be anticipated or provided for, through regions absolutely untraversed and very nearly unknown, should be monotonous, may seem strange. But in truth the novelties of the situation, such as they were, though intensely striking and interesting, were each in turn speedily examined, realised, and, so to speak, exhausted; and this once done, there was no greater occupation to the mind in the continuance of strange than in that of familiar scenery. The infinitude of surrounding blackness, filled as it were with points of light more or less brilliant, when once its effects had been scrutinised, and when nothing more remained to be noted, afforded certainly a more agreeable, but scarcely a more interesting or absorbing, outlook than the dead grey circle of sea, the dead grey hemisphere of cloud, which form the prospect from the deck of a packet in mid-Atlantic; while of change without or incident in the vessel herself there was, of course, infinitely less than is afforded in an ocean voyage by the variations of weather, not to mention the solace of human society. Everything around me, except in the one direction in which the Earth's disc still obscured the Sun, remained unchanged for hours and days; and the management of my machinery required no more than an occasional observation of my instruments and a change in the position of the helm, which occupied but a few minutes some half-dozen times in the twenty-four hours. There was not even the change of night and day, of sun

and stars, of cloud or clear sky. Were I to describe the manner in which each day's leisure was spent, I should bore my readers even more than—

they will perhaps be surprised by the confession—I was bored myself.

My sleep was of necessity more or less broken. I wished to have eight hours of rest, since, though seven of continuous sleep might well have sufficed me, even if my brain had been less quiet and unexcited during the rest of the twenty-four, it was impossible for me to enjoy that term of unbroken slumber. I therefore decided to divide my sleep into two portions of rather more than four hours each, to be taken as a rule after noon and after midnight; or rather, since noon and midnight had no meaning for me, from 12h. to 16h. and from 24h. to 4.h. But of course sleep and everything else, except the necessary management of the machine, must give way to the chances of observation; it would be better to remain awake for forty-eight hours at a stretch than to miss any important phenomenon the period of whose occurrence could be even remotely calculated.

At 8h., I employed for the first time the apparatus which I may call my window telescope, to observe, from a position free from the difficulties inflicted on terrestrial astronomers by the atmosphere, all the celestial objects within my survey. As I had anticipated, the absence of atmospheric disturbance and diffusion of light was of extreme advantage. In the first place, I ascertained by the barycrite and the discometer my distance from the Earth, which appeared to be about 120 terrestrial radii. The light of the halo was of course very much narrower than when I first observed it, and its scintillations or coruscations no longer distinctly visible. The Moon presented an exquisitely fine thread of light, but no new object of interest on the very small portion of her daylight hemisphere turned towards me.

Mars was somewhat difficult to observe, being too near what may be called my zenith. But the markings were far more distinct than they appear, with greater magnifying powers than I employed, upon the Earth. In truth, I should say that the various disadvantages due to the atmosphere deprive the astronomer of at least one-half of the available light-collecting power of his telescope, and consequently of the defining power of the eye-piece; that with a 200 glass he sees less than a power of 100 reveals to an eye situated

in space; though, from the nature of the lens through which I looked, I cannot speak with certainty upon this point. With a magnifying power of 300 the polar spots of Mars were distinctly visible and perfectly defined.

They were, I thought, less white than they appeared from the Earth, but their colour was notably different from that of the planet's general surface, differing almost as widely from the orange hue of what I supposed to be land as from the greyish blue of the water. The orange was, I thought, deeper than it appears through a telescope of similar power on Earth. The seas were distinctly grey rather than blue, especially when, by covering the greater part of the field, I contrived for a moment to observe a sea alone, thus eliminating the effect of contrast. The bands of Jupiter in their turn were more notably distinct; their variety of colour as well as the contrast of light and shade much more definite, and their irregularities more unmistakable. A satellite was approaching the disc, and this afforded me an opportunity of realising with especial clearness the difference between observation through seventy or a hundred miles of terrestrial atmosphere outside the object glass and observation in space. The two discs were perfectly rounded and separately discernible until they touched. Moreover, I was able to distinguish upon one of the darker bands the disc of the satellite itself, while upon a lighter band its round black shadow was at the same time perfectly defined. This wonderfully clear presentation of one of the most interesting of astronomical phenomena so absorbed my attention that I watched the satellite and shadow during their whole course, though the former, passing after a time on to a light band, became comparatively indistinct. The moment, however, that the outer edge passed off the disc of Jupiter, its outline became perfectly visible against the black background of sky. What was still more novel was the occultation for some little time of a star, apparently of the tenth magnitude, not by the planet but by the satellite, almost immediately after it passed off the disc of the former.

Whether the star actually disappeared at once, as if instantaneously extinguished, or whether, as I thought at the moment, it remained for some tenth of a second partially visible, as if refracted by an atmosphere belonging to the satellite, I will not venture to say. The bands and rings of Saturn, the division between the two latter, and the seven satellites, were

also perfectly visible, with a distinctness that a much greater magnifying power would hardly have attained under terrestrial conditions. I was perplexed by two peculiarities, not, so far as I know, hitherto mentioned by astronomers. The circumference did not appear to present an even curvature.

I mean that, apart from the polar compression, the shape seemed as if the spheroid were irregularly squeezed; so that though not broken by projection or indentation, the limb did not present the regular quasi-circular curvature exhibited in the focus of our telescopes. Also, between the inner ring and the planet, with a power of 500, I discerned what appeared to be a dark purplish ring, semi-transparent, so that through it the bright surface of Saturn might be discerned as through a veil. Mercury shone brightly several degrees outside the halo surrounding the Earth's black disc; and Venus was also visible; but in neither case did my observations allow me to ascertain anything that has not been already noted by astronomers. The dim form of Uranus was better defined than I had previously seen it, but no marking of any kind was perceptible.

Rising from my second, or, so to speak, midday rest, and having busied myself for some little time with what I may call my household and garden duties, I observed the discometer at 1h. (or 5 P.M.). It indicated about two hundred terrestrial radii of elevation. I had, of course, from the first been falling slightly behind the Earth in her orbital motion, and was no longer exactly in opposition; that is to say, a line drawn from the Astronaut to the Earth's centre was no longer a prolongation of that joining the centres of the Earth and Sun. The effect of this divergence was now perceptible. The earthly corona was unequal in width, and to the westward was very distinctly brightened, while on the other side it was narrow and comparatively faint. While watching this phenomenon through the lower lens, I thought that I could perceive behind or through the widest portion of the halo a white light, which at first I mistook for one of those scintillations that had of late become scarcely discernible. But after a time it extended visibly beyond the boundary of the halo itself, and I perceived that the edge of the Sun's disc had come at last into view. It was but a

minute and narrow crescent, but was well worth watching. The brightening and broadening of the halo at this point I perceived to be due, not to the Sun's effect upon the atmosphere that produced it, but chiefly to the twilight now brightening on that limb of the Earth's disc; or rather to the fact that a small portion of that part of the Earth's surface, where, if the Sun were not visible, he was but a very little below the horizon, had been turned towards me. I saw through the telescope first a tiny solar crescent of intense brightness, then the halo proper, now exceedingly narrow, and then what looked like a silver terrestrial crescent, but a mere thread, finer and shorter than any that the Moon ever displays even to telescopic observers on Earth; since, when such a minute portion of her illuminated surface is turned towards the Earth, it is utterly extinguished to our eyes by the immediate vicinity of the Sun, as was soon the case with the terrestrial crescent in question. I watched long and with intense interest the gradual change, but I was called away from it by a consideration of no little practical moment. I must now be moving at a rate of nearly, if not quite, 40,000 miles an hour, or about a million miles per diem. It was not my intention, for reasons I shall presently explain, ever greatly to exceed this rate; and if I meant to limit myself to a fixed rate of speed, it was time to diminish the force of the apergic current, as otherwise before its reduction could take effect I should have attained an impulse greater than I desired, and which could not be conveniently or easily diminished when once reached. Quitting, therefore, though reluctantly, my observation of the phenomena below me, I turned to the apergion, and was occupied for some two or three hours in gradually reducing the force as measured by the cratometer attached to the downward conductor, and measuring with extreme care the very minute effect produced upon the barycrite and the discometer. Even the difference between 200 and 201 radii of elevation or apogaic distance was not easily perceptible on either. It took, of course, much more minute observation and a much longer time to test the effect produced by the regulation of the movement, since whether I traveller forty, forty-five, or forty-two thousand miles in the course of one hour made scarcely any difference in the diameter of the Earth's disc, still less, for reasons above given, in the gravity. By midnight, however, I was

satisfied that I had not attained quite 1,000,000 miles, or 275 terrestrial radii; also that my speed was not greater than 45,000 miles (11-1\4 radii) per hour, and was not, I thought, increasing. Of this last point, however, I could better satisfy myself at the end of my four hours' rest, to which I now betook myself.

I woke about 4h. 30m., and on a scrutiny of the instruments, felt satisfied that I was not far out in my calculations. A later hour, however, would afford a more absolute certainty. I was about to turn again to the interesting work of observation through the lens in the floor, when my attention was diverted by the sight of something like a whitish cloud visible through the upper window on my left hand. Examined by the telescope, its widest diameter might be at most ten degrees. It was faintly luminous, presenting an appearance very closely resembling that of a star cluster or nebula just beyond the power of resolution. As in many nebulae, there was a visible concentration in one part; but this did not occupy the centre, but a position more resembling that of the nucleus of a small tailless comet. The cloudlet might be a distant comet, it might be a less distant body of meteors clustering densely in some particular part of their orbit; and, unfortunately, I was not likely to solve the problem. Gradually the nebula changed its position, but not its form, seeming to move downwards and towards the stern of my vessel, as if I were passing it without approaching nearer. By the time that I was satisfied of this, hunger and even faintness warned me that I must not delay preparing my breakfast.

When I had finished this meal and fulfilled some necessary tasks, practical and arithmetical, the hand of the chronometer indicated the eighth hour of my third day. I turned again somewhat eagerly to the discometer, which showed an apparent distance of 360 terrestrial radii, and consequently a movement which had not materially varied from the rate of 11-1/4 radii per hour. By this time the diameter of the Earth was not larger in appearance than about 19', less than two-thirds that of the Sun; and she consequently appeared as a black disc covering somewhat more than one-third of his entire surface, but by no means concentrical. The halo had of course completely disappeared; but with the vernier it was possible to discern a narrow band or line of hazy grey around the black limb of the

planet. She was moving, as seen from the Astronaut, very slightly to the north, and more decidedly, though very slowly, to the eastward; the one motion due to my deliberately chosen direction in space, the other to the fact that as my orbit enlarged I was falling, though as yet slowly, behind her. The sun now shone through, the various windows, and, reflected from the walls, maintained a continuous daylight within the Astronaut, as well diffused as by the atmosphere of Earth, strangely contrasting the star-spangled darkness outside.

At the beginning as at the end of my voyage, I steered a distinct course, governed by considerations quite different from those which controlled the main direction of my voyage. Thus far I had simply risen straight from the Earth in a direction somewhat to the southward, but on the whole "in opposition," or right away from the Sun. So, at the conclusion of my journey, I should have to devote some days to a gradual descent upon Mars, exactly reversing the process of my ascent from the Earth. But between these two periods I had comparatively little to do with either planet, my course being governed by the Sun, and its direction and rate being uniform. I wished to reach Mars at the moment of opposition, and during the whole of the journey to keep the Earth between myself and the Sun, for a reason which may not at first be obvious. The moment of opposition is not necessarily that at which Mars is nearest to the Earth, but is sufficiently so for practical calculation. At that moment, according to the received measurement of planetary distances, the two would be more than 40 millions of miles apart. In the meantime the Earth, travelling on an interior or smaller orbit, and also at a greater absolute speed, was gaining on Mars. The Astronaut, moving at the Earth's rate under an impulse derived from the Earth's revolution round the Sun (that due to her rotation on her own axis having been got rid of, as aforesaid), traveller in an orbit constantly widening, so that, while gaining on Mars, I gained on him less than did the Earth, and was falling behind her. Had I used the apergy only to drive me directly outward from the Sun, I should move under the impulse derived from the Earth about 1,600,000 miles a day, or 72 millions of miles in forty-five days, in the direction common to the two planets. The effect of the constantly widening orbit would be much as if the whole

motion took place on one midway between those of the Earth and Mars, say 120 millions of miles from the Sun. The arc described on this orbit would be equivalent to 86 millions of miles on that of Mars. The entire arc of his orbit between the point opposite to that occupied by the Earth when I started and the point of opposition—the entire distance I had to gain as measured along his path—was about 116 millions of miles; so that, trusting to the terrestrial impulse alone, I should be some 30 millions behindhand at the critical moment. The apergic force must make up for this loss of ground, while driving me in a direction, so to speak, at right angles with that of the orbit, or along its radius, straight outward from the Sun, forty odd millions of miles in the same time. If I succeeded in this, I should reach the orbit of Mars at the point and at the moment of opposition, and should attain Mars himself. But in this I might fail, and I should then find myself under the sole influence of the Sun's attraction; able indeed to resist it, able gradually to steer in any direction away from it, but hardly able to overtake a planet that should lie far out of my line of advance or retreat, while moving at full speed away from me. In order to secure a chance of retreat, it was desirable as long as possible to keep the Earth between the Astronaut and the Sun; while steering for that point in space where Mars would lie at the moment when, as seen from the centre of the Earth, he would be most nearly opposite the Sun,—would cross the meridian at midnight. It was by these considerations that the course I henceforward steered was determined. By a very simple calculation, based on the familiar principle of the parallelogram of forces, I gave to the apergic current a force and direction equivalent to a daily motion of about 750,000 miles in the orbital, and rather more than a million in the radial line. I need hardly observe that it would not be to the apergic current alone, but to a combination of that current with the orbital impulse received at first from the Earth, that my progress and course would be due. The latter was the stronger influence; the former only was under my control, but it would suffice to determine, as I might from time to time desire, the resultant of the combination. The only obvious risk of failure lay in the chance that, my calculations failing or being upset, I might reach the desired point too soon or too late. In either case, I should be dangerously far from Mars, beyond

his orbit or within it, at the time when I should come into a line with him and the Sun; or, again, putting the same mischance in another form, behind him or before him when I attained his orbit. But I trusted to daily observation of his position, and verification of my "dead reckoning"

thereby, to find out any such danger in time to avert it.

The displacement of the Earth on the Sun's face proved it to be necessary that the apergic current should be directed against the latter in order to govern my course as I desired, and to recover the ground I had lost in respect to the orbital motion. I hoped for a moment that this change in the action of the force would settle a problem we had never been able to determine. Our experiments proved that apergy acts in a straight line when once collected in and directed along a conductor, and does not radiate, like other forces, from a centre in all directions. It is of course this radiation—

diffusing the effect of light, heat, or gravity over the surface of a sphere, which surface is proportionate to the square of the radius—that causes these forces to operate with an energy inversely proportionate, not to the distance, but to its square. We had no reason to think that apergy, exempt as it is from this law, would be at all diminished by distance; and this view the rate of acceleration as I rose from the Earth had confirmed, and my entire experience has satisfied me that it is correct. None of our experiments, however, had indicated, or could well indicate, at what rate this force can travel through space; nor had I yet obtained any light upon this point. From the very first the current had been continuous, the only interruption taking place when I was not five hundred miles from the Earth's surface. Over so small a distance as that, the force would move so instantaneously that no trace of the interruption would be perceptible in the motion of the Astronaut. Even now the total interruption of the action of apergy for a considerable time would not affect the rate at which I was already moving. It was possible, however, that if the current had been hitherto wholly intercepted by the Earth, it might take so long a time in reaching the Sun that the interval between the movement of the helm and the response of the Astronaut's course thereto might afford some indication of the time occupied by the current in traversing the 96-1/2 millions of miles which parted me from the Sun. My hope, however, was wholly

disappointed. I could neither be sure that the action was instantaneous, nor that it was otherwise.

At the close of the third day I had gained, as was indicated by the instruments, something more than two millions of miles in a direct line from the Sun; and for the future I might, and did, reckon on a steady progress of about one and a quarter million miles daily under the apergic force alone—a gain in a line directly outward from the Sun of about one million. Henceforward I shall not record my observations, except where they implied an unexpected or altered result.

On the sixth day, I perceived another nebula, and on this occasion in a more promising direction. It appeared, from its gradual movement, to lie almost exactly in my course, so that if it were what I suspected, and were not at any great distance from me, I must pass either near or through it, and it would surely explain what had perplexed and baffled me in the case of the former nebula. At this distance the nature of the cloudlet was imperceptible to the naked eye. The window telescope was not adjustable to an object which I could not bring conveniently within the field of view of the lenses. In a few hours the nebula so changed its form and position, that, being immediately over the portion of the roof between the front or bow lens and that in the centre of the roof, its central section was invisible; but the extremities of that part which I had seen in the first instance through the upper plane window of the bow were now clearly visible from the upper windows of either side. What had at first been a mere greatly elongated oval, with a species of rapidly diminishing tail at each extremity, had now become an arc spanning no inconsiderable part of the space above me, narrowing rapidly as it extended downwards and sternwards.

Presently it came in view through the upper lens, but did not obscure in the least the image of the stars which were then visible in the metacompass.

I very soon ascertained that the cloudlet consisted, as I had supposed in the former case, of a multitude of points of light less brilliant than the stars, the distance between which became constantly wider, but which for some time were separately so small as to present no disc that any magnifying power at my command could render measurable. In the meantime, the extremities

visible through the other windows were constantly widening out till lost in the spangled darkness. By and by, it became impossible with the naked eye to distinguish the individual points from the smaller stars; and shortly after this the nearest began to present discs of appreciable size but somewhat irregular shape. I had now no doubt that I was about to pass through one of those meteoric rings which our most advanced astronomers believe to exist in immense numbers throughout space, and to the Earth's contact with or approach to which they ascribe the showers of falling, stars visible in August and November. Ere long, one after another of these bodies passed rapidly before my sight, at distances varying probably from five yards to five thousand miles. Where to test the distance was impossible, anything like accurate measurement was equally out of the question; but my opinion is, that the diameters of the nearest ranged from ten inches to two hundred feet. One only passed so near that its absolute size could be judged by the marks upon its face. This was a rock-like mass, presenting at many places on the surface distinct traces of metallic veins or blotches, rudely ovoid in form, but with a number of broken surfaces, one or two of which reflected the light much more brilliantly than others. The weight of this one meteoroid was too insignificant as compared with that of the Astronaut seriously to disturb my course. Fortunately for me, I passed so nearly through the centre of the aggregation that its attraction as a whole was nearly inoperative. So far as I could judge, the meteors in that part of the ring through which I passed were pretty evenly distributed; and as from the appearance of the first which passed my window to the disappearance of the last four hours elapsed, I conceived that the diameter of the congeries, measured in the direction of my path, which seemed to be nearly in the diameter of their orbit, was about 180,000 miles, and probably the perpendicular depth was about the same.

I may mention here, though somewhat out of place, to avoid interrupting the narrative of my descent upon Mars, the only interesting incident that occurred during the latter days of my journey—the gradual passage of the Earth off the face of the Sun. For some little time after this the Earth was entirely invisible; but later, looking through the telescope adjusted to the lens on that side, I discerned two very minute and bright crescents, which,

from their direction and position, were certainly those of the Earth and Moon, indeed could hardly be anything else.

Towards the thirtieth day of my voyage I was disturbed by the conflicting indications obtained from different instruments and separate observations.

The general result came to this, that the discometer, where it should have indicated a distance of 333, actually gave 347. But if my speed had increased, or I had overestimated the loss by changes of direction, Mars should have been larger in equal proportion. This, however, was not the case. Supposing my reckoning to be right, and I had no reason to think it otherwise, except the indication of the discometer, the Sun's disc ought to have diminished in the proportion of 95 to 15, whereas the diminution was in the proportion of 9 to 1. So far as the barycrite could be trusted, its very minute indications confirmed those of the discometer; and the only conclusion I could draw, after much thought and many intricate calculations, was that the distance of 95 millions of miles between the Earth and the Sun, accepted, though not very confidently, by all terrestrial astronomers, is an over-estimate; and that, consequently, all the other distances of the solar system have been equally overrated. Mars consequently would be smaller, but also his distance considerably less, than I had supposed. I finally concluded that the solar distance of the Earth was less than 9 millions of miles, instead of more than 95. This would involve, of course, a proportionate diminution in the distance I had to traverse, while it did not imply an equal error in the reckoning of my speed, which had at first been calculated from the Earth's disc, and not from that of the Sun. Hence, continuing my course unchanged, I should arrive at the orbit of Mars some days earlier than intended, and at a point behind that occupied by the planet, and yet farther behind the one I aimed at. Prolonged observation and careful calculation had so fully satisfied me of the necessity of the corrections in question, that I did not hesitate to alter my course accordingly, and to prepare for a descent on the thirty-ninth instead of the forty-first day. I had, of course, to prepare for the descent very long before I should come within the direct influence of the attraction of Mars. This would not prevail over the Sun's attraction till I had come within a little more than 100,000 miles of the surface, and this distance

would not allow for material reduction of my speed, even were I at once to direct the whole force of the apergic current against the planet. I estimated that arriving within some two millions of miles of him, with a speed of 45,000 miles per hour, and then directing the whole force of the current in his direction, I should arrive at his surface at a speed nearly equal to that at which I had ascended from the Earth. I knew that I could spare force enough to make up for any miscalculation possible, or at least probable. Of course any serious error might be fatal. I was exposed to two dangers; perhaps to three: but to none which I had not fully estimated before even preparing for my voyage. If I should fail to come near enough to the goal of my journey, and yet should go on into space, or if, on the other hand, I should stop short, the Astronaut might become an independent planet, pursuing an orbit nearly parallel to that of the Earth; in which case I should perish of starvation. It was conceivable that I might, in attempting to avert this fate, fall upon the Sun, though this seemed exceedingly improbable, requiring a combination of accidents very unlikely to occur. On the other hand, I might by possibility attain my point, and yet, failing properly to calculate the rate of descent, be dashed to pieces upon the surface of Mars.

Of this, however, I had very little fear, the tremendous power of the apergy having been so fully proved that I believed that nothing but some disabling accident to myself—such as was hardly to be feared in the absence of gravitation, and with the extreme simplicity of the machinery I employed—could prevent my being able, when I became aware of the danger, to employ in time a sufficient force to avert it. The first of these perils, then, was the graver one, perhaps the only grave one, and certainly to my imagination it was much the most terrible. The idea of perishing of want in the infinite solitude of space, and being whirled round for ever the dead denizen of a planet one hundred feet in diameter, had in it something even more awful than grotesque.

On the thirty-ninth morning of my voyage, so far as I could calculate by the respective direction and size of the Sun and of Mars, I was within about 1,900,000 miles from the latter. I proceeded without hesitation to direct the whole force of the current permitted to emerge from the apergion directly against the centre of the planet. His diameter increased with great rapidity,

till at the end of the first day I found myself within one million of miles of his surface. His diameter subtended about 15', and his disc appeared about one-fourth the size of the Moon. Examined through the telescope, it presented a very different appearance from that either of the Earth or of her satellite. It resembled the former in having unmistakably air and water.

But, unlike the Earth, the greater portion of its surface seemed to be land; and, instead of continents surrounded by water, it presented a number of separate seas, nearly all of them land-locked. Around the snow-cap of each pole was a belt of water; around this, again, a broader belt of continuous land; and outside this, forming the northern and southern boundary between the arctic and temperate zones, was another broader band of water, connected apparently in one or two places with the central, or, if one may so call it, equatorial sea. South of the latter is the one great Martial ocean. The most striking feature of this new world, as seen from this point, was the existence of three enormous gulfs, from three to five thousand miles in length, and apparently varying in breadth from one hundred to seven hundred miles. In the midst of the principal ocean, but somewhat to the southward, is an island of unique appearance. It is roughly circular, and, as I perceived in descending, stands very high, its table-like summit being some 4000 feet, as I subsequently ascertained, above the sea-level. Its surface, however, was perfectly white—scarcely less brilliant, consequently, than an equal area of the polar icefields. The globe, of course, revolved in some 4-1/ hours of earthly time, and, as I descended, presented successively every part of its surface to my view. I speak of descent, but, of course, I was as yet ascending just as truly as ever, the Sun being visible through the lens in the floor, and reflected upon the mirror of the discometer, while Mars was now seen through the upper lens, and his image received in the mirror of the metacompass. A noteworthy feature in the meteorology of the planet became apparent during the second day of the descent. As magnified by the telescope adjusted to the upper lens, the distinctions of sea and land disappeared from the eastern and western limbs of the planet; indeed, within 15° or an hour of time from either. It was plain, therefore, that those regions in which it was late evening or early morning were hidden from view; and, independently of the whitish light reflected from them, there could be little doubt that the obscuration was due to clouds or mists. Had the whitish light covered the land alone, it might have been attributed to a snowfall, or, perhaps, even to a very severe hoar frost congealing a dense moisture. But this last seemed highly improbable; and that mist or cloud was the true explanation became more and more apparent as, with a nearer approach, it became possible to discern dimly a broad expanse of water contrasting the orange tinge of the land through this annular veil. At 4h. on the second day of the descent, I was about 500,000 miles from Mars, the micrometer verifying, by the increased angle subtended by the diameter, my calculated rate of approach.

On the next day I was able to sleep in security, and to devote my attention to the observation of the planet's surface, for at its close I should be still 15,000 miles from Mars, and consequently beyond the distance at which his attraction would predominate over that of the Sun. To my great surprise, in the course of this day I discerned two small discs, one on each side of the planet, moving at a rate which rendered measurement impossible, but evidently very much smaller than any satellite with which astronomers are acquainted, and so small that their non-discovery by terrestrial telescopes was not extraordinary. They were evidently very minute, whether ten, twenty, or fifty miles in diameter I could not say; neither of them being likely, so far as I could calculate, to come at any part of my descent very near the Astronaut, and the rapidity of their movement carrying them across the field, even with the lowest power of my telescopes, too fast for measurement. That they were Martial moons, however, there could be no doubt.

About 10h. on the last day of the descent, the effect of Mars' attraction, which had for some time so disturbed the position of the Astronaut as to take his disc completely out of the field of the meta-compass, became decidedly predominant over that of the Sun. I had to change the direction of the apergic current first to the left-hand conductor, and afterwards, as the greater weight of the floor turned the Astronaut completely over, bringing the planet immediately below it, to the downward one. I was, of course, approaching Mars on the daylight side, and nearly in the centre.

This, however, did not exactly suit me. During the whole of this day it was impossible that I should sleep for a minute; since if at any point I should find that I had miscalculated my rate of descent, or if any other unforeseen accident should occur, immediate action would be necessary to prevent a shipwreck, which must without doubt be fatal. It was very likely that I should be equally unable to sleep during the first twenty-four hours of my sojourn upon Mars, more especially should he be inhabited, and should my descent be observed. It was, therefore, my policy to land at some point where the Sun was setting, and to enjoy rest during such part of the twelve hours of the Martial night as should not be employed in setting my vessel in order and preparing to evacuate it. I should have to ascertain exactly the pressure of the Martial atmosphere, so as not to step too suddenly from a dense into what was probably a very light one. If possible, I intended to land upon the summit of a mountain, so high as to be untenanted and of difficult access. At the same time it would not do to choose the highest point of a very lofty range, since both the cold and the thinness of the air might in such a place be fatal. I wished, of course, to leave the Astronaut secure, and, if not out of reach, yet not within easy reach; otherwise it would have been a simple matter to watch my opportunity and descend in the dark from my first landing-place by the same means by which I had made the rest of my voyage.

At 18h. I was within 8000 miles of the surface, and could observe Mars distinctly as a world, and no longer as a star. The colour, so remarkable a feature in his celestial appearance, was almost equally perceptible at this moderate elevation. The seas are not so much blue as grey. Masses of land reflected a light between yellow and orange, indicating, as I thought, that orange must be as much the predominant colour of vegetation as green upon Earth. As I came still lower, and only parts of the disc were visible at once, and these through the side and end windows, this conviction was more and more strongly impressed upon my mind. What, however, was beyond denial was, that if the polar ice and snow were not so purely and distinctly white as they appear at a distance upon Earth, they were yet to a great extent devoid of the yellow tinge that preponderated everywhere else. The most that could be said was, that whereas on Earth the snow is of that white which we consider absolute, and call, as such, snow-white, but

which really has in it a very slight preponderance of blue, upon Mars the polar caps are rather cream-white, or of that white, so common in our flowers, which has in it an equally slight tinge of yellow. On the shore, or about twenty miles from the shore of the principal sea to the southward of the equator, and but a few degrees from the equator itself, I perceived at last a point which appeared peculiarly suitable for my descent. A very long range of mountains, apparently having an average height of about 14,000

feet, with some peaks of probably twice or three times that altitude, stretched for several hundred miles along the coast, leaving, however, between it and the actual shore-line an alluvial plain of some twenty to fifty miles across. At the extremity of this range, and quite detached from it, stood an isolated mountain of peculiar form, which, as I examined it through the telescope, appeared to present a surface sufficiently broken and sloped to permit of descent; while, at the same time, its height and the character of its summit satisfied me that no one was likely to inhabit it, and that though I might descend-it in a few hours, to ascend it on foot from the plain would be a day's journey. Towards this I directed my course, looking out from time to time carefully for any symptoms of human habitation or animal life. I made out by degrees the lines of rivers, mountain slopes covered by great forests, extensive valleys and plains, seemingly carpeted by a low, dense, rich vegetation. But my view being essentially of a bird's-eye character, it was only in those parts that lay upon my horizon that I could discern clearly the height of any object above the general level; and as yet, therefore, there might well be houses and buildings, cultivated fields and divisions, which I could not see.

Before I had satisfied myself whether the planet was or was not inhabited, I found myself in a position from which its general surface was veiled by the evening mist, and directly over the mountain in question, within some twelve miles of its summit. This distance I descended in the course of a quarter of an hour, and landed without a shock about half an hour, so far as I could judge, after the Sun had disappeared below the horizon. The sunset, however, by reason of the mists, was totally invisible.

CHAPTER IV - A NEW WORLD.

I will not attempt to express the intensity of the mingled emotions which overcame me as I realised the complete success of the most stupendous adventure ever proposed or even dreamed by man. I don't think that any personal vanity, unworthy of the highest lessons I had received, had much share in my passionate exultation. The conception was not original; the means were furnished by others; the execution depended less on a daring and skill, in which any courageous traveller or man of science knowing what I knew might well have excelled me, than on the direct and manifest favour of Providence. But this enterprise, the greatest that man had ever attempted, had in itself a charm, a sanctity in my eyes that made its accomplishment an unspeakable satisfaction. I would have laid down life a dozen times not only to achieve it myself, but even to know that it had been achieved by others. All that Columbus can have felt when he first set foot on a new hemisphere I felt in tenfold force as I assured myself that not, as often before, in dreams, but in very truth and fact, I had traversed forty million miles of space, and landed in a new world. Of the perils that might await me I could hardly care to think. They might be greater in degree.

They could hardly be other in kind, than those which a traveller might incur in Papua, or Central Africa, or in the North-West Passage. They could have none of that wholly novel, strange, incalculable character which sometimes had given to the chances of my etherial voyage a vague horror and mystery that appalled imagination. For the first time during my journey I could neither eat nor sleep; yet I must do both. I might soon meet with difficulties and dangers that would demand all the resources of perfect physical and mental condition, with heavy calls on the utmost powers of nerve and muscle. I forced myself, therefore, to sup and to slumber, resorting for the first time in many years to the stimulus of brandy for the one purpose, and to the aid of authypnotism for the other.

When I woke it was 8h. by my chronometer, and, as I inferred, about 5h.

after midnight of the Martial meridian on which I lay. Sleep had given me an appetite for breakfast, and necessary practical employment calmed the excitement natural to my situation. My first care, after making ready to quit

the Astronaut as soon as the light around should render it safe to venture into scenes so much more utterly strange, unfamiliar, and unknown than the wildest of the yet unexplored deserts of the Earth, was to ascertain the character of the atmosphere which I was presently to breathe. Did it contain the oxygen essential to Tellurian lungs? Was it, if capable of respiration, dense enough to sustain life like mine? I extracted the plug from the tubular aperture through which I had pumped in the extra quantity of air that the Astronaut contained; and substituted the sliding valve I had arranged for the purpose, with a small hole which, by adjustment to the tube, would give the means of regulating the air-passage at pleasure. The difficulty of this simple work, and the tremendous outward pressure of the air, showed that the external atmosphere was very thin indeed. This I had anticipated. Gravity on the surface of Mars is less than half what it is on Earth; the total mass of the planet is as two to fifteen.

It was consequently to be expected that the extent of the Martial atmosphere, and its density even at the sea-level, would be far less than on the heavier planet. Rigging the air-pump securely round the aperture, exhausting its chamber, and permitting the Martial air to fill it, I was glad to find a pressure equal to that which prevails at a height of 16,000 feet on Earth. Chemical tests showed the presence of oxygen in somewhat greater proportion than in the purest air of terrestrial mountains. It would sustain life, therefore, and without serious injury, if the change from a dense to a light atmosphere were not too suddenly made. I determined then gradually to diminish the density of the internal atmosphere to something not very much greater than that outside. For this purpose I unrigged the air-pump apparatus, and almost, but not quite, closed the valve, leaving an aperture about the twentieth part of an inch in diameter. The silence was instantly broken by a whistle the shrillest and loudest I had ever heard; the dense compressed atmosphere of the Astronaut rushing out with a force which actually created a draught through the whole vessel, to the great discomfiture of the birds, which roughed their feathers and fluttered about in dismay. The pressure gauge fell with astonishing rapidity, despite the minuteness of the aperture; and in a few minutes indicated about 24 barometrical inches. I then checked the exit of the air for a time, while I

proceeded to loosen the cement around the window by which I had entered, and prepared for my exit. Over a very light flannel under-vesture I put on a mail-shirt of fine close-woven wire, which had turned the edge of Mahratta tulwars, repelled the thrust of a Calabrian stiletto, and showed no mark of three carbine bullets fired point-blank. Over this I wore a suit of grey broadcloth, and a pair of strong boots over woollen socks, prepared for cold and damp as well as for the heat of a sun shining perpendicularly through an Alpine atmosphere. I had nearly equalised the atmospheric pressure within and without, at about 17 inches, before the first beams of dawn shone upward on the ceiling of the Astronaut. A few minutes later I stepped forth on the platform, some two hundred yards in circumference, whereon the vessel rested. The mist immediately around me was fast dispersing; five hundred feet below it still concealed everything. On three sides descent was barred by sheer precipices; on the fourth a steep slope promised a practicable path, at least as far as my eye could reach. I placed the weaker and smaller of my birds in portable cages, and then commenced my experiment by taking out a strong-winged cuckoo and throwing him downwards over the precipice. He fell at first almost like a stone; but before he was quite lost to sight in the mist, I had the pleasure of seeing that he had spread his wings, and was able to sustain himself. As the mist was gradually dissolving, I now ventured to begin my descent, carrying my bird-cages, and dismissing the larger birds, several of which, however, persistently clung about me. I had secured on my back an air-gun, arranged to fire sixteen balls in succession without reloading, while in my belt, scabbarded in a leathern sheath, I had placed a well and often tried two-edged sword. I found the way practicable, though not easy, till I reached a point about 1000 feet below the summit, where farther progress in the same direction was barred by an abrupt and impassable cleft some hundred feet deep. To the right, however, the mountain side seemed to present a safe and sufficiently direct descent. The sun was a full hour above the horizon, and the mist was almost gone. Still I had seen no signs of animal life, save, at some distance and in rapid motion, two or three swarms of flying insects, not much resembling any with which I was acquainted. The vegetation, mostly small, was of a yellowish colour, the

flowers generally red, varied by occasional examples of dull green and white; the latter, however, presenting that sort of creamy tinge which I had remarked in the snow. Here I released and dismissed my birds one by one.

The stronger and more courageous flew away downwards, and soon disappeared; the weakest, trembling and shivering, evidently suffering from the thinness of the atmosphere, hung about me or perched upon the cages.

The scene I now contemplated was exceedingly novel and striking. The sky, instead of the brilliant azure of a similar latitude on earth, presented to my eye a vault of pale green, closely analogous to that olive tint which the effect of contrast often throws over a small portion of clear sky distinguished among the golden and rose-coloured clouds of a sunset in our temperate zones.

The vapours which still hung around the north-eastern and south-eastern horizon, though dispelled from the immediate vicinity of the Sun, were tinged with crimson and gold much deeper than the tints peculiar to an earthly twilight. The Sun himself, when seen by the naked eye, was as distinctly golden as our harvest moon; and the whole landscape, terrestrial, aerial, and celestial, appeared as if bathed in a golden light, wearing generally that warm summer aspect peculiar to Tellurian landscapes when seen through glass of a rich yellow tint. It was a natural inference from all I saw that there takes place in the Martial atmosphere an absorption of the blue rays which gives to the sunlight a predominant tinge of yellow or orange. The small rocky plateau on which I stood, like the whole of the mountainside I had descended, faced the extremity of the range of which this mountain was an outpost; and the valley which separated them was not from my present position visible. I saw that I should have to turn my back upon this part of the landscape as I descended farther, and therefore took note at this point of the aspect it presented. The most prominent object was a white peak in the distant sky, rising to a height above my actual level, which I estimated conjecturally at 25,000 feet, guessing the distance at fifty miles. The summit was decidedly more angular and pointed, less softened in outline by atmospheric influences, than those of mountains on

Earth. Beyond this in the farthest distance appeared two or three peaks still higher, but of which, of course, only the summits were visible to me. On this side of the central peak an apparently continuous double ridge extended to within three miles of my station, exceedingly irregular in level, the highest elevations being perhaps 20,000, the lowest visible depressions 3000 feet above me. There appeared to be a line of perpetual snow, though in many places above, this line patches of yellow appeared, the nearer of which were certainly and the more distant must be inferred to be covered with a low, close herbaceous vegetation. The lower slopes were entirely clothed with yellow or reddish foliage. Between the woods and snow-line lay extensive pastures or meadows, if they might be so called, though I saw nothing whatever that at all resembled the grass of similar regions on Earth. Whatever foliage I saw as yet I had not passed near anything that could be called a tree, and very few shrubs—consisted distinctly of leaves analogous to those of our deciduous trees, chiefly of three shapes: a sort of square rounded at the angles, with short projecting fingers; an oval, slightly pointed where it joined the stalk; and lanceolate or sword-like blades of every size, from two inches to four feet in length. Nearly all were of a dull yellow or copper-red tinge. None were as fine as the beech-leaf, none succulent or fleshy; nothing resembling the blades of grass or the bristles of the pine and cedar tribes was visible.

My path now wound steadily downward at a slope of perhaps one in eight along the hillside, obliging me to turn my back to the mountains, while my view in front was cut off by a sharp cross-jutting ridge immediately, before me. By the time I turned this, all my birds had deserted me, and I was not, I think, more than 2000 feet from the valley below. Just before reaching this point I first caught sight of a Martial animal. A little creature, not much bigger than a rabbit, itself of a sort of sandy-yellow colour, bounded from among some yellow herbage by my feet, and hopped or sprang in the manner of a kangaroo down the steep slope on my left. When I turned the ridge, a wide and quite new landscape burst upon my sight. I was looking upon an extensive plain, the continuation apparently of a valley of which the mountain range formed the southern limit. To the southward this plain was bounded by the sea, bathed in the peculiar light I have tried to

describe, and lying in what seemed from this distance a glassy calm. To eastward and northward the plain extended to the horizon, and doubtless far beyond it; while from the valley north of the mountain range emerged a broad river, winding through the plain till it was lost at the horizon. Plain I have called it, but I do not mean to imply that it was by any means level.

On the contrary, its surface was broken by undulations, and here and there by hills, but all so much lower than the point on which I stood that the general effect was that of an almost flat surface. And now the question of habitation, and of human habitation, seemed to be solved. Looking through my field-glass, I saw, following the windings of the river, what must surely be a road; serving also, perhaps, as an embankment, since it was raised many feet above the level of the stream. It seemed, too, that the plain was cultivated. Everywhere appeared extensive patches, each of a single colour, in every tint between deep red and yellowish green, and so distinctly rectangular in form as irresistibly to suggest the idea of artificial, if not human, arrangement. But there were other features of the scene that dispelled all doubt upon this point. Immediately to the south-eastward, and about twenty miles from where I stood, a deep arm of the sea ran up into the land, and upon the shores of this lay what was unquestionably a city. It had nothing that looked like fortifications, and even at this distance I could discern that its streets were of remarkable width, with few or no buildings so high as mosques, churches, State-offices, or palaces in Tellurian cities. Their colours were most various and brilliant, as if reflected from metallic surfaces; and on the waters of the bay itself rode what I could not doubt to be ships or rafts. More immediately beneath me, and scattered at intervals over the entire plain, clustering more closely in the vicinity of the city, were walled enclosures, and in the centre of each was what could hardly be anything but a house, though not apparently more than twelve or fourteen feet high, and covering a space sufficient for an European or even American street or square. Upon the lower slopes of the hill whereon I stood were moving figures, which, seen through the binocular, proved to be animals; probably domestic animals, since they never ranged very far, and presented none of those signs of watchfulness and alarm which are peculiar to creatures not protected by man from their

less destructive enemies, and taught to lay aside their dread of man himself. I had descended, then, not only into an inhabited world—not only into a world of men, who, however they might differ in outward form, must resemble in their wants, ideas, and habits, in short, in mind if not in body, the lords of my own planet—but into a civilised world and among a race living under a settled order, cultivating the soil, and taming the brutes to their service.

And now, as I came on lower ground, I found at each step new objects of curiosity and interest. A tree with dark-yellowish leaves, taller than most timber trees on Earth, bore at the end of drooping twigs large dark-red fruits—fruits with a rind something like that of a pomegranate, save for the colour and hardness, and about the size of a shaddock or melon. One of these, just within reach of my hand, I gathered, but found it impossible to break the thin, dry rind or shell, without the aid of a knife. Having pierced this, a stream of red juice gushed out, which had a sweet taste and a strong flavour, not unlike the juice expressed from cherries, but darker in colour.

Dissecting the fruit completely, I found it parted by a membrane, essentially of the same nature as the rind, but much thinner and rather tough than hard, into sixteen segments, like those of an orange divided across the middle, each of which enclosed a seed. These seeds were all joined at the centre, but easily separated. They were of a yellow colour and about as large as an almond kernel. Some fruits that, being smaller, I concluded to be less ripe, were of a reddish-yellow. After walking for about a mile through a grove of such trees, always tending downwards, I came to another of more varied character. The most prevalent tree here was of lower stature and with leaves of great length and comparatively narrow, the fruit of which, though protected by a somewhat similar rind, was of rich golden colour, not so easily seen among the yellowish leaves, and contained one solid kernel of about the size of an almond, enclosed entirely in a sort of spongy material, very palatable to the taste, and resembling more the inside of roasted maize than any other familiar vegetable. As I emerged entirely from the grove, I came upon a ditch about twice as broad as deep. On Earth I certainly could not have leaped it; but since landing on Mars, I had forgotten the weightless life of the Astronaut, and felt as if on

Earth, but enjoying great increase of strength and energy; and with these sensations had come instinctively an exalted confidence in my physical powers. I took, therefore, a vigorous run, and leaping with all my strength, landed, somewhat to my own surprise, a full yard on the other side of the ditch.

Having done so, I found myself in what was beyond doubt a cultivated field, producing nothing but one crimson-coloured plant, about a foot in height. This carpeted the soil with broad leaves shaped something like those of the laurel, and in colour exactly resembling a withered laurel leaf, but somewhat thicker, more metallic and brighter in appearance, and perfectly free from the bitter taste of the bay tribe. At a little distance I saw half-a-dozen animals somewhat resembling antelopes, but on a second glance still more resembling the fabled unicorn. They were like the latter, at all events, in the single particular from which it derived its name: they had one horn, about eight inches in length, intensely sharp, smooth and firm in texture as ivory, but marbled with vermilion and cream white. Their skins were cream-coloured, dappled with dark red. Their ears were large and protected by a lap which fell down so as to shelter the interior part of the organ, but which they had not quite lost the power to erect at the approach of a sound that startled them. They looked up at me, at first without alarm, afterwards with some surprise, and presently bounded away; as if my appearance, at first familiar, had, on a closer examination, presented some unusual particulars, frightening them, as everything unusual frightens even those domestic animals on Earth best acquainted with man and most accustomed to his caprices. I noticed that all were female, and their abnormally large udders suggested that they were domestic creatures kept for their milk. Not being able to see a path through the field, I went straight forward, endeavouring to trample the pasture as little as I could, but being surprised to remark how very little the plants had been injured by the feet of the animals. The leaves had been grazed, but the stems were seldom or never broken. In fact, the animals seemed to have gathered their food as man would do, with an intelligent or instinctive care not to injure the plant so as to deprive it of the power of reproducing their sustenance.

In another minute I discerned the object of my paramount interest, of whose vicinity I had thus far seen nearly every imaginable evidence except himself. It was undoubtedly a man, but a man very much smaller than myself. His eyes were fixed upon the ground as if in reverie, and he did not perceive me till I had come within fifty yards of him, so that I had full time to remark the peculiarities of his form and appearance. He was about four feet eight or nine inches in height, with legs that seemed short in proportion to the length and girth of the body, but only because, as was apparent on more careful scrutiny, the chest was proportionately both longer and wider than in our race; otherwise he greatly resembled the fairer families of the Aryan breed, the Swede or German. The yellow hair, unshaven beard, whiskers, and moustache were all close and short. The dress consisted of a sort of blouse and short pantaloons, of some soft woven fabric, and of a vermilion colour. The head was protected from the rays of an equatorial sun by a species of light turban, from which hung down a short shade or veil sheltering the neck and forehead. His bare feet were guarded by sandals of some flexible material just covering the toes and bound round the ankle by a single thong. He carried no weapon, not even a staff; and I therefore felt that there was no immediate danger from him. On seeing me he started as with intense surprise and not a little alarm, and turned to run. Size and length of limb, however, gave me immense advantage in this respect, and in less than a minute I had come up with and laid my hand upon him.

He looked up at me, scanning my face with earnest curiosity. I took from my pocket first a jewel of very exquisite construction, a butterfly of turquoise, pearl, and rubies, set on an emerald branch, upon which he looked without admiration or interest, then a watch very small and elaborately enamelled and jewelled. To the ornament he paid no attention whatever; but when I opened the watch, its construction and movement evidently interested him. Placing it in his hands and endeavouring to signify to him by signs that he was to retain it, I then held his arm and motioned to him to guide me towards the houses visible in the distance.

This he seemed willing to do, but before we had gone many paces he repeated two or three times a phrase or word which sounded like "r'mo-ah-

el" ("whence-who-what" do you want?). I shook my head; but, that he might not suppose me dumb, I answered him in Latin. The sound seemed to astonish him exceedingly; and as I went on to repeat several questions in the same tongue, for the purpose of showing him that I could speak and was desirous of doing so, I observed that his wonder grew deeper and deeper, and was evidently mingled first with alarm and afterwards with anger, as if he thought I was trying to impose upon him. I pointed to the sky, to the summit of the mountain from which I had descended, and then along the course by which I had come, explaining aloud at the same time the meaning of my signs. I thought that he had caught the latter, but if so, it only provoked an incredulous indignation, contempt of a somewhat angry character being the principal expression visible in his countenance. I saw that it was of little use to attempt further conversation for the present, and, still holding his hand and allowing him to direct me, looked round again at the scenes through which we were passing. The lower hill slopes before us appeared to be divided into fields of large extent, perhaps some 100 acres each, separated by ditches. We followed a path about two yards broad, raised two or three inches above the level of the ground, and paved with some kind of hard concrete. Each ditch was crossed by a bridge of planks, in the middle of which was a stake or short pole, round which we passed with ease, but which would obviously baffle a four-footed animal of any size. The crops were of great variety, and wonderfully free from weeds.

Most of them showed fruit of one kind or another, sometimes gourd-like globes on the top of upright stalks, sometimes clusters of a sort of nut on vines creeping along the soil, sometimes a number of pulpy fruits about the size of an orange hanging at the end of pendulous stalks springing from the top of a stiff reed-like stem. One field was bare, its surface of an ochreish colour deeper than that of clay, broken and smoothed as perfectly as the surface of the most carefully tended flower-bed. Across this was ranged a row of birds, differing, though where and how I had hardly leisure to observe, from the form of any earthly fowl, about twice the size of a crow, and with beaks apparently at least as powerful but very much longer. Extending entirely across the field, they kept line with wonderful accuracy, and as they marched across it, slowly and constantly dug their

beaks into the soil as if seeking grubs or worms beneath the surface. They went on with their work perfectly undisturbed by our presence. In the next field was a still odder sight; here grew gourd-like heads on erect reed-like stems, and engaged in plucking the ripe purple fruit, carefully distinguishing them from the scarlet unripened heads, were half-a-score of creatures which, from their occupation and demeanour, I took at first to be human; but which, as we approached nearer, I saw were only about half the size of my companion, and thickly covered with hair, with bushy tails, which they kept carefully erect so as not to touch the ground; creatures much resembling monkeys in movement, size, and length, and flexibility of limb, but in other respects more like gigantic squirrels. They held the stalks of the fruit they plucked in their mouths, filling with them large bags left at intervals, and from the manner in which they worked I suspected that they had no opposable thumbs—that the whole hand had to be used like the paw of a squirrel to grasp an object. I pointed to these, directing my companion's attention and asking, "What are they?" "Ambau," he said, but apparently without the slightest interest in their proceedings. Indeed, the regularity and entire freedom from alarm or vigilance which characterised their movements, convinced me that both these and the birds we passed were domesticated creatures, whose natural instincts had been turned to such account by human training.

After a few moments more, we came in sight of a regular road, in a direction nearly at right angles to that which followed the course of the river. Like the path, it was constructed of a hard polished concrete. It was about forty paces broad, and in the centre was a raised way about four inches higher than the general surface, and occupying about one-fourth of the entire width. Along the main way on either side passed from time to time with great rapidity light vehicles of shining metal, each having three wheels, one small one in front and two much larger behind, with box-like seat and steering handle; otherwise resembling nothing so much as the velocipedes I have seen ridden for amusement by eccentric English youths.

It was clear, however, that these vehicles were not moved by any effort on the part of their drivers, and their speed was far greater than that of the swiftest mail-coach:—say, from fifteen to thirty miles an hour. All risk of

collision was avoided, as those proceeding in opposite directions took opposite sides of the road, separated by the raised centre I have described.

Crossing the road with caution, we came upon a number of small houses, perhaps twenty feet square, each standing in the midst of a garden marked out by a narrow ditch, some of them having at either side wings of less height and thrown a little backward. In the centre of each, and at the end of the wings where these existed, was what seemed to be a door of some translucent material about twelve feet in height. But I observed that these doors were divided by a scarcely perceptible line up to six feet from the ground, and presently one of these parted, and a figure, closely resembling that of my guide, came out.

We had now reached another road which led apparently towards the larger houses I had seen in the distance, and were proceeding along the raised central pathway, when some half-dozen persons from the cottages followed us. At a call from my guide, these, and presently as many more, ran after and gathered around us. I turned, took down my air-gun from my back, and waving it around me, signalled to them to keep back, not choosing to incur the danger of a sudden rush, since their bearing, if not plainly hostile, was not hospitable or friendly. Thus escorted, but not actually assailed, I passed on for three or four miles, by which time we were among the larger dwellings of which I have spoken. Each of them stood in grounds enclosed by walls about eight feet high, each of some uniform colour, contrasting agreeably with that chosen for the exterior of the house. The enclosures varied in size from about six to sixty acres. The houses were for the most part some twelve feet in height, and from one to four hundred feet square. On several flat roofs, guarded by low parapets, other persons, all about the size of my guide, now showed themselves, all of them interested, and, as it seemed, somewhat excited by my appearance.

In a few cases groups differently dressed, and, from their somewhat smaller stature, slighter figures, and the long hair here and there visible, probably consisting of women, were gathered on a remoter portion of the roof. But these, when seen by those in front, were always waived back with an impatient or threatening gesture, and instantly retired. Presently two or three men more richly dressed than my escort, and in various colours,

came out upon the road. Addressing one of these, I pointed again to the sky, and again endeavoured to describe my journey, holding out to him at the same time, as the thing most likely to conciliate him, a watch somewhat larger than that I had bestowed upon my guide. He, however, did not come within arm's length; and when I repeated my signs, he threw back his head with a sort of sneer and uttered a few words in a sharp tone, at which my escort rushed upon and attempted to throw me down. For this, however, I had been long prepared, and striking right and left with my air-gun—for I was determined not to shed blood except in the last extremity—

I speedily cleared a circle round me, still grasping my guide with the left hand, from a providential instinct which suggested that his close contiguity might in some way protect me. A call from the chief of my antagonists was answered from the roof of a neighbouring house. I heard a whizzing through the air, and presently something like a winged serpent, but with a slender neck, and shoulders of considerable breadth, and a head much larger than a serpent's in proportion to the body, and shaped more like a bird's, with a sharp, short beak, sprang upon and coiled round my left arm.

That it was trying to sting with an erectile organ placed about midway between the shoulders and the tail I became instinctively aware, and presently felt something like a weak electric thrill over all my body, while my left hand, which was naked, sustained a severe shock, completely numbing it for the moment. I caught the beast by the neck, and flung him with all my force right in the face of my chief antagonist, who fell with a cry of terror. Looking in the direction from which this dangerous assailant had come, I perceived another in the air, and saw that not a moment was to be lost. Dropping my gun with the muzzle between my feet, and holding it so far as I could with my numbed left hand—releasing also my guide, but throwing him to the ground as I released him—I drew my sword; and but just in time, with the same motion with which I drew it, I cut right through the neck of the dragon that had been launched against me. My principal enemy had quickly recovered his feet and presence of mind, and spoke very loudly and at some length to the person who had launched the dragons. The latter disappeared, and at the same time the group around me began to disperse. Whatever suited them was certain not to suit me,

and accordingly, still holding my sword, I caught one of them with each hand. It was well I had done so, for within another minute the owner of the dragons reappeared with a weapon not wholly unlike a long cannon of very small bore fixed upon a sort of stand. This he levelled at me, and I, seeing that a danger of whose magnitude and nature I could form no exact estimate was impending, caught up instinctively one of my prisoners, and held him as a shield between myself and the weapon pointed at me. This checked my enemy, who for the moment seemed almost as much at a loss as myself. Fortunately his hostile intention evidently endangered not only my life but all near me, and secured me from any close attack.

At this moment a somewhat remarkable personage came to the front of the group which had gathered some few yards before me. He wore a long frock of emerald green and trousers of the same colour, gathered in at the waist by a belt of a red metal. On earth I should have taken him for a hale and vigorous gentleman of some fifty years; he was two inches short of five feet, but well proportioned as a man of middle size. Gentleman I say emphatically; for something of dignity, gravity, and calm good-breeding, was conspicuous in his manner, as authority unmixed with menace was evident in his tone. He called, somewhat peremptorily as I thought, to the man who was still aiming his weapon at my head, then waived back those behind him, and presently advanced towards me, looking me straight in the eyes with a steadiness and intensity of gaze far exceeding, both in expressiveness and in effect, the most fixed stare of the most successful mesmerists I have known. I doubt whether I should have had the power to resist his will had I thought it wise to do so. But I was perfectly aware that, however successful in repelling the first tumultuous attack, prolonged self-defence was hopeless.

I must, probably at the next move, certainly in a few minutes, succumb to the enemies around me. I could not conciliate those whose malignity I could not comprehend. I had done them no injury, and they could hardly be maddened by fear, since my size and strength did not seem to overawe them save at close quarters, and of my weapons they were certainly less afraid than I of theirs. My only chance must lie in finding favour with an

individual protector. When, therefore, the new-comer fearlessly laid his hand on an arm which could have killed him at a blow, and rather by gesture than by force released my captives, policy as well as instinct dictated submission. I allowed him to disarm and make me in some sense his prisoner without a show of resistance. He took me by the left hand, first placing my fingers upon his own wrist and then grasping mine, and led me quietly through the crowd, which gave way before him reluctantly and not without angry murmurs, but with a certain awe as before one superior either in power or rank.

Thus he led me for about half a mile, till we reached the crystal gate of an enclosure of exceptional size, the walls of which, like the gate itself, were of a pale rose-colour. Through grounds laid out in symmetrical alternation of orchard and grove, shrubbery, close-carpeted field, and garden beds, arranged with evident regard to effect in form and colour, as well as to fitting distribution of shade and sun, we followed a straight path which sloped under a canopy of flowering creepers up to the terrace on which stood the house itself. There were some eight or nine crystal doors (or windows) in the front, and in the centre one somewhat larger than the others, which, as we came immediately in front of it, opened, not turning on hinges, but, like every other door I had seen, dividing and sliding rapidly into the walls to the right and left. We entered, and it immediately closed behind us in the same way. Turning my head for a moment, I was surprised to observe that, whereas I could see nothing through the door from the outside, the scene without was as visible from within as through the most perfectly transparent glass. The chamber in which I found myself had walls of bright emerald green, with all the brilliant transparency of the jewel; their surface broken by bas-reliefs of minutely perfect execution, and divided into panels—each of which seemed to contain a series of distinct scenes, one above the other—by living creepers with foliage of bright gold, and flowers sometimes pink, sometimes cream-white of great size, both double and single; the former mostly hemispherical and the latter commonly shaped as hollow cones or Avide shallow champagne glasses.

In these walls two or three doors appeared, reaching, from the floor to the roof, which was coloured like the walls, and seemingly of the same

material. Through one of these my guide led me into a passage which appeared to run parallel with the front of the house, and turning down this, a door again parted on the right hand, through which he led me into a similar but smaller apartment, some twenty feet in width and twenty-five in length. The window—if I should so call that which was simply another door—of this apartment looked into one corner of a flower-garden of great extent, beyond and at each end of which were other portions of the dwelling. The walls of this chamber were pink, the surface appearing as before of jewel-like lustre; the roof and floor of a green lighter than that of the emerald. In two corners were piles of innumerable cushions and pillows covered with a most delicate satin-like fabric, embroidered with gold, silver, and feathers, all soft as eider-down and of all shapes and sizes.

There were three or four light tables, apparently of metal, silver, or azure, or golden in colour, in various parts of the chamber, with one or two of different form, more like small office-tables or desks. In one of the walls was sunk a series of shelves closed by a transparent sheet of crystal of pale yellow tinge. There were three or four movable seats resembling writing or easy-chairs, but also of metal, luxurious all though all different. In the corner to the left, farthest from the inner court or peristyle, was a screen, which, as my host showed me, concealed a bath and some other convenient appurtenances. The bath was a cylinder some five feet in depth and about two in diameter, with thin double walls, the space between which was filled with an apparatus of small pipes. By pressing a spring, as my protector pointed out, countless minute jets of warm perfumed water were thrown from every part of the interior wall, forming the most delicious and perfect shower-bath that could well be devised.

My host then led me to a seat among the cushions, and placed himself beside me, looking for some time intently and gravely into my face, but with nothing of offensive curiosity, still less of menace in his gaze. It appeared to me as if he wished to read the character and perhaps the thoughts of his guest. The scrutiny seemed to satisfy him. He stretched out his left hand, and grasping mine, placed it on his heart, and then dropping my hand, placed his upon my breast. He then spoke in words whose meaning I could not guess, but the tone sounded to me as that of inquiry.

The question most likely to be asked concerned my character and the place from which I had come. I again explained, again pointing upward. He seemed dubious or perplexed, and it occurred to me that drawing might assist explanation; since, from the bas-reliefs and tracery, it was evident that the art was carried to no common excellence in Mars. I drew, therefore, in the first place, a globe to represent the Earth, traced its orbit round the Sun, and placed a crescent Moon at some little distance, indicating its path round the Earth. It was evident that my host understood my meaning, the more clearly when I marked upon the form of the Earth a crescent, such as she would often present through a Martial telescope. Sketches in outline roughly exhibiting different stages of my voyage, from the first ascent to the final landing, appeared to convince my host of my meaning, if not of my veracity. Signing to me to remain where I was, he left the room. In a few minutes he returned, accompanied by one of the strange squirrel-like animals I had seen in the fields. I was right in conjecturing that the creature had no opposable thumb; but a little ingenuity had compensated this so far as regarded the power of carrying. A little chain hung down from each wrist, and to these was suspended a tray, upon which were arranged a variety of fruits and what seemed to be small loaves of various materials.

Breaking one of these and cutting open with a small knife, apparently of silver, one of the fruits, my host tasted each and then motioned to me to eat. The attendant had placed the tray upon a table, disengaged the chains, and disappeared; the door opening and closing as he trod, somewhat more heavily than had been necessary for my host, upon particular points of the floor.

The food offered me was very delicious and various in flavour. My host showed me how to cut the top from some of the hard-rind fruits, so as to have a cup full of the most delicately-flavoured juice, the whole pulp having been reduced to a liquid syrup by a process with which some semicivilised cultivators on Earth are familiar. When I had finished my meal, my host whistled, and the attendant, returning, carried away the tray. His master gave him at the same time what was evidently an order, repeating it twice, and speaking with signal clearness of intonation. The little creature bowed its head, apparently as a sign of intelligence, and in a

few minutes returned with what seemed like a pencil or stylus and writing materials, and with a large silver-like box of very curious form. To one side was affixed a sort of mouthpiece, consisting of a truncated cone expanding into a saucer-shaped bowl. Across the wider and outer end of the cone was stretched a membrane or diaphragm about three inches in diameter. Into the mouth of the bowl, two or three inches from the diaphragm, my host spoke one by one a series of articulate but single sounds, beginning with â, a, aa, au, o, oo, ou, u, y or ei (long), i (short), oi, e, which I afterwards found to be the twelve vowels of their language. After he had thus uttered some forty distinct sounds, he drew from the back of the instrument a slip of something like goldleaf, on which as many weird curves and angular figures were traced in crimson. Pointing to these in succession, he repeated the sounds in order. I made out that the figures in question represented the sounds spoken into the instrument, and taking out my pencil, marked under each the equivalent character of the Roman alphabet, supplemented by some letters not admitted therein but borrowed from other Aryan tongues. My host looked on with some interest whilst I did this, and bent his head as if in approval. Here then was the alphabet of the Martial tongue—an alphabet not arbitrary, but actually produced by the vocal sounds it represented! The elaborate machinery modifies the rough signs which are traced by the mere aerial vibrations; but each character is a true physical type, a visual image, of the spoken sound; the voice, temper, accent, sex, of a speaker affect the phonograph, and are recognisable in the record. The instrument wrote, so to speak, different hands under my voice and under Esmo's; and those who knew him could identify his phonogram, as my friends my manuscript.

After I had been employed for some time in fixing these forms and the corresponding sounds in my memory, my host advanced to the window, and opening it, led me into the interior garden; which, as I had supposed, was a species of central court around which the house was built.

The construction of the house was at once apparent. It consisted of a front portion, divided by the gallery of which I have spoken, all the rooms on one side thereof looking, like the chamber I first entered, into the outer

enclosure; those on the other into the interior garden or peristyle. Beyond the latter was a single row of chambers opening upon it, appropriated to the ladies and children of the household. The court was roofed over with the translucent material of the windows. It was about 360 feet in length by 300 in width. At either end were chambers entirely formed of the same material as the roof, in one of which the various birds and animals employed either in domestic service or in agriculture, in another the various stores of the household, were kept. In front of these, two inclined planes of the same material as the walls of the house led up to the several parts of the roof. The court was divided by broad concrete paths into four gardens. In the centre of each was a basin of water and a fountain, above which was a square opening of some twenty feet in the roof. Each garden was, so to speak, turfed with minute plants, smaller than daisy roots, and even more closely covering the soil than English lawn grass. These were of different colours—emerald, gold, and purple—arranged in bands. This turf was broken by a number of beds of all shapes, the crescent, circle, and six-rayed star being apparently the chief favourites. The smaller of these were severally filled with one or two flowers; in the larger, flowers of different colours were set in patterns, generally rising from the outside to the centre, and never allowing the soil to be seen through a single interval. The contrast of colours and tints was admirably ordered; the size, form, and structure of the flowers wonderfully various and always exquisitely beautiful. The exact tints of silver and gold were frequent and especially favoured, At each corner of every garden was a hollow silvery pillar, up which creepers with flowers of marvellous size and beauty, and foliage of hues almost as striking as those of the flowers, were conducted to form a perfect arch overhead, parting off the gardens from the walks. In each basin were fishes whose brilliancy of colouring and beauty of form far surpassed anything I have seen in earthly seas or rivers.

At the meeting of the four cross paths was a wide space covered with a soft woven carpet, upon which were strown cushions similar to those in my room. On these several ladies were reclining, who rose as the head of the family approached. One who seemed by her manner to be the mistress, and by her resemblance to some of her younger companions the mother, of the

family, wore a sort of light golden half-helmet on the head, and over this, falling round her half-way to the waist, a crimson veil, intended apparently to protect her head and neck from the sun as much as to conceal them. Her face was partially uncovered. The dress of all was, except in colour and in certain omissions and additions, much the same. The under-garments must have been slight in material and few in number. Nothing was to be seen of them save the sleeves, which were of a delicate substance, resembling that of the finest Parisian kid gloves, but far softer and finer. Over all was a robe almost without shape, save what it took from the figure to which it closely adapted itself, suspended by broad ribbons and jewelled clasps from the shoulders, falling nearly to the ankles, and gathered in by a zone at the waist. This garment left the neck, shoulders, and the upper part of the bosom uncovered; but the veil, whether covering the head completely, drawn round all save the face, or consisting only of two separate muslin falls behind either ear, was always so arranged as to render the general effect far more decorous than the "low dresses" of European matrons and maidens. The ankles and feet were entirely bare, save for sandals with an embroidered velvety covering for the toes, and silver bands clasped round the ankles. The eldest lady wore a pale green robe of a fine but very light silken-seeming fabric. Three younger ones wore a similar material of pink, with silver head-dresses and veils hiding everything but the eyes. All these had sleeves reaching to the wrist, ending in gloves of the same fabric. Two young girls were robed in white gauze, with gauze veils attached over either ear to a very slight silver coronal; their arms bare till the sleeve of the under-robe appeared, a couple of inches below the shoulder; their bright soft faces and their long hair (which fell freely down the back, kept in graceful order here and there by almost invisible silver clasps or bands) were totally uncovered. "A maiden," says the Martialist, "may make the most of her charms; a wife's beauty is her lord's exclusive right." One of the girls, my host's daughters, might almost have veiled her entire form above the knees in the masses of rich soft brown hair inherited from her father, but mingled with tresses of another tinge, shimmering like gold under certain lights. Her eyes, of deepest violet, were shaded by dark thick lashes, so long that when the lids were closed they traced a clear black curve on

either cheek. The other maiden had, like their mother, and, I believe, like the younger matrons, the bright hair—flaxen in early childhood, pale gold in maturer years—and the blue or grey eyes characteristic of the race. My host spoke two or three words to the chief of the party, indicating me by a graceful and courteous wave of the hand, upon which the person addressed slightly bent her head, laying her hand at the same time upon her heart. The others acknowledged the introduction by a similar but slighter inclination, and all resumed their places as soon as my host, seating himself between us, signed to me to occupy some pillows which one of the young ladies arranged on his left hand, I had observed by this time that the left hand was used by preference, as we use the right, for all purposes, and therefore was naturally extended in courtesy; and the left side was, for similar reasons, the place of honour.

Three or four children were playing in another part of the court. All, with one exception, were remarkably beautiful and healthy-looking, certainly not less graceful in form and movement than the happiest and prettiest in our own world. Their tones were soft and gentle, and their bearing towards each other notably kind and considerate. One unfortunate little creature differed from the rest in all respects. It was slightly lame, misshapen rather than awkward, and with a face that indicated bad health, bad temper, or both. Its manner was peevish and fractious, its tones sharp and harsh, and its actions rough and hasty. I took it for a mother's sickly favourite, deformed in character to compensate for physical deformity. Watching them for a short time, I saw the little creature repeatedly break out in all the humours of an ill-tempered, over-indulged youngest-born in an ill-managed family; snatching toys from the others, and now and then slapping or pinching them. But they never returned either word or blow, even when pain or vexation brought the tears to their eyes. When its caprices became intolerable most of its companions withdrew; one, however, always remaining on the watch, even if driven from the immediate neighbourhood by its intolerably provoking temper, tones, and acts.

Before sunset we were joined by a young man, who, first approaching my host with a respectful inclination of the head, stood before him till apparently desired by a few quiet words to speak; when he addressed the head of the family in some short sentences, and then, at a sign from him, turned to two of the squirrel-like animals, "ambau," which followed him.

These then laid at my feet two large baskets, or open bags of golden network, containing many of the smaller objects left in the Astronaut.

Emptying these, they brought several more, till they had laid before me the whole of my wardrobe and my store of intended presents, books, and drawings, with such of my instruments as were not attached to the walls. It was evident that great care had been taken not to injure or dismantle the vessel. Nothing that actually belonged to it had been taken away, and of the articles brought not one had been broken or damaged. It was equally evident that there was no intention or idea of appropriating them. They were brought and handed over to me as a host on Earth might send for the baggage of an unexpected guest. Of the various toys and ornaments that I had brought for the purpose, I offered several of the most precious to my host. He accepted one of the smallest and least valuable, rather declining to understand than refusing the offer of the rest. The bringer did the same.

Then placing in the chief's hands an open jewel-box containing a variety of the choicest jewellery, I requested by signs his permission to offer them to the ladies. The elder ones imitated his example, and graciously accepted one or two tasteful feminine ornaments, of far less beauty and value than any of the few splendid jewels that adorned their belts and clasped their robes at the shoulder, or fastened their veils. The white-robed maidens shrank back shyly until the box was pressed upon them, when each, at a word from the mistress, selected some small gold or silver locket or chain; each at once placing the article accepted about her person, with an evident intention of adding to the grace with which it was received and acknowledging the intended courtesy. How valueless the most valuable of these trifles must have been in their eyes I had begun to suspect from what I saw, and was afterwards made fully aware. As the shades of evening fell, the fountains ceased to play, the young man pressed electric springs which closed the openings in the roof, and, finally, turning a small handle, caused

a bright light to diffuse itself over the whole garden, and through the doors into the chambers opening upon it. At the same time a warmer air gradually spread throughout the interior of the building. A meal was then served in small low trays, which was eaten by all of us reclining on our cushions; after which the ladies retired, and my host conducted me back to my chamber, and left me to repose.

My books and sketches, as well as the portfolios of popular prints which I had selected to assist me in describing the life and scenery of our world, were, with my wardrobe and other properties, arranged on my shelves by the ambau, under the direction of Kevimâ, the young gentleman who had superintended their removal and conveyance to his father's house. The portfolios gave me occasional means and topics of pleasant intercourse with the family of my host, before we could converse at ease in their language. The children, though never troublesome or importunate, took frequent opportunities of stealing into the room to look over the prints I produced for their amusement. The ladies also, particularly the violet-eyed maiden, who seemed to be the especial guardian of the little ones, would draw near to look and listen. The latter, though she never entered the room or directly addressed me, often assisted in explaining my broken sentences to her charges, some of them not many years younger than herself. I took sincere pleasure in the children's company and growing confidence, but they were not the less welcome because they drew their sisters to listen to my descriptions of an existence so strange and so remote in habits and character, as well as in space. Perhaps their gentle governess learned more than any other member of the family respecting Earth-life, and my own adventures by land and water, in air and space. For, though just not child enough to share the children's freedom, she took in all they heard; she listened in silence during our evening gatherings to the conversation in which her father and brother encouraged me to practise the language I was laboriously studying. She had, therefore, double opportunities of acquiring a knowledge which seemed to interest her deeply; naturally, since it was so absolutely novel, and communicated by one whose very presence was the most marvellous of the marvels it attested. How much she understood I could not judge. Except her mother, the ladies did not take a direct part in

my talk with the children, and but very seldom interposed, through my host, a shy brief question when the evening brought us all together. The maidens, despite their theoretical privileges, were even more reserved than their elders, and the dark-haired Eveena the most silent and shy of all.

I learned afterwards that the privilege of intercourse with the ladies of the household, restricted as it was, was wholly exceptional, and even in this family was conceded only out of consideration for one who could not safely be allowed to leave the house.

CHAPTER V - LANGUAGE, LAWS, AND LIFE.

Though treated with the greatest kindness and courtesy, I soon found reason to understand that I was, at least for the present, a prisoner. My host or his son never failed to invite me each day to spend some time in the outer enclosure, but never intentionally left me alone there. On one occasion, when Kevimâ had been called away and I ventured to walk down towards the gate, my host's youngest child, who had been playing on the roof, ran after me, and reaching me just as my foot was set on the spring that opened the gate or outer door, caught me by the hand, and looking up into my face, expressed by glance and gesture a negative so unmistakable that I thought it expedient at once to comply and return to the house. There my time was occupied, for as great a part of each day as I could give to such a task without extreme fatigue, in mastering the language of the country. This was a much simpler task than might have been supposed. I soon found that, unlike any Terrestrial tongue, the language of this people had not grown but been made—constructed deliberately on set principles, with a view to the greatest possible simplicity and the least possible taxation of the memory. There were no exceptions or irregularities, and few unnecessary distinctions; while words were so connected and related that the mastery of a few simple grammatical forms and of a certain number of roots enabled me to guess at, and by and by to feel tolerably sure of, the meaning of a new word. The verb has six tenses, formed by the addition of a consonant to the root, and six persons, plural and singular, masculine and feminine.

Singular. | Masc. | Fem. || Plural. | Masc. | Fem.
I am | avâ | ava || We are | avau | avaa
Thou art | avo | avoo || You are | avou | avu
He or she is | avy | ave || They are | avoi | avee

The terminations are the three pronouns, feminine and masculine, singular and plural, each represented by one of twelve vowel characters, and declined like nouns. When a nominative immediately follows the verb, the pronominal suffix is generally dropped, unless required by euphony. Thus,

"a man strikes" is dak klaftas, but in the past tense, dakny klaftas, the verb without the suffix being unpronounceable. The past tense is formed by the insertion of n (avnâ: "I have been"), the future by m: avmâ. The imperative, avsâ; which in the first person is used to convey determination or resolve; avsâ, spoken in a peremptory tone, meaning "I will be," while avso, according to the intonation, means "be" or "thou shalt be;" i.e., shalt whether or no. R forms the conditional, avrâ, and ren the conditional past, avrenâ, "I should have been." The need for a passive voice is avoided by the simple method of putting the pronoun in the accusative; thus, dâcâ signifies "I strike," dâcal (me strike) "I am struck." The infinitive is avi; avyta, "being;" avnyta, "having been;" avmyta, "about to be." These are declined like nouns, of which latter there are six forms, the masculine in â, o, and y, the feminine in a, oo, and e; the plurals being formed exactly as in the pronominal suffixes of the verb. The root-word, without inflexion, alone is used where the name is employed in no connection with a verb, where in every terrestrial language the nominative would be employed.

Thus, my guide had named the squirrel-monkeys ambau (sing. ambâ); but the word is declined as follows:—

Singular. Plural.
Nominative ambâs ambaus
Accusative ambâl ambaul
Dative, to or in ambân ambaun
Ablative, by or from ambâm ambaum

The five other forms are declined in the same manner, the vowel of the last syllable only differing. Adjectives are declined like nouns, but have no comparative or superlative degree; the former being expressed by prefixing the intensitive syllable ca, the latter, when used (which is but seldom) by the prefix ela, signifying the in an emphatic sense, as his Grace of Wellington is in England called The Duke par excellence. Prepositions and adverbs end in t or d.

Each form of the noun has, as a rule, its special relation to the verb of the same root: thus from dâc, "strike," are derived dâcâ, "weapon" or

"hammer;", dâco, a "stroke" or "striking" [as given] both masculine; dâca,

"anvil;" dâcoo, "blow" or "beating" [as received]; and dâke, "a thing beaten,"

feminine. The sixth form, dâky, masculine, has in this case no proper signification, and not being wanted, is not used. Individual letters or syllables are largely employed in combination to give new and even contradictory meanings to a root. Thus n, like the Latin in, signifies

"penetration," "motion towards," or simply "remaining in a place," or, again, "permanence." M, like the Latin ab or ex, indicates "motion from." R

expresses "uncertainty" or "incompleteness," and is employed to convert a statement into a question, or a relative pronoun into one of inquiry. G, like the Greek a or anti, generally signifies "opposition" or "negation;" ca is, as aforesaid, intensive, and is employed, for

42

example, to convert âfi, "to breathe," into câfi, "to speak." Cr is by itself an interjection of abhorrence or disgust; in composition it indicates detestation or destruction: thus, crâky signifies "hatred;" crâvi, "the destruction of life" or "to kill." L for the most part indicates passivity, but with different effect according to its place in the word. Thus mepi signifies "to rule;" mepil, "to be ruled;" melpi, "to control one's self;" lempi, "to obey." The signification of roots themselves is modified by a modification of the principal vowel or consonant, i.e., by exchanging the original for one closely related. Thus avi, "exist;" âvi, "be,"

in the positive sense of being this or that; afi, "live;" âfi, "breathe." Z is a diminutive; zin, "with," often abbreviated to zn, "combination," "union."

Thus znaftau means "those who were brought into life together," or "brethren."

I may add, before I quit this subject, that the Martial system of arithmetic differs from ours principally in the use of a duodecimal instead of a decimal basis. Figures are written on a surface divided into minute squares, and the value of a figure, whether it signify so many units, dozens, twelve dozens, and so forth, depends upon the square in which it is placed. The central square of a line represents the unit's place, and is marked by a line drawn above it. Thus a figure answering to our I, if placed in the fourth square to the left, represents 1728. In the third place to the right, counting the unit square in both cases, it signifies 1/144, and so forth.

In less than a fortnight I had obtained a general idea of the language, and was able to read easily the graven representations of spoken sound which I have described; and by the end of a month (to use a word which had no meaning here) I could speak intelligibly if not freely. Only in a language so simple could my own anxiety to overcome as soon as possible a fatal obstacle to all investigation of this new world, and the diligent and patient assistance given by my host or his son for a great part of every day, have enabled me to make such rapid progress. I had noted even, during the short evening gatherings when the whole family was assembled, the extreme taciturnity of both sexes; and by the time I could make myself understood, I was not surprised to learn that the Martials have scarcely the idea of what we mean by conversation, not talking for the sake of talking, or speaking unless they have something to discuss, explain, or communicate. I found, again, that a new and much more difficult task, though fortunately one not so indispensable, was still in store for me. The Martials have two forms of writing: the one I have described, which is simply a mechanical rendering of spoken words into artificially simplified visible signs; the other, written by hand, with a fine pencil of some chemical material on a prepared surface, textile or metallic. The characters of the latter are, like ours wholly arbitrary; but the contractions and abbreviations are so numerous that the mastery of the mere alphabet, the forty or fifty single letters employed, is but a single step in the first stage of the hard task of learning to read. In no country on Earth, except China, is this task half so severe as in Mars. On the other hand, when it is once mastered, a far superior instrument has been gained; the Martial writing being a most terse but perfectly legible shorthand. Every Martial can write at least as quickly as he can speak, and can read the written character more rapidly than the quickest eye can peruse the best Terrestrial print. Copies, whether of the phonographic or stylographic writing, are multiplied with extreme facility and perfection. The original, once inscribed in either manner upon the above-mentioned tafroo or gold-leaf, is placed upon a sheet of a species of linen, smoother than paper, called difra. A current of electricity sent through the former reproduces the writing exactly upon the latter, which has been previously steeped in some chemical composition;

the effect apparently depending on the passage of the electricity through the untouched metal, and its absolute interception by the ink, if I may so call it, of the writing, which bites deeply into the leaf. This process can be repeated almost ad libitum; and it is equally easy to take at any time a fresh copy upon tafroo, which serves again for the reproduction of any number of difra copies. The book, for the convenience of this mode of reproduction, consists of a single sheet, generally from four to eight inches in breadth and of any length required. The writing intended to be thus copied is always minute, and is read for the most part through magnifying spectacles. A roller is attached to each end of the sheet, and when not in use the latter is wound round that attached to the conclusion. When required for reading, both rollers are fixed in a stand, and slowly moved by clockwork, which spreads before the eyes of the reader a length of about four inches at once.

The motion is slackened or quickened at the reader's pleasure, and can be stopped altogether, by touching a spring. Another means of reproducing, not merely writings or drawings, but natural objects, consists in a simple adaptation of the camera obscura. [The only essential difference from our photographs being that the Martial art reproduces colour as well as outline, I omit this description.]

While I was practising myself in the Martial language my host turned our experimental conversations chiefly, if not exclusively, upon Terrestrial subjects; endeavouring to learn all that I could convey to him of the physical peculiarities of the Earth, of geology, geography, vegetation, animal life in all its forms, human existence, laws, manners, social and domestic order. Afterwards, when, at the end of some fifty days, he found that we could converse, if not with ease yet without fear of serious misapprehension, he took an early opportunity of explaining to me the causes and circumstances of my unfriendly reception among his people.

"Your size and form," he said, "startled and surprised them. I gather from what you have told me that on Earth there are many nations very imperfectly known to one another, with different dress, language, and manners. This planet is now inhabited by a single race, all speaking the same tongue, using much the same customs, and differing from one

another in form and size much less widely than (I understand) do men upon your Earth. There you might have been taken for a visitor from some strange and unexplored country. Here it was clear that you were not one of our race, and yet it was inconceivable what else you could be. We have no giants; the tallest skeleton preserved in our museums is scarcely a hand's breadth taller than myself, and does not, of course, approach to your stature. Then, as you have pointed out, your limbs are longer and your chest smaller in proportion to the rest of the body; probably because, as you seem to say, your atmosphere is denser than ours, and we require ampler lungs to inhale the quantity of air necessary at each breath for the oxidation of the blood. Then you were not dumb, and yet affected not to understand our language and to speak a different one. No such creature could have existed in this planet without having been seen, described, and canvassed. You did not, therefore, belong to us. The story you told by signs was quickly apprehended, and as quickly rejected as an audacious impossibility. It was an insult to the intelligence of your hearers, and a sufficient ground for suspecting a being of such size and physical strength of some evil or dangerous design. The mob who first attacked you were probably only perplexed and irritated; those who subsequently interfered may have been animated also by scientific curiosity. You would have been well worth anatomisation and chemical analysis. Your mail-shirt protected you from the shock of the dragon, which was meant to paralyse and place you at the mercy of your assailants; the metal distributing the current, and the silken lining resisting its passage. Still, at the moment when I interposed, you would certainly have been destroyed but for your manoeuvre of laying hold of two of your immediate escort. Our destructive weapons are far superior to any you possess or have described. That levelled at you by my neighbour would have sent to ten times your distance a small ball, which, bursting, would have asphyxiated every living thing for several yards around. But our laws regarding the use of such weapons are very stringent, and your enemy dared not imperil the lives of those you held. Those laws would not, he evidently thought, apply to yourself, who, as he would have affirmed, could not be regarded as a man and an object of legal protection."

He explained the motives and conduct of his countrymen with such perfect coolness, such absence of surprise or indignation, that I felt slightly nettled, and answered sarcastically, "If the slaughter of strangers whose account of themselves appears improbable be so completely a matter of course among you, I am at a loss to understand your own interference, and the treatment I have received from yourself and your family, so utterly opposite in spirit as well as in form to that I met from everybody else."

"I do not," he answered, "always act from the motives in vogue among my fellow-creatures of this planet; but why and how I differ from them it might not be well to explain. It is for the moment of more consequence to tell you why you have been kept in some sense a prisoner here. My neighbours, independently of general laws, are for certain reasons afraid to do me serious wrong. While in my company or in my dwelling they could hardly attempt your life without endangering mine or those of my family.

If you were seen alone outside my premises, another attempt, whether by the asphyxiator or by a destructive animal, would probably be made, and might this time prove successful. Till, therefore, the question of your humanity and right to the protection of our law is decided by those to whom it has been submitted, I will beg you not to venture alone beyond the bounds that afford you security; and to believe that in this request, as in detaining you perforce heretofore, I am acting simply for your own welfare, and not," he added, smiling, "with a view to secure the first opportunity of putting your relation to our race to the tests of the dissecting table and the laboratory."

"But my story explained everything that seemed inexplicable; why was it not believed? It was assumed that I could not belong to Mars; yet I was a living creature in the flesh, and must therefore have come from some other planet, as I could hardly be supposed to be an inhabitant of space."

"We don't reason on impossibilities," replied my friend. "We have a maxim that it is more probable that any number of witnesses should lie, that the senses of any number of persons should be deluded, than that a miracle should be true; and by a miracle we mean an interruption or violation of the known laws of nature."

"One eminent terrestrial sceptic," I rejoined, "has said the same thing, and masters of the science of probabilities have supported his assertion. But a miracle should be a violation not merely of the known but of all the laws of nature, and until you know all those laws, how can you tell what is a miracle? The lifting of iron by a magnet—I suppose you have iron and loadstones here as we have on Earth—was, to the first man who witnessed it, just as complete a violation of the law of gravity as now appears my voyage through space, accomplished by a force bearing some relation to that which acts through the magnet."

"Our philosophers," he answered, "are probably satisfied that they know nearly all that is to be known of natural laws and forces; and to delusion or illusion human sense is undeniably liable."

"If," I said, "you cannot trust your senses, you may as well disbelieve in your own existence and in everything around you, for you know nothing save through those senses which are liable to illusion. But we know practically that there are limits to illusion. At any rate, your maxim leads directly and practically to the inference that, since I do not belong to Mars and cannot have come from any other world, I am not here, and in fact do not exist. Surely it was somewhat illogical to shoot an illusion and intend to dissect a spectre! Is not a fact the complete and unanswerable refutation of its impossibility?"

"A good many facts to which I could testify," he replied, "are in this world confessed impossibilities, and if my neighbours witnessed them they would pronounce them to be either impostures or illusions."

"Then," said I, somewhat indignantly, "they must prefer inferences from facts to facts themselves, and the deductions of logic to the evidence of their senses. Yet, if that evidence be wanting in certainty, then, since no chain can be stronger than its weakest point, inferences are doubly uncertain; first, because they are drawn from facts reported by sense, and, secondly, because a flaw in the logic is always possible."

"Do not repeat that out of doors," he answered, smiling. "It is not permitted here to doubt the infallibility of science; and any one who ventures to
affirm persistently a story which science pronounces impossible (like your voyage through space), if he do not fall at once a victim to popular piety, would be consigned to the worse than living death of life-long confinement in a lunatic hospital."

"In that case I fear very much that I have little chance of being put under the protection of your laws, since, whatever may be the impression of those who have seen me, every one else must inevitably pronounce me non-existent; and a nonentity can hardly be the subject of legal wrong or have a right to legal redress."

"Nor," he replied, "can there be any need or any right to annihilate that which does not exist. This alternative may occupy our Courts of Justice, for aught I know, longer than you or I can hope to live. What I have asked is that, till these have decided between two contradictory absurdities, you shall be provisionally and without prejudice considered as a human reality and an object of legal protection."

"And who," I asked, "has authority ad interim to decide this point?"

"It was submitted," he answered, "in the first place, to the Astyntâ (captain, president) who governs this district; but, as I expected, he declined to pronounce upon it, and referred it to the Meptâ (governor) of the province.

Half-an-hour's argument so bewildered the latter that he sent the question immediately to the Zamptâ (Regent) of this dominion, and he, after hearing by telegraph the opening of the case, at once pronounced that, as affecting the entire planet, it must be decided by the Camptâ or Suzerain. Now this gentleman is impatient of the dogmatism of the philosophers, who have tried recently to impose upon him one or two new theoretical rules which would limit the amount of what he calls free will that he practically enjoys; and as the philosophers are all against you, and as, moreover, he has a strong though secret hankering after curious phenomena—it would not do to say, after impossibilities—I do not think he will allow you to be destroyed, at least till he has seen you."

"Is it possible," I said, "that even your monarch cherishes a belief in the incredible or logically impossible, and yet escapes the lunatic asylum with which you threaten me?"

"I should not escape grave consequences were I to attribute to him a heresy so detestable," said my host. "Even the Camptâ would not be rash enough to let it be said that he doubts the infallibility of science, or of public opinion as its exponent. But as it is the worst of offences to suggest the existence of that which is pronounced impossible or unscientific, the supreme authority can always, in virtue of the enormity of the guilt, insist on undertaking himself the executive investigation of all such cases; and generally contrives to have the impossibility, if a tangible one, brought into the presence either as evidence or as accomplice."

"Well," I rejoined, after a few minutes' reflection, "I don't know that I have much right to complain of ideas which, after all, are but the logical development of those which, are finding constantly more and more favour among our most enlightened nations. I can quite believe, from what I have seen of our leading scientists, that in another century it may be dangerous in my own country for my descendants to profess that belief in a Creator and a future life which I am superstitious enough to prefer to all the revelations of all the material sciences."

"As you value your life and freedom," he replied, "don't speak of such a belief here, save to the members of my own family, and to those with whom I may tell you you are safe. Such ideas were held here, almost as generally as you say they now are on Earth, some twelve thousand years ago, and twenty thousand years ago their profession was compulsory. But for the last hundred centuries it has been settled that they are utterly fatal to the progress of the race, to enlightenment, to morality, and to the practical devotion of our energies to the business of life; and they are not merely disavowed and denounced, but hated with an earnestness proportioned to the scientific enthusiasm of classes and individuals."

"But," said I, "if so long, so severely, and so universally discountenanced, how can their expression by one man here or there be considered perilous?"

"Our philosophers say," he replied, "that the attractiveness of these ideas to certain minds is such that no reasoning, no demonstration of their absurdity, will prevent their exercising a mischievous influence upon weak, and especially upon feminine natures; and perhaps the suspicion that they are still held in secret may contribute to keep alive the bitterness with which they are repudiated and repressed. But if they are so held, if there be any who believe that the order of the universe was at first established, and that its active forces are still sustained and governed, by a conscious Intelligence—if there be those who think that they have proof positive of the continued existence of human beings after death—their secret has been well kept. For very many centuries have elapsed since the last victim of such delusions, as they were solemnly pronounced by public vote in the reign of the four-hundredth predecessor of the present Camptâ, was sent as incurable to the dangerous ward of our strictest hospital for the insane."

A tone of irony, and at the same time an air of guarded reserve, seemed to pervade all my host's remarks on this subject, and I perceived that for some reason it was so unpleasant to him that courtesy obliged me to drop it. I put, therefore, to turn the conversation, some questions as to the political organisation of which his words had afforded me a glimpse; and in reply he undertook to give me a summary of the political history of his planet during the last few hundred generations.

"If," he said, "in giving you this sketch of the process by which our present social order has been established, I should mention a class or party who have stood at certain times distinctly apart from or in opposition to the majority, I must, in the first place, beg you to ask no questions about them, and in the next not to repeat incautiously the little I may tell you, or to show, by asking questions of others, what you have heard from me."

I gave my promise frankly, of course, and he then gave me the following sketch of Martial history:—

We date events from the union of all races and nations in a single State, a union which was formally established 13,218 years ago. At that time the large majority of the inhabitants of this planet possessed no other property
than their houses, clothes, and tools, their furniture, and a few other trifles.

The land was owned by fewer than 400,000 proprietors. Those who possessed movable wealth may have numbered thrice as many. Political and social power was in the hands of the owners of property, and of those, generally connected with them by birth or marriage, who were at any rate not dependent on manual labour for their bread. But among these there were divisions and factions on various questions more or less trivial, none of them approaching in importance or interest to the fundamental and irreconcilable conflict sure one day to arise between those who had accumulated wealth and those who had not. To gain their ends in one or another of these frivolous quarrels, each party in turn admitted to political influence section after section of what you call the proletariat; till in the year 3278 universal suffrage was granted, every man and woman over the age of twelve years being entitled to a single and equal vote.

About the same time the change in opinion of which I have spoken had taken general effect, and the vast majority of the men, at any rate, had ceased to believe in a future life wherein the inequalities and iniquities of this might be redressed. It followed that they were fiercely impatient of hardships and suffering, especially such as they thought might be redressed by political and social changes. The leaders of the multitude, for the most part men belonging to the propertied classes who had either wasted their wealth or never possessed any, demanded the abolition of private ownership, first of land, then of movable wealth; a demand which fiercely excited the passions of those who possessed neither, and as bitterly provoked the anger and alarm of those who did. The struggle raged for some generations and ended by an appeal to the sword; in which, since the force of the State was by law in the hands of the majority, the intelligent, thrifty, careful owners of property with their adherents were signally defeated. Universal communism was established in 3412, none being permitted to own, or even to claim, the exclusive use of any portion of the planet's surface, or of any other property except the share of food and clothing allotted to him. One only privilege was allowed to certain sectaries who still clung to the habits of the past, to the permanence and privacy of family life. They were permitted to have houses or portions of houses to

themselves, and to live there on the share of the public produce allotted to the several members of each household. It had been assumed as matter of course by the majority that when every one was forced to work there would be more than enough for all; that public spirit, and if necessary coercion, would prove as effectual stimulants to exertion and industry as interest and necessity had done under the system of private ownership.

Those who relied on the refutation of this theory forgot that with poor and suffering men who look to no future, and acknowledge no law but such as is created by their own capricious will and pleasure, envy is even a more powerful passion than greed. The Many preferred that wealth and luxury should be destroyed, rather than that they should be the exclusive possession of the Few. The first and most visible effect of Communism was the utter disappearance of all perishable luxuries, of all food, clothing, furniture, better than that enjoyed by the poorest. Whatever could not be produced in quantities sufficient to give each an appreciable share was not produced at all. Next, the quarrels arising out of the apportionment of labour were bitter, constant, and savage. Only a grinding despotism could compose them, and those who wielded such despotism for a short time excited during the period of their rule such fierce and universal hatred, that they were invariably overturned and almost invariably murdered before their very brief legal term of office had closed. It was not only that those engaged in the same kind of labour quarrelled over the task assigned to each, whether allotted in proportion to his strength, or to the difficulty of his labour, or by lot equally to all. Those to whom the less agreeable employments were assigned rebelled or murmured, and at last it was necessary to substitute rotation for division of labour, since no one would admit that he was best fitted for the lower or less agreeable. Of course we thus wasted silver tools in doing the work of iron, and reduced enormously the general production of wealth. Next, it was found that since one man's industry or idleness could produce no appreciable effect upon the general wealth, still less upon the particular share assigned to him, every man was as idle as the envy and jealousy of his neighbours would allow. Finally, as the produce annually diminished and the number of mouths to be fed became a serious consideration, the parents of many children were

regarded as public enemies. The entire independence of women, as equal citizens, with no recognised relation to individual men, was the inevitable outcome, logically and practically, of the Communistic principle; but this only made matters worse. Attempts were of course made to restrain multiplication by law, but this brought about inquisitions so utterly intolerable that human nature revolted against them. The sectaries I have mentioned—around whom, without adopting or even understanding their principles, gradually gathered all the better elements of society, every man of intellect and spirit who had not been murdered, with a still larger proportion of women—seceded separately or in considerable numbers at once; established themselves in those parts of the planet whose less fertile soil or less genial climate had caused them to be abandoned, and there organised societies on the old principles of private ownership and the permanence of household ties. By and by, as they visibly prospered, they attracted the envy and greed of the Communists. They worked under whatever disadvantage could be inflicted by climate and soil, but they had a much more than countervailing advantage in mutual attachment, in freedom from the bitter passions necessarily excited by the jealousy and incessant mutual interference inseparable from the Communistic system, and in their escape from the caprice and instability of popular government—these societies, whether from wisdom or mere reaction, submitting to the rule of one or a few chief magistrates selected by the natural leaders of each community. Moreover, they had not merely the adhesion of all the more able, ambitious, and intellectual who seceded from a republic in which neither talent nor industry could give comfort or advantage, but also the full benefit of inventive genius, stimulated by the hope of wealth in addition to whatever public spirit the habits of Communism had not extinguished. They systematically encouraged the cultivation of science, which the Communists had very early put down as a withdrawal of energy from the labour due to the community at large. They had a monopoly of machinery, of improvement, of invention both in agriculture, in manufactures, and in self-defence. They devised weapons far more destructive than those possessed by the old régime, and still more superior to such as, after centuries of anarchy and decline, the Communists

were able to procure. Finally, when assailed by the latter, vast superiority of numbers was annulled by immeasurable superiority in weapons and in discipline. The secessionists were animated, too, by a bitter resentment against their assailants, as the authors of the general ruin and of much individual suffering; and when the victory was gained, they not infrequently improved it to the utter destruction of all who had taken part in the attack. Whichever side were most to blame in the feud, no quarter was given by either. It was an internecine war of numbers, ignorance, and anarchy against science and order. On both sides there still remained much of the spirit generated in times when life was less precious than the valour by which alone it could be held, and preserved through milder ages by the belief that death was not annihilation—enough to give to both parties courage to sacrifice their lives for the victory of their cause and the destruction of their enemies. But after a few crushing defeats, the Communists were compelled to sue for peace, and to cede a large part of their richest territory. Driven back into their own chaotic misery, deterred by merciless punishment from further invasion of their neighbours'

dominions, they had leisure to contrast their wretched condition with that of those who prospered under the restored system of private ownership, family interest, strong, orderly, permanent government, material and intellectual civilisation. Machinery did for the new State, into which the seceding societies were consolidated by the necessity of self-defence, much more than it had done before Communism declared war on it. The same envy which, if war had been any longer possible, would have urged the Communists again and again to plunder the wealth that contrasted so forcibly their own increasing poverty, now humbled them to admire and covet the means which had produced it. At last, after bitter intestine struggles, they voluntarily submitted to the rule of their rivals, and entreated the latter to accept them as subjects and pupils. Thus in the 39th century order and property were once more established throughout the planet.

"But, as I have said, what you call religion had altogether disappeared—

had ceased, at least as an avowed principle, to affect the ideas and conduct of society or of individuals. The re-establishment of peace and order

concentrated men's energies on the production of material wealth and the achievement of physical comfort and ease. Looking forward to nothing after death, they could only make the best of the short life permitted to them and do their utmost to lengthen it. In the assurance of speedy separation, affection became a source of much more anxiety and sorrow than happiness. All ties being precarious and their endurance short, their force became less and less; till the utmost enjoyment of the longest possible life for himself became the sole, or almost the sole, animating motive, the one paramount interest, of each individual. The equality which logic had established between the sexes dissolved the family tie. It was impossible for law to dictate the conditions on which two free and equal individuals should live together, merely because they differed in sex. All the State could do it did; it insisted on a provision for the children. But when parental affection was extinguished, such provision could only be secured by handing over the infant and its portion to the guardianship of the State.

As children were troublesome and noisy, the practice of giving them up to public officers to be brought up in vast nurseries regulated on the strictest scientific principles became the general rule, and was soon regarded as a duty; what was at first almost openly avowed selfishness soon justifying and glorifying itself on the ground that the children were better off under the care of those whose undivided attention was given to them, and in establishments where everything was regulated with sole regard to their welfare, than they could be at home. No law compels us to send our children to these establishments. In rare cases a favourite will persuade her lord to retain her pet son and make him heir, but both the Courts and public opinion discountenance this practice. Some families, like my own, systematically retain their children and educate them at home; but it is generally thought that in doing so we do them a wrong, and our neighbours look askance upon so signal a deviation from custom; the more so, perhaps, that they half suspect us of dissenting from their views on other subjects, on which our opinions do not so directly or so obviously affect our conduct, and on which therefore we are not so easily convicted of free choice" [heresy]. Here I inquired whether the birth and parentage of

the children sent to the public establishments were registered, so as to permit their being reclaimed or inheriting property.

"No," he replied. "Inheritance by mere descent is a notion no longer favoured. I believe that young mothers sometimes, before parting with their children, impress upon them some indelible mark by which it may be possible hereafter to recognise them; but such recognitions seldom occur.

Maternal affection is discountenanced as a purely animal instinct, a survival from a lower grade of organisation, and does not generally outlast a ten years' separation; while paternal love is utterly scouted as an absurdity to which even the higher animals are not subject. Boys are kept in the public establishments until the age of twelve, those from ten to twelve being separated from the younger ones and passing through the higher education in separate colleges. The girls are educated apart till they complete their tenth year, and are almost invariably married in the course of the next. At first, under the influence of the theory of sexual equality, both received their intellectual instruction in the same classes and passed through the same examinations. Separation was soon found necessary; but still girls passed through the same intellectual training as their brothers.

Experience, however, showed that this would not answer. Those girls who distinguished themselves in the examinations were, with scarcely an exception, found unattractive as wives and unfit to be mothers. A very much larger number, a number increasing in every generation, suffered unmistakably from the severity of the mental discipline to which they were subjected. The advocates of female equality made a very hard fight for equal culture; but the physical consequences were perfectly clear and perfectly intolerable. When a point was reached at which one half the girls of each generation were rendered invalids for life, and the other half protected only by a dense stupidity or volatile idleness which no school punishments could overcome, the Equalists were driven from one untenable point to another, and forced at last to demand a reduction of the masculine standard of education to the level of feminine capacities. Upon this ground they took their last stand, and were hopelessly beaten. The reaction was so complete that for the last two hundred and forty generations, the standard of female education has been lowered to that

which by general confession ordinary female brains can stand without injury to the physique. The practical consequences of sexual equality have re-established in a more absolute form than ever the principle that the first purpose of female life is marriage and maternity; and that, for their own sakes as for the sake of each successive generation, women should be so trained as to be attractive wives and mothers of healthy children, all other considerations being subordinated to these. A certain small number of ladies avail themselves of the legal equality they still enjoy, and live in the world much as men. But we regard them as third-rate men in petticoats, hardly as women at all. Marriage with one of them is the last resource to which a man too idle or too foolish to earn his own living will betake himself. Whatever their education, our women have always found that such independence as they could earn by hard work was less satisfactory than the dependence, coupled with assured comfort and ease, which they enjoy as the consorts, playthings, or slaves of the other sex; and they are only too glad to barter their legal equality for the certainty of protection, indolence, and permanent support."

"Then your marriages," I said, "are permanent?"

"Not by law," he replied. "Nothing like what our remote ancestors called marriage is recognised at all. The maidens who come of age each year sell themselves by a sort of auction, those who purchase them arranging with the girls themselves the terms on which the latter will enter their family.

Custom has fixed the general conditions which every girl expects, and which only the least attractive are forced to forego. They are promised a permanent maintenance from their master's estate, and promise in return a fixed term of marriage. After two or three years they are free to rescind the contract, after ten or twelve they may leave their husbands with a stipulated pension. They receive an allowance for dress and so forth proportionate to their personal attractions or to the fancy of the suitor; and of course the richest men can offer the best terms, and generally secure the most agreeable wives, in whatever number they please or think they can without inconvenience support."

"Then," I said, "the women can divorce themselves at pleasure, but the men cannot dismiss them! This hardly looks like equality."

"The practical result," he answered, "is that men don't care for a release which would part them from complaisant slaves, and that women dare not seek a divorce which can only hand them over to another master on rather worse terms. When the longer term has expired, the latter almost always prefer the servitude to which they are accustomed to an independent life of solitude and friendlessness."

"And what becomes," I asked, "of the younger men who must enter the world without property, without parents or protectors?"

"We are, after youth has passed, an indolent race. We hardly care, as a rule, to cultivate our fields or direct our factories; but prefer devoting the latter half at least of our lives to a somewhat easy-going cultivation of that division of science which takes hold of our fancy. These divisions are such as your conversation leads me to think you would probably consider absurdly minute. A single class of insects, a single family of plants, the habits of one race of fishes, suffice for the exclusive study of half a lifetime.

Minds of a more active or more practical bent will spend an equal time over the construction of a new machine more absolutely automatic than any that has preceded it. Physical labour is thrown as much as possible on the young; and even they are now so helped by machinery and by trained animals, that the eight hours' work which forms their day's labour hardly tires their muscles. Our tastes render us very anxious to devolve upon others as soon as possible the preservation and development of the property we have acquired. A man of moderate means, long before he has reached his thirtieth year, generally seeks one assistant; men of larger fortune may want two, five, or ten. These are chosen, as a rule, by preference from those who have passed the most stringent and successful collegiate examination. Martial parents are not prolific, and the mortality in our public nurseries is very large. I impute it to moral influences, since the chief cause of death is low vitality, marked nervous depression and want of animal spirits, such as the total absence of personal tenderness and sympathy must produce in children. It is popularly ascribed to the over-

cultivation of the race, as plants and animals highly civilised—that is, greatly modified and bred to an artificial excellence by human agency—are certainly delicate, unprolific, and especially difficult to rear. There is little disease in the nurseries, but there is little health and a deficiency of nervous energy. One fact is significant, however interpreted, and bears directly on your last question. Since the wide extension of polygamy, female births are to male about as seven to six; but the deaths in public nurseries between the first and tenth years are twenty-nine in twelve dozen admissions in the stronger sex, and only about ten in the weaker. Read these facts as we may, they ensure employment to the young men when their education is completed—the two last years of severe study adding somewhat to the mortality among them.

"A large number find employment in superintending the property of others. To give them a practical interest in its preservation and improvement, they are generally, after a shorter or longer probation, adopted by their employers as heirs to their estate; our experience of Communism having taught us that immediate and obvious self-interest is the only motive that certainly and seriously affects human action. The distance at which they are kept, and the absolute seclusion of our family life, enables us easily to secure ourselves against any over-anxiety on their part to anticipate their inheritance. The minority who do not thus find a regular place in society are employed in factories, as artisans, or on the lands belonging to the State. To ensure their zeal, the last receive a fixed proportion of the produce, or are permitted to rent land at fixed rates, and at the end of ten years receive a part thereof in full property. By these means we are free from all the dangers and difficulties of that state of society which preceded the Communistic cataclysm. We have poor men, and men who can live only by daily labour; but these have dissipated their wealth, or are looking forward at no very distant period to a sufficient competence. The entire population of our planet does not exceed two hundred millions, and is not much increased from generation to generation. The area of cultivable land is about ten millions of square miles, and half a square mile in these equatorial continents, which alone are at all generally inhabited, will, if well cultivated and cared for, furnish the largest household with every luxury that man's heart can desire. Eight hours' labour in the day for ten years of life will secure to the least fortunate a reasonable competence; and an ambitious man, with quick intelligence and reasonable industry, may always hope to become rich, if he thinks wealth worth the labour of invention or of exceptionally troublesome work."

"Mars ought, then," I said, "to be a material paradise. You have attained nearly all that our most advanced political economists regard as the perfection of economical order—a population nearly stationary, and a soil much more than adequate to their support; a general distribution of property, total absence of permanent poverty, and freedom from that gnawing anxiety regarding the future of ourselves or our children which is the great evil of life upon Earth and the opprobrium of our social arrangements. You have carried out, moreover, the doctrines of our most advanced philosophers; you have absolute equality before the law, competitive examination among the young for the best start in life, with equal chances wherever equality is possible; and again, perfect freedom and full legal equality as regards the relations of the sexes. Are your countrymen satisfied with the results?"

"Yes," answered my host, "in so far, at least, that they have no wish to change them, no idea that any great social or political reforms could improve our condition. Our lesson in Communism has rendered all agitation on such matters, all tendency to democratic institutions, all appeals to popular passions, utterly odious and alarming to us. But that we are happy I will venture neither to affirm nor to deny. Physically, no doubt, we have great advantages over you, if I rightly understand your description of life on Earth. We have got rid of old age, and, to a great extent, of disease. Many of our scientists persist in the hope to get rid of death; but, since all that has been accomplished in this direction was accomplished some two thousand years back, and yet we continue to die, general opinion hardly concurs in this hope."

"How do you mean," I inquired, "that you have got rid of old age and of disease?"

"We have," he replied, "learned pretty fully the chemistry of life. We have found remedies for that hardening of the bones and weakening of the muscles which used to be the physical characteristics of declining years.

Our hair no longer whitens; our teeth, if they decay, are now removed and naturally replaced by new ones; our eyes retain to the last the clearness of their sight. A famous physician of five thousand years back said in controversy on this subject, that 'the clock was not made to go for ever;' by which he meant that human bodies, like the materials of machines, wore out by lapse of time. In his day this was true, since it was impossible fully to repair the waste and physical wear and tear of the human frame. This is no longer so. The clock does not wear out, but it goes more and more slowly and irregularly, and stops at last for some reason that the most skilful inspection cannot discover. The body of him who dies, as we say,

'by efflux of time' at the age of fifty is as perfect as it was at five-and twenty. Yet few men live to be fifty-five, and most have ceased to take much interest in practical life, or even in science, by forty-five."

"That seems strange," I said. "If no foreign body gets into the machinery, and the machinery itself does not wear out, it is difficult to understand why the clock should cease to go."

"Would not some of your race," he asked, "explain the mystery by suggesting that the human frame is not a clock, but contains, and owes its life to, an essence beyond the reach of the scalpel, the microscope, and the laboratory?"

"They hold that it is so. But then it is not the soul but the body that is worn out in seventy or eighty of the Earth's revolutions."

"Ay," he said; "but if man were such a duplex being, it might be that the wearing out of the body was necessary, and had been adapted to release the soul when it had completed its appropriate term of service in the flesh."

I could not answer this question, and he did not pursue the theme.

Presently I inquired, "If you allow no appeal to popular feeling or passion, to what was I so nearly the victim? And what is the terrorism that makes it

dangerous to avow a credulity or incredulity opposed to received opinion?"

"Scientific controversies," he replied, "enlist our strongest and angriest feelings. It is held that only wickedness or lunacy can resist the evidence that has convinced a vast majority. By arithmetical calculation the chances that twelve men are wrong and twelve thousand right, on a matter of inductive or deductive proof, are found to amount to what must be taken for practical certainty; and when the twelve still hold out, they are regarded as madmen or knaves, and treated accordingly by their fellows. If it be thought desirable to invoke a legal settlement of the issue, a council of all the overseers of our scientific colleges is called, and its decision is by law irrevocable and infallible, especially if ratified by the popular voice. And if a majority vote be worth anything at all, I think this modern theory at least as sound as the democratic theory of politics which prevailed here before the Communistic revolution, and which seems by your account to be gaining ground on Earth."

"And what," I inquired, "is your political constitution? What are the powers of your rulers; and how, in the absence of public discussion and popular suffrage, are they practically limited?"

"In theory they are unlimited," he answered; "in practice they are limited by custom, by caution, and, above all, by the lack of motives for misrule. The authority of each prince over those under him, from the Sovereign to the local president or captain, is absolute. But the Executive leaves ordinary matters of civil or criminal law to the Courts of Justice. Cases are tried by trained judges; the old democratic usage of employing untrained juries having been long ago discarded, as a worse superstition than simple decision by lot. The lot is right twelve times in two dozen; the jury not oftener than half-a-dozen times. The judges don't heat or bias their minds by discussion. They hear all that can be elicited from parties, accuser, accused, and witnesses, and all that skilled advocates can say. Then the secretary of the Court draws up a summary of the case, each judge takes it home to consider, each writes out his judgment, which is read by the secretary, none but the author knowing whose it is. If the majority be five to two, judgment is given; if less, the case is tried again before a higher tribunal of twice as many judges. If no decision can be reached, the accused is acquitted for the time, or, in a civil dispute, a compromise is imposed.

The rulers cannot, without incurring such general anger as would be fatal to their power, disregard our fundamental laws. Gross tyranny to individuals is too dangerous to be carried far. It is a capital crime for any but the officers of the Sovereign and of the twelve Regents to possess the fearfully destructive weapons that brought our last wars to an end. But any man, driven to desperation, can construct and use similar weapons so easily that no ruler will drive a man to such revengeful despair. Again, the tyranny of subordinate officials would be checked by their chief, who would be angry at being troubled and endangered by misconduct in which he had no direct interest. And finally, personal malice is not a strong passion among us; and our manners render it unlikely that a ruler should come into such collision with any of his subjects as would engender such a feeling. Of those immediately about him, he can and does at once get rid as soon as he begins to dislike, and before he has cause to hate them. It is our maxim that greed of wealth or lust of power are the chief motives of tyranny. Our rulers cannot well hope to extend a power already autocratic, and we take care to leave them nothing to covet in the way of wealth. We can afford to give them all that they can desire of luxury and splendour. To enrich to the uttermost a few dozen governors costs us nothing comparable to the cost of democracy, with its inseparable party conflicts, maladministration, neglect, and confusion."

"A clever writer on Earth lately remarked that it would be easy to satiate princes with all personal enjoyments, but impossible to satiate all their hangers-on, or even all the members of their family."

"You must remember," he replied, "that we have here, save in such exceptional cases as my own, nothing like what you call a family. The ladies of a prince's house have everything they can wish for within their bounds and cannot go outside of these. As for dependents, no man here, at least of such as are likely to be rulers, cares for his nearest and dearest friends enough to incur personal peril, public displeasure, or private

resentment on their account. The officials around a ruler's person are few in number, so that we can afford to make their places too comfortable and too valuable to be lightly risked. Neglect, again, is pretty sure to be punished by superior authority. Activity in the promotion of public objects is the only interest left to princes, while tyranny is, for the reasons I have given, too dangerous to be carried far."

CHAPTER VI - AN OFFICIAL VISIT.

At this point of our conversation an ambâ entered the room and made certain signs which my host immediately understood.

"The Zamptâ," he said, "has called upon me, evidently on your account, and probably with some message from his Suzerain. You need not be afraid," he added. "At worst they would only refuse you protection, and I could secure you from danger under my own roof, and in the last extremity effect your retreat and return to your own planet; supposing for a moment," he added, smiling, "that you are a real being and come from a real world."

The Regent of that dominion, the only Martialist outside my host's family with whom I had yet been able to converse, awaited us in the hall or entrance chamber. I bowed low to him, and then remained standing. My host, also saluting his visitor, at once took his seat. The Regent, returning the salute and seating himself, proceeded to address us; very little ceremony on either side being observed between this autocratic deputy of an absolute Sovereign and his subjects.

"Esmo dent Ecasfen" said the Regent, "will you point out the person you declare yourself to have rescued from assault and received into your house on the 431st day of this year?"

"That is the person, Regent," said my host, pointing to me.

The visitor then asked my name, which I gave, and addressing me thereby, he continued—

"The Camptâ has requested me to ascertain the truth regarding your alleged size, so far exceeding anything hitherto known among us. You will permit me, therefore, to measure your height and girth."

I bowed, and he proceeded to ascertain that I was about a foot taller and some ten inches larger round the waist than himself. Of these facts he took note, and then proceeded—

"The signs you made to those who first encountered you were understood to mean that you descended from the sky, in a vessel which is now left on the summit of yonder mountain, Asnyca."

"I did not descend from the sky," I replied, "for the sky is, as we both know, no actual vault or boundary of the atmospheric depths. I ascended from a world nearer to the Sun, and after travelling for forty days through space, landed upon this planet in the vessel you mention."

"I am directed," he answered, "to see this vessel, to inspect your machinery and instruments, and to report thereon to the Suzerain. You will doubtless be ready to accompany me thither to-morrow two hours after sunrise. You may be accompanied, if you please, by your host or any members of his family; I shall be attended by one or more of my officers. In the meantime I am to inform you that, until my report has been received and considered, you are under the protection of the law, and need not apprehend any molestation of the kind you incurred at first. You will not, however, repeat to any one but myself the explanation you have offered of your appearance—which, I understand, has been given in fuller detail to Esmo—until the decision of the Camptâ shall have been communicated to you."

I simply bowed my assent; and after this brief but sufficient fulfilment of the purpose for which he had called, the Regent took his leave.

"What," I asked, when we re-entered my chamber, "is the meaning of the title by which the Regent addressed you?"

"In speaking to officials," he replied, "of rank so high as his, it is customary to address them simply by their titles, unless more than one of the same rank be present, in which case we call them, as we do inferior officials, by their name with the title appended. For instance, in the Court of the Sovereign our Regent would be called Endo Zamptâ. Men of a certain age and social position, but having no office, are addressed by their name and that of their residence; and, asfe meaning a town or dwelling, usage gives me the name of Esmo, in or of the town of Eca.

"I am sorry," he went on, "that neither my son nor myself can accompany you to-morrow. All the elder members of my family are engaged to attend at some distance hence before the hour at which you can return. But I should not like you to be alone with strangers; and, independently of this consideration, I should perhaps have asked of you a somewhat unusual favour. My daughter Eveena, who, like most of our women" (he laid a special emphasis on the pronoun) "has received a better education than is now given in the public academies, has been from the first greatly interested in your narrative and in all you have told us of the world from which you come. She is anxious to see your vessel, and I had hoped to take her when I meant to visit it in your company. But after to-morrow I cannot tell when you may be summoned to visit the Camptâ, or whether after that visit you are likely to return hither. I will ask you, therefore, if you do not object to what I confess is an unusual proceeding, to take Eveena under your charge to-morrow."

"Is it," I inquired, "permissible for a young lady to accompany a stranger on such an excursion?"

"It is very unusual," returned my host; "but you must observe that here family ties are, as a rule, unknown. It cannot be usual for a maiden to be attended by father or brother, since she knows neither. It is only by a husband that a girl can, as a rule, be attended abroad. Our usages render such attendance exceedingly close, and, on the other hand, forbid strangers to interrupt or take notice thereof. In Eveena's presence the Regent will find it difficult to draw you into conversation which might be inconvenient or dangerous; and especially cannot attempt to gratify, by questioning you, any curiosity as to myself or my family."

"But," I said, "from what you say, it seems that the Regent and any one who might accompany him would draw inferences which might not be agreeable to you or to the young lady."

"I hardly understand you," he replied. "The only conjecture they could make, which they will certainly make, is that you are, or are about to be, married to her; and as they will never see her again, and, if they did, could not recognise her—as they will not to-morrow know anything save that she

belongs to my household, and certainly will not speak to her—I do not see how their inference can affect her. When I part with her, it will be to some one of my own customs and opinions; and to us this close confinement of girls appears to transcend reasonable restraint, as it contradicts the theoretical freedom and equality granted by law to the sex, but utterly withheld by the social usages which have grown out of that law."

"I can only thank you for giving me a companion more agreeable than the official who is to report upon my reality," I said.

"I do not desire," he continued, "to bind you to any reserve in replying to questions, beyond what I am sure you will do without a pledge—namely, to avoid betraying more than you can help of that which is not known outside my own household. But on this subject I may be able to speak more fully after to-morrow. Now, if you will come into the peristyle, we shall be in time for the evening meal."

Eveena's curiosity had in nowise overcome her silent shyness. She might possibly have completed her tenth year, which epoch in the life of Mars is about equivalent to the seventeenth birthday of a damsel nurtured in North-Western Europe. I hardly think that I had addressed her directly half-a-dozen times, or had received from her a dozen words in return. I had been attracted, nevertheless, not only by her grace and beauty, but by the peculiar sweetness of her voice and the gentleness of her manner and bearing when engaged in pacifying dispute or difficulty among the children, and particularly in dealing with the half-deformed spoilt infant of which I have spoken. This evening that little brat was more than usually exasperating, and having exhausted the patience or repelled the company of all the rest, found itself alone, and set up a fretful, continuous scream, disagreeable even to me, and torturing to Martial ears, which, adapted to hear in that thin air, are painfully alive to strident, harsh, or even loud sounds. Instantly obeying a sign from her mother, Eveena rose in the middle of a conversation to which she had listened with evident interest, and devoted herself for half-an-hour to please and pacify this uncomfortable child. The character and appearance of this infant, so utterly unlike all its companions, had already excited my curiosity, but I had

found no opportunity of asking a question without risking an impertinence. On this occasion, however, I ventured to make some remark on the extreme gentleness and forbearance with which not only Eveena but the children treated their peevish and exacting brother.

"He is no brother of theirs," said Zulve, the mistress of the house. "You would hardly find in any family like ours a child with so irritable a temper or a disposition so selfish, and nowhere a creature so hardly treated by Nature in body as well as mind."

"Indeed," I said, hardly understanding her answer.

"No," said my host. "It is the rule to deprive of life, promptly and painlessly, children to whom, from physical deformity or defect, life is thought unlikely to be pleasant, and whose descendants might be a burden to the public and a cause of physical deterioration to the race. It is, however, one of the exceptional tenets to which I have been obliged to allude, that man should not seek to be wiser than Nature; and that life should neither be cut short, except as a punishment for great crimes, nor prolonged artificially contrary to the manifest intention, or, as our philosophers would say, the common course of Nature. Those who think with me, therefore, always endeavour, when we hear in time of their approaching fate, to preserve children so doomed. Precautions against undue haste or readiness to destroy lives that might, after all, grow up to health and vigour are provided by law. No single physician or physiologist can sign a death-warrant; and I, though no longer a physician by craft, am among the arbiters, one or more of whom must be called in to approve or suspend the decision. On these occasions I have rescued from extinction several children of whose unfitness to live, according to the standard of the State Nurseries, there was no question, and placed them in families, mostly childless, that were willing to receive them. Of this one it was our turn to take charge; and certainly his chance is better for being brought up among other children, and under the influence of their gentler dispositions and less exacting temperaments."

"And is such ill-temper and selfishness," I asked, "generally found among the deformed?"

"I don't think," replied Esmo, "that this child is much worse than most of my neighbours' children, except that physical discomfort makes him fretful. What you call selfishness in him is only the natural inheritance derived from an ancestry who for some hundred generations have certainly never cared for anything or any one but themselves. I thought I had explained to you by what train of circumstances and of reasoning family affection, such as it is reputed to have been thousands of years ago, has become extinct in this planet; and, family affection extinguished, all weaker sentiments of regard for others were very quickly withered up."

"You told me something of the kind," I said; "but the idea of a life so utterly swallowed up in self that no one even thinks it necessary to affect regard for and interest in others, was to me so unintelligible and inconceivable that I did not realise the full meaning of your account. Nor even now do I understand how a society formed of such members can be held together.

On Earth we should expect them either to tear one another to pieces, or to relapse into isolation and barbarism lower than that of the lowest tribe which preserves social instincts and social organisation. A society composed of men resembling that child, but with the intelligence, force, and consistent purpose of manhood, would, I should have thought, be little better than a congregation of beasts of prey."

"We have such beasts," said Esmo, "in the wild lands, and they are certainly unsociable and solitary. But men, at least civilised men, are governed not only by instinct but by interest, and the interest of each individual in the preservation of social co-operation and social order is very evident and very powerful. Experience and school discipline cure children of the habit of indulging mere temper and spite before they come to be men, and they are taught by practice as well as by precept the absolute necessity of co-operation. Egotism, therefore, has no tendency to dissolve society as a mere organisation, though it has utterly destroyed society as a source of pleasure."

"Does your law," I asked, "confine the principle of euthanasia to infants, or do you put out of the world adults whose life is supposed, for one reason or another, to be useless and joyless?"

"Only," he answered, "in the case of the insane. When the doctors are satisfied that a lunatic cannot be cured, an inquest is held; and if the medical verdict be approved, he is quietly and painlessly dismissed from existence. Logically, of course, the same principle should be applied to all incurable disease; and I suspect—indeed I know—that it is applied when the household have become weary, and the patient is utterly unable to protect himself or appeal to the law. But the general application of the principle has been successfully resisted, on the ground that the terror it would cause, the constant anxiety and alarm in which men would live if the right of judging when life had become worthless to them were left to others, would far outweigh any benefit which might be derived from the legalised extinction of existences which had become a prolonged misery; and such cases, as I have told you, are very rare among us. A case of hopeless bodily suffering, not terminating very speedily in death, does not occur thrice a year among the whole population of the planet, except through accident. We have means of curing at the outset almost all of those diseases which the observance for hundreds of generations of sound physical conditions of life has not extirpated; and in the worst instances our anæsthetics seldom fail to extinguish the sense of pain without impairing intellect. Of course, any one who is tired of his life is at liberty to put an end to it, and any one else may assist him. But, though the clinging to existence is perhaps the most irrational of all those purely animal instincts on emancipation from which we pride ourselves, it is the strongest and the most lasting. The life of most of my countrymen would be to me intolerable weariness, if only from the utter want, after wealth is attained, of all warmer and less isolated interest than some one pet scientific pursuit can afford; and yet more from the total absence of affection, family duties, and the various mental occupations which interest in others affords. But though the question whether life is worth living has long ago been settled among us in the negative, suicide, the logical outcome of that conviction, is the rarest of all the methods by which life is terminated."

"Which seems to show that even in Mars logic does not always dominate life and prevail over instinct. But what is the most usual cause of death, where neither disease nor senility are other than rare exceptions?"

"Efflux of time," Esmo replied with an ironical smile. "That is the chief fatal disease recognised by our physicians."

"And what is its nature?"

"Ah, that neither I nor any other physician can tell you. Life 'goes out,' like a lamp when the materials supplying the electric current are exhausted; and yet here all the waste of which physic can take cognisance is fully repaired, and the circuit is not broken."

"What are the symptoms, then?"

"They are all reducible to one—exhaustion of the will, the prime element of personality. The patient ceases to care. It is too much trouble to work; then too much trouble to read; then too much trouble to exert even those all but mechanical powers of thought which are necessary to any kind of social intercourse—to give an order, to answer a question, to recognise a name or a face: then even the passions die out, till the patient cannot be provoked to rate a stupid ambâ or a negligent wife; finally, there is not energy to dress or undress, to rise up or sit down. Then the patient is allowed to die: if kept alive perforce, he would finally lack the energy to eat or even to breathe.

And yet, all this time, the man is alive, the self is there; and I have prolonged life, or rather renewed it, for a time, by some chance stimulus that has reached the inner sight through the thickening veil, and shocked the essential man into willing and thinking once more as he thought and willed when he was younger than his grandchildren are now.... It is well that some of us who know best how long the flesh may be kept in life, are, in right of that very knowledge, proof against the wish to keep the life in the flesh for ever."

CHAPTER VII - ESCORT DUTY.

Immediately after breakfast the next morning my host invited me to the gate of his garden, where stood one of the carriages I had seen before in the distance, but never had an opportunity of examining. It rested on three wheels, the two hind ones by far larger than that in front, which merely served to sustain the equilibrium of the body and to steer. The material was the silver-like metal of which most Martial vessels and furniture are formed, every spar, pole, and cross-piece being a hollow cylinder; a construction which, with the extreme lightness of the metal itself, made the carriage far lighter than any I had seen on Earth. The body consisted of a seat with sides, back, and footboard, wide enough to accommodate two persons with ease. It was attached by strong elastic fastenings to a frame consisting of four light poles rising from the framework in which the axles turned; completely dispensing with the trouble of springs, while affording a more complete protection from anything like jolting. The steering gear consisted of a helm attached to the front wheel and coming up within easy reach of the driver's hand. The electric motive power and machinery were concealed in a box beneath the seat, which was indeed but the top of this most important and largest portion of the carriage. The poles sustained a light framework supporting a canopy, which could be drawn over the top and around three sides of the carriage, leaving only the front open. This canopy, in the present instance, consisted of a sort of very fine silken material, thickly embroidered within and without with feathers of various colours and sizes, combined in patterns of exquisite beauty. My host requested me to mount the carriage with him, and drove for some distance, teaching me how to steer, and how, by pressing a spring, to stop or slacken the motion of the vehicle, also how to direct it over rough ground and up or down the steepest slope on which it was available. When we returned, the Regent's carriage was standing by the gate, and two others were waiting at a little distance in the rear. The Regent, with a companion, was already seated, and as soon as we reached the gate, Eveena appeared. She was enveloped from head to foot in a cloak of something like swans-down covering her whole figure, loose, like the ordinary outer garments of both sexes, and gathered in at the waist by a narrow zone of silver, with a sort of

clasp of some bright green jewel; and a veil of white satin-looking material covered the whole head and face, and fell half-way to the waist. Her gloved right hand was hidden by the sleeve of her cloak; that of the left arm was turned back, and the hand which she gave me as I handed her to the seat on my left was bare—a usage both of convenience and courtesy. At Esmo's request, the Regent, who led the way, started at a moderate pace, not exceeding some ten miles an hour. I observed that on the roofs of all the houses along the road the inhabitants had gathered to watch us; and as my companion was so completely veiled, I did not baulk their curiosity by drawing the canopy. I presently noticed that the girl held something concealed in her right sleeve, and ventured to ask her what she had there.

"Pardon me," she said; "if we had been less hurried, I meant to have asked your permission to bring my pet esvè with me." Drawing back her sleeve, she showed a bird about the size of a carrier-pigeon, but with an even larger and stronger beak, white body, and wings and tail, like some of the plumage of the head and neck, tinted with gold and green. Around its neck was a little string of silver, and suspended from this a small tablet with a pencil or style. Since by her look and manner she seemed to expect an answer, I said—

"I am very glad you have given me the opportunity of making acquaintance with another of those curiously tame and manageable animals which your people seem to train to such wonderful intelligence and obedience. We have birds on Earth which will carry a letter from a strange place to their home, but only homewards."

"These," she answered, "will go wherever they are directed, if they have been there before and know the name of the place; and if this bird had been let loose after we had left, he would have found me, if not hidden by trees or other shelter, anywhere within a score of miles."

"And have your people," I asked, "many more such wonderfully intelligent and useful creatures tamed to your service, besides the ambau, the tyree, and these letter-carriers?"

"Oh yes!" she answered. "Nearly all our domestic animals will do anything they are told which lies within their power. You have seen the tyree marching in a line across a field to pick up every single worm or insect, or egg of such, within the whole space over which they move, and I think you saw the ambau gathering fruit. It is not very usual to employ the latter for this purpose, except in the trees. Have you not seen a big creature—I should call it a bird, but a bird that cannot fly, and is covered with coarse hair instead of feathers? It is about as tall as myself, but with a neck half as long as its body, and a very sharp powerful beak; and four of these carvee would clear a field the size of our garden (some 160 acres) of weeds in a couple of days. We can send them, moreover, with orders to fetch a certain number of any particular fruit or plant, and they scarcely ever forget or blunder. Some of them, of course, are cleverer than others. The cleverest will remember the name of every plant in the garden, and will, perhaps, bring four or even six different kinds at a time; but generally we show them a leaf of the plant we want, or point out to them the bed where it is to be found, and do not trouble their memory with more than two different orders at a time. The Unicorns, as you call them, come regularly to be milked at sunset, and, if told beforehand, will come an hour earlier or later to any place pointed out to them. There were many beasts of burden before the electric carriages were invented, so intelligent that I have heard the rider never troubled himself to guide them except when he changed his purpose, or came to a road they had not traversed before. He would simply tell them where to go, and they would carry him safely. The only creature now kept for this purpose is the largest of our birds (the caldecta), about six feet long from head to tail, and with wings measuring thrice as much from tip to tip. They will sail through the air and carry their rider up to places otherwise inaccessible. But they are little used except by the hunters, partly because the danger is thought too great, partly because they cannot rise more than about 4000 feet from the sea-level with a rider, and within that height there are few places worth reaching that cannot be reached more safely. People used to harness them to balloons till we found means to drive these by electricity—the last great invention in the way of

locomotion, which I think was completed within my grandfather's memory."

"And," I asked, "have you no animals employed in actually cultivating the soil?"

"No," she replied, "except the weeding birds of whom I have told you.

When we have a piece of ground too small for our electric ploughs, we sometimes set them to break it up, and they certainly reduce the soil to a powder much finer than that produced by the machine."

"I should like to see those machines at work."

"Well," answered Eveena, "I have no doubt we shall pass more than one of them on our way."

As she said this we reached the great road I had crossed on my arrival, and turning up this for a short distance, sufficient, however, to let me perceive that it led to the seaport town of which I have spoken, we came to a break in the central footpath, just wide enough to allow us to pass. Looking back on this occasion, I observed that we were followed by the two other carriages I have mentioned, but at some distance. We then proceeded up the mountain by a narrow road I had not seen in descending it. On either side of this lay fields of the kind already described, one of which was in course of cultivation, and here I saw the ploughs of which my companion had spoken. Evidently constructed on the same principle as the carriages, but of much greater size, and with heavier and broader wheels, they tore up and broke to pieces a breadth of soil of some two yards, working to a depth of some eighteen inches, with a dozen sharp powerful triangular shares, and proceeding at a rate of about fifty yards per minute. Eveena explained that these fields were generally from 200 to 600 yards square.

The machine having traversed the whole field in one direction, then recommenced its work, ploughing at right angles to the former, and carrying behind it a sort of harrow, consisting of hooks supported by light, hollow, metallic poles fixed at a certain angle to the bar forming the rearward extremity of the plough, by which the surface was levelled and the soil beaten into small fragments; broken up, in fact, as I had seen, not

less completely than ordinary garden soil in England or Flanders. When it reached the end of its course, the plough had to be turned; and this duty required the employment of two men, one at each end of the field, who, however, had no other or more difficult labour than that of turning the machine at the completion of each set of furrows. In another field, already doubly ploughed, a sowing machine was at work. The large seeds were placed singly by means of an instrument resembling a magnified ovipositor, such as that possessed by many insects, which at regulated intervals made a hole in the ground and deposited a seed therein. Eveena explained that where the seed and plant were small, a continuous stream was poured into a small furrow made by a different instrument attached to the same machine, while another arm, placed a little to the rear, covered in the furrow and smoothed the surface. In reply to another question of mine—"There are," she said, "some score of different wool or hair bearing animals, which are shorn twice in the year, immediately after the rains, and furnish the fibre which is woven into most of the materials we use for dress and other household purposes. These creatures adapt themselves to the shearing machines with wonderful equanimity and willingness, so that they are seldom or never injured."

"Not even," I asked, "by inexperienced or clumsy hands?"

"Hands," she said, "have nothing to do with the matter. They have only to send the animal into the machine, and, indeed, each goes in of his own accord as he sees his fellow come out."

"And have you no vegetable fibres," I said, "that are used for weaving?"

"Oh yes," she answered, "several. The outer dress I wear indoors is made of a fibre found inside the rind of the fruit of the algyro tree, and the stalks of three or four different kinds of plants afford materials almost equally soft and fine."

"And your cloak," I asked, "is not that made of the skin of some animal?"

"Yes," she replied, "and the most curious creature I have heard of. It is found only in the northern and southern Arctic land-belts, to which indeed nearly all wild animals, except the few small ones that are encouraged

because they prey upon large and noxious insects, are now confined. It is about as large as the Unicorns, and has, like them, four limbs; but otherwise it more resembles a bird. It has a bird's long slight neck, but a very small and not very bird-like head, with a long horny snout, furnished with teeth, something between a beak and a mouth. Its hind limbs are those of a bird, except that they have more flesh upon the lowest joints and are covered with this soft down. Its front limbs, my father says, seem as if nature had hesitated between wings and arms. They have attached to them several long, sharp, featherless quills starting from a shrivelled membrane, which make them very powerful and formidable weapons, so that no animal likes to attack it; while the foot has four fingers or claws with, which it clasps fish or small dragons, especially those electric dragons of which you have seen a tame and very much enlarged specimen, and so holds them that they cannot find a chance of delivering their electric shock.

But for the Thernee these dragons, winged as they are, would make those lands hardly habitable either for man, or other beasts. All our furs are obtained from those countries, and the creatures from which they are derived are carefully preserved for that purpose, it being forbidden to kill more than a certain number of each every year, which makes these skins by far the costliest articles we use."

By this time we had reached the utmost point to which the carriages could take us, about a furlong from the platform on which I had rested during my descent. Seeing that the Regent and his companion had dismounted, I stopped and sprang down from my carriage, holding out my hand to assist Eveena's descent, an attention which I thought seemed to surprise her. Up to the platform the path was easy enough; after that it became steep even for me, and certainly a troublesome and difficult ascent for a lady dressed as I have described, and hardly stronger than a child of the same height and size on earth. Still my companion did not seem to expect, and certainly did not invite assistance. That she found no little difficulty in the walk was evident from her turning back both sleeves and releasing her bird, which hovered closely round her. Very soon her embarrassments and stumbles threatened such actual danger as overcame my fear of committing what, for aught I knew, might be an intrusion. Catching her as she fell, and

raising her by the left hand, I held it fast in my own right, begging to be permitted to assist her for the rest of the journey. Her manner and the tone of her voice made it evident that such an attention, if unusual, was not offensive; but I observed that those who were following us looked at us with some little surprise, and spoke together in words which I could not catch, but the tone of which was not exactly pleasant or complimentary.

The Regent, a few steps in advance of us, turned back from time to time to ask me some trivial question. At last we reached the summit, and here I released my companion's hand and stepped forward a pace or two to point out to the Regent the external structure of the Astronaut. I was near enough, of course, to be heard by Eveena, and endeavoured to address my explanations as much to her as to the authority to whom I was required to render an account. But from the moment that we had actually joined him she withdrew from all part and all apparent interest in the conversation.

When our companions moved forward to reach the entrance, which I had indicated, I again offered my hand, saying, "I am afraid you will find some little difficulty in getting into the vessel by the window by which I got out."

The Regent, however, had brought with him several light metal poles, which I had not observed while carried by his companion, but which being put together formed a convenient ladder of adequate length. He desired me to ascend first and cut the riband by means of which the window had been sealed; the law being so strict that even he would not violate the symbol of private ownership which protected my vessel. Having done this and opened the window, I sprang down, and he, followed by his companion, ascended the ladder, and resting himself upon the broad inner ledge of the window—which afforded a convenient seat, since the crystal was but half the thickness of the wall—first took a long look all round the interior, and then leaped down, followed by his attendant. Eveena drew back, but was at last persuaded to mount the ladder with my assistance, and rest on the sill till I followed her and lifted her down inside. The Regent had by this time reached the machinery, and was examining it very curiously, with greater apparent appreciation of its purpose than I should have expected. When we joined them, I found little difficulty in explaining the purpose and working of most parts of the apparatus. The nature and

generation of the apergic power I took care not to explain. The existence of such a repulsive force was the point on which the Regent professed incredulity; as it was, of course, the critical fact on which my whole narrative turned—on which its truth or falsehood depended. I resolved ere the close of the inspection to give him clear practical evidence on this score.

In the meantime, listening without answer to his expressions of doubt, I followed him round the interior, explaining to him and to Eveena the use and structure of the thermometer, barycrite, and other instruments. My fair companion seemed to follow my explanation almost as easily as the officials. Our followers, who had now entered the vessel, kept within hearing of my remarks; but, evidently aware that they were there on sufferance, asked no questions, and made their comments in a tone too low to allow me to understand their purport. The impression made on the Regent by the instruments, so far as I could gather from his brief remarks and the expression of his face, was one of contemptuous surprise rather than the interest excited by the motive machinery. Most of them were evidently, in his opinion, clumsy contrivances for obtaining results which the scientific knowledge and inventive genius of his countrymen had long ago secured more completely and more easily. But he was puzzled by the combination of such imperfect knowledge or semi-barbaric ignorance with the possession of a secret of such immense importance as the repulsive current, not yet known nor, as I gathered, even conceived by the inhabitants of this planet. When he had completed his inspection, he requested permission to remove some of the objects I had left there; notably many of the dead plants, and several books of drawings, mathematical, mechanical, and ornamental, which I had left, and which had not been brought away by my host's son when he visited the vessel. These I begged him to present to the Camptâ, adding to them a few smaller curiosities, after which I drew him back towards the machinery. He summoned his attendant, and bade him take away to the carriages the articles I had given him, calling upon the intruders to assist.

I was thus left with him and with Eveena alone in the building; and with a partly serious, partly mischievous desire to prove to him the substantial reality of objects so closely related to my own disputed existence, and to

demonstrate the truth of my story, I loosened one of the conductors, connected it with the machinery, and, directing it against him, sent through it a very slight apergic current. I was not quite prepared for the result. His Highness was instantly knocked head over heels to a considerable distance.

Turning to interrupt the current before going to his assistance, I was startled to perceive that an accident of graver moment, in my estimation at least, than the discomfiture of this exalted official, had resulted from my experiment. I had not noticed that a conductive wire was accidentally in contact with the apergion, while its end hung down towards the floor Of this I suppose Eveena had carelessly taken hold, and a part of the current passing through it had lessened the shock to the Regent at the expense of one which, though it could not possibly have injured her, had from its suddenness so shaken her nerves as to throw her into a momentary swoon.

She was recovering almost at soon as I reached her; and by the time her fellow-sufferer had picked himself up in great disgust and astonishment, was partly aware what had happened. She was, however; much more anxious to excuse herself, in the manner of a frightened child, for meddling with the machinery than to hear my apologies for the accident. Noting her agitation, and seeing that she was still trembling all over, I was more anxious to get her into the open air, and out of reach of the apparatus she seemed to regard with considerable alarm, than to offer any due apology to the exalted personage to whom I had afforded much stronger evidence, if not of my own substantiality, yet of the real existence of a repulsive energy, than I had seriously intended. With a few hurried words to him, I raised Eveena to the window, and lifted her to the ground outside. I felt, however, that I could not leave the Regent to find his own way out, the more so that I hardly saw how he could reach the window from the inside without my assistance. I excused myself, therefore, and seating her on a rock close to the ladder, promised to return at once. This, however, I found impossible.

By the time the injured officer had recovered the physical shock to his nerves and the moral effect of the disrespect to his person, his anxiety to verify what he had heard entirely occupied his mind; and he requested further experiments, not upon himself, which occupied some half-hour. He listened and spoke, I must admit, with temper; but his air of displeasure

was evident enough, and I was aware that I had not entitled myself to his good word, whether or not he would permit his resentment to colour his account of facts. He was compelled, however, to request my help in reaching the window, which I gave with all possible deference.

But, to my alarm, when we reached the foot of the ladder, Eveena was nowhere to be seen. Calling her and receiving no reply, calling again and hearing what sounded like her voice, but in a faint tone and coming I knew not whither, I ran round the platform to seek her. I could see nothing of her; but at one point, just where the projecting edge of the platform overhung the precipice below, I recognised her bird fluttering its wings and screaming as if in pain or terror. The Regent was calling me in a somewhat imperious tone, but of course received neither answer nor attention. Reaching the spot, I looked over the edge and with some trouble discovered what had happened. Not merely below but underneath the overhanging edge was a shelf about four feet long and some ten inches in breadth, covered with a flower equally remarkable in form and colour, the former being that of a hollow cylindrical bell, about two inches in diameter; the latter a bluish lilac, the nearest approach to azure I have seen in Mars—

the whole ground one sheet of flowers. On this, holding in a half-insensible state to the outward-sloping rock above her, Eveena clung, her veil and head-dress fallen, her face expressing utter bewilderment as well as terror.

I saw, though at the moment I hardly understood, how she had reached this point. A very narrow path, some hundred feet in length, sloped down from the table-rock of the summit to the shelf on which she stood, with an outer hedge of shrubs and the summits of small trees, which concealed, and in some sort guarded, the precipice below, so that even a timid girl might pursue the path without fear. But this path ended several feet from the commencement of the shelf. Across the gap had lain a fallen tree, with boughs affording such a screen and railing on the outward side as might at once conceal the gulf below, and afford assistance in crossing the chasm.

But in crossing this tree Eveena's footsteps had displaced it, and it had so given way as not only to be unavailable, but a serious obstacle to my passage. Had I had time to go round, I might have been able to leap the chasm; I certainly could not return that way with a burden even so light as

that of my precious charge. The only chance was to lift her by main force directly to where I stood; and the outward projection of the rock at this point rendered this peculiarly difficult, as I had nothing to cling or hold by.

The Regent had by this time reached me, and discerned what had occurred.

"Hold me fast," I said, "or sit upon me if you like, to hold me with your weight whilst I lean over." The man stood astounded, not by the danger of another but by the demand on himself; and evidently without the slightest intention of complying.

"You are mad!" he said. "Your chance is ten times greater to lose your own life than to save hers."

"Lose my life!" I cried. "Could I dare return alive without her? Throw your whole weight on me, I say, as I lean over, and waste no more time!"

"What!" he rejoined. "You are twice as heavy as I, and if you are pulled over I shall probably go over too. Why am I to endanger myself to save a girl from the consequences of her folly?"

"If you do not," I swore, "I will fling you where the carcass of which you are so careful shall be crushed out of the very form of the manhood you disgrace."

Even this threat failed to move him. Meantime the bird, fluttering on my shoulder, suggested a last chance; and snatching the tablet round its neck, I wrote two words thereon, and calling to it, "Home!" the intelligent creature flew off at fullest speed.

"Now," I said, "if you do not help me I will kill you here and now. If you pretend to help and fail me, that bird carries to Esmo my request to hold you answerable for our lives."

I invoked, in utter desperation, the awe with which, as his hints and my experience implied, Esmo was regarded by his neighbours; and slender as seemed this support, it did not fail me. The Regent's countenance fell, and I saw that I might depend at least on his passive compliance. Clasping his arm with my left hand, I said, "Pull back with all your might. If I go over, you shall go over too." Then pulling him down with me, and stretching myself over the precipice so far that but for this additional support I must

have fallen, I reached Eveena, whose closed eyes and relaxing limbs indicated that another moment's delay might be fatal.

"Give me your hand," I cried in despair, seeing how tightly she still grasped the tough fibrous shoots growing in the crevices of the rock, whereof she had taken hold. "Give me your hand, and let go!"

To give me her hand was beyond the power of her will; to let go without giving me hold would have been fatal. Reaching over to the uttermost, I contrived to lay a firm grasp upon her wrist. But this would not do. I could hardly drag her up by one arm, especially if she would not relax her grasp.

I must release the Regent and depend upon his obedience, or forfeit the chance of saving her, as in a few more moments she would certainly swoon and fall.

"Throw yourself upon me, and sit firm, if you value your life," I cried, and I relaxed my hold on his arm, stretching both hands to grasp Eveena. I felt the man's weight on my body, and with both arms extended to the uttermost hanging over the edge, I caught firm bold of the girl's shoulders.

Even now, with any girl of her age on earth, and for aught I know with many Martial damsels, the case would have been hopeless. My whole strength was required to raise her; I had none to spare to force her loose from her hold. Fortunately my rough and tight clasp seemed to rouse her.

Her eyes half opened, and semi-consciousness appeared to have returned.

"Let go!" I cried in that sharp tone of imperious anger which—with some tempers at least—is the natural expression of the outward impulse produced by supreme and agonizing terror. Obedience is the hereditary lesson taught to her sex by the effects of equality in Mars. Eveena had been personally trained in a principle long discarded by Terrestrial women; and not half aware what she did, but yielding instinctively to the habit of compliance with imperative command spoken in a masculine voice, she opened her hands just as I had lost all hope. With one desperate effort I swung her fairly on to the platform, and, seeing her safe there, fell back myself scarcely more sensible than she was.

The whole of this terrible scene, which it has taken so long to relate, did not occupy more than a minute in action. I know not whether my readers can understand the full difficulty and danger of the situation. I know that no words of mine can convey the impression graven into my own memory, never to be effaced or weakened while consciousness remains. The strongest man on Earth could not have done what I did; could not, lying half over the precipice, have swung a girl of eighteen right out from underneath him, and to his own level. But Eveena was of slighter, smaller frame than a healthy French girl of twelve, while I retained the full strength of a man adapted to the work of a world where every weight is twice as heavy as on Mars. What I had practically to do was to lift not seven or eight stone of European girlhood, not even the six Eveena might possibly have weighed on Earth, but half that weight. And yet the position was such that all the strength I had acquired through ten years of constant practice in the field and in the chase, all the power of a frame in healthful maturity, and of muscles whose force seemed doubled by the tension of the nerves, hardly availed. When I recovered my own senses, and had contrived to restore Eveena's, my unwilling assistant had disappeared.

It was an hour before Eveena seemed in a condition to be removed, and perhaps I was not very urgent to hurry her away. I had done no more than any man, the lowest and meanest on Earth, must have done under the circumstances. I can scarcely enter into the feelings of the fellow-man who, in my position, could have recognised a choice but between saving and perishing with the helpless creature entrusted to his charge. But hereditary disbelief in any power above the physical forces of Nature, in any law higher than that of man's own making, has rendered human nature in Mars something utterly different from, perhaps, hardly intelligible to, the human nature of a planet forty million miles nearer the Sun. Though brought up in an affectionate home, Eveena shared the ideas of the world in which she was born; and so far accepted its standards of opinion and action as natural if not right, that the risk I had run, the effort I had made to save her, seemed to her scarcely less extraordinary than it had appeared to the Zamptâ. She rated its devotion and generosity as highly as he appreciated its extravagance and folly; and if he counted me a madman, she was

disposed to elevate me into a hero or a demi-god. The tones and looks of a maiden in such a temper, however perfect her maidenly reserve, would, I fancy, be very agreeable to men older than I was, either in constitution or even in experience. I doubt whether any man under fifty would have been more anxious than myself to cut short our period of repose, broken as it was, when I refused to listen to her tearful penitence and self-reproach, by occasional words and looks of gratitude and admiration. I did, however, remember that it was expedient to refasten the window, and re-attach the seals, before departing. At the end of the hour's rest I allowed my charge and myself, I had recovered more or less completely the nervous force which had been for a while utterly exhausted, less by the effort than by the terror that preceded it. I was neither surprised, nor perhaps as much grieved as I should have been, to find that Eveena could hardly walk; and felt to the full the value of those novel conditions which enabled me to carry her the more easily in my arms, though much oppressed even by so slight an effort in that thin air, to the place where we had left our carriage—

no inconsiderable distance by the path we had to pursue. Before starting on our return I had, in despite of her most earnest entreaties, managed to recover her head-dress and veil, at a risk which, under other circumstances, I might not have cared to encounter. But had she been seen without it on our return, the comments of the whole neighbourhood would have been such as might have disturbed even her father's cool indifference. We reached her home in safety, and with little notice, having, of course, drawn the canopy around us as completely as possible. I was pleased to find that only her younger sister, to whose care I at once committed her, was there at present, the elders not having yet returned. I took care to detach from the bird's neck the tablet which had served its purpose so well. The creature had found his way home within half-an-hour after I dismissed him, and had frightened Zevle [Stella] not a little; though the message, which a fatal result would have made sufficiently intelligible to Esmo, utterly escaped her comprehension.

CHAPTER VIII - A FAITH AND ITS FOUNDER.

On the return of the family, my host was met at the door with such accounts of what had happened as led him at once to see and question his daughter. It was not, therefore, till he had heard her story that I saw him.

More agitated than I should have expected from one under ordinary circumstances so calm and self-possessed, he entered my room with a face whose paleness and compressed lips indicated intense emotion; and, laying his hand on my shoulder, expressed his feeling rather in look and tone than in his few broken and not very significant words. After a few moments, however, he recovered his coolness, and asked me to supply the deficiencies of Eveena's story. I told him briefly but exactly what had passed from the moment when I missed her to that of her rescue. He listened without the slightest symptom of surprise or anger to the tale of the Regent's indifference, and seemed hardly to understand the disgust and indignation with which I dwelt upon it. When I had finished—

"You have made," he said, "an enemy, and a dangerous one; but you have also secured friends against whose support even the anger of a greater than the Zamptâ might break as harmlessly as waves upon a rock. He behaved only as any one else would have done; and it is useless to be angry with men for being what they habitually and universally are. What you did for Eveena, one of ourselves, perhaps, but no other, might have risked for a first bride on the first day of her marriage. Indeed, though I am most thankful to you, I should, perhaps, have withheld my consent to my daughter's request had I supposed that you felt so strongly for her."

"I think," I replied with some displeasure, "that I may positively affirm that I have spoken no word to your daughter which I should not have spoken in your presence. I am too unfamiliar with your ideas to know whether your remark has the same force and meaning it would have borne among my own people; but to me it conveys a grave reproach. When I accepted the charge of your daughter during this day's excursion, I thought of her only as every man thinks of a young, pretty, and gentle girl of whom he has seen and knows scarcely anything. To avail myself of what has since

happened to make a deeper impression on her feelings than you might approve would have seemed to me unpardonable treachery."

"You do utterly misunderstand me," he answered. "It may be that Eveena has received an impression which will not be effaced from her mind. It may be that this morning, could I have foreseen it, I should have decidedly wished to avoid anything that would so impress her. But that feeling, if it exist, has been caused by your acts and not by your words. That you should do your utmost, at any risk to yourself, to save her, is consistent with what I know of your habit of mind, and ought not much to surprise me. But, from your own account of what you said to the Zamptâ, you were not merely willing to risk life for life. When you deemed it impossible to return without her, you spoke as few among us would seriously speak of a favourite bride."

"I spoke and felt," I replied, "as any man trained in the hereditary thought of my race and rank would have spoken of any woman committed to his care. All that I said and did for Eveena, I should have said and done, I hope, for the least attractive or least amiable maiden in this planet who had been similarly entrusted to my charge. How could any but the vilest coward return and say to a father, 'You trusted your daughter to me, and she has perished by my fault or neglect'?"

"Not so," he answered, "Eveena alone was to blame—and much to blame.

She says herself that you had told her to remain where you left her till your return; and if she had not disobeyed, neither her life nor yours would have been imperilled."

"One hardly expects a young lady to comply exactly with such requests," I said. "At any rate, Terrestrial feelings of honour and even of manhood would have made it easier to leap the precipice than to face you and the world if, no matter by whose fault, my charge had died in such a manner under my eyes and within my reach."

Esmo's eyes brightened and his cheek flushed a little as I spoke, with more of earnestness or passion than any incident, however exciting, is wont to provoke among his impassive race.

"Of one thing," he said, "you have assured me—that the proposal I was about to make rather invites honour than confers it. I have been obliged, in speaking of the manners and ideas of my countrymen, to let you perceive not only that I differ from them, but that there are others who think and act as I do. We have for ages formed a society bound together by our peculiar tenets. That we individually differ in conduct, and, therefore, probably in ideas, from our countrymen, they necessarily know; that we form a body apart with laws and tenets of our own, is at least suspected. But our organisation, its powers, its methods, its rules of membership, and its doctrines are, and have always been, a secret, and no man's connection with it is avowed or provable. Our chief distinctive and essential doctrines you hold as strongly as we do—the All-perfect Existence, the immortal human soul. From these necessarily follow conceptions of life and principles of conduct alien to those that have as necessarily grown up among a race which repudiates, ignores, and hates our two fundamental premises. After what has happened, I can promise you immediate and eager acceptance among those invested with the fullest privileges of our order. They will all admire your action and applaud your motives, though, frankly speaking, I doubt whether any of us would carry your views so far as you have done. The best among us would have flinched, unless under the influence of the very strongest personal affection, from the double peril of which you seemed to think so lightly. They might indeed have defied the Regent but it would have been in reliance on the protection of, a power superior to his of which you knew nothing."

"Then," I said, "I suppose your engagement of to-day was a meeting of this society?"

"Yes," he answered, "a meeting of the Chamber to which I and the elder members of my household, including my son and his wife, belong." "But," I said, "if you are more powerful than the rulers of your people, what need of such careful secrecy?"

"You will understand the reason," he answered, "when you learn the nature of our powers. Hundreds among millions, we are no match for the fighting force of our unbelieving countrymen. Our safety lies in the terror inspired

by a tradition, verified by repeated and invariable experience, that no one who injures one of us but has reason to rue it, that no mortal enemy of the Star has ever escaped signal punishment, more terrible for the mystery attending it. Were we known, were our organisation avowed, we might be hunted down and exterminated, and should certainly suffer frightful havoc, even if in the end we were able to frighten or overcome our enemies. But if you are disposed to accept my offer—and enrolment among us gives you at once your natural place in this planet and your best security against the enmity you have incurred and will incur here—I should prefer to make the rest of the explanation that must precede your admission in presence of my family. The first step, the preliminary instruction in our creed and our simpler mysteries, which is the work of the Novitiate, is a solemn epoch in the lives of our children. They are not trusted with our secret till we can rely on the maturity of their intelligence and loyalty of their nature. Eveena would in any case have been received as a novice within some dozen days. It will now be easy for me, considering her education and intelligence and my own position in the Order, to obtain, for her as for you, exemption from the usual probation on proof that you both know all that is usually taught therein, and admission on the same occasion; and it will add solemnity and interest to her first initiation, that this chief lesson of her life should be shared this evening with him to whom she owes it that she lives to enter the society, to which her ancestors have belonged since its institution."

We passed into the peristyle, where the ladies were as usual assembled; but the children had been dismissed, and of the maidens Eveena only was present. Fatigue and agitation had left her very pale, and she was resting at full length on the cushions with her head pillowed on her mother's knee.

As we approached, however, they all rose, the other ladies greeting me eagerly and warmly, Eveena rising with difficulty and faltering the welcome which the rest had spoken with enthusiastic earnestness.

Forgetting for the moment the prudence which ignorance of Martial customs had hitherto dictated, I lifted to my lips the hand that she, following the example of the rest, but shyly and half reluctantly, laid on my shoulder—a form very different to the distant greeting I had heretofore

received, and marking that I was no longer to be treated as a stranger to the family. My unusual salute brought the colour back to her cheeks, but no one else took notice of it. I observed, however, that on this occasion, instead of interposing himself between me and the ladies as usual, her father left vacant the place next to her; and I seated myself at her feet. She would have exchanged her reclining posture for that of the others, but her mother gently drew her down to her former position.

"Eveena," said my host, "I have told our friend, what you know, that there is in this world a society, of which I am a member, whose principles are not those of our countrymen, but resemble rather those which supplied the impulses on which he acted to-day. This much you know. What you would have learned a few days hence, I mean that you and he shall now hear at the same time."

"Before you enter on that subject," interposed Zulve timidly—for it is most unusual for a lady to interfere in her husband's conversation, much more to offer a suggestion or correction—but yet earnestly, "let me say, on my own part, what I am sure you must have said already on yours. If there be now, or ever shall be, anything we can do for our guest, anything we can give that he would value, not in requital, but in memory of what he has done for us—whatever it should cost us, though he should ask the most precious thing we possess, it will be our pride and pleasure—the greatest pleasure he can afford us—to grant it."

The time and the surroundings were not perhaps exactly suitable to the utterance of the wish suggested by these words; but I knew so little what might be in store for me, and understood so well the difficulty and uncertainty of finding future opportunities of intercourse with the ladies at least of the family, that I dared not lose the present. I spoke at once upon the impulse of the moment, with a sense of reckless desperation not unlike that with which an artillerist fires the train whose explosion may win for him the obsidional wreath or blow him into atoms. "You and my host," I said, "have one treasure that I have learned to covet, but it is exactly the most precious thing you possess, and one which it would be presumptuous to ask as reward; even had I not owed to Esmo the life I perilled for

Eveena, and if I had acted from choice and freely, instead of doing only what only the vilest of cowards could have failed to attempt. In asking it indeed, I feel that I cancel whatever claim your extravagant estimate of that act can possibly ascribe to me."

"We don't waste words," answered Esmo, "in saying what we don't mean, and I confirm fully what my wife has said. There is nothing we possess that we shall not delight to give as token of regard and in remembrance of this day to the saviour of our child."

"If," I said, "I find a neighbour's purse containing half his fortune, and return it to him, he may offer me what reward I ask, but would hardly think it reasonable if I asked for the purse and its contents. But you have only one thing I care to possess—that which I have, by God's help, been enabled to save to-day. If I must ask a gift, give me Eveena herself."

Utilitarianism has extinguished in Mars the use of compliment and circumlocution; and until I concluded, their looks of mild perplexity showed that neither Zulve nor her husband caught my purpose. I fancied—for, not daring to look them in the face, I had turned my downcast glance on Eveena—that she had perhaps somewhat sooner divined the object of my thoughts. However, a silence of surprise—was it of reluctance?—followed, and then Zulve bent over her daughter and looked into her half-averted face, while Esmo answered—

"What you should ask I promised to give; what you have asked I give, in so far as it is mine to give, in willing fulfilment of my pledge. But, of course, what I can give is but my free permission to my daughter to answer for herself. You will be, I hope, within a few days at furthest, one of those in whose possession alone a woman of my house could be safe or content; and, free by the law of the land to follow her own wish, she is freed by her father's voice from the rule which the usage of ten thousand years imposes on the daughters of our brotherhood."

Zulve then looked up, for Eveena had hidden her face in her mother's robe, and said—

"If my child will not speak for herself I must speak for her, and in my own name and in hers I fulfil her father's promise. And now let my husband tell his story, for nothing can solemnise more appropriately the betrothal of a daughter of the Star, than her admission to the knowledge of the Order whose privileges are her heritage."

"At the time," Esmo began, "when material science had gained a decided ascendant, and enforced the recognition of its methods as the only ones whereby certain knowledge and legitimate belief could be attained, those who clung most earnestly to convictions not acquired or favoured by scientific logic were sorely dismayed. They were confounded, not so much by the yet informal but irrevocable majority-vote against them, as by an instinctive misgiving that Science was right; and by irrepressible doubts whether that which would not bear the application of scientific method could in any sense be true or trustworthy knowledge. At the same time, to apply a scientific method to the cherished beliefs threatened only to dissolve them. Fortunately for them and their successors, there was living at that time one of the most remarkable and original thinkers whom our race has produced. From him came the suggestions that gave impulse to our learning and birth to our Order. 'The reasonings, the processes of Science,' he affirmed,'are beyond challenge. Their trustworthiness depends not on their subject-matter, but on their own character; not on their relation to outward Nature, but on their conformity to the laws of thought. Their upholders are right in affirming that what will

not ultimately bear the test of their application cannot be knowledge, and probably—for the practical purposes of human life we may say certainly—cannot be truth. They are wrong in alleging that the ideas for which they can find no foundation in the subjects to which scientific method has hitherto been applied, are therefore unscientific, or sure to disappear under scientific investigation. I hold that the existence of a Creator and Ruler of the Universe can be logically deduced from first principles, as well as justly inferred from cumulative evidences of overwhelming weight. The existence of something in Man that is not merely corporeal, of powers that can act beyond the reach of any corporeal instruments at his command, or without the range of their application, is not proven; it may be, only because the facts that
  indicate without proving it have never yet been subject to systematic verification or scientific analysis. But of such facts there exists a vast accumulation; unsifted, untested, and therefore as yet ineffective for proof, but capable, I can scarcely doubt, of reduction to methodical order and scientific treatment. There are records and traditions of every degree of value, from utter worthlessness to the worth of the most authentic history, preserving the evidences of powers which may be generally described as spiritual. Through all ages, among all races, the living have alleged themselves from time to time to have seen the forms and even heard the voices of the dead. Scientific men have been forced by the actual and public exercise of the power under the most crucial tests—for instance, to produce insensibility in surgical operations—to admit that the will of one man can control the brain, the senses, the physical frame of another without material contact, perhaps at a distance. There are narratives of marvels wrought by human will, chiefly in remote, but occasionally in recent times, transcending and even contradicting or overruling the known laws of Nature. All these evidences point to one conclusion; all corroborate and confirm one another. The men of science ridicule them because in so many cases the facts are imperfectly authenticated, and because in others the action of the powers is uncertain, dependent on conditions imperfectly ascertained, and not of that material kind to which material science willingly submits. But if they be facts, if they relate to any element of human nature, all these things can be systematically investigated, the true separated from the false, the proven from the unproven. The powers can be investigated, their conditions of action laid down. Probably they may be so developed as to be exercised with comparative certainty, whether by every one or only by those special constitutions in which they may inhere. Such investigations will at present only enlist the attention and care of a few qualified persons, and, that they may be carried on in peace and safety, should be carried on in secrecy. But upon them may, I hope, be founded a certainty as regards the higher side of man's nature not less complete than that which science, by similar methods, has gradually acquired in regard to its purely physical aspects.'

"For this end he instituted a secret society, which has subsisted in constantly increasing strength and cohesion to the present hour. It has collected evidence, conducted experiments, investigated records, studied methodically the abnormal phenomena you call occult or spiritual, and reduced them to something like the certainty of science. Discoveries from the first curious and interesting have become more and more complete, practical, and effective. Our results have surpassed the hopes of our Founder, and transcend in importance, while they equal in certainty, the contemporary achievements of physical science,—some of the chief of which belong to us. All that profound knowledge of human nature could suggest to bring its weakness to the support of its strength, and enlist both in the work, was done by our Founder, and by those who have carried out his scheme. The corporate character of the society, its rites and formularies, its grades and ranks, are matter of deep interest to all its members, have linked them together by an inviolable bond, and given them a strength infinitely greater than numbers without such cohesion could possibly have afforded. The Founder left us no moral code, imposed on us none of his own most cherished ethical convictions, as he pledged us to none of the conclusions which his own occult studies had led him to anticipate, nearly all of which have been verified by later investigation. Such rules as he imposed were directed only to the cohesion and efficiency of the Order.

Our creed still consists only of the two fundamental doctrines; two settled principles only are laid down by our aboriginal law. We are taught to cultivate the closest personal affection, the most intimate and binding ties among ourselves; to defend the Order and one another, whether by strenuous resistance or severe reprisals, against all who injure us individually or collectively, and especially against persecutors of the Order. But the few laws our Founder has left are given in the form of striking precepts, brief, and often even paradoxical. For example, the law of defence or reprisal is concentrated in one antithetic phrase:—Gavart dax Zveltâ, gavart gedex Zinta [Never let the member strike, never let the Order spare]. As it is a rule with us to embody none of our symbols, forms, or laws in writing, this manner of statement served to impress them on the memory, as well as to leave the utmost freedom in their application, by the

gathered experience of ages, and the prudence of those who had to deal with the circumstances of each successive period. Another maxim says,

'Who kisses a brother's hand may kick the Camptâ,' thus enforcing at once the value of ceremonial courtesy, and the power conferred by union. We observe more ceremony in family life than others in the most formal public relations. Their theory of life being utterly utilitarian, no form is observed that serves no distinct practical purpose. We wish to make life graceful and elegant, as well as easy. Principles originally inculcated upon us by the necessity of self-protection have been enforced and graven on our very nature, by the reaction of our experience against the rough and harsh relations, the jarring and often unfriendly intercourse, of external society.

Aliens to our Order—that is, ninety-nine hundredths of our race—take delight in the infliction of petty personal annoyance, at least never take care not to 'jar each other's elbow-nerves,' or set on edge the teeth that never bit them. We are careful not to wound the feelings or even the weaknesses of a brother. Punctilious courtesy, frank apology for unintentional wrong, is with us a point of honour. Disputes, when by any chance they arise, are referred to the arbitration of our chiefs, who never consider their work done till the disputants are cordially reconciled. Envy, the most dangerous source of ill-will among men, can hardly exist among us. Rank has been well earned by its holder, or in a few cases by his ancestors; and authority is a trust never to be used for its holder's benefit. Wealth never provokes covetousness, since no member is ever allowed to be poor. Not only the Order but each member is bound to take every opportunity of assisting every other by every method within his power. We employ them, we promote them, we give them the preference in every kind of patronage at our command. But these obligations are points of honour rather than of law. Only apostasy or treason to the Order involve compulsory penalties; and the latter, if it ever occurred in these days, would be visited with instant death,—inflicted, as it is inflicted upon irreconcilable enemies, in such a manner that none could know who passed the sentence, or by whom it was executed."

"And have you," I asked, "no apostates, as you have no traitors?"

"No," he said. "In the first place, none who has lived among us could endure to fall into the ordinary Martial life. Secondly, the foundations of our simple creed are so clear, so capable of being made apparent to every one, that none once familiar with the evidences can well cease to believe them."

Here he paused, and I asked, "How is it possible that the means you employ to punish those who have wronged you should not, in some cases at least, indicate the person who has employed them?"

"Because," he said, "the means of vengeance are not corporeal; the agency does not in the least resemble any with which our countrymen, or apparently your race on Earth, are acquainted. A traitor would be found dead with no sign of suffering or injury, and the physician would pronounce that he had died of apoplexy or heart disease. A persecutor, or one who had unpardonably wronged any of the Children of the Star, might go mad, might fling himself from a precipice, might be visited with the most terrible series of calamities, all natural in their character, all distinctly traceable to natural causes, but astonishing and even apparently supernatural in their accumulation, and often in their immediate appropriateness to the character of his offence. Our neighbours would, of course, destroy the avenger, if they could find him out—would attempt to exterminate our society, could they prove its agency."

"But surely your countrymen must either disbelieve in such agency, in which case they can hardly fear your vengeance, or they must believe it, and then would deem it just and necessary to retaliate."

"No," he said. "They disbelieve in the possibility while they are forced to see the fact. It is impossible, they would say, that a man should be injured in mind or body, reputation or estate, that the forces of Nature or the feelings of men should be directed against him, without the intervention of any material agent, by the mere will of those who take no traceable means to give that will effect. At the same time, tradition and even authentic history record, what experience confirms, that every one who has wronged us deeply has come to some terrible, awe-striking end. Each man would ridicule heartily a neighbour who should allege such a ground for fearing

to injure one of us; but there is none who is so true to his own unbelief as to do that which, in every instance, has been followed by signal and awful disaster. Moreover, we do by visible symbols suggest a relation between the vengeance and the crime. Over the heart of criminals who have paid with their lives, no matter by what immediate agency, for wrong to us, is found after death the image of a small blood-red star; the only case in which any of our sacred symbols are exposed to profane eyes."

"Surely," I said, "in the course of generations, and with your numbers, you must be often watched and traced; and some one spy, on one out of a million occasions, must have found access to your meetings and heard and seen all that passed."

"Our meetings," he said, "are held where no human eye can possibly see, no human ear hear what passes. The Chambers meet in apartments concealed within the dwellings of individual members. When we meet the doors are guarded, and can be passed only by those who give a token and a password. And if these could become known to an enemy, the appearance of a stranger would lead to questions that would at once expose his ignorance of our simplest secrets. He would learn nothing, and would never tell his story to the outer world." ...

Opening the door, or rather window, of his private chamber, Esmo directed our eyes to a portrait sunk in the wall, and usually concealed by a screen which fitted exactly the level and the patterns of the general surface.

It displayed, in a green vesture not unlike his own, but with a gold ribbon and emerald symbol like the cross of an European knighthood over the right shoulder, a spare soldierly form, with the most striking countenance I have ever seen; one which, once seen, none could forget. The white long hair and beard, the former reaching the shoulders, the latter falling to the belt, were not only unlike the fashion of this generation, but gave tokens of age never discerned in Mars for the last three or four thousand years. The form, though erect and even stately, was that of one who had felt the long since abolished infirmity of advancing years. The countenance alone bore no marks of old age. It was full, unwrinkled, firm in physical as in moral character; calm in the unresisted power of intellect and will over the

passions, serene in a dignity too absolute and self-contained for pride, but expressing a consciousness of command over others as evident as the unconscious, effortless command of self to which it owed its supreme and sublime quietude. The lips were not set as with a habit of reserve or self-restraint, but close and even as in the repose to which restraint had never been necessary. The features were large, clearly defined, and perfect in shape, proportion, and outline. The brow was massive and broad, but strangely smooth and even; the head had no single marked development or deficiency that could have enlightened a phrenologist, as the face told no tale that a physiognomist could read. The dark deep eyes were unescapable; while in presence of the portrait you could not for a moment avoid or forget their living, fixed, direct look into your own. Even in the painted representation of that gaze, almost too calm in its absolute mastery to be called searching or scrutinising, yet seeming to look through the eyes into the soul, there was an almost mesmeric influence; as if, across the abyss of ten thousand years, the Master could still control the wills and draw forth the inner thoughts of the living, as he had dominated the spirits of their remotest ancestors.

CHAPTER IX - MANNERS AND CUSTOMS.

Next morning Esmo asked me to accompany him on a visit to the seaport I have mentioned. In the course of this journey I had opportunities of learning many things respecting the social and practical conditions of human life and industry on Mars that had hitherto been unknown to me, and to appreciate the enormous advance in material civilisation which has accompanied what seems to me, as it would probably seem to any other Earth-dweller, a terrible moral degeneration. Most of these things I learned partly from my own observation, partly from the explanations of my companion; some exclusively from what he told me. We passed a house in process of building, and here I learned the manner in which the wonders of domestic architecture, which had so surprised me by their perfection and beauty, are accomplished. The material employed in all buildings is originally liquid, or rather viscous. In the first place, the foundation is excavated to a depth of two or three feet, the ground beaten hard, and the liquid concrete poured into the level tank thus formed. When this has hardened sufficiently to admit of their erection, thin frames of metal are erected, enclosing the spaces to be occupied by the several outer and interior walls.

These spaces are filled with the concrete at a temperature of about 80° C.

The tracery and the bas-reliefs impressed on the walls are obtained by means of patterns embossed or marked upon thinner sheets placed inside the metallic frames. The hardening is effected partly by sudden cooling, partly by the application of electricity under great hydraulic pressure. The flat roof is constructed in the same manner, the whole mass, when the fluid concrete is solidified, being simply one continuous stone, as hard and cohesive as granite. Where a flat roof would be liable to give way or break from its own weight, the arch or dome is employed to give the required strength, and consequently all the largest Martial buildings are constructed in the form of vaults or domes. As regards the form of the building, individual or public taste is absolutely free, it being just as easy to construct a circular or octagonal as a rectangular house or chamber; but the latter form is almost exclusively employed for private dwellings. The jewel-like

lustre and brilliancy I have described are given to the surfaces of the walls by the simultaneous action of cold, electricity, and pressure, the principle of which Esmo could not so explain as to render it intelligible to me.

Almost the whole physical labour is done by machinery, from the digging and mixing of the materials to their conveyance and delivery into the place prepared for them by the erection of the metallic frames, and from the erection to the removal of the latter. The translucent material for the windows I have described is prepared by a separate process, and in distinct factories, and, ready hardened and cut into sheets of the required size, is brought to the building and fixed in its place by machinery. It can be tinted to the taste of the purchaser; but, as a rule, a tintless crystal is preferred.

The entire work of building a large house, from the foundation to the finishing and removal of the metallic frames, occupies from half-a-dozen to eighteen workmen from four to eight days. This, like most other labour in Mars, goes on continuously; the electric lamps, raised to a great height on hollow metallic poles, affording by night a very sufficient substitute for the light of the sun. All work is done by three relays of artisans; the first set working from noon till evening, the next from evening till morning, and the third from morning to noon. The Martial day, which consists of about twenty-four hours forty minutes of our time, is divided in a somewhat peculiar manner. The two-hour periods, of which "mean" sunrise and sunset are severally the middle points, are respectively called the morning and evening zydau. Two periods of the same length before and after noon and midnight are distinguished as the first and second dark, the first and second mid-day zyda. There remain four intervals of three hours each, popularly described as the sleeping, waking, after-sunrise, and fore-sunset zyda respectively. This is the popular reckoning, and that marked upon the instruments which record time for ordinary purposes, and by these the meals and other industrial and domestic epochs are fixed. But for purposes of exact calculation, the day, beginning an hour before mean sunrise, is distributed into twelve periods, or antoi, of a little more than two terrestrial hours each. These again are subdivided by twelve into periods of a little more than 10m., 50s., 2-1/2s., and 5/24s respectively; but of these the second and last are alone employed in common speech. The uniform

employment of twelve as the divisor and multiplier in tables of weight, distance, time, and space, as well as in arithmetical notation, has all the conveniences of the decimal system of France, and some others besides due to the greater convenience of twelve as a base. But as regards the larger divisions of time, the Martials are placed at a great disadvantage by the absence of any such intermediate divisions as the Moon has suggested to Terrestrials. The revolutions of the satellites are too rapid and their periods too brief to be of service in dividing their year of 668-2/3 solar days.

Martial civilisation having taken its rise within the tropics—indeed the equatorial continents, which only here and there extend far into the temperate zone, and two minor continents in the southern ocean, are the only well-peopled portions of the planet—the demarcation of the seasons afforded by the solstices have been comparatively disregarded. The year is divided into winter and summer, each beginning with the Equinox, and distinguished as the North and South summer respectively. But these being exceedingly different in duration—the Northern half of the planet having a summer exceeding by seventy-six days that of the Southern hemisphere—

are of no use as accurate divisions of time. Time is reckoned, accordingly, from the first day of the year; the 669th day being incomplete, and the new year beginning at the moment of the Equinox with the 0th day. In remote ages the lapse of time was marked by festivals and holidays occurring at fixed periods; but the principle of utility has long since abolished all anniversaries, except those fixed by Nature, and these pass without public observance and almost without notice.

The climate is comparatively equable in the Northern hemisphere, the summer of the South being hotter and the winter colder, as the planet is much nearer the Sun during the former. On an average, the solar disc seems about half as large as to eyes on Earth; but the continents lying in a belt around the middle of the planet, nearly the whole of its population enjoy the advantages of tropical regularity. There are two brief rainy seasons on the Equator and in its neighbourhood, and one at each of the tropics. Outside these the cold of winter is aggravated by cloud and mist.

The barometer records from 20 inches to 21 inches at the sea-level. Storms are slight, brief, and infrequent; the tides are insignificant; and sea-voyages

were safe and easy even before Martial ingenuity devised vessels which are almost independent of weather. During the greater part of the year a clear sky from the morning to the evening zyda may be reckoned upon with almost absolute confidence. A heavy dew, thoroughly watering the whole surface, rendering the rarity of rain no inconvenience to agriculture, falls during the earlier hours of the night, which nevertheless remains cloudy; while the periods of sunset and sunrise are, as I have already said, marked almost invariably by dense mist, extending from one to four thousand feet above the sea-level, according to latitude and season. From the dissipation of the morning to the fall of the evening mist, the tropical temperature ranges, according to the time of the day and year, from 24° to 35° C. A very sudden change takes place at sunset. Except within 28° of the Equator, night frosts prevail during no small part of the year. Fine nights are at all times chilly, and men employed out of doors from the fall of the evening to the dispersal of the morning mists rely on an unusually warm under-dress of soft leather, as flexible as kid, but thicker, which is said to keep in the warmth of the body far better than any woven material. Women who, from whatever reason, venture out at night, wear the warmest cloaks they can procure. Those of limited means wear a loosely woven hair or woollen over-robe in lieu of their usual outdoor garment, resembling tufted cotton.

Those who can afford them substitute for the envelope of down, described a while back, warm skin or fur overgarments, obtained from the sub-arctic lands and seas, and furnished sometimes by a creature not very unlike our Polar bear, but passing half his time in the water and living on fish; sometimes by a mammal more resembling something intermediate between the mammoth and the walrus, with the habits of the hippopotamus and a fur not unlike the sealskin so much affected in Europe.

Outside the city, at a distance protecting it from any unpleasant vapours, which besides were carried up metallic tubes of enormous height, were several factories of great extent, some chemical, some textile, others reducing from their ores, purifying, forging, and producing in bulk and forms convenient for their various uses, the numerous metals employed in Mars. The most important of these—zorinta—is obtained from a tenacious

soil much resembling our own clay. It is far lighter than tin, has the colour and lustre of silver, and never tarnishes, the only rust produced by oxidation of its surface being a white loose powder, which can be brushed or shaken off without difficulty. Of this nearly all Martial utensils and furniture are constructed; and its susceptibility to the electric current renders it especially useful for mechanical purposes, electricity supplying the chief if not the sole motive-power employed in Martial industry. The largest factories, however, employ but a few hands, the machinery being so perfect as to perform, with very little interposition from human hands, the whole work, from the first purification to the final arrangement. I saw a mass of ore as dug out from the ground put into one end of a long series of machines, which came out, without the slightest manual assistance, at the close of a course of operations so directed as to bring it back to our feet, in the form of a thin sheet of lustrous metal. In another factory a mass of dry vegetable fibre was similarly transformed by machinery alone into a bale of wonderfully light woven drapery resembling satin in lustre, muslin or gauze in texture.

The streets were what, even in the finest and latest-built American cities, would be thought magnificent in size and admirable in construction. The roadway was formed of that concrete, harder than granite, which is the sole material employed in Martial building, and which, as I have shown, can take every form and texture, from that of jewels or of the finest marble to that of plain polished slate. Along each side ran avenues of magnificent trees, whose branches met at a height of thirty feet over the centre. Between these and the houses was a space reserved for the passage of light carriages exclusively. The houses, unlike those in the country, were from two to four stories in height.

All private dwellings, however, were built, as in the country, around a square interior garden, and the windows, except those of the front rooms employed for business purposes, looked out upon this. The space occupied, however, was of course much smaller than where ground was less precious, few dwellings having four chambers on the same floor and front.

The footway ran on the level of what we call the first story, over a part of the roof of the ground floor; and the business apartments were always the front chambers of the former, while the stores of the merchants were collected in a single warehouse occupying the whole of the ground front.

No attempt was made to exhibit them as on Earth. I entered with my host a number of what we should call shops. In every case he named exactly the article he wanted, and it was either produced at once or he was told that it was not to be had there, a thing which, however, seldom happened. The traders are few in number. One or two firms engaged in a single branch of commerce do the whole business of an extensive province. For instance, all the textile fabrics on sale in the province were to be seen in one or other of two warehouses; all metals in sheets, blocks, and wires in another; in a third all finished metal-work, except writing materials; all writing, phonographic, and telegraphic conveniences in a fourth; all furs, feathers, and fabrics made from these in a fifth. The tradesman sells on commission, as we say, receiving the goods from the manufacturer, the farmer, or the State, and paying only for what are sold at the end of each year, reserving to himself one-twenty-fourth of the price. Prices, however, do not vary from year to year, save when, on rare occasions, an adverse season or a special accident affects the supply and consequently the price of any natural product—choice fruit, skins, silver, for instance—obtained only from some peculiarly favoured locality.

The monetary system, like so many other Martial institutions, is purely artificial and severely logical. It is held that the exchange value of any article of manufacture or agricultural produce tends steadily downwards, while any article obtained by mining labour, or supplied by nature alone, tends to become more and more costly. The use of any one article of either class as a measure of value tends in the long-run to injustice either towards creditors or debtors. Labour may be considered as the most constant in intrinsic value of all things capable of sale or barter; but the utmost ingenuity of Martial philosophers has failed to devise a fixed standard by which one kind of labour can be measured against another, and their respective productive force, and consequently their value in exchange, ascertained. One thing alone retains in their opinion an intrinsic value always the same, and if it increase in value, increases only in proportion as

all produce is obtained in greater quantities or with greater facility. Land, therefore, is in their estimation theoretically the best available measure of value—a dogma which has more practical truth in a planet where population is evenly diffused and increases very slowly, if at all, than it might have in the densely but unevenly peopled countries of Europe or Asia. A staltâ, or square of about fifty yards (rather more than half an acre), is the primary standard unit of value. For purposes of currency this is represented by a small engraved document bearing the Government stamp, which can always at pleasure be exchanged for so much land in a particular situation. The region whose soil is chosen as the standard lies under the Equator, and the State possesses there some hundreds of square miles, let out on terms thought to ensure its excellent cultivation and the permanence of its condition. The immediate convertibility of each such document, engraven on a small piece of metal about two inches long by one in breadth, and the fortieth part of an inch in thickness, is the ultimate cause and permanent guarantee of its value. Large payments, moreover, have to be made to the State by those who rent its lands or purchase the various articles of which it possesses a monopoly; or, again, in return for the services it undertakes, as lighting roads and supplying water to districts dependent on a distant source. Great care is taken to keep the issue of these notes within safe limits; and as a matter of fact they are rather more valuable than the land they represent, and are in consequence seldom presented for redemption therein. To provide against the possibility of such an over-issue as might exhaust the area of standard land at command of the State, it is enacted that, failing this, the holder may select his portion of State domain wherever he pleases, at twelve years' purchase of the rental; but in point of fact these provisions are theoretically rather than practically important, since not one note in a hundred is ever redeemed or paid off. The "square measure," upon which the coinage, if I may so call it is based, following exactly the measure of length, each larger area in the ascending scale represents 144 times that below it. Thus the styly being a little more than a foot, the steely is about 13 feet, or one-twelfth of the stâly; but the steeltâ (or square steely) is 1/144th part of the stâltâ. The stoltâ, again, is about 600 yards square, or 360,000 square yards, 144 times the stâltâ. The highest note, so to speak, in circulation represents this last area; but all calculations are made in staltau, or twelfths thereof. The stâltâ will purchase about six ounces of gold. Notes are issued for the third, fourth, and twelfth parts of this: values smaller than the latter are represented by a token coinage of square medals composed of an alloy in which gold and silver respectively are the principal elements. The lowest coin is worth about threepence of English money.

Stopping at the largest public building in the city, a central hexagon with a number of smaller hexagons rising around it, we entered one of the latter, each side of which might be some 30 feet in length and 15 in height. Here were ranged a large number of instruments on the principle of the voice-writer, but conveying the sound to a vast distance along electric wires into one which reverses the voice-recording process, and repeats the vocal sound itself. Through one of these, after exchanging a few words with one of the officials in charge of them, Esmo carried on a conversation of some length, the instrument being so arranged that while the mouth is applied to one tube another may be held to the ear to receive the reply. In the meantime I fell in with one of the officers, apparently very young, who was strongly interested at the sight of the much-canvassed stranger, and, perhaps on this account, far more obliging than is common among his countrymen. From him I learnt that this, with another method I will presently describe, is the sole means of distant communication employed in Mars. Those who have not leisure or do not care to visit one of the offices, never more than twelve-miles distant from one another, in which the public instruments are kept, can have a wire conveyed to their own house. Almost every house of any pretension possesses such a wire.

Leading me into the next apartment, my friend pointed out an immense number of instruments of a box-like shape, with a slit in which a leaf of about four inches by two was placed. These were constantly ejected and on the instant mechanically replaced. The fallen leaves were collected and sorted by the officers present, and at once placed in one or other of another set of exactly similar instruments. Any one possessing a private wire can write at his own desk in the manual character a letter or message on one of these slips. Placing it in his own instrument, it at once reproduces itself

exactly in his autograph, and with every peculiarity, blot, or erasure, at the nearest office. Here the copy is placed in the proper box, and at once reproduced in the office nearest the residence of the person to whom it is addressed, and forwarded in the same manner to him. A letter, therefore, covering one of these slips, and saying as much as we could write in an average hand upon a large sheet of letter-paper, is delivered within five minutes at most from the time of despatch, no matter how great the distance.

I remarked that this method of communication made privacy impossible.

"But," replied the official, "how could we possibly have time to indulge in curiosity? We have to sort hundreds of these papers in an hour. We have just time to look at the address, place them in the proper box, and touch the spring which sets the electric current at work. If secrecy were needed a cipher would easily secure it, for you will observe that by this telegraph whatever is inscribed on the sheet is mechanically reproduced; and it would be as easy to send a picture as a message."

I learnt that a post of marvellous perfection had, some thousand years ago, delivered letters all over Mars, but it was now employed only for the delivery of parcels. Perhaps half the commerce of Mars, except that in metals and agricultural produce, depends on this post. Purchasers of standard articles describe by the telegraph-letter to a tradesman the exact amount and pattern of the goods required, and these are despatched at once; a system of banking, very completely organised, enabling the buyer to pay at once by a telegraphic order.

When Esmo had finished his business, we walked down, at my request, to the port. Around three sides of the dock formed by walls, said to be fifty feet in depth and twenty in thickness, ran a road close to the water's edge, beyond which was again a vast continuous warehouse. The inner side was reserved for passenger vessels, and everywhere the largest ships could come up close, landing either passengers or cargo without even the intervention of a plank. The appearance of the ships is very unlike that of Terrestrial vessels. They have no masts or rigging, are constructed of the zorinta, which in Mars serves much more effectively all the uses of iron,

and differ entirely in construction as they are intended for cargo or for travel. Mercantile ships are in shape much like the finest American clippers, but with broad, flat keel and deck, and with a hold from fifteen to twenty feet in depth. Like Malayan vessels, they have attached by strong bars an external beam about fifty feet from the side, which renders overturning almost impossible. Passenger ships more resemble the form of a fish, but are alike at both ends. Six men working in pairs four hours at a time compose the entire crew of the largest ship, and half this number are required for the smallest that undertakes a voyage of more than twelve hours.

I may here mention that the system of sewage is far superior to any yet devised on Earth. No particle of waste is allowed to pollute the waters. The whole is deodorised by an exceedingly simple process, and, whether in town or country, carried away daily and applied to its natural use in fertilising the soil. Our practice of throwing away, where it is an obvious and often dangerous nuisance, material so valuable in its proper place, seemed to my Martial friends an inexplicable and almost incredible absurdity.

As we returned, Esmo told me that he had been in communication with the Camptâ, who had desired that I should visit him with the least possible delay.

"This," he said, "will hurry us in matters where I at any rate should have preferred a little delay. The seat of Government is by a direct route nearly six thousand miles distant, and you will have opportunity of travelling in all the different ways practised on this planet. A long land-journey in our electric carriages, with which you are not familiar, is, I think, to be avoided.

The Camptâ would wish to see your vessel as well as yourself; but, on the whole, I think it is safer to leave it where it is. Kevimâ, and I propose to accompany you during the first part of your journey. At our first halt, we will stay one night with a friend, that you may be admitted a brother of our Order."

"And," said I, "what sort of a reception may I expect at the end of my journey?"

"I think," he answered, "that you are more likely to be embarrassed by the goodwill of the Camptâ than by the hostility of some of those about him.

His character is very peculiar, and it is difficult to reckon upon his action in any given case. But he differs from nearly all his subjects in having a strong taste for adventure, none the less if it be perilous; and since his position prevents him from indulging this taste in person, he is the more disposed to take extreme interest in the adventures of others. He has, moreover, a great value for what you call courage, a virtue rarely needed and still more rarely shown among us; and I fancy that your venture through space has impressed him with a very high estimate of your daring. Assuredly none of us, however great his scientific curiosity, would have dreamed of incurring such a peril, and incurring it alone. But I must give you one warning. It is not common among us to make valuable gifts: we do not care enough for any but ourselves to give except with the idea of getting something valuable in return. Our princes are, however, so wealthy that they can give without sacrifice, and it is considered a grave affront to refuse any present from a superior. Whatever, then, our Suzerain may offer you—

and he is almost sure, unless he should take offence, to give you whatever he thinks will induce you to settle permanently in the neighbourhood of his Court—
you must accept graciously, and on no account, either then or afterwards, lead him to think that you slight his present."

"I must say," I replied, "that while I wish to remain in your world till I have learnt, if not all that is to be learnt, yet very much more than I at present know about it, the whole purpose of my voyage would be sacrificed if I could not effect my return to Earth."

"I suppose so," he answered, "and for that reason I wish to keep your vessel safe and within your reach; for to get away at all you may have to depart suddenly. But you will not do wisely to make the Prince suspect that such is your intention. Tell him of what you wish to see and to explore in this world; tell him freely of your own, for he will not readily fancy that you prefer it to this; but say as little as possible of your hopes of an ultimate return, and, if you are forced to acknowledge them, let them seem as indefinite as possible."

By this time, returning by another road, Esmo stopped the carriage at the gate of an enclosed garden of moderate size, about two miles from Ecasfe.

Entering alone, he presently returned with another gentleman, wearing a dress of grey and silver, with a white ribbon over the shoulder; a badge, I found, of official rank or duties. Mounting his own carriage, this person accompanied us home.

CHAPTER X - WOMAN AND WEDLOCK.

We arrived at home in the course of some few minutes, and here my host requested us to wait in the hall, where in about half-an-hour he rejoined us, accompanied by all the members of his family, the ladies all closely veiled.

Looking among them instinctively for Eveena, I observed that she had exchanged her usual light veil for one fuller and denser, and wore, contrary to the wont of maidens indoors, sleeves and gloves. She held her father's hand, and evinced no little agitation or alarm. The visitor stood by a table on which had been placed the usual pencils or styles, and a sort of open portfolio, on one side of which was laid a small strip of the golden tafroo, inscribed with crimson characters of unusual size, leaving several blanks here and there. Most of these he filled up, and then, leading forward his daughter, Esmo signed to me also to approach the table. The others stood just behind us, and the official then placed the document in Eveena's hand.

She looked through it and replaced it on the table with the gesture of assent usual among her people, inclining her head and raising her left hand to her lips. The document was then handed to me, but I, of course, was unable to read it. I said so, and the official read it aloud:—

"Between Eveena, daughter of Esmo dent Ecasfen, and —— reclamomortâ (the alleged arch-traveller), covenant: Eveena will live with —— in wedlock for two years, foregoing during that period the liberty to quit his house, or to receive any one therein save by his permission. In consideration whereof he will maintain her, clothing her to her satisfaction, at a cost not exceeding five stâltau by the year. He will provide for any child or children she may bear while living with him, or within twice twelve dozen days thereafter. And if at any time he shall dismiss her or permit her to leave him, or if she shall desire to leave him after the expiration of eight years, he will ensure to her for her life an annual payment of fifteen stâltau. Neither shall appeal to a court of law or public authority against the other on account of anything done during the time they shall live together, except for attempt to kill or for grave bodily injury."

Such is the form of marriage covenant employed in Mars. The occasion was unfit for discussion, and I simply intimated my acceptance of the covenants, oo which Eveena and myself forthwith were instructed to write our names where they appear in the above translation. The official then inquired whether I recognised the lady standing beside me as Eveena, daughter of Esmo. It then struck me that, though I felt pretty certain of her identity, marriage under such conditions might occasionally lead to awkward mistakes. There was no such difference between my bride and her companions as, but for her dress and her agitation, would have enabled me positively to distinguish them, veiled and silent as all were. I expressed no doubt, however, and the official then proceeded to affix his own stamp to the document; and then lifting up that on which our names had actually been written, showed that, by some process I hardly understand, the signature had been executed and the agreement filled up in triplicate, the officer preserving one copy, the others being given to the bride and bridegroom respectively. The ladies then retired, Esmo, his son, and the official remaining, when two ambau brought in a tray of refreshments. The official tasted each article offered to him, evidently more as a matter of form than of pleasure. I took this opportunity to ask some questions regarding the Martial cuisine, and learnt that all but the very simplest cookery is performed by professional confectioners, who supply twice a day the households in their vicinity; unmarried men taking their meals at the shop. The preparation of fruit, roasted grain, beverages consisting of juices mixed with a prepared nectar, and the vegetables from the garden, which enter into the composition of every meal, are the only culinary cares of the ladies of the family. Everything can be warmed or freshened on the stove which forms a part of that electric machinery by which in every household the baths and lights are supplied and the house warmed at night. The ladies have therefore very little household work, and the greater part of this is performed under their superintendence by the animals, which are almost as useful as any human slaves on earth, with the one unquestionable advantage that they cannot speak, and therefore cannot be impertinent, inquisitive, or treacherous. No fermented liquors form part of

the Martial diet; but some narcotics resembling haschisch and opium are much relished. When the official had retired, I said to my host—

"I thought it best to raise no question or objection in signing the contract put before me with your sanction; but you must be aware, in the first place, that I have no means here of performing the pecuniary part of the covenant, no means of providing either maintenance or pin-money."

The explanation of the latter phrase, which was immediately demanded, produced not a little amusement, after which Esmo replied gravely—

"It will be very easy for you, if necessary, to realise a competence in the course of half a year. A book relating your adventures, and describing the world you have left, would bring you in a very comfortable fortune; and you might more than double this by giving addresses in each of our towns, which, if only from the curiosity our people would entertain to see you with their own eyes, would attract crowded audiences. You could get a considerable sum for the exclusive right to take your likeness; and, if you chose to explain it, you might fix your own price on the novel motive power you have introduced. But there is another point in regard to the contract which you have overlooked, but which I was bound to bear in mind. What you have promised is, I believe, what Eveena would have obtained from any suitor she was likely to accept. But since you left the matter entirely to my discretion, I am bound to make it impossible that you should be a loser; and this document (and he handed me a small slip very much like that which contained the marriage covenant) imposes on my estate the payment of an income for Eveena's life equal to that you have promised her."

With much reluctance I found myself obliged to accept a dowry which, however natural and proper on Earth, was, I felt, unusual in Mars. I may say that such charges do not interfere with the free sale of land. They are registered in the proper office, and the State trustee collects them from the owner for the time being as quit-rents are collected in Great Britain or land revenue in India. Turning to another but kindred question, I said—

"Your marriage contract, like our own laws, appears to favour the weaker sex more than strict theoretical equality would permit. This is quite right and practically inevitable; but it hardly agrees with the theory which supposes bride and bridegroom, husband and wife, to enter on and maintain a coequal voluntary partnership."

"How so?" he inquired.

"The right of divorce," I said, "at the end of two years belongs to the wife alone. The husband cannot divorce her except under a heavy penalty."

"Observe," he answered, "that there is a grave practical inequality which even theory can hardly ignore. The wife parts with something by the very fact of marriage. At the end of two years, when she has borne two, three, or four children, her value in marriage is greatly lessened. Her capacity of maintaining herself, in the days when women did work, was found practically to be even smaller than before marriage. You may say that this really amounts to a recognition by custom of the natural inequality denied by law; but at any rate, it is an inequality which it was scarcely possible to overlook. Examine the practical working of the covenants, and you will find that in affecting to treat unequals as equals they merely make the weaker the slave of the stronger."

"Surely," I said, "husband and wife are so far equal, where neither is tied to the children, that each can make the other heartily glad to assent to a divorce."

"Perhaps, where law interferes to enforce monogamy, and thereby to create an artificial equality of mutual dependence. But our law cannot dictate to equals, whose sex it ignores, the terms or numbers of partnership. So, the terms of the contract being voluntary, men of course insist on excluding legal interference in household quarrels; and before the prohibitive clause was generally adopted, legal interposition did more harm than good. As you will find, equality before the law gives absolute effect to the real inequality, and chiefly through its coarsest element, superior physical force. The liberty that is a necessary logical consequence of equality takes

from the woman her one natural safeguard—the man's need of her goodwill, if not of her affection."

"In our world," I replied, "I always held that even slaves, so they be household slaves, are secure against gross cruelty. The owner cannot make life a burden to them without imperilling his own. To reduce the question to its lowest terms—malice will always be a match for muscle, and poison an efficient antidote to the ferula."

"So," rejoined Esmo, "our men have perceived, and consequently they have excepted attempts to murder, as the women have excepted serious bodily injury, from the general rule prohibiting appeals to a court of law."

"And," said I, "are there many such appeals?"

"Not one in two years," he replied; "and for a simple reason. Our law, as matter of course and of common sense, puts murder, attempted or accomplished, on the same footing, and visits both with its supreme penalty. Consequently, a wife detected in such an attempt is at her husband's mercy; and if he consent to spare her life, she must submit to any infliction, however it may transgress the covenanted limit. In fact, if he find her out in such an attempt, he may do anything but put her to death on his own authority."

"Still," I answered, "as long as she remains in the house, she must have frequent opportunity of repeating her attempt at revenge; and to live in constant fear of assassination would break down the strongest nerves."

"Our physicians," he said, "are more skilful in antidotes than our women in poisons, even when the latter have learned chemistry. No poisonous plants are grown near our houses; and as wives never go out alone, they have little chance of getting hold of any fatal drug. I believe that very few attempts to poison are successful, and that many women have suffered very severely on mere suspicion."

"And what," I asked, "is the legal definition of 'grave bodily injury'?"

"Injury," he said, "of which serious traces remain at the end of twenty-four days; the destruction of a limb, or the deprivation, partial or total, of a sense. I have often thought bitterly," he continued, "of that boasted logic
and liberality of our laws under which my daughters might have to endure almost any maltreatment from their husbands, so long as these have but the sense not to employ weapons that leave almost ineffaceable marks. This is one main reason why we so anxiously avoid giving them save to those who are bound by the ties of our faith to treat them as kindly as children—
for whom, at the worst, they remain sisters of the Order. If women generally had parents, our marriage law could never have carried out the fiction of equality to its logical perfection and practical monstrosity."

"Equality, then, has given your women a harder life and a worse position than that of those women in our world who are, not only by law but by fact and custom, the slaves of their husbands?"

"Yes, indeed," he said; "and our proverbs, though made by men, express this truth with a sharpness in which there is little exaggeration. Our school textbooks tell us that action and reaction are equal and opposite; and this familiar phrase gives meaning to the saw, Pelmavè dakâl dakè, 'She is equal, the thing struck to the hammer,' meaning that woman's equality to man is no more effective than the reaction of the leather on the mallet.

'Bitterer smiles of twelve than tears of ten' (referring to the age of marriage). Thleen delkint treen lalfe zevleen, "Twixt fogs and clouds she dreams of stars.'"

"What does that mean?"

"Would you not render it in the terminology of the hymn you translated for us, 'Between Purgatory and Hell, one dream of Heaven?' Still puzzled?

'Between the harshness of school and the misery of marriage, the illusions of the bride.' Again, Zefoo zevleel, zave marneel, clafte cratheneel, 'A child
[cries] for the stars, a maiden for the matron's dress, a woman for her shroud.'"

"Do you mean to say that that is not exaggerated?"

"I suppose it is, as women are even less given to suicide than men. That is perhaps the ugliest proverb of its kind. I will only quote one more, and that is two-edged—

'"Fool he who heeds a woman's tears, to woman's tongue replies;
 Fool she who braves man's hand—but when was man or woman wise?"'

Here Zulve came to the door and made a sign to her husband. Waiting courteously to ascertain that I had finished speaking, and until his son had somewhat ceremoniously taken leave of me, he led me to the door of a chamber next to that I had hitherto occupied. Pausing here himself, he motioned me to go on, and the door parting, I found myself in a room I had not before entered, about the same size as my own and similarly furnished, but differently coloured, now communicating with it by a door which I knew had not previously existed. Here were Eveena's mother and sister, dressed as usual.

Eveena herself had exchanged her maiden white for the light pink of a young matron, but was closely veiled in a similar material. Her mother and sister kissed her with much emotion, though without the tears and lamentations, real or affected, with which—alike among the nomads of Asia and the most cultivated races of Europe—even those relatives who have striven hardest to marry a daughter or sister think it necessary to celebrate the fulfilment of their hopes, and the termination of their often prolonged and wearisome labours. I was then left alone with my bride, who remained half-seated, half-crouching on the cushions in a corner of the room. I could not help feeling keenly how much a marriage so uncermonious and with so little previous acquaintance, or rather so great a reserve and distance in our former intercourse, intensified the awkwardness many a man on Earth feels when first left alone with the partner of his future life. But a single glance at the small drooping figure half-hidden in the cushions brought the reflection that a situation, embarrassing to the bridegroom, must be in the last degree alarming and distressing to the bride. But for her visit to the Astronaut we should have been almost strangers; I could hardly have recognised even her voice. I must, however, speak; and naturally my first sentence was a half-articulate request that she would remove her veil.

"No," she whispered, rising, "you must do that."

Taking off the glove of her left hand, she came up to me shyly and slowly, and placed it in my right—a not unmeaning ceremony. Having obeyed her

instruction, my lips touched for the first time the brow of my young wife.

That she was more than shy and startled, was even painfully agitated and frightened, became instantly apparent now that her countenance was visible. What must be the state of Martial brides in general, when the signature of the contract immediately places them at the disposal of an utter stranger, it was beyond the power of my imagination to conceive, if their feelings were at all to be measured by Eveena's under conditions sufficiently trying, but certainly far better than theirs. Nothing was so likely to quiet her as perfect calmness on my side; and, though with a heart beating almost as fast as her own, if with very different emotions, I led her gently back to her place, and resting on a cushion just out of reach, began to talk to her. Choosing as the easiest subject our adventure of yesterday, I asked what could have induced her to place herself in a situation so dangerous.

"Do not be angry with me now," she pleaded. "I am exceedingly fond of flowers; they have been my only amusement except the training of my pets. You can see how little women have to do, how little occupation or interest is permitted us. The rearing of rare flowers, or the creation of new ones, is almost the only employment in which we can find exercise for such intelligence as we possess. I had never seen before the flower that grew on that shelf. I believe, indeed, that it only grows on a few of our higher mountains below the snow-line, and I was anxious to bring it home and see what could be made of it in the garden. I thought it might be developed into something almost as beautiful as that bright leenoo you admired so greatly in my flower-bed."

"But," said I, "the two flowers are not of the same shape or colour; and, though I am not learned in botany, I should say hardly belong to the same family."

"No," she said. "But with care, and with proper management of our electric apparatus, I accomplished this year a change almost as great. I can show you in my flower-bed one little white flower, of no great beauty and conical in shape, from which I have produced in two years another, saucer-shaped, pink, and of thrice the size, almost exactly realising an imaginary

flower, drawn by my sister-in-law to represent one of which she had dreamed. We can often produce the very shape, size, and colour we wish from something that at first seems to have no likeness to it whatever; and I have been told that a skilful farmer will often obtain a fruit, or, what is more difficult, an animal, to answer exactly the ideal he has formed."

"Some of our breeders," I said, "profess to develop a sort of ideal of any given species; but it takes many generations, by picking and choosing those that vary in the right direction, to accomplish anything of the kind; and, after all, the difference between the original and the improved form is mere development, not essential change."

She hardly seemed to understand this, but answered—

"The seedling or rootlet would be just like the original plant, if we did not from the first control its growth by means of our electric frames. But if you will allow me, I will show you to-morrow what I have done in my own flower-bed, and you will have opportunities of seeing afterwards how very much more is done by agriculturists with much more time and much more potent electricities."

"At any rate," I said, "if I had known your object, you certainly should have had the flowers for which you risked so much: and if I remain here three days longer, I promise you plenty of specimens for your experiment."

"You do not mean to go back to the Astronaut?" she asked, with an air of absolute consternation.

"I had not intended to do so," I replied, "for it seems to be perfectly safe under your father's seal and your stringent laws of property. But now, if time permit, I must get these flowers to which you tell me I am so deeply indebted."

"You are very kind," returned Eveena earnestly, "but I entreat you not to venture there again. I should be utterly miserable while you were running such a risk again, and for such a trifle."

"It is no such terrible risk to me, and to please you is not quite a trifle.

Besides, I ought to deserve my prize better than I have yet done. But you seem to have some especial spite against the unlucky vessel that brought

me here; and that," I added, smiling, "seems hardly gracious in a bride of an hour."

"No, no!" she murmured, evidently much distressed; "but the vessel that brought you here may take you away."

"I will not pain you yet by saying that I hope it may. At all events, it shall not do so till you are content that it should."

She made no answer, and seemed for some time to hesitate, as if afraid or unwilling to say something which rose irrepressibly to her lips. A few persuasive words, however, encouraged her, and she found her voice, though with a faltering accent, which greatly surprised me when I learned at last the purport of her request.

"I do not understand," she said, "your ideas or customs, but I know they are different from ours. I have found at least that they make you much more indulgent and tender to women than our own; and I hope, therefore, you will forgive me if I ask more than I have any right to do."

"I could scarcely refuse my bride's first request, whatever it might be. But your hesitation and your apologies might make me fear that you are about to ask something which one or both of us may wish hereafter had neither been asked nor granted."

She still hesitated and faltered, till I began to fancy that her wish must have a much graver import than I at first supposed. Perhaps to treat the matter lightly and sportively would be the course most likely to encourage her to explain it.

"What is it, child," I asked, "which you think the stranger of another world more likely to grant than one of your own race, and which is so extravagant, nevertheless, that you tremble to ask it even from me? Is it too much to be bound not to appeal against me to the law, which cannot yet determine whether I am a reality or a fiction? Or have I proved my arm a little too substantial? Must the giant promise not to exercise the masculine prerogative of physical force safely conceded to the dwarf? Fie, Eveena! I am almost afraid to touch you, lest I should hurt you unawares; lest

tenderness itself should transgress the limit of legal cruelty, and do grave bodily harm to a creature so much more like a fairy than a woman!"

"No, no!" she expostulated, not at all reciprocating the jesting tone in which I spoke. "If you would consent to give such a promise, it is just one of those we should wish unmade. How could I ask you to promise that I may behave as ill as I please? I dare say I shall be frightened to tears when you are angry; but I shall never wish you to retain your anger rather than vent it and forgive. The proverb says, 'Who punishes pardons; who hates awaits.' No, pray do not play with me; I am so much in earnest. I know that I don't understand where and why your thoughts and ways are so unlike ours. But—but—I thought—I fancied—you seemed to hold the tie between man and wife something more—faster—more lasting—than—our contract has made it."

"Certainly! With us it lasts for life at least; and even here, where it may be broken at pleasure, I should not have thought that, on the very bridal eve, the coldest heart could willingly look forward to its dissolution."

She was too innocent of such a thought—perhaps too much absorbed by her own purpose—to catch the hint of unjust reproach.

"Well, then," she said, with a desperate effort, in a voice that trembled between the fear of offending by presumption or exaction, and the desire to give utterance to her wish—"I want ... will you say that—if by that time you do not think that I have been too faulty, too undeserving—that I shall go with you when you quit this world?" And, her eagerness at last overpowering her shyness, she looked up anxiously into my face.

We wholly misconceived each other. She drooped in bitter disappointment, mistaking my blank surprise for displeasure; her words brought over my mind a rush of that horror with which I ever recall the scenes I witnessed but too often at Indian funerals.

"That, of course, will rest with yourself. But even should I hereafter deserve and win such love as would prompt the wish, I trust you will never dream of cutting short your life because—in the ordinary course of nature—mine should end long before the term of yours."

Her face again brightened, and she looked up more shyly but not less earnestly.

"I did not make my meaning clear," she replied. "I spoke not, as my father sometimes speaks, of leaving this world, when he means to remind us that death is only a departure to another; though that was, not so long ago, the only meaning the words could bear. I was thinking of your journey, and I want you to take me with you when you go."

"You have quite settled in your own mind that I shall go! And in truth you have now removed, as you yesterday created, the only obstacle. If you would not go with me, I might, rather than give you up, have given up the whole purpose of my enterprise, and have left my friends, and the world from which I came, ignorant whether it had ever been accomplished. But if you accompany me, I shall certainly try to regain my own planet."

"Then," she said hopefully, but half confidently, "when you go, if I have not given you cause of lasting displeasure, you will take me with you? Most men do not think much of promises, especially of promises made to women; but I have heard you speak as if to break a plighted word were a thing impossible."

"I promise," I returned earnestly, very much moved by a proof of real affection such as I had no right to expect, and certainly had not anticipated.

"I give you the word of one who has never lied, that if, when the time comes, you wish to go with me, you shall. But by that time, you will probably have a better idea what are the dangers you are asking to share."

"What can that matter?" she answered. "I suppose in almost any case we should escape or die together? To leave me here is to inflict certainly, and at once, the worst that can possibly befall me; to take me gives me the hope of living or dying with you; and even if I were killed, I should be with you, and feel that you were kind to me, to the last."

"I little thought," said I, hesitating long for some expression of tenderness, which the language of Mars refuses to furnish,—"I little thought to find in a world of which selfishness seems to be the paramount principle, and the absence of real love even between man and woman the most prevalent

characteristic, a wife so true to the best and deepest meaning of wedlock. Still less could I have hoped to find such a wife in one who had scarcely spoken to me twenty-four hours before our marriage. If my unexampled adventure had had no other reward—if I had cared nothing for the triumph of discovering a new world with all its wonders—Eveena, this discovery alone is reward in full for all my studies, toils, and perils. For all I have done and risked already, for all the risks of the future, I am tenfold repaid in winning you."

She looked up at these words with an expression in which there was more of bewilderment and incredulity than of satisfaction, evidently touched by the earnestness of my tone, but scarcely understanding my words better than if I had spoken in my own tongue. It would not be worth while to record the next hour's conversation; I would only note the strong and painful impression it left upon my mind. There was in Eveena's language and demeanour a timidity—a sort of tentative fearful venturing as on dangerous ground, feeling her way, as it were, in almost every sentence—

which could not be wholly attributed to the shyness of a very young and very suddenly wedded bride. There was enough and to spare of this shyness; but more of the sheer physical or nervous fear of a child suddenly left in hands whose reputed severity has thoroughly frightened her; not daring to give offence by silence, but afraid at each word to give yet more fatal offence in speaking. Longer experience of a world in which even the first passion of love is devoid of tenderness—in which asserted equality has long since deprived women of that claim to indulgence which can only rest on acknowledged weakness—taught me but too well the meaning of this fearful, trembling anxiety to please, or rather not to offend. I suppose that even a brutal master hardly likes to see a child cower in his presence as if constantly expecting a blow; and this cowering was so evident in my bride's demeanour, that, after trying for a couple of hours to coax her into confidence and unreserved feminine fluency, I began to feel almost impatient. It was fortunate that, just as my tone involuntarily betrayed to her quick and watchful ear some shade of annoyance, just as I caught a furtive upward glance that seemed to ask what error she had committed and how it might be repaired, a scratching on the door startled her. She did

not, however, venture to disengage herself from the hand which now held her own, but only moved half-imperceptibly aside with a slight questioning look and gesture, as if tacitly asking to be released. As I still held her fast, she was silent, till the unnoticed scratching had been two or three times repeated, and then half-whispered, "Shall I tell them to come in?" When I released her, there appeared to my surprise at her call, no human intruder, but one of the ambau, bearing on a tray a goblet, which, as he placed it on a table beside us, I perceived to contain a liquid rather different from any yet offered me. The presence of these mute servants is generally no more heeded than that of our cats and dogs; but I now learnt that Martial ideas of delicacy forbid them, even as human servants would be forbidden, to intrude unannounced on conjugal privacy. When the little creature had departed, I tasted the liquid, but its flavour was so unpleasant that I set down the vessel immediately. Eveena, however, took it up, and drinking a part of it, with an effort to control the grimace of dislike it provoked, held it up to me again, so evidently expecting and inviting me to share it that courtesy permitted no further demur. A second sign or look, when I set it down unemptied, induced me to finish the draught.

Regarding the matter as some trivial but indispensable ceremonial, I took no further notice of it; but, thankful for the diversion it had given to my thoughts, continued my endeavours to soothe and encourage my fair companion. After a few minutes it seemed as if she were somewhat suddenly gaining courage and confidence. At the same time I myself became aware of a mental effect which I promptly ascribed to the draught.

Nor was I wrong. It contained one of those drugs which I have mentioned; so rarely used in this house that I had never before seen or tasted any of them, but given, as matter of course, on any occasion that is supposed to involve unusual agitation or make an exceptional call on nerves or spirits.

But for the influence of this cup I should still have withheld the remark which, nevertheless, I had resolved to make as soon as I could hope to do so without annoying or alarming Eveena.

"Are you afraid of me?" I asked somewhat abruptly. The question may have startled her, but I was more startled by the answer.

"Of course," she said in a tone which would have been absolutely matter of fact, except that the doubt evidently surprised her. "Ought I not to be so?

But what made you ask? And what had I done to displease you, just before they sent us the 'courage cup'?"

"I did not mean to show anything like displeasure," I replied. "But I was thinking then, and I may tell you now, that you remind me not of the women of my own Earth, but of petted children suddenly transferred to a harsh school. You speak and look like such a child, as if you expected each moment at least to be severely scolded, if not beaten, without knowing your fault."

"Not yet," she murmured, with a smile which seemed to me more painful than tears would have been. "But please don't speak as if I should fear anything so much as being scolded by you. We have a saying that 'the hand may bruise the skin, the tongue can break the heart.'"

"True enough," I said; "only on Earth it is mostly woman's tongue that breaks the heart, and men must not in return bruise the skin."

"Why not?" she asked. "You said to my mother the other day that Argâ (the fretful child of Esmo's adoption) deserved to be beaten."

"Women are supposed," I answered, "to be amenable to milder influences; and a man must be drunk or utterly brutal before he could deal harshly with a creature so gentle and so fragile as yourself."

"Don't spoil me," she said, with a pretty half-mournful, half-playful glance.

"'A petted bride makes an unhappy wife.' Surely it is no true kindness to tempt us to count on an indulgence that cannot last."

"There is among us," I rejoined, "a saying about 'breaking a butterfly on the wheel'—as if one spoke of driving away the tiny birds that nestle and feed in your flowers with a hammer. To apply your proverbs to yourself would be to realise this proverb of ours. Can you not let me pet and spoil my little flower-bird at least till I have tamed her, and trust me to chastise her as soon as she shall give reason—if I can find a tendril or flower-stem light enough for the purpose?"

"Will you promise to use a hammer when you wish to be rid of her?" said she, glancing up for one moment through her drooping lashes with a look exactly attuned to the mingled archness and pathos of her tone.

CHAPTER XI - A COUNTRY DRIVE.

Like all Martialists, I had been accustomed since my landing to wake with the first light of dawn; but the draught, though its earlier effects were anything but narcotic or stupifying, deepened and prolonged my sleep. It was not till the rays of sunlight came clear and full through the crystal roof of the peristyle, and the window of our bridal chamber, that my eyes unclosed. The first object on which they opened startled me into full waking recollection. Exactly where the sunbeams fell, just within reach of my hand, Eveena stood; the loveliest creature I ever beheld, a miniature type of faultless feminine grace and beauty. By the standard of Terrestrial humanity she was tiny rather than small: so light, so perfect in proportion, form, and features, so absolutely beautiful, so exquisitely delicate, as to suggest the ideal Fairy Queen realised in flesh and blood, rather than any properly human loveliness. In the transparent delicacy of a complexion resembling that of an infant child of the fairest and most tenderly nurtured among the finest races of Europe, in the ideally perfect outline of face and features—the noble but even forehead—the smooth, straight, clearly pencilled eyebrows—the large almond-shaped eyes and drooping lids, with their long, dark, soft fringe—the little mouth and small, white, even regular teeth—the rosy lips, slightly compressed, save when parted in speech, smile, or eager attention—she exhibited in their most perfect but by no means fullest development the characteristics of Martial physiognomy; or rather the characteristic beauty of a family in which the finest traits of that physiognomy are unmixed with any of its meaner or harsher peculiarities. The hands, long, slight, and soft, the unsandalled feet, not less perfectly shaped, could only have belonged to the child of ancestors who for more than a hundred generations have never known hard manual toil, rough exposure, or deforming, cramping costume; even as every detail of her beauty bore witness to an immemorial inheritance of health unbroken by physical infirmity, undisturbed by violent passions, and developed by an admirable system of physical and mental discipline and culture. The absence of veil and sleeves left visible the soft rounded arms and shoulders, in whose complexion a tinge of pale rose seemed to shine through a skin itself of translucent white; the small head, and the

perfection of the slender neck, with the smooth unbroken curve from the ear to the arm. Her long hair, fastened only by a silver band woven in and out behind the small rounded ears, fell almost to her knee; and, as it caught the bright rays of the morning sun, I discerned for the first time the full beauty of that tinge of gold which varied the colour of the rich, soft, brown tresses. As her sex are seldom exposed to the cold of the night or the mists, their underclothing is slight and close fitting. Eveena's thin robe, of the simplest possible form—two wide straight pieces of a material lustrous as satin but rivalling the finest cambric in texture (lined with the same fabric reversed), sewn together from the hem of the skirt to the arm, and fastened again by the shoulder clasps—fell perfectly loose save where compressed by the zone or by the movements of the wearer; and where so compressed, defined the outlines of the form as distinctly as the lightest wet drapery of the studio. Her dress, in short, achieved in its pure simplicity all at which the artistic skill of matrons, milliners, and maidens aims in a Parisian ball costume, without a shadow of that suggestive immodesty from which ball costumes are seldom wholly free. Exactly reversing Terrestrial practice, a Martial wife reserves for strictest domestic privacy that undressed full-dress, that frank revelation of her beauty, which the matrons of London, Paris, or New York think exclusively appropriate to the most public occasions. Till now, while still enjoying the liberty allowed to maidens in this respect, Eveena, by the arrangement of her veil, had always given to her costume a reserve wholly unexceptionable, even according to the rules enforced by the customs of Western Europe on young girls not yet presented in the marriage market of society. A new expression, or one, at least, which I had never before seen there, gave to her face a strange and novel beauty; the beauty, I wish to think, of shy, but true happiness; felt, it may be, for the first time, and softened, I fear, by a doubt of its possible endurance which rendered it as touching as attractive. Never was the sleep even of the poet of the Midsummer Night's Dream visited by a lovelier vision—especially lovely as the soft rose blush suffused her cheeks under my gaze of admiration and delight. Springing up, I caught her with both hands and drew her on my knee. Some minutes passed before either of us cared to speak. Probably as she rested her head on my arm and looked into

my eyes, each read the other's character more truly and clearly than words the most frank and open could ever enable us to do. I had taught her last night a few substitutes in the softest tongue I knew for those words of natural tenderness in which her language is signally deficient: taught her to understand them, certainly not to use them, for it was long before I could even induce her to address me by name.

"My father bade me yesterday," she said at last, "ask you in future to wear the dress of our people. Not that you will be the less an object of attention and wonder, but that in retaining a distinction which depends entirely on your own choice, you will seem intentionally to prefer your own habits to ours."

"I comply of course," I observed. "Naturally the dress of every country is best suited to its own conditions. Yet I should have thought that a preference for my own world, even were it wholly irrational, might seem at least natural and pardonable."

"People don't," she answered simply, "like any sign of individual fancy or opinion. They don't like any one to show that he thinks them wrong even on a matter of taste."

"I fear, then, carissima, that I must be content with unpopularity. I may wear the costume of your people; but their thought, their conduct, their inner and outer life, as your father reports them, and as thus far I have seen them, are to me so unnatural, that the more I resemble them externally the more my unlikeness in all else is likely to attract notice. I am sorry for this, because women are by nature prone to judge even their nearest and dearest by the standard of fashion, and to exact from men almost as close a conformity to that standard as they themselves display. I fear you will have to forgive many heresies in my conduct as well as in my thoughts."

"You cannot suppose," she answered earnestly—she seemed incapable of apprehending irony or jest,—"that I should wish you more like others than you are. Whatever may happen hereafter, I shall always feel myself the happiest of women in having belonged to one who cares for something beside himself, and holds even life cheaper than love." "I hope so,carissima.

But in that matter there was scarcely more of love than of choice. What I did for you I must have done no less for Zevle [her sister]. If I had feared death as much as the Regent does, I could not have returned alive and alone. My venture into infinite space involved possibilities of horror more appalling than the mere terrors of death. You asked of me as my one bridal gift leave to share its perils. How unworthy of you should I be, if I did not hold the possession of Eveena, even for the two years of her promise, well worth dying for!"

The moral gulf between the two worlds is wider than the material. Utterly unselfish and trustful, Eveena was almost pained to be reminded that the service she so extravagantly overprized was rendered to her sex rather than herself; while yet more deeply gratified, though still half incredulous, by the commonplace that preferred love to life. I had yet to learn, however, that Eveena's nature was as utterly strange in her own world as the ideas in which she was educated would seem in mine.

I left her for a few minutes to dress for the first time in the costume which Esmo's care had provided. The single under-vestment of softest hide, closely fitting from neck to knees, is of all garments the best adapted to preserve natural warmth under the rapid and extreme changes of the external atmosphere. The outer garb consisted of blouse and trousers, woven of a fabric in which a fine warp of metallic lustre was crossed by a strong silken weft, giving the effect of a diapered scarlet and silver; both fastened by the belt, a broad green strap of some species of leather, clasped with gold. Masculine dress is seldom brilliant, as is that of the women, but convenient and comfortable beyond any other, and generally handsome and elegant. The one part of the costume which I could never approve is the sandal, which leaves the feet exposed to dust and cold. Rejoining my bride, I said—

"I have had no opportunity of seeing much of this country, and I fancy from what I have seen of feminine seclusion that an excursion would be as much a holiday treat to you as to myself. If your father will lend us his carriage, would you like to accompany me to one or two places Kevimâ has described not far from this, and which I am anxious to visit?"

She bent her head, but did not answer; and fancying that the proposal was not agreeable to her, I added—

"If you prefer to spend our little remaining time here with your mother and sister, I will ask your brother to accompany me, though I am selfishly unwilling to part with you to-day."

She looked up for a moment with an air of pain and perplexity, and as she turned away I saw the tears gather in her eyes.

"What is the matter?" I asked, surprised and puzzled as one on Earth who tries to please a woman by offering her her own way, and finds that, so offered, it is the last thing she cares to have. It did not occur to me that, even in trifles, a Martial wife never dreams that her taste or wish can signify, or be consulted where her lord has a preference of his own. To invite instead of commanding her companionship was unusual; to withdraw the expression of my own wish, and bid her decide for herself, was in Eveena's eyes to mark formally and deliberately that I did not care for her society.

"What have I done," she faltered, "to be so punished? I have not, save the day before yesterday, left the house this year; and you offer me the greatest of pleasures only to snatch it away the next moment."

"Nay, Eveena!" I answered. "If I had not told you, you must know that I cannot but wish for your company; but by your silence I fancied you disliked my proposal, yet did not like to decline it."

The expression of surprise and perplexity in her face, though half pathetic, seemed so comical that I with difficulty suppressed a laugh, because for her it was evidently no laughing matter. After giving her time, as I thought, to recover herself, I said—

"Well, I suppose we may now join them at the morning meal?"

Something was still wrong, the clue to which I gathered by observing her shy glance at her head-dress and veil.

"Must you wear those?" I asked—a question which gave her some such imperfect clue to my thoughts as I had found to hers.

"How foolish of me," she said, smiling, "to forget how little you can know of our customs! Of course I must wear my veil and sleeves; but to-day you must put on the veil, as you removed it last night."

The awkwardness with which I performed this duty had its effect in amusing and cheering her; and the look of happiness and trust had come back to her countenance before the veil concealed it.

I made my request to Esmo, who answered, with some amusement—

"Every house like ours has from six to a dozen larger or lighter carriages.

Of course they cost nothing save the original purchase. They last for half a lifetime, and are not costly at the outset. But I have news for you which, I venture to think, will be as little agreeable to you as to ourselves. Your journey must begin tomorrow, and this, therefore, is the only opportunity you will have for such an excursion as you propose."

"Then," I said, "will Eveena still wish to share it?"

Even her mother's face seemed to ask what in the world that could matter; but a movement of the daughter's veiled head reminded me that I was blundering; and pressing her little hand as she lay beside me, I took her compliance for granted.

The morning mist had given place to hot bright sunshine when we started.

At first our road lay between enclosures like that which surrounded Esmo's dwelling.

Presently the lines were broken here and there by such fields as I had seen in descending from Asnyca; some filled with crops of human food, some with artificial pastures, in which Unicorns or other creatures were feeding.

I saw also more than one field wherein the carvee were weeding or gathering fruit, piling their burdens in either case as soon as their beaks were full into bags or baskets. Pointing out to Eveena the striking difference of colour between the cultivated fields and gardens and the woods or natural meadows on the mountain sides, I learned from her that this distinction is everywhere perceptible in Mars. Natural objects, plants or animals, rocks and soil, are for the most part of dimmer, fainter, or darker tints than on Earth; probably owing to the much less intense light of

the Sun; partly, perhaps, to that absorption of the blue rays by the atmosphere, which diminishes, I suppose, even that light which actually reaches the planet. But uncultivated ground, except on the mountains above the ordinary range of crops or pastures, scarcely exists in the belt of Equatorial continents; the turf itself, like the herbage or fruit shrubs in the fields, is artificial, consisting of plants developed through long ages into forms utterly unlike the native original by the skill and ingenuity of man.

Even the great fruit trees have undergone material change, not only in the size, flavour, and appearance of the fruits themselves, which have been the immediate object of care, but, probably through some natural correlation between, the different organs, in the form and colour of the foliage, the arrangement of the branches, and the growth of the trunk, all of which are much more regular, and, so to speak, more perfect, than is the case either here or on Earth with those left to the control of Nature and locality, or the effects of the natural competition, which is in its way perhaps as keen among plants and animals as among men. Martialists have the same delight in bright colours as Orientals, with far greater taste in selection and combination; and the favourite hues not only of their flowers, tame birds, fishes, and quadrupeds, but of plants in whose cultivation utility has been the primary object, contrast signally, as I have said, with the dull tints of the undomesticated flora and fauna, of which comparatively scanty remnants were visible here and there in this rich country.

Presently we came within sight of the river, over which was a single bridge, formed by what might be called a tube of metal built into strong walls on either bank. In fact, however, the sides were of open work, and only the roof and floor were solid. The river at this, its narrowest point, was perhaps a furlong in breadth, and it was not without instinctive uneasiness that I trusted to the security of a single piece of metal spanning, without even the strength afforded by the form of the arch, so great a space.

The first object we were to visit lay at some distance down the stream. As we approached the point, we passed a place where the river widened considerably. The main channel in the centre was kept clear and deep to

afford an uninterrupted course for navigation; but on either side were rocks that broke the river into pools and shallows, such as here, no less than on Earth, form the favourite haunts or spawning places of the fish. In some of the lesser pools birds larger than the stork, bearing under the throat an expansible bag like that of the pelican, were seeking for prey.

They were watched and directed by a master on the shore, and carried to a square tank, fixed on a wheeled frame not unlike that of the ordinary carriage, which accompanied him, each fish they took. I observed that the latter were carefully seized, with the least possible violence or injury, placed by a jerk head-downmost in the throat-bag, which, though when empty it was scarcely perceptible, would contain prey of very considerable size and weight, and as carefully disgorged into the tank. In one of the most extensive pools, too deep for these birds, a couple of men had spread a sort of net, not unlike those used on Earth, but formed of twisted metal threads with very narrow meshes, enclosing the whole pool, a space of perhaps some 400 square yards. In the centre of this an electric lamp was let down into the water, some feet below the surface. The fish crowded towards it, and a sudden shock of electricity transmitted through the meshes of the net, as well as from the wires of the lamp circuit, stunned for a few minutes all life within the enclosure. The fish then floated on the surface, the net was drawn together, and they were collected and sorted; some which, as I afterwards learned, were required for breeding, being carefully and separately preserved in a smaller tank, those fit for food cast into the larger one, those too small for the one purpose and not needed for the other being thrown back into the water. I noted, however, that many fish apparently valuable were among those thus rejected. I spoke to one of the fishermen, who, regarding me with great surprise and curiosity, at last answered briefly that a stringent law forbids the catching of spawning fish except for breeding purposes. Those, therefore, for which the season was close-time were invariably spared.

In sea-fishing a much larger net, sometimes enclosing more than 10,000

square yards, is employed. This fishing is conducted chiefly at night, the electric lamp being then much more effective in attracting the prey, and lowered only a few inches below the surface. Many large destructive

creatures, unfit for food, generally of a nature intermediate between fish and reptiles, haunt the seas. It is held unwise to exterminate them, since they do their part in keeping down an immense variety of smaller creatures, noxious for one reason or another, and also in clearing the water from carrion and masses of seaweed which might otherwise taint the air of the sea-coasts, especially near the mouths of large tropical rivers. But these sea-monsters devour enormous quantities of fish, and the hunters appointed to deal with them are instructed to limit their numbers to the minimum required. Their average increase is to be destroyed each year. If at any time it appear that, for whatever cause, the total number left alive is falling off, the chief of this service suspends it partially or wholly at his discretion.

We now came to the entrance of a vast enclosure bordering on the river, the greatest fish-breeding establishment on this continent, or indeed in this world. One of its managers courteously showed me over it. It is not necessary minutely to describe its arrangements, from the spawning ponds and the hatching tanks—the latter contained in a huge building, whose temperature is preserved with the utmost care at the rate found best suited to the ova—to the multitude of streams, ponds, and lakes in which the different kinds of fish are kept during the several stages of their existence.

The task of the breeders is much facilitated by the fact that the seas of Mars are not, like ours, salt; and though sea and river fish are almost as distinct as on Earth, each kind having its own habitat, whose conditions are carefully reproduced in the breeding or feeding reservoirs, the same kind of water suits all alike. It is necessary, however, to keep the fishes of tropical seas and streams in water of a very different temperature from that suited to others brought from arctic or sub-arctic climates; and this, like every other point affecting the natural peculiarities and habits of the fish, is attended to with minute and accurate care. The skill and science brought to bear on the task of breeding accomplish this and much more difficult operations with marvellous ease and certainty.

On one of the buildings I observed one of the most remarkable, largest, and most complete timepieces I had yet seen; and I had on this occasion an
opportunity of examining it closely. The dial was oblong, enclosed in a case of clear transparent crystal, somewhat resembling in form the open portion of a mercurial barometer. At the top were three circles of different colours, divided by twelve equidistant lines radiating from the centres and subdivided again and again by the same number. Exactly at the uppermost point of each was a golden indicator. One of these circles marked the temperature, graduated from the lowest to the highest degree ever known in that latitude. Another indicated the direction of the wind, while the depth of colour in the circle itself, graduated in a manner carefully explained to me, but my notes of which are lost, showed the exact force of the atmospheric current. The third served the purpose of a barometer. A coloured band immediately below indicated by the variations of tint the character of the coming weather. This band stretched right across the face; below it were figures indicating the day of the year. The central portion of the face was occupied by a larger circle, half-green and half-black; the former portion representing the colour of the daylight sky, the latter emblematic of night. On this circle the Sun and the planets were represented by figures whose movement showed exactly the actual place of each in the celestial sphere. The two Moons were also figured, their phases and position at each moment being accurately presented to the eye.

Around this circle was a narrow band divided into strips of different length of various colours, each representing one of the peculiar divisions of the Martial day; that point which came under the golden indicator showing the zyda and the exact moment of the zyda, while the movement of the inner circle fixed with equal accuracy the period of day or night. Below were other circles from which the observer could learn the amount of moisture in the atmosphere, the intensity of the sunlight, and the electric tension at the moment. Each of the six smaller circles registered on a moving ribbon the indications of every successive moment, these ribbons when unrolled forming a perfect record of temperature, atmospheric pressure, wind, and so forth, in the form of a curve—a register kept for more than 8000 Martial years.

Four times during the revolution of the great circle each large clock emits for a couple of minutes a species of chime, the nature of which my
ignorance of music renders me unable to describe:—viz., when the line dividing the green and black semicircles is horizontal at noon and midnight, and an hour before, at average

sunrise and sunset, it becomes perpendicular. The individual character of the several chimes, tunes, or peals, whatever they should be called, is so distinct that even I appreciated it. Further, as the first point of the coloured strip distinguishing each several zyda reaches the golden indicator, a single slightly prolonged sound—I fancy what is known on Earth as a single chord—is emitted. Of these again each is peculiar, so that no one with an ear for music can doubt what is the period of the day announced. The sound is never, even in the immediate vicinity of the clock, unpleasantly loud; while it penetrates to an amazing distance. It would be perfectly easy, if needful, to regulate all clocks by mechanical control through the electric network extended all over the face of the planet; but the perfect accuracy of each individual timepiece renders any such check needless. In those latitudes where day and night during the greater part of the year are not even approximately equal, the black and green semicircles are so enlarged or diminished by mechanical means, that the hour of the day or night is represented as accurately as on the Equator itself.

The examination of this establishment occupied us for two or three hours, and when we remounted our carriage it seemed to me only reasonable that Eveena should be weary both in mind and body. I proposed, therefore, to return at once, but against this she earnestly protested.

"Well," I said, "we will finish our excursion, then. Only remember that whenever you do feel tired you must tell me at once. I do not know what exertion you can bear, and of course it would be most inconsiderate to measure your endurance by my own."

She promised, and we drove on for another hour in the direction of a range of hills to the north-eastward. The lower and nearer portion of this range might be 400 feet above the general level of the plain; beyond, the highest peaks rose to perhaps 1500 feet, the average summit being about half that height. Where our road brought us to the foot of the first slope, large groves of the calmyra, whose fruit contains a sort of floury pulp like

roasted potato, were planted on ground belonging to the State, and tenanted by young men belonging to that minority which, as Esmo had told me not being fortunate enough to find private employment, is thus provided for. Encountering one of these, he pointed out to us the narrow road which, winding up the slope, afforded means of bringing down in waggons during the two harvest seasons, each of which lasts for about fifty days, the fruit of these groves, which furnishes a principal article of food.

The trees do not reach to a higher level than about 400 feet; and above this we had to ascend on foot by a path winding through meadows, which I at first supposed to be natural. Eveena, however, quickly undeceived me, pointing out the prevalence of certain plants peculiar to the cultivated pastures we had seen in the plain. These were so predominant as to leave no reasonable doubt that they had been originally sown by the hand of man, though the irregularity of their arrangement, and the encroachment of one species upon the ground of another, enabled my companion to prove to me with equal clearness that since its first planting the pasture had been entirely neglected. It was, she thought, worth planting once for all with the most nutritious herbage, but not worth the labour of subsequent close cultivation. Any lady belonging to a civilised people, and accustomed to a country life, upon Earth might easily have perceived all that Eveena discovered; but considering how seldom the latter had left her home, how few opportunities she had to see anything of practical agriculture, the quickness of her perception and the correctness of her inferences not a little surprised me. The path we pursued led directly to the object of our visit. The waters of the higher hills were collected in a vast tank excavated in an extensive plateau at the mid-level. At the summit of the first ascent we met and were escorted by one of the officials entrusted with the charge of these works, which supply water of extraordinary purity to a population of perhaps a quarter of a million, inhabiting a district of some 10,000 square miles in extent. The tank was about sixty feet in depth, and perhaps a mile in length, with half that breadth. Its sides and bottom were lined with the usual concrete. Our guide informed me that in many cases tanks were covered with the crystal employed for doors and windows; but in the-pure air of these hills such a precaution was thought

unnecessary, as it would have been exceedingly costly. The water itself was of wonderful purity, so clear that the smallest object at the bottom was visible where the Sun, still high in the heavens, shone directly upon the surface. But this purity would by no means satisfy the standard of Martial sanitary science. In the first place, it is passed into a second division of the tank, where it is subjected to some violent electric action till every kind of organic germ it may contain is supposed to be completely destroyed. It is then passed through several covered channels and mechanically or chemically cleansed from every kind of inorganic impurity, and finally oxygenated or aerated with air which has undergone a yet more elaborate purification. At every stage in this process, a phial of water is taken out and examined in a dark chamber by means of a beam of light emanating from a powerful electric lamp and concentrated by a huge crystal lens. If this beam detect any perceptible dust or matter capable of scattering the light, the water is pronounced impure and passed through further processes. Only when the contents of the bottle remain absolutely dark, in the midst of an atmosphere whose floating dust renders the beam visible on either side, so that the phial, while perfectly transparent to the light, nevertheless interrupts the beam with a block of absolute darkness, is it considered fit for human consumption. It is then distributed through pipes of concrete, into which no air can possibly enter, to cisterns equally, air-tight in every house. The water in these is periodically examined by officers from the waterworks, who ascertain that it has contracted no impurity either in the course of its passage through hundreds of miles of piping or in the cisterns themselves. The Martialists consider that to this careful purification of their water they owe in great measure their exemption from the epidemic diseases which were formerly not infrequent. They maintain that all such diseases are caused by organic self-multiplying germs, and laugh to scorn the doctrine of spontaneous generation, either of disease, or of even such low organic life as can propagate it. I suggested that the atmosphere itself must, if their theory were true, convey the microscopic seeds of disease even more freely and universally than the water.

"Doubtless," replied our guide, "it would scatter them more widely; but it does not enable them to penetrate and germinate in the body half so easily

as when conveyed by water. You must be aware that the lining of the upper air-passages arrests most of the impurities contained in the inhaled air before it comes into contact with the blood in the lungs themselves.

Moreover, the extirpation of one disease after another, the careful isolation of all infectious cases, and the destruction of every article that could preserve or convey the poisonous germs, has in the course of ages enabled us utterly to destroy them."

This did not seem to me consistent with the confession that disorders of one kind or another still not infrequently decimate their highly-bred domestic animals, however the human race itself may have been secured against contagion. I did not, however, feel competent to argue the question with one who had evidently studied physiology much more deeply than myself; and had mastered the records of an experience infinitely longer, guided by knowledge far more accurate, than is possessed by the most accomplished of Terrestrial physiologists.

The examination of these works of course occupied us for a long time, and obliged us to traverse several miles of ground. More than once I had suggested to Eveena that we should leave our work unfinished, and on every opportunity had insisted that she should rest. I had been too keenly interested in the latter part of the explanation given me, to detect the fatigue she anxiously sought to conceal; but when we left the works, I was more annoyed than surprised to find that the walk down-hill to our carriage was too much for her. The vexation I felt with myself gave, after the manner of men, some sharpness to the tone of my remonstrance with her.

"I bade you, and you promised, to tell me as soon as you felt tired; and you have let me almost tire you to death! Your obedience, however strict in theory, reminds me in practice of that promised by women on Earth in their marriage-vow—and never paid or remembered afterwards."

She did not answer; and finding that her strength was utterly exhausted, I carried her down the remainder of the hill and placed her in the carriage.

During our return neither of us spoke. Ascribing her silence to habit or fatigue, perhaps to displeasure, and busied in recalling what I had seen and

heard, I did not care to "make conversation," as I certainly should have done had I guessed what impression my taciturnity made on my companion's mind. I was heartily glad for her sake when we regained the gate of her father's garden. Committing the carriage to the charge of an ambâ, I half led, half carried Eveena along the avenue, overhung with the grand conical bells—gold, crimson, scarlet, green, white, or striped or variegated with some or all these colours—of the glorious leveloo, the Martial convolvulus. Its light clinging stems and foliage hid the astyra's arched branches overhead, and formed a screen on either side. From its bells flew at our approach a whole flock of the tiny and beautiful caree, which take the chief part in rendering to the flora of Mars such services as the flowers of Earth receive from bees and butterflies. They feed on the nectar, farina, syrup, and other secretions, sweet or bitter, in which the artificial flowers of Mars are peculiarly abundant, and make their nests in the calyx or among the petals. These lovely little birds—about the size of a hornet, but perfect birds in miniature, with wings as large as those of the largest Levantine papilio, and feathery down equally fine and soft—are perhaps the most shy and timid of all creatures familiar with the presence of Martial humanity. The varied colours of their plumage, combined and intermingled in marvellously minute patterns, are all of those subdued or dead tints agreeable to the taste of Japanese artists, and perhaps to no other. They signally contrast the vivid and splendid colouring of objects created or developed by human genius and patience, from the exquisite decorations and jewel-like masses of domestic and public architecture to the magnificent flowers and fruit produced, by the labour of countless generations, from originals so dissimilar that only the records of past ages can trace or the searching comparisons of science recognise them. I am told that the present race of flower-birds themselves are a sort of indirect creation of art. They certainly vary in size, shape, and colour according to the flower each exclusively frequents; and those which haunt the cultivated bells of the leveloo present an amazing contrast to the far tinier and far less beautiful careewhich have not yet abandoned the wildflowers for those of the garden. Above two hundred varieties distinguished by ornithologists frequent only the domesticated flowers.

The flight of this swarm of various beauty recalled the conversation of last night; and breaking off unobserved a long fine tendril of the leveloo, I said lightly—

"Flower-birds are not so well-trained as esvee, bambina."

Never forgetting a word of mine, and never failing to catch with quick intelligence the sense of the most epigrammatic or delicate metaphor, Eveena started and looked up, as if stung by a serious reproach. Fancying that overpowering fatigue had so shaken her nerves, I would not allow her to speak. But I did not understand how much she had been distressed, till in her own chamber, cloak and veil thrown aside, she stood beside my seat, her sleeveless arms folded behind her, drooping like a lily beaten down by a thunderstorm. Then she murmured sadly—

"I did not think of offending. But you are quite right; disobedience should never pass."

"Certainly not," I replied, with a smile she did not see. Taking both the little hands in my left, I laid the tendril on her soft white shoulders, but so gently that in her real distress she did not feel the touch. "You see I can keep my word; but never let me tire you again. My flower-bird cannot take wing if she anger me in earnest."

"Are you not angered now?" she asked, glancing up in utter surprise.

My eyes, or the sight of the leveloo, answered her; and a sweet bright smile broke through her look of frightened, penitent submission, as she snatched the tendril and snapped it in my hand.

"Cruel!" she said, with a pretty assumption of ill-usage, "to visit a first fault with the whip."

"You are hard to please, bambina! I knew no better. Seriously, until I can measure your strength more truly, never again let me feel that in inviting your company I have turned my pleasure into your pain."

"No, indeed," she urged, once more in earnest. "Girls so seldom pass the gate, and men never walk where a carriage will go, or I should not have

been so stupid. But if I had blistered my feet, and the leveloo had been a nut-vine, the fruit was worth the scratches."

"What do you know, my child, either of blisters or stripes?"

"You will teach me——No, you know I don't mean that! But you will take me with you sometimes till I learn better! If you are going to leave me at home in future "——

"My child, can you not trust me to take you for my own pleasure?"

The silvery tone of her low sweet laugh was truly perfectly musical.

"Forgive me," she said, nestling in the cushions at my knee, and seeking with upturned eyes, like a child better assured of pardon than of full reconciliation, to read my face, "it is very naughty to laugh, and very ungrateful, when you speak to please me; but is it real kindness to say what I should be very silly to believe?"

"You will believe whatever I tell you, child. If you wish to anger a man, even with you, tell him that he is lying."

"I do nothing but misbehave," she said, in earnest despondency.

"I——" But I sealed her lips effectually for the moment.

"Why did you not speak as we came home?"

"You were tired, and I was thinking over all I had seen. Besides, who talks air?" [makes conversation].

"You always talk when you are pleased. The lip-sting (scolding) and silence frightened me so, you nearly heard me crying."

"Crying for fear? You did well to break the leveloo!... And so you think I must be tired of my bride, before the colours have gone round on the dial?"

"Not tired of her. You will like a little longer to find her in the cushions when you are vexed or idle; but you don't want her where her ignorance wearies and her weakness hampers you."

"Are you an esve, to be caged at home, and played with for lack of better employment? We shall never understand each other, child."

"What more can I be? But don't say we shall never understand each other,"

she pleaded earnestly. "It took time and trouble to make my pet understand and obey each word and sign. Zevle gave hers more slaps and fewer sweets, and it learned sooner. But, like me, you want your esve to be happy, not only to fly straight and play prettily. She will try hard to learn if you will teach her, and not be so afraid of hurting her, as if she expected sweets from both hands. It is easy for you to see through her empty head: do not give her up till she has had time to look a little way into your eyes."

"Eveena," I answered, almost as much pained as touched by the unaffected humility which had so accepted and carried out my ironical comparison,

"one simple magnet-key would unlock the breast whose secrets seem so puzzling; but it has hardly a name in your tongue, and cannot yet be in your hands."

"Ah, yes!" she said softly, "you gave it me; do you think I have lost it in two nights? But the esve cannot be loved as she loves her master. I could half understand the prodigal heart that would buy a girl's life with yours, and all that is bound up in yours. No other man would have done it—in our world," she added, answering my gesture of dissent; "but they say that the terrible kargynda will stand by his dying mate till he is shot down. You bought my heart, my love, all I am, when you bought my life, and never asked the cost." She continued almost in a whisper, her rose-suffused cheeks and moist eyes hidden from my sight as the lips murmured their loving words into my ear,—"Though the nestling never looked from under the wing, do you think she knows not what to expect when she is bought from the nest? She dares not struggle in the hand that snatches her; much more did she deserve to be rated and rapped for fluttering in that which saved her life. Bought twice over, caged by right as by might—was her thought midnight to your eyes, when she wondered at the look that watched her so quietly, the hand that would not try to touch lest it should scare her, the patience that soothed and coaxed her to perch on the outstretched finger, like a flower-bird tamed at last? Do you think that name, given her by lips which softened even their words of fondness for her ear, did not go to her heart straight as the esve flies home, or that it

could ever be forgotten? There is a chant young girls are fond of, which tells more than I can say."

Her tones fell so low that I should have lost them, had her lips not actually touched my ear while she chanted the strange words in the sweetest notes of her sweet voice:—

"Never yet hath single sun
Seen a flower-bird tamed and won;
Sun and stars shall quit the sky
Ere a bird so tamed shall fly.
"Never human lips have kissed
Flower-bird tamed 'twixt mist and mist;
Bird so tamed from tamer's heart
Night of death shall hardly part."

CHAPTER XII - ON THE RIVER.

The next morning saw our journey commenced. Eveena's wardrobe, with my own and my books, portfolios, models, and specimens of Terrestrial art and mechanism, were packed in light metallic cases adapted to the larger form of carriage whereof I have made mention. I was fortunate in escaping the actual parting scene between Eveena and her family, and my own leave-taking was hurried. Esmo and his son accompanied us, leading the way in one carriage, while Eveena and myself occupied that which we had used on our memorable trip to the Astronaut. Half an hour brought us to the road beside the river, and a few minutes more to the point at which a boat awaited us. The road being some eight or ten feet above the level of the water, a light ladder not three feet long was ready to assist our descent to the deck. The difference of size between the Martial race and my own was forcibly impressed upon me, in seeing that Esmo and his son found this assistance needful, or at least convenient, while I simply stepped rather than jumped to the deck, and lifted Eveena straight from her carriage to her seat under the canopy that covered the stern of the vessel. Intended only for river navigation, propelled by a small screw like two fishtails set at right angles, working horizontally; the vessel had but two cabins, one on either side of the central part occupied by the machinery. The stern apartment was appropriated to myself and my bride, the forecastle, if I may so call it, to our companions, the boatmen having berths in the corners of the machine-room. The vessel was flat-bottomed, drawing about eighteen inches of water and rising about five feet from the surface, leaving an interior height which obliged me to be cautious in order not to strike my head against every projection or support of the cabin roof. We spent the whole of the day, however, on deck, and purposely slackened the speed of the boat, which usually travels some thirty miles an hour, in order to enjoy the effect and observe the details of the landscape. For the first few miles our voyage lay through the open plain. Then we passed, on the left as we ascended the stream, the mountain on whose summit I tried with my binocular to discern the Astronaut, but unsuccessfully, the trees on the lower slopes intercepting the view. Eveena, seeing my eyes fixed on that point, extended her hand and gently drew the glass out of mine.

"Not yet," she said; which elicited from me the excuse—

"That mountain has for me remembrances more interesting than those of my voyage, or even than the hopes of return."

Presently, as we followed the course of the stream, we lost sight altogether of the rapidly dwindling patches of colour representing the enclosures of Ecasfe. On our left, at a distance varying from three to five miles, but constantly increasing as the stream bent to the northward, was the mountain range I had scanned in my descent. On our right the plain dipped below the horizon while still but a few feet above the level of the river; but in the distant sky we discerned some objects like white clouds, which from their immobility and fixedness of outline I soon discovered to be snow-crowned hills, lower, however, than those to the northward, and perhaps some forty miles distant. The valley is one of the richest and most fertile portions of this continent, and was consequently thoroughly cultivated and more densely peopled than most parts even of the Equatorial zone. An immediate river frontage being as convenient as agreeable, the enclosures on either bank were continuous, and narrow in proportion to their depth; the largest occupying no more than from one hundred and fifty to two hundred yards of the bank, the smaller from half to one quarter of that length. Most had a tunnel pierced under the road bordering the river, through which the water was admitted to their grounds and carried in a minute stream around and even through the house; for ornament rather than for use, since every house in a district so populous has a regular artificial water supply, and irrigation, as I have explained, is not required. The river itself was embellished with masses of water-flowers; and water-birds, the smallest scarcely larger than a wagtail, the largest somewhat exceeding the size of a swan, of a different form and dark grey plumage, but hardly less graceful, seemed to be aware of the stringent protection they enjoyed from the law. They came up to our boat and fed out of Eveena's hand with perfect fearlessness. I could not induce any of them to be equally familiar with myself, my size probably surprising them as much as their masters, and leading them to the same doubt whether I were really and wholly human. The lower slopes of the hills

were covered with orchards of every kind, each species occupying the level best suited to it, from the reed-supported orange-like alva of the lowlands to the tall astyra, above which stretched the timber forests extending as high as trees could grow, while between these and the permanent snow-line lay the yellowish herbage of extensive pastures. A similar mountain range on earth would have presented a greater variety of colouring and scenery, the total absence of glaciers, even in the highest valleys, creating a notable difference. The truth is that the snows of Mars are nowhere deep, and melt in the summer to such an extent that that constant increase whose downward tendency feeds Terrestrial glaciers cannot take place. Probably the thin atmosphere above the snow-line can hold but little watery vapour.

Esmo was of opinion that the snow on the highest steeps, even on a level plateau, was never more than two feet in depth; and in more than one case a wind-swept peak or pinnacle was kept almost clear, and presented in its grey, green, or vermilion rocks a striking contrast to the masses of creamy white around it. This may explain the very rapid diminution of the polar ice-caps in the summer of either, but especially of the Southern hemisphere; and also the occasional appearance of large dark spots in their midst, where the shallow snow has probably been swept away by the rare storms of this planet from an extensive land surface. It is supposed that no inconsiderable part of the ice and snow immediately surrounding the poles covers land; but, though balloon parties have of late occasionally reached the poles, they have never ventured to remain there long enough to disembark and ascertain the fact.

Towards evening the stream turned more decidedly to the north, and at this point Esmo brought out an instrument constructed somewhat on the principle of a sextant or quadrant, but without the mirror, by which we were enabled to take reliable measures of the angles. By a process which at that time I did not accurately follow, and which I had not subsequently the means of verifying, the distance as well as the angle subtended by the height was obtained. Kevimâ, after working out his father's figures, informed me that the highest peak in view—the highest in Mars—was not less than 44,000 feet. No Martial balloonist, much less any Martial mountain-climber, has ever, save once, reached a greater height than 16,000 feet—the air at the sea-level being scarcely more dense than ours at 10,000

feet. Kevimâ indicated one spot in the southern range of remarkable interest, associated with an incident which forms an epoch in the records of Martial geography. A sloping plateau, some 19,000 feet above the sea-level, is defined with remarkable clearness in the direction from which we viewed it. The forests appeared to hide, though they do not of course actually approach, its lower edge. On one side and to the rear it is shut in by precipices so abrupt that the snow fails to cling to them, while on the remaining side it is separated by a deep, wide cleft from the western portion of the range. Here for centuries were visible the relics of an exploring party, which reached this plateau and never returned. Attempts have, since the steering of balloons has become an accomplished fact, been made to reach the point, but without success, and those who have approached nearest have failed to find any of the long-visible remains of an expedition which perished four or five thousand years ago. Kevimâ thought it probable that the metallic poles even then employed for tents and for climbing purposes might still be intact; but if so, they were certainly buried in the snow, and Esmo believed it more likely that even these had perished.

As the mists of evening fell we retreated to our cabin, which was warmed by a current of heated air from the electric machinery. Here our evening meal was served, at which Esmo and his son joined us, Eveena resuming, even in their presence, the veil she had worn on deck but had laid aside the moment we were alone. An hour or two after sunset, the night (an unusual occurrence in Mars) was clear and fine, and I took this opportunity of observing from a new standpoint the familiar constellations. The scintillation so characteristic of the fixed stars, especially in the temperate climates of the Earth, was scarcely perceptible. Scattered once more over the surface of a defined sky, it was much easier than in space to recognise the several constellations; but their new and strange situations were not a little surprising at first sight, some of those which, as seen on Earth revolved slowly in the neighbourhood of the poles, being now not far from the tropics, and some, which had their place within the tropics, now lying far to north or south. Around the northern pole the Swan swings by its tail,

as in our skies the Lesser Bear; Arided being a Pole-Star which needs no Pointers to indicate its position. Vega is the only other brilliant star in the immediate neighbourhood; and, save for the presence of the Milky Way directly crossing it, the arctic circle is distinctly less bright than our own.

The south pole lies in one of the dullest regions of the heavens, near the chief star of the Peacock. Arcturus, the Great Bear, the Twins, the Lion, the Scorpion, and Fomalhaut are among the ornaments of the Equatorial zone: the Cross, the Centaur, and the Ship of our antarctic constellations, are visible far into the northern hemisphere. On the present occasion the two Moons were both visible in the west, the horns of both crescents pointing in the same direction, though the one was in her last, the other in her first phase.

As we were watching them, Eveena, wrapped in a cloak of fur not a little resembling that of the silver fox, but far softer, stole her hand into mine and whispered a request that I would lend her the instrument I was using.

With some instruction and help she contrived to adjust it, her sight requiring a decided alteration of the focus and an approach of the two eye-pieces; the eyes of her race being set somewhat nearer than in an average Aryan countenance. She expressed no little surprise at the clearness of definition, and the marked enlargement of the discs of the two satellites, and would have used the instrument to scan the stars and visible planets had I not insisted on her retirement; the light atmosphere, as is always the case on clear nights, when no cloud-veil prevents rapid radiation from the surface, being bitterly cold, and her life not having accustomed her to the night air even in the most genial season.

As we could, of course, see nothing of the country through which we passed during the night, and as Esmo informed me that little or nothing of special interest would occur during this part of our voyage, our vessel went at full speed, her pilot being thoroughly acquainted with the river, and an electric light in the bow enabling him to steer with perfect confidence and safety. When, therefore, we came on deck after the dissipation of the morning mist, we found ourselves in a scene very different from that which we had left. Our course was north by west. On
either bank lay a country cultivated indeed, but chiefly pastoral, producing a rich herbage, grazed by innumerable herds, among which I observed with interest several flocks of large birds, kept, as Esmo informed me, partly for their plumage. This presented remarkable combinations of colour, far surpassing in brilliancy and in variety of pattern the tail of the peacock, and often rivalling in length and delicacy, while exceeding in beauty of colouring, the splendid feathers which must have embarrassed the Bird of Paradise, even before they rendered him an object of pursuit by those who have learnt the vices and are eager to purchase the wares of civilised man. Immediately across our course, at a distance of some thirty miles, stretched a range of mountains. I inquired of Esmo how the river turned in order to avoid them, since no opening was visible even through my glass.

"The proper course of the river," he said, "lies at the foot of those hills. But this would take us out of our road, and, moreover, the stream is not navigable for many stoloi above the turning-point. We shall hold on nearly in the same direction as the present till we land at their foot."

"And how," I said, "are we to cross them?"

"At your choice, either by carriage or by balloon," he said. "There is at our landing-place a town in which we shall easily procure either."

"But," said I, "though our luggage is far less heavy than would be that of a bride on Earth, and Eveena's forms the smallest portion of it, I should fancy that it must be inconveniently heavy for a balloon."

"Certainly," he replied; "but we could send it by carriage even over the mountain roads. The boat, however, will go on, and will meet us some thirty miles beyond the point where we leave it."

"And how is the boat to pass over the hills?"

"Not over, but under," he said, smiling. "There is no natural passage entirely through the range, but there is within it a valley the bottom of which is not much higher than this plain. Of the thirty miles to be traversed, about one-half lies in the course of this valley, along which an artificial canal has been made. Through the hills at either end a tunnel has
been cut, the one of six, the other of about nine miles in length, affording a perfectly safe and easy course for the boat; and it is through these that nearly all the heavy traffic passing in this direction is conveyed."

"I should like," I said, "if it be possible, to pass through one at least of these tunnels, unless there be on the mountains themselves something especially worth seeing."

"Nothing," he replied. "They are low, none much exceeding the height of that from which you descended."

Eveena now joined us on deck, and we amused ourselves for the next two hours in observing the different animals, of which such numbers were to be seen at every turn, domesticated and trained for one or other of the many methods in which the brutes can serve the convenience, the sustenance, or the luxury of man. Animal food is eaten on Mars; but the flesh of birds and fish is much more largely employed than that of quadrupeds, and eggs and milk enter into the cuisine far more extensively than either. In fact, flesh and fish are used much as they seem to have been in the earlier period of Greek civilisation, as relish and supplement to fruits, vegetables, and farinaceous dishes, rather than as the principal element of food. As their training and their extreme tameness indicate, domestic creatures, even those destined only to serve as food or to furnish clothing, are treated not indeed with tenderness, but with gentleness, and without either the neglect or the cruelty which so revolt humane men in witnessing the treatment of Terrestrial animals by those who have personal charge of them. To describe any considerable number of the hundred forms I saw during this short period would be impossible. I have drawings, or rather pictures, of most, taken by the light-painting process, which I hope herewith to remit to Earth, and which at least serve to give a general idea of the points in which the Martial chiefly differs from the Terrestrial fauna. Those animals whose coats furnish a textile fibre more resemble reindeer and goats than sheep; their wool is softer, longer, and less curly, free also from the greasiness of the sheep.

It seemed to me that an extreme quaintness characterised the domestic creatures kept for special purposes. This was not the effect of mere novelty,

for animals like the ambâ and birds like the esve, trained to the performance of services congenial to their natural habits, however dissimilar to Terrestrial species, had not the same air of singularity, or rather of monstrosity. But in the creatures bred to furnish wool, feathers, or the like, some single feature was always exaggerated into disproportionate dimensions. Thus the elnerve is loaded with long plumes, sometimes twice the length of the body, and curled upward at the extremity, so that it can neither fly nor run; and though its plumage is exquisitely beautiful, the creature itself is simply ludicrous. It bears the same popular repute for sagacity as the goose of European farmyards. The angasto has hair or wool so long that its limbs are almost hidden, just before shearing-time, in the tresses that hang from the body half way to the ground. The calperze, a bird no larger than a Norfolk turkey, has the hinder part developed to an enormous size, so that the graceful peacock-like neck and shoulders appear as if lost in the huge proportions of the body, and the little wings are totally unfit to raise it in the air; while it lays almost daily eggs as large as those of the ostrich and of peculiar richness and flavour. Nearly all the domestic birds kept for the sake of eggs or feathers have wings that look as if they had been clipped, and are incapable of flight. Creatures valued for their flesh, such as the quorno (somewhat like the eland, but with the single horn so common among its congeners in Mars, and with a soft white hide), and the viste, a bird about the size of the peacock, with the form of the partridge and the flavour of grouse or black game, preserve more natural proportions. The wing-quills of the latter, however, having been systematically plucked for hundreds of generations, are now dwarfed and useless. These animals are not encouraged to make fat on the one hand, or to develop powerful muscles and sinews on the other. They are fed for part of the year on the higher and thinner pastures of the mountains. When brought down to the meadows of the plain, they are allowed to graze only for a few hours before sunset and after sunrise. They thus preserve much of the flavour of game or mountain sheep and cattle, which the oxen and poultry of Europe have lost; flavour, not quantity, being the chief object of care with Martial graziers. Sometimes, however, some peculiarity perfectly useless, or even inconvenient, appears to be naturally associated with that

which is artificially developed. Thus the beak of the elnerve is weak and often splits, so as to render its rearing troublesome and entail considerable losses; while the horns of the wool-bearing animals are long and strong enough to be formidable, but so rough and coarsely grained that they are turned to no account for use or ornament.

We were rapidly approaching the foot of the hills, where the river made another and abrupt turn. At this point the produce of the whole upper valley is generally embarked, and supplies from all other quarters are here received and distributed. In consequence, a town large and important for this planet, where no one who can help it prefers the crowded street to the freedom and expanse of the country, had grown up, with about a hundred and fifty houses, and perhaps a thousand inhabitants. It was so much matter of course that voyagers should disembark to cross the hills or to pursue their journey along the upper part of the river by road, that half-a-dozen different partnerships made it their business to assist in the transfer of passengers and light wares. Ahead of us was a somewhat steep hill-slope, in the lower part of which a wall absolutely perpendicular had been cut by those who pierced the tunnel, the mouth of which was now clearly visible immediately before us. It was about twelve feet in height, and perhaps twenty feet in width. The stream, which, like nearly all Martial rivers, is wide and shallow, had during the last fifty miles of our course grown narrower, with a depth at the same time constantly lessening, so that some care was required on the part of the pilot to avoid running aground. A stream of twenty inches in depth, affording room for two boats to pass abreast, is considered navigable for vessels only carrying passengers; thirty inches are required to afford a course which for heavy freight is preferable to the road. Eveena had taken it for granted that we should disembark here, and it was not till we had come within a hundred yards of the landing-place—where the bank was perpendicular and levelled to a height above the water, which enabled passengers to step directly from the deck of the boat—without slackening our speed, that the possibility of our intending to accompany the boat on its subterrene course occurred to her. As she did not speak, but merely drew closer to me, and held fast my hand, I had no idea of her real distress till we were actually at

the mouth of the black and very frightful-looking passage, and the pilot had lighted the electric lamp. As the boat shot under the arch she could not repress a cry of terror. Naturally putting my arm round her at this sign of alarm, I felt that she was trembling violently, and a single look, despite her veil, convinced me that she was crying, though in silence and doing her utmost to conceal her tears.

"Are you so frightened, child?" I asked. "I have been through many subterranean passages, though none so long and dark as this. But you see our lamp lights up not only the boat but the whole vault around and before us, and there can be no danger whatever."

"I am frightened, though," she said, "I cannot help it. I never saw anything of the kind before; and the darkness behind and before us, and the black water on either side, do make me shiver."

"Stop!" I called to the boatman.

"Now, Eveena," I said, "I do not care to persist in this journey if it really distresses you. I wished to see so wonderful a work of engineering; but, after all, I have been in a much uglier and more wonderful place, and I can see nothing here stranger than when I was rowed for three-quarters of a mile on the river in the Mammoth Cave. In any case I shall see little but a continuation of what I see already; so if you cannot bear it, we will go back."

By this time Esmo, who had been in the bows, had joined us, wishing to know why I had stopped the boat.

"This child," I said, "is not used to travelling, and the tunnel frightens her; so that I think, after all, we had better take the usual course across the mountains."

"Nonsense!" he answered. "There is no danger here; less probably than in an ordinary drive, certainly less than in a balloon. Don't spoil her, my friend. If you begin by yielding to so silly a caprice as this, you will end by breaking her heart before the two years are out."

"Do go on," whispered Eveena. "I was very silly; I am not so frightened now, and if you will hold me fast, I will not misbehave again."

Esmo had taken the matter out of my hands, desiring the boatman to proceed; and though I sympathised with my bride's feminine terror much more than her father appeared to do, I was selfishly anxious, in spite of my declaration that there could be no novelty in this tunnel, to see one thing certainly original—the means by which so narrow and so long a passage could be efficiently ventilated. The least I could do, however, was to appease Eveena's fear before turning my attention to the objects of my own curiosity. The presence of physical strength, which seemed to her superhuman, produced upon her nerves the quieting effect which, however irrationally, great bodily force always exercises over women; partly, perhaps, from the awe it seems to inspire, partly from a yet more unreasonable but instinctive reliance on its protection even in dangers against which it is obviously unavailing.

Presently a current of air, distinctly warmer than that of the tunnel, which had been gradually increasing in force for some minutes, became so powerful that I could no longer suppose it accidental. Kevimâ being near us, I asked him what it meant.

"Ventilation," he answered. "The air in these tunnels would be foul and stagnant, perhaps unbreathable, if we did not drive a constant current of air through them. You did not notice, a few yards from the entrance, a wheel which drives a large fan. One of these is placed at every half mile, and drives on the air from one end of the tunnel to the other. They are reversed twice in a zyda, so that they may create no constant counter-current outside."

"But is not the power exerted to drive so great a body of air exceedingly costly?"

"No," he answered. "As you are aware, electricity is almost our only motive power, and we calculate that the labour of two men, even without the help of machines, could in their working zydau [eight hours] collect and reduce a sufficient amount of the elements by which the current is created to do the work of four hundred men during a whole day and night."

"And how long," I inquired, "has electricity had so complete a monopoly of mechanical work?"

"It was first brought into general use," he replied, "about eight thousand years ago. Before that, heated air supplied our principal locomotive force, as well as the power of stationary machines wherever no waterfall of sufficient energy was at hand. For several centuries the old powers were still employed under conditions favourable to their use. But we have found electricity so much cheaper than the cheapest of other artificial forces, so much more powerful than any supplied by Nature, that we have long discontinued the employment of any other. Even when we obtain electricity by means of heat, we find that the gain in application more than compensates the loss in the transmutation of one force into another."

In the course of little more than half an hour we emerged from the tunnel, whose gloom, when once the attraction of novelty was gone, was certainly unpleasant to myself, if not by any means so frightful as Eveena still found it. There was nothing specially attractive or noticeable in the valley through which our course now ran, except the extreme height of its mountain walls, which, though not by any means perpendicular, rose to a height of some 3000 feet so suddenly that to climb their sides would have been absolutely impossible. Only during about two hours in the middle of the day is the sun seen from the level of the stream; and it is dark in the bottom of this valley long before the mist has fallen on the plain outside. We had presently, however, to ascend a slope of some twenty-five feet in the mile, and I was much interested in the peculiar method by which the ascent was made. A mere ascent, not greater than that of some rapids up which American boatmen have managed to carry their barques by manual force, presented no great difficulty; but some skill is required at particular points to avoid being overturned by the rush of the water, and our vessel so careened as to afford much more excuse for Eveena's outbreak of terror than the tunnel had done. Had I not held her fast she must certainly have been thrown overboard, the pilot, used to the danger, having forgotten to warn us. For the rest, in the absence of rocks, the vessel ascended more easily than a powerful steamer, if she could find sufficient depth, could

make her way up the rapids of the St. Lawrence or similar streams. We entered the second tunnel without any sign of alarm from Eveena perceptible to others; only her clinging to my hand expressed the fear of which she was ashamed but could not rid herself. Emerging from its mouth, we found ourselves within sight of the sea and of the town and harbour of Serocasfe, where we were next day to embark. Landing from the boat, we were met by the friend whose hospitality Esmo had requested.

At his house, half a mile outside the town, for the first time since our marriage I had to part for a short period with Eveena, who was led away by the veiled mistress of the house, while we remained in the entrance chamber or hall. The evening meal was anticipated by two hours, in order that we might attend the meeting at which my bride and I were to receive our formal admission into the Zinta.

CHAPTER XIII - THE CHILDREN OF LIGHT.

"Probably," said Esmo, when, apparently at a sign from him, our host left us for some minutes alone, "much through which you are about to pass will seem to you childish or unmeaning. Ceremonial rendered impressive to us by immemorial antiquity, and cherished the more because so contrary to the absence of form and ceremony in the life around us—symbolism which is really the more useful, the more valuable, because it contains much deeper meaning than is ever apparent at first sight—have proved their use by experience; and, as they are generally witnessed for the first time in early youth, make a sharper impression than they are likely to effect upon a mind like yours. But they may seem strangely inconsistent with a belief which is in itself so limited, and founded so absolutely upon logical proof or practical evidence. The best testimony to the soundness of our policy in this respect is the fact that our vows, and the rites by which they are sanctioned, are never broken, that our symbols are regarded with an awe which no threats, no penalties, can attach to the highest of civil authorities or the most solemn legal sanctions. The language of symbol, moreover, has for us two great advantages—one dependent upon the depth of thought and knowledge with which the symbols themselves were selected by our Founder, owing to which each generation finds in them some new truth of which we never dreamed before; the other arising from the fact that we are a small select body in the midst of a hostile and jealous race, from whom it is most important to keep the key of communications which, without the appearance, have all the effect of ciphers."

"I find," I replied, "in my own world that every religion and every form of occult mysticism, nay, every science, in its own way and within its own range, attaches great importance to symbols in themselves apparently arbitrary. Experience shows that these, symbols often contain a clue to more than they were originally meant to convey, and can be employed in reasonings far beyond the grasp of those who first invented or adopted them. That a body like the Zinta could be held together without ceremonial and without formalities, which, if they had no other value, would have the attraction of secrecy and exclusiveness, seems obviously impossible."

Here our host rejoined us. We passed into the gallery, where several persons were awaiting us; the men for the most part wearing a small vizor dependent from the turban, which concealed their faces; the women all, without exception, closely veiled. As soon as Esmo appeared, the party formed themselves into a sort of procession two and two. Motioning me to take the last place, Esmo passed himself to its head. If the figure beside me were not at once recognised, I could not mistake the touch of the hand that stole into my own. The lights in the gallery were extinguished, and then I perceived a lamp held at the end of a wand of crystal, which gleamed above Esmo's head, and sufficed to guide us, giving light enough to direct our footsteps and little more. Perhaps this half-darkness, the twilight which gave a certain air of mystery to the scene and of uncertainty to the forms of objects encountered on our route, had its own purpose. We reached very soon the end of the gallery, and then the procession turned and passed suddenly into another chamber, apparently narrow, but so faintly lighted by the lamp in our leader's hands that its dimensions were matter of mere conjecture. That we were descending a somewhat steep incline I was soon aware; and when we came again on to level ground I felt sure that we were passing through a gallery cut in natural rock. The light was far too dim to enable me to distinguish any openings in the walls; but the procession constantly lengthened, though it was impossible to see where and when new members joined. Suddenly the light disappeared. I stood still for a moment in surprise, and when I again went forward I became speedily conscious that all our companions had vanished, and that we stood alone in utter darkness. Fearing to lead Eveena further where my own steps were absolutely uncertain, I paused for some time, and with little difficulty decided to remain where I was, until something should afford an indication of the purpose of those who had brought us so far, and who must know, if they had not actual means of observing, that in darkness and solitude I should not venture to proceed.

Presently, as gradually as in Northern climates the night passes into morning twilight, the darkness became less absolute. Whence the light came it was impossible to perceive. Diffused all around and slowly broadening, it just enabled me to discern a few paces before us the verge of

a gulf. This might have been too shallow for inconvenience, it might have been deep enough for danger. I waited till my eyes should be able to penetrate its interior; but before the light entered it I perceived, apparently growing across it, really coming gradually into view under the brightening gleam, a species of bridge which—when the twilight ceased to increase, and remained as dim as that cast by the crescent moon—assumed the outline of a slender trunk supported by wings, dark for the most part but defined along the edge by a narrow band of brightest green, visible in a gleam too faint to show any object of a deeper shade. Somewhat impatient of the obvious symbolism, I hurried Eveena forward. Immediately on the other side of the bridge the path turned almost at right angles; and here a gleam of light ahead afforded a distinct guidance to our steps.

Approaching it, we were challenged, and I gave the answer with which I had been previously furnished; an answer which may not be, as it never has been, written down. A door parted and admitted us into a small vestibule, at the other end of which a full and bright light streamed through a portal of translucent crystal. A sentinel, armed only with the antiquated spear which may have been held by his first predecessor in office ten thousand Martial years ago, now demanded our names. Mine he simply repeated, but as I gave that of Eveena, daughter of Esmo, he lowered his weapon in the salute still traditional among Martial sentries; and bending his head, touched with his lips the long sleeve of the cloak of therne-down in which she was on this occasion again enveloped. This homage appeared to surprise her almost as much as myself, but we had no leisure for observation or inquiry. From behind the crystal door another challenge was uttered. To this it was the sentry's part to reply, and as he answered the door parted; that at the other end of the vestibule having, I observed, closed as we entered, and so closed that its position was undiscoverable. Before us opened a hall of considerable size, consisting of three distinct vaults, defined by two rows of pillars, slender shafts resembling tall branchless trees, the capital of each being formed by a branching head like that of the palm. The trunks were covered with golden scales; the fern-like foliage at the summit was of a bright sparkling emerald. It was evident to my observation that the entire hall had been

excavated from solid rock, and the pillars left in their places. Each of the side aisles, if I may so call them, was occupied by four rows of seats similarly carved in the natural stone; but lined after Martial fashion, with cushions embroidered in feathers and metals, and covered by woven fabrics finer than any known to the looms of Lyons or Cashmere. About two-thirds of the seats were occupied; those to the right as we entered (that is, on the left of the dais at the end of the hall) by men, those opposite by women. All, I observed, rose for a moment as Eveena's name was announced, from the further end of the hall, by the foremost of three or four persons vested in silver, with belts of the crimson metal which plays the part of our best-tempered steel, and bearing in their hands wands of a rose-coloured jewel resembling a clouded onyx in all but the hue. Each of them wore over his dress a band or sash of gold, fastened on the left shoulder and descending to the belt on the right, much resembling the ribbons of European knighthood. These supported on the left breast a silver star, or heraldic mullet, of six points. Throughout the rest of the assembly a similar but smaller star glimmered on every breast, supported, however, by green or silver bands, the former worn by the body of the assembly, the latter by a few persons gathered together for the most part at the upper end of the chamber.... The chief who had first addressed us bade us pass on, and we left the Hall of the Novitiate as accepted members of the Order.... That into which we next entered was so dark that its form and dimensions were scarcely defined to my eyes. I supposed it, however, to be circular, surmounted by a dome resembling in colour the olive green Martial sky and spangled by stars, among which I discerned one or two familiar constellations, but most distinctly, brightened far beyond its natural brilliancy, the arch of the Via Lactea. Presently, not on any apparent sheet or screen but as in the air before us, appeared a narrow band of light crossing the entire visible space. It resembled a rope twisted of three strands, two of a deep dull hue, the one apparently orange, the other brown or crimson, contrasting the far more brilliant emerald strand that formed the third portion of the threefold cord. I had learnt by this time that metallic cords so twined serve in Mars most of the uses for which

chains are employed on Earth, and I assumed that this symbol possessed the significance which poetry or ritual might attach to the latter.

This cord or band retained its position throughout, crossing the dark background of the scenes now successively presented, each of which melted into its successor—rapidly, but so gradually that there was never a distinct point of division, a moment at which it was possible to say that any new feature was first introduced.

A bright mist of various colours intermixed in inextricable confusion, an image of chaos but for the dim light reflected from all the particles, filled a great part of the space before us, but the cord was still discernible in the background. Presently, a bright rose-coloured point of light, taking gradually the form of an Eye, appeared above the cord and beyond the mist; and, emanating from it, a ray of similar light entered the motionless vapour. Then a movement, whose character it was not easy to discern, but which constantly became more and more evidently rhythmical and regular, commenced in the mist. Within a few moments the latter had dissolved, leaving in its place the semblance of stars, star-clusters, and golden nebulae, as dim and confused as that in the sword-belt of Orion, or as well defined as any of those called by astronomers planetary. "What seest thou?"

said a voice whose very direction I could not recognise.

"Cosmos evolved out of confusion by Law; Law emanating from Supreme Wisdom and irresistible Will."

"And in the triple band?"

"The continuity of Time and Space preserved by the continuity of Law, and controlled by the Will that gave Law."

While I spoke a single nebula grew larger, brighter, and filled the entire space given throughout to the pictures presented to us; stars and star-clusters gradually fading away into remoter distance. This nebula, of spherical shape—formed of coarser particles than the previous mist, and reflecting or radiating a more brilliant effulgence—was in rapid whirling motion. It flattened into the form of a disc, apparently almost circular, of considerable depth or thickness, visibly denser in the centre and thinner

towards the rounded edge. Presently it condensed and contracted, leaving at each of the several intervals a severed ring. Most of these rings broke up, their fragments conglomerated and forming a sphere; one in particular separating into a multitude of minuter spheres, others assuming a highly elliptical form, condensing here and thinning out there; while the central mass grew brighter and denser as it contracted; till there lay before me a perfect miniature of the solar system, with planets, satellites, asteroids, and meteoric rings.

"What seest thou?" again I heard.

"Intelligence directing Will, and Will by Law developing the microcosm of which this world is one of the smallest parts."

The orb which represented Mars stood still in the centre of the space, and this orb soon occupied the whole area. It assumed at first the form of a vast vaporous globe; then contracted to a comparatively small sphere, glowing as if more than red-hot, and leaving as it contracted two tiny balls revolving round their primary. The latter gradually faded till it gave out no light but that which from some unseen source was cast upon it, one-half consequently contrasting in darkness the reflected brightness of the other.

Ere long it presented the appearance of sea and land, of cloud, of snow, and ice, and became a perfect image of the Martial sphere. Then it gave place to a globe of water alone, within which the processes of crystallisation, as exhibited first in its simpler then in its more complicated forms, were beautifully represented. Then there appeared, I knew not how, but seemingly developed by the same agency and in the same manner as the crystals, a small transparent sphere within the watery globe, containing itself a spherical nucleus. From this were evolved gradually two distinct forms, one resembling very much some of the simplest of those transparent creatures which the microscope exhibits to us in the water drop, active, fierce, destructive in their scale of size and life as the most powerful animals of the sea and land. The other was a tiny fragment of tissue, gradually shaping itself into the simplest and smallest specimens of vegetable life. The watery globe disappeared, and these two were left alone. From each gradually emerged, growing in size, complexity, and distinctness, one form after another of higher organisation.

"What seest thou?"

"Life called out of lifelessness by Law."

Again, so gradually that no step of the process could be separately distinguished, formed a panorama of vegetable and animal life; a landscape in which appeared some dozen primal shapes of either kingdom. Each of these gradually dissolved, passing by slow degrees into several higher or more perfect shapes, till there stood before our eyes a picture of life as it exists at present; and Man in its midst, more obviously even than on Earth, dominating and subduing the fellow-creatures of whom he is lord. From which of the innumerable animal forms that had been presented to us in the course of these transmutations this supreme form had arisen, I did not note or cannot remember. But that no true ape appeared among them, I do distinctly recollect, having been on the watch for the representation of such an epoch in the pictured history.

What was now especially noteworthy was that, solid as they appeared, each form was in some way transparent. From the Emblem before mentioned a rose-coloured light pervaded the scene; scarcely discernible in the general atmosphere, faintly but distinctly traceable in every herb, shrub, and tree, more distinguishable and concentrated in each animal. But in plant or animal the condensed light was never separated and individualised, never parted from, though obviously gathered and agglomerated out of, the generally diffused rosy sheen that tinged the entire landscape. It was as though the rose-coloured light formed an atmosphere which entered and passed freely through the tissues of each animal and plant, but brightened and deepened in those portions which at any moment pervaded any organised shape, while it flowed freely in and out of all. The concentration was most marked, the connection with the diffused atmosphere least perceptible, in those most intelligent creatures, like the ambâ and carve, which in the service of man appear to have acquired a portion of human intelligence. But turning to the type of Man himself, the light within his body had assumed the shape of the frame it

filled and appeared to animate. In him the rose-coloured image which exactly corresponded to the body that encased it was perfectly individualised, and had no other connection with the remainder of the light than that it appeared to emanate and to be fed from the original source.

As I looked, the outward body dissolved, the image of rosy light stood alone, as human and far more beautiful than before, rose upward, and passed away.

"What seest thou?" was uttered in an even more earnest and solemn tone than heretofore.

"Life," I said, "physical and spiritual; the one sustained by the other, the spiritual emanating from the Source of Life, pervading all living forms, affording to each the degree of individuality and of intelligence needful to it, but in none forming an individual entity apart from the race, save in Man himself; and in Man forming the individual being, whereof the flesh is but the clothing and the instrument."

The whole scene suddenly vanished in total darkness; only again in one direction a gleam of light appeared, and guided us to a portal through which we entered another long and narrow passage, terminating in a second vestibule before a door of emerald crystal, brilliantly illuminated by a light within. Here, again, our steps were arrested. The door was guarded by two sentries, in whom I recognised Initiates of the Order, wearers of the silver sash and star. The password and sign, whispered to me as we left the Hall of the Novitiate, having been given, the door parted and exposed to our view the inmost chamber, a scene calculated to strike the eye and impress the mind not more by its splendour and magnificence than by the unexpected character it displayed. It represented a garden, but the boundaries were concealed by the branching trees, the arches of flowering creepers, the thickets of flowers, shrubs, and tall reeds, which in every direction imitated so perfectly the natural forms that the closest scrutiny would have been required to detect their artificiality. The general form, however, seemed to be that of a square entered by a very short, narrow passage, and divided by broad paths, forming a cross of equal arms. At the central point of this cross was placed on a pedestal of emerald a statue in

gold, which recalled at once the features of the Founder. The space might have accommodated two thousand persons, but on the seats—of a material resembling ivory, each of them separately formed and gathered in irregular clusters—there were not, I thought, more than four hundred or five hundred men and women intermingled; the former dressed for the most part in green, the latter in pink or white, and all wearing the silver band and star. At the opposite end, closing the central aisle, was a low narrow platform raised by two steps carved out of the natural rock, but inlaid with jewellery imitating closely the variegated turf of a real garden. On this were placed, slanting backward towards the centre, two rows of six golden seats or thrones, whose occupants wore the golden band over silver robes.

That next the interval, but to the left, was filled by Esmo, who to my surprise wore a robe of white completely covering his figure, and contrasting signally the golden sash to which his star was attached. On his left arm, bare below the elbow, I noticed a flat thick band of plain gold, with an emerald seal, bearing the same proportion to the bracelet as a large signet to its finger ring. What struck me at once as most remarkable was, that the seats on the dais and the forms of their occupiers were signally relieved against a background of intense darkness, whose nature, however, I could not discern. The roof was in form a truncated pyramid; its material a rose-coloured crystal, through which a clear soft light illuminated the whole scene. Across the floor of the entrance, immediately within the portal, was a broad band of the same crystal, marking the formal threshold of the Hall. Immediately inside this stood the same Chief who had received us in the former Hall; and as we stood at the door, stretching forth his left hand, he spoke, or rather chanted, what, by the rhythmical sequence of the words, by the frequent recurrence of alliteration and irregular rhyme, was evidently a formula committed to the verse of the Martial tongue: a formula, like all those of the Order, never written, but handed down by memory, and therefore, perhaps, cast in a shape which rendered accurate remembrance easier and more certain.

"Ye who, lost in outer night,
Reach at last the Source of Light,
Ask ye in that light to dwell?

None we urge and none repel;
Opens at your touch the door,
Bright within the lamp of lore.
Yet beware! The threshold passed,
Fixed the bond, the ball is cast.
Failing heart or faltering feet
Find nor pardon nor retreat.
Loyal faith hath guerdon given
Boundless as the star-sown Heaven;
Horror fathomless and gloom
Rayless veil the recreant's doom.
Warned betimes, in time beware—Freely
turn, or frankly swear."

"What am I to swear?" I asked.

A voice on my left murmured in a low tone the formula, which I repeated, Eveena accompanying my words in an almost inaudible whisper—

"Whatsoe'er within the Shrine
Eyes may see or soul divine,
Swear we secret as the deep,
Silent as the Urn to keep.
By the Light we claim to share,
By the Fount of Light, we swear."

As these words were uttered, I became aware that some change had taken place at the further end of the Hall. Looking up, the dark background had disappeared, and under a species of deep archway, behind the seats of the Chiefs, was visible a wall diapered in ruby and gold, and displaying in

various interwoven patterns the several symbols of the Zinta. Towards the roof, exactly in the centre, was a large silver star, emitting a light resembling that which the full moon sheds on a tropical scene, but far more brilliant. Around this was a broad golden circle or band; and beneath, the silver image of a serpent—perfectly reproducing a typical terrestrial snake, but coiled, as no snake ever coils itself, in a double circle or figure of eight, with the tail wound around the neck. On the left was a crimson shield or what seemed to be such, small, round, and swelling in the centre into a sharp point; on the right three crossed spears of silver with crimson blades pointed upward. But the most remarkable object—immediately filling the interval between the seats of the Chiefs, and carved from a huge cubic block of emerald—was a Throne, ascended on each side by five or six steps, the upper step or seat extending nearly across the whole some two feet below the surface, the next forming a footstool thereto. Above this was a canopy, seemingly self-supported, of circular form. A chain formed by interlaced golden circles was upheld by four great emerald wings. Within the chain, again, was the silver Serpent, coiled as before and resting upon a surface of foliage and flowers. In the centre of all was repeated the silver Star within the golden band; the emblem from which the Order derives its name, and in which it embodies its deepest symbolism. Following again the direction of my unseen prompter, I repeated words which may be roughly translated as follows:—

"By the outer Night of gloom,
By the ray that leads us home,
By the Light we claim to share,
By the Fount of Light, we swear.
Prompt obedience, heart and hand,
To the Signet's each command:
For the Symbols, reverence mute,
In the Sense faith absolute.

Link by link to weld the Chain,
 Link with link to bear the strain;
Cherish all the Star who wear,
As the Starlight's self—we swear.
By the Life the Light to prove,
In the Circle's bound to move;
Underneath the all-seeing Eye
Act, nor speak, nor think the lie;
Live, as warned that Life shall last,
And the Future reap the Past:
Clasp in faith the Serpent's rings,
Trust through death the Emerald Wings,
Hand and voice we plight the Oath:
Fade the life ere fail the troth!"

Rising from his seat and standing immediately before and to the left of the Throne, Esmo replied. But before he had spoken half-a-dozen words, a pressure on my arm drew my eyes from him to Eveena. She stood fixed as if turned to stone, in an attitude which for one fleeting instant recalled that of the sculptured figures undergoing sudden petrifaction at the sight of the Gorgon's head. This remembered resemblance, or an instinctive sympathy, at once conveyed to me the consciousness that the absolute stillness of her attitude expressed a horror or an awe too deep for trembling. Looking into her eyes, which alone were visible, their gaze fixed intently on the Throne, at once caught and controlled my own; and raising my eyes again to the same point, I stood almost equally petrified by consternation and amazement. I need not say how many marvels of no common character I have seen on Earth; how many visions that, if I told them, none who have not shared them would believe; wonders that the few who have seen them can never forget, nor—despite all experience and all theoretical explanation—recall without renewing the thrill of awe-stricken dismay with which the sight was first beheld. But no marvel of the Mystic Schools,

no spectral scene, objective or subjective, ever evoked by the rarest of occult powers, so startled, so impressed me as what I now saw, or thought I saw. The Throne, on which but a few moments before my eyes had been steadily fixed, and which had then assuredly been vacant, was now occupied; and occupied by a Presence which, though not seen in the flesh for ages, none who had ever looked on the portrait that represented it could forget or mistake. The form, the dress, the long white hair and beard, the grave, dignified countenance, above all the deep, scrutinising, piercing eyes of the Founder—as I had seen them on a single occasion in Esmo's house—were now as clearly, as forcibly, presented to my sight as any figure in the flesh I ever beheld. The eyes were turned on me with a calm, searching, steady gaze, whose effect was such as Southey ascribes to Indra's:—

"The look he gave was solemn, not severe;
No hope to Kailyal it conveyed,
And yet it struck no fear."

For a moment they rested on Eveena's veiled and drooping figure with a widely different expression. That look, as I thought, spoke a grave but passionless regret or pity, as of one who sees a child unconsciously on the verge of peril or sorrow that admits neither of warning nor rescue. That look happily she did not read; but we both saw the same object and in the same instant; we both stood amazed and appalled long enough to render our hesitation not only apparent, but striking to all around, many of whom, following the direction of my gaze, turned their eyes upon the Throne.

What they saw or did not see I know not, and did not then care to think.

The following formula, pronounced by Esmo, had fallen not unheard, but almost unheeded on my ears, though one passage harmonised strangely with the sight before me:—

"Passing sign and fleeting breath
Bind the Soul for life and death!
Lifted hand and plighted word
Eyes have seen and ears have heard;
  Eyes have seen—nor ours alone;
Fell the sound on ears unknown.
Age-long labour, strand by strand,
Forged the immemorial band;
Never thread hath known decay,
Never link hath dropped away."

Here he paused and beckoned us to advance. The sign, twice repeated before I could obey it, at last broke the spell that enthralled me. Under the most astounding or awe-striking circumstances, instinct moves our limbs almost in our own despite, and leads us to do with paralysed will what has been intended or is expected of us. This instinct, and no conscious resolve to overcome the influence that held me spell-bound, enabled me to proceed; and I led Eveena forward by actual if gentle force, till we reached the lower step of the platform. Here, at a sign from her father, we knelt, while, laying his hands on our heads, and stooping to kiss each upon the brow—Eveena raising her veil for one moment and dropping it again—he continued—

"So we greet you evermore,
Brethren of the deathless Lore;
So your vows our own renew,
Sworn to all as each to you.
Yours at once the secrets won
Age by age, from sire to son;
Yours the fruit through countless years
Grown by thought and toil and tears.
He who guards you guards his own,
He who fails you fails the Throne."

The last two lines were repeated, as by a simultaneous impulse, in a low but audible tone by the whole assembly. In the meantime Esmo had invested each of us with the symbol of our enrolment in the Zinta, the silver sash and Star of the Initiates. The ceremonial seemed to me to afford that sort of religious sanction and benediction which had been so signally wanting to the original form of our union. As we rose I turned my eyes for a moment upon the Throne, now vacant as at first. Another Chief, followed by the voices of the assembly, repeated, in a low deep tone, which fell on our ears as distinctly as the loudest trumpet-note in the midst of absolute silence, the solemn imprecation—

"Who denies a brother's need,
Who in will, or word, or deed,
Breaks the Circle's bounded line,
Rends the Veil that guards the Shrine,
Lifts the hand to lips that lie,
Fronts the Star with soothless eye:—.
Dreams of horror haunt his rest,
Storms of madness vex his breast,
Snares surround him, Death beset,
Man forsake—and God forget!"

It was probably rather the tone of profound conviction and almost tremulous awe with which these words were slowly enunciated by the entire assemblage, than their actual sense, though the latter is greatly weakened by my translation, that gave them an effect on my own mind such as no oath and no rite, however solemn, no religious ceremonial, no forms of the most secret mysteries, had ever produced. I was not surprised that Eveena was far more deeply affected. Even the earlier words of the imprecation had caused her to shudder; and ere it closed she would have sunk to the ground, but for the support of my arm. Disengaging the bracelet, Esmo held out to our lips the signet, which, as I now perceived, reproduced in miniature the symbols that formed the canopy above the throne. A few moments of deep and solemn silence had elapsed, when one

of the Chiefs, who, except Esmo, had now resumed their seats, rose, and addressing himself to the latter, said—

"The Initiate has shown in the Hall of the Vision a knowledge of the sense embodied in our symbols, of the creed and thoughts drawn from them, which he can hardly have learned in the few hours that have elapsed since you first spoke to him of their existence. If there be not in his world those who have wrought out for themselves similar truths in not dissimilar forms, he must possess a rare and almost instinctive power to appreciate the lessons we can teach. I will ask your permission, therefore, to put to him but one question, and that the deepest and most difficult of all."

Esmo merely bent his head in reply.

"Can you," said the speaker, turning to me with marked courtesy, "draw meaning or lesson from the self-entwined coil of the Serpent?"

I need not repeat an answer which, to those familiar with the oldest language of Terrestrial symbolism, would have occurred as readily as to myself; and which, if they could understand it, it would not be well to explain to others. The three principal elements of thought represented by the doubly-coiled serpent are the same in Mars as on Earth, confirming in so far the doctrine of the Zinta, that their symbolic language is not arbitrary, but natural, formed on principles inherent in the correspondence between things spiritual and physical. Some similar but trivial query, whose purport I have now forgotten, was addressed by the junior of the Chiefs to Eveena; and I was struck by the patient courtesy with which he waited till, after two or three efforts, she sufficiently recovered her self-possession to understand and her voice to answer. We then retired, taking our place on seats remote from the platform, and at some distance from any of our neighbours.

On a formal invitation, one after another of the brethren rose and read a brief account of some experiment or discovery in the science of the Order.

The principles taken for granted as fundamental and notorious truths far transcend the extremest speculations of Terrestrial mysticism. The powers claimed as of course so infinitely exceed anything alleged by the most

ardent believers in mesmerism, clairvoyance, or spiritualism, that it would be useless to relate the few among these experiments which I remember and might be permitted to repeat. I observed that a phonographic apparatus of a peculiarly elaborate character wrote down every word of these accounts without obliging the speakers to approach it; and I was informed that this automatic reporting is employed in every Martial assembly, scientific, political, or judicial.

I listened with extreme interest, and was more than satisfied that Esmo had even underrated the powers claimed by and for the lowest and least intelligent of his brethren, when he said that these, and these alone, could give efficient protection or signal vengeance against all the tremendous physical forces at command of those State authorities, one of the greatest of whom I had made my personal enemy. One battalion of Martial guards or police, accompanied by a single battery of what I may call their artillery, might, even without the aid of a balloon-squadron, in half-an-hour annihilate or scatter to the winds the mightiest and bravest army that Europe could send forth. Yet the Martial State had deliberately, and, I think, with only a due prudence, shrunk during ages from an open conflict of power with the few thousand members of this secret but inevitably suspected organisation.

Esmo called on me in my turn to give such account as I might choose of my own world, and my journey thence. I frankly avowed my indisposition to explain the generation and action of the apergic force. The power which a concurrent knowledge of two separate kinds of science had given to a very few Terrestrials, and which all the science of a far more enlightened race had failed to attain, was in my conscientious conviction a Providential trust; withheld from those in whose hands it might be a fearful temptation and an instrument of unbounded evil. My reserve was perfectly intelligible to the Children of the Star, and evidently raised me in their estimation. I was much impressed by the simple and unaffected reliance placed on my statements, as on those of every other member of the Order. As a rule, Martialists are both, and not without reason, to believe any unsupported statement that might be prompted by interest or vanity. But the Zveltau

can trust one another's word more fully than the followers of Mahomet that of his strictest disciples, or the most honest nations of the West the most solemn oaths of their citizens; while that bigotry of scientific unbelief, that narrowness of thought which prevails among their countrymen, has been dispelled by their wider studies and loftier interests. They have a saying, whose purport might be rendered in the proverbial language of the Aryans by saying that the liar "kills the goose that lays the golden eggs." Again,

"The liar is like an opiatised tunneller" (miner), i.e., more likely to blow himself to pieces than to effect his purpose. Again, "The liar drives the point into a friend's heart, and puts the hilt into a foe's hand." The maxim that "a lie is a shield in sore need, but the spear of a scoundrel," affirms the right in extremity to preserve a secret from impertinent inquisitiveness.

Rarely, but on some peculiarly important occasions, the Zveltau avouch their sincerity by an appeal to their own symbols; and it is affirmed that an oath attested by the Circle and the Star has never, in the lapse of ages, been broken or evaded.

Before midnight Esmo dismissed the assembly by a formula which dimly recalled to memory one heard in my boyhood. It is not in the power of my translation to preserve the impressive solemnity of the immemorial ritual of the Zinta, deepened alike by the earnestness of its delivery, and the reverence of the hearers. There was something majestic in the mere antiquity of a liturgy whereof no word has ever been committed to writing.

Five hundred generations have, it is alleged, gathered four times in each year in the Hall of Initiation; and every meeting has been concluded by the utterance from the same spot and in the same words of the solemn but simple Zulvakalfe [word of peace]:—

"Peace be with you, near and far,
Children of the Silver Star;
Lore undoubting, conscience clean,
Hope assured, and life serene.
By the Light that knows no flaw,
By the Circle's perfect law,
By the Serpent's life renewed,
By the Wings' similitude—
Peace be yours no force can break;
Peace not death hath power to shake;
Peace from passion, sin, and gloom,
Peace of spirit, heart, and home;
Peace from peril, fear, and pain;
Peace, until we meet again—
Meet—before yon sculptured stone,
Or the All-Commander's Throne."

Before we finally parted, Esmo gave me two or three articles to which he attached especial value. The most important of these was a small cube of translucent stone, in which a multitude of diversely coloured fragments were combined; so set in a tiny swivel or swing of gold that it might be conveniently attached to the watch-chain, the only Terrestrial article that I still wore. "This," he said, "will test nearly every poison known to our science; each poison discolouring for a time one or another of the various substances of which it is composed; and poison is perhaps the weapon least unlikely to be employed against you when known to be connected with myself, and, I will hope, to possess the favour of the Sovereign. If you are curious to verify its powers, the contents of the tiny medicine-chest I have given you will enable you to do so. There is scarcely one of those medicines which is not a single or a combined poison of great power. I need not warn you to be careful lest you give to any one the means of reaching them. I have shown you the combination of magnets which will open each of your cases; that demanded by the chest is the most complicated of all, and one which can hardly be hit upon by accident. Nor can any one force or pick open a case locked by our electric apparatus, save by cutting to pieces the metal of the case itself, and this only special tools will accomplish; and, unless peculiarly skilful, the intruder would 'probably be maimed or paralysed, if not killed by ...

"Thoughts he sends to each planet, Uranus, Venus, and Mars;
Soars to the Centre to span it,
Numbers the infinite Stars."
Courthope's Paradise of Birds

CHAPTER XIV - BY SEA.

An hour after sunrise next morning. Esmo, his son, and our host accompanied us to the vessel in which we were to make the principal part of our journey. We were received by an officer of the royal Court, who was to accompany us during the rest of our journey, and from whom, Esrno assured me, I might obtain the fullest information regarding the various objects of interest, to visit which we had adopted an unusual and circuitous course. We embarked on a gulf running generally from east to west, about midway between the northern tropic and the arctic circle. As this was the summer of the northern hemisphere, we should thus enjoy a longer day, and should not suffer from the change of climate. After taking leave of our friends, we went down below to take possession of the fore part of the vessel, which was assigned as our exclusive quarters. Immediately in front of the machine-room, which occupied the centre of the vessel, were two cabins, about sixteen feet square, reaching from side to side. Beyond these, opening out of a passage running along one side, were two smaller cabins about eight feet long. All these apartments were furnished and ornamented with the luxury and elegance of chambers in the best houses on shore. In the foremost of the larger cabins were a couple of desks, and three or four writing or easy chairs. In the outer cabin nearest to the engine-room, and entered immediately by the ladder descending from the deck, was fixed a low central table. In all we found abundance of those soft exquisitely covered and embroidered cushions which in Mars, as in Oriental countries, are the most essential and most luxurious furniture. The officer had quarters in the stern of the vessel, which was an exact copy of the fore part.

But the first of these rooms was considered as public or neutral ground.

Leaving Eveena below, I went on deck to examine, before she started, the construction of the vessel. Her entire length was about one hundred and eighty feet, her depth, from the flat deck to the wide keel, about one half of her breadth; the height of the cabins not much more than eight feet; her draught, when most completely lightened, not more than four feet. Her electric machinery drew in and drove out with great force currents of water which propelled her with a speed greater than that afforded by the most powerful paddles. It also pumped in or out, at whatever depth, the quantity of water required as ballast, not merely to steady the vessel, but to keep her in position on the surface or to sink her to the level at which the pilot might choose to sail. At either end was fixed a steering screw, much resembling the tail-fin of a fish, capable of striking sideways, upwards, or downwards, and directing our course accordingly.

Ergimo, our escort, had not yet reached middle age, but was a man of exceptional intellect and unusual knowledge. He had made many voyages, and had occupied for some time an important official post on one of those Arctic continents which are inhabited only by the hunters employed in collecting the furs and skins furnished exclusively by these lands. The shores of the gulf were lofty, rocky, and uninteresting. It was difficult to see any object on shore from the deck of the vessel, and I assented, therefore, without demur, after the first hour of the voyage, to his proposal that the lights, answering to our hatches, should be closed, and that the vessel should pursue her course below the surface. This was the more desirable that, though winds and storms are, as I have said, rare, these long and narrow seas with their lofty shores are exposed to rough currents, atmospheric and marine, which render a voyage on the surface no more agreeable than a passage in average weather across the Bay of Biscay. After descending I was occupied for some time in studying, with Ergimo's assistance, the arrangement of the machinery, and the simple process by which electric force is generated in quantities adequate to any effort at a marvellously small expenditure of material. In this form the Martialists assert that they obtain without waste all the potential energy stored in …

[About half a score lines, or two pages of an ordinary octavo volume like this, are here illegible.] She (Eveena?) was somewhat pale, but rose quickly, and greeted me with a smile of unaffected cheerfulness, and was evidently surprised as well as pleased that I was content to remain alone with her, our conversation turning chiefly on the lessons of last night. Our time passed quickly till, about the middle of the day, we were startled by a shock which, as I thought, must be due to our having run aground or struck against a rock. But when I passed into the engine-room, Ergimo explained that the pilot was nowise in fault. We had encountered one of those inconveniences, hardly to be called perils, which are peculiar to the

waters of Mars. Though animals hostile or dangerous to man have been almost extirpated upon the land, creatures of a type long since supposed to be extinct on Earth still haunt the depths of the Martial seas; and one of these—a real sea-serpent of above a hundred feet in length and perhaps eight feet in circumference—had attacked our vessel, entangling the steering screw in his folds and trying to crush it, checking, at the same time, by his tremendous force the motion of the vessel.

"We shall soon get rid of him, though," said Ergimo, as I followed him to the stern, to watch with great interest the method of dealing with the monster, whose strange form was visible through a thick crystal pane in the stern-plate. The asphyxiator could not have been used without great risk to ourselves. But several tubes, filled with a soft material resembling cork, originally the pith of a Martial cane of great size, were inserted in the floor, sides, and deck of the vessel, and through the centre of each of these passed a strong metallic wire of great conducting power. Two or three of those in the stern were placed in contact with some of the electric machinery by which the rudder was usually turned, and through them were sent rapid and energetic currents, whose passage rendered the covering of the wires, notwithstanding their great conductivity, too hot to be touched. We heard immediately a smothered sound of extraordinary character, which was, in truth, no other than a scream deadened partly by the water, partly by the thick metal sheet interposed between us and the element. The steering screw was set in rapid motion, and at first revolving with some difficulty, afterwards moving faster and more regularly, presently released us. Its rotation was stopped, and we resumed our course. The serpent had relaxed his folds, stunned by the shock, but had not disentangled himself from the screw, till its blades, no longer checked by the tremendous force of his original grasp, striking him a series of terrific blows, had broken the vertebrae and paralysed if not killed the monstrous enemy.

At each side of the larger chambers and of the engine-room were fixed small thick circular windows, through which we could see from time to time the more remarkable objects in the water. We passed along one

curious submarine bank, built somewhat like our coral rocks, not by insects, however, but by shellfish, which, fixing themselves as soon as hatched on the shells below or around them, extended slowly upward and sideways. As each of these creatures perished, the shell, about half the size of an oyster, was filled with the same sort of material as that of which its hexagonic walls were originally formed, drawn in by the surrounding and still living neighbours; and thus, in the course of centuries, were constructed solid reefs of enormous extent. One of these had run right across the gulf, forming a complete bridge, ceasing, however, within some five feet of the surface; but on this a regular roadway had been constructed by human art and mechanical labour, while underneath, at the usual depth of thirty feet, several tunnels had been pierced, each large enough to admit the passage of a single vessel of the largest size. At every fourth hour our vessel rose to the surface to renew her atmosphere, which was thus kept purer than that of an ordinary Atlantic packet between decks, while the temperature was maintained at an agreeable point by the warmth diffused from the electric machinery.

On the sixth day of our voyage, we reached a point where the Gulf of Serocasfe divides, a sharp jutting cape or peninsula parting its waters. We took the northern branch, about fifteen miles in width, and here, rising to the surface and steering a zigzag course from coast to coast, I was enabled to see something of the character of this most extraordinary strait. Its walls at first were no less than 2000 feet in height, so that at all times we were in sight, so to speak, of land. A road had been cut along the sea-level, and here and there tunnels ascending through the rock rendered this accessible from the plateau above. The strata, as upon Earth, were of various character, none of them very thick, seldom reproducing exactly the geology of our own planet, but seldom very widely deviating in character from the rocks with which we are acquainted. The lowest were evidently of the same hard, fused, compressed character as those which our terminology calls plutonic. Above these were masses which, bike the carboniferous strata of Earth, recalled the previous existence of a richer but less highly organised form of vegetation than at present exists anywhere upon the surface. Intermixed with these were beds of the peculiar submarine shell-

rock whose formation I have just described. Above these again come strata of diluvial gravel, and about 400 feet below the surface rocks that bore evident traces of a glacial period. As we approached the lower end of the gulf the shores sloped constantly downward, and where they were no more than 600 feet in height I was able to distinguish an upper stratum of some forty yards in depth, preserving through its whole extent traces of human life and even of civilisation. This implied, if fairly representative of the rest of the planet's crust, an existence of man upon its surface ten, twenty, or even a hundred-fold longer than he is supposed to have enjoyed upon Earth. About noon on the seventh day we entered the canal which connects this arm of the gulf with the sea of the northern temperate zone. It varies in height from 400 to 600 feet, in width from 100 to 300 yards, its channel never exceeds 20 feet in depth, Ergimo explained that the length had been thought to render a tunnel unsuitable, as the ordinary method of ventilation could hardly have been made to work, and to ventilate such a tunnel through shafts sunk to so great a depth would have been almost as costly as the method actually adopted. A much smaller breadth might have been thought to suffice, and was at first intended; but it was found that the current in a narrow channel, the outer sea being many inches higher than the water of the gulf, would have been too rapid and violent for safety. The work had occupied fifteen Martial years, and had been opened only for some eight centuries. The water was not more than twenty feet in depth; but the channel was so perfectly scoured by the current that no obstacle had ever arisen and no expense had been incurred to keep it a clear. We entered the Northern sea where a bay ran up some half dozen miles towards the end of the gulf, shortening the canal by this distance. The bay itself was shallow, the only channel being scarcely wider than the canal, and created or preserved by the current setting in to the latter; a current which offered a very perceptible resistance to our course, and satisfied me that had the canal been no wider than the convenience of navigation would have required in the absence of such a stream, its force would have rendered the work altogether useless. We crossed the sea, holding on in the same direction, and a little before sunset moored our vessel at the wharf of

a small harbour, along the sides of which was built the largest town of this subarctic landbelt, a village of some fifty houses named Askinta.

CHAPTER XV - FUR-HUNTING.

Ergimo landed to make arrangements for the chase, to witness which was the principal object of this deviation from what would otherwise have been our most convenient course. Not only would it be possible to take part in the pursuit of the wild fauna of the continent, but I also hoped to share in a novel sport, not unlike a whale-hunt in Baffin's Bay. A large inland sea, occupying no inconsiderable part of the area of this belt, lay immediately to the northward, and one wide arm thereof extended within a few miles of Askirita, a distance which, notwithstanding the interposition of a mountain range, might be crossed in a couple of hours. One or two days at most would suffice for both adventures. I had not yet mentioned my intention to Eveena. During the voyage I had been much alone with her, and it was then only that our real acquaintance began. Till then, however close our attachment, we were, in knowledge of each other's character and thought, almost as strangers. While her painful timidity had in some degree worn off, her anxious and watchful deference was even more marked than before. True to the strange ideas derived chiefly from her training, partly from her own natural character, she was the more careful to avoid giving the slightest pain or displeasure, as she ceased to fear that either would be immediately and intentionally visited upon herself. She evidently thought that on this account there was the greater danger lest a series of trivial annoyances, unnoticed at the time, might cool the affection she valued so highly. Diffident of her own charms, she knew how little hold the women of her race generally have on the hearts of men after the first fever of passion has cooled. It was difficult for her to realise that her thoughts or wishes could truly interest me, that compliance with her inclinations could be an object, or that I could be seriously bent on teaching her to speak frankly and openly. But as this new idea became credible and familiar, her unaffected desire to comply with all that was expected from her drew out her hitherto undeveloped powers of conversation, and enabled me day by day to appreciate more thoroughly the real intelligence and soundness of judgment concealed at first by her shyness, and still somewhat obscured by her childlike simplicity and absolute inexperience. In the latter respect, however, she was, of course, at the less disadvantage with a stranger to the

manners and life of her world. A more perfectly charming companion it would have been difficult to desire and impossible to find. If at first I had been secretly inclined to reproach her with exaggerated timidity, it became more and more evident that her personal fears were due simply to that nervous susceptibility which even men of reputed courage have often displayed in situations of sudden and wholly unfamiliar peril. Her tendency to overrate all dangers, not merely as they affected herself, but as they might involve others, and above all her husband, I ascribed to the ideas and habits of thought now for so many centuries hereditary among a people in whom the fear of annihilation—and the absence of all the motives that impel men on earth to face danger and death with calmness, or even to enjoy the excitement of deadly peril—have extinguished manhood itself.

I could not, however, conceal from Eveena that I was about to leave her for an adventure which could not but seem to her foolhardy and motiveless.

She was more than terrified when she understood that I really intended to join the professional hunters in an enterprise which, even on their part, is regarded by their countrymen with a mixture of admiration and contempt, as one wherein only the hope of large remuneration would induce any sensible man to share; and which, from my utter ignorance of its conditions, must be obviously still more dangerous to me. The confidence she was slowly learning from what seemed to her extravagant indulgence, to me simply the consideration due to a rational being, wife or comrade, slave or free, first found expression in the freedom of her loving though provoking expostulations.

"You must be tired of me," she said at last, "if you are so ready to run the risk of parting out of mere curiosity."

"Sheer petulance!" I answered. "You know well that you are dearer to me every day as I learn to understand you better; but a man cannot afford to play the coward because marriage has given new value to life. And you might remember that I have threefold the strength which emboldens your hunters to incur all the dangers that seem to your fancy so terrible."

That no shade of mere cowardice or feminine affectation influenced her remonstrance was evident from her next words.

"Well, then, if you will go, however improper and outrageous the thing may be, let me go with you. I cannot bear to wait alone, fancying at every moment what may be happening to you, and fearing to see them carry you back wounded or killed."

Touched by the unselfishness of her terror, and feeling that there was some truth in her representation of the state of mind in which she would spend the hours of my absence, I tried to quiet her by caresses and soft words. But these she received as symptoms of yielding on my part; and her persistence brought upon her at last the resolute and somewhat sharp rebuke with which men think it natural and right to repress the excesses of feminine fear.

"This is nonsense, Eveena. You cannot accompany me; and, if you could, your presence would multiply tenfold the danger to me, and utterly unnerve me if any real difficulty should call for presence of mind. You must be content to leave me in the hands of Providence, and allow me to judge what becomes a man, and what results are worth the risks they may involve. I hear Ergimo's step on deck, and I must go and learn from him what arrangements he has been able to make for to-morrow."

My escort had found no difficulty in providing for the fulfilment of both my wishes. We were to beat the forests which covered the southern seabord in the neighbourhood, driving our game out upon the open ground, where alone we should have a chance of securing it. By noon we might hope to have seen enough of this sport, and to find ourselves at no great distance from that part of the inland sea where a yet more exciting chase was to employ the rest of the day. Failing to bring both adventures within the sixteen hours of light which at this season and in this latitude we should enjoy, we were to bivouac for the night on the northern sea-coast and pursue our aquatic game in the morning of the morrow, returning before dark to our vessel.

Ergimo, however, was more of Eveena's mind than of mine. "I have complied," he said, "with your wishes, as the Camptâ ordered me to do.

But I am equally bound, by his orders and by my duty, to tell you that in my opinion you are running risks altogether out of proportion to any object our adventure can serve. Scarcely any of the creatures we shall hunt are other than very formidable. Eyen the therne, with the spikes on its fore-limbs, can inflict painful if not dangerous wounds, and its bite is said to be not unfrequently venomous. You are not used to our methods of hunting, to the management of the caldecta, or to the use of our weapons. I can conceive no reason why you should incur what is at any rate a considerable chance, not merely of death, but of defeating the whole purpose of your extraordinary journey, simply to do or to see the work on which we peril only the least valuable lives among us."

I was about to answer him even more decidedly than I had replied to Eveena, when a pressure on my arm drew my eyes in the other direction; and, to my extreme mortification, I perceived that Eveena herself, in all-absorbing eagerness to learn the opinion of an intelligent and experienced hunter, had stolen on deck and had heard all that had passed. I was too much vexed to make any other reply to Ergimo's argument than the single word, "I shall go." Really angry with her for the first and last time, but not choosing to express my displeasure in the presence of a third person, I hurried Eveena down the ladder into our cabin.

"Tell me," I said, "what, according to your own rules of feminine reserve and obedience, you deserve? What would one of your people say to a wife who followed him without leave into the company of a stranger, to listen to that which she knew she was not meant to hear?"

She answered by throwing off her veil and head-dress, and standing up silent before me.

"Answer me, child," I repeated, more than half appeased by the mute appeal of her half-raised eyes and submissive attitude. "I know you will not tell me that you have not broken all the restraints of your own laws and customs. What would your father, for instance, say to such an escapade?"

She was silent, till the touch of my hand, contradicting perhaps the harshness of my words, encouraged her to lift her eyes, full of tears, to mine.

"Nothing," was her very unexpected reply.

"Nothing?" I rejoined. "If you can tell me that you have not done wrong, I shall be sorry to have reproved you so sharply."

"I shall tell you no such lie!" she answered almost indignantly. "You asked what would be said."

I was fairly at a loss. The figure which Martial grammarians call "the suppressed alternative" is a great favourite, and derives peculiar force from the varied emphasis their syntax allows. But, resolved not to understand a meaning much more distinctly conveyed in her words than in my translation, I replied, "I shall say nothing then, except—don't do it again;"

and I extricated myself promptly if ignominiously from the dilemma, by leaving the cabin and closing the door, so sharply and decidedly as to convey a distinct intimation that it was not again to be opened.

We breakfasted earlier than usual. My gentle bride had been subdued into a silence, not sullen, but so sad that when her wistful eyes followed my every movement as I prepared to start, I could willingly, to bring back their brightness, have renounced the promise of the day. But this must not be; and turning to take leave on the threshold, I said—

"Be sure I shall come to no harm; and if I did, the worst pang of death would be the memory of the first sharp words I have spoken to you, and which, I confess, were an ill return for the inconvenient expression of your affectionate anxiety."

"Do not speak so," she half whispered. "I deserved any mark of your displeasure; I only wish I could persuade you that the sharpest sting lies in the lips we love. Do remember, since you would not let me run the slightest risk of harm, that if you come to hurt you will have killed me."

"Rest assured I shall come to no serious ill. I hope this evening to laugh with you at your alarms; and so long as you do not see me either in the

flesh or in the spirit, you may know that I am safe. I could not leave you for ever without meeting you again."

This speech, which I should have ventured in no other presence, would hardly have established my lunacy more decisively in Martial eyes than in those of Terrestrial common sense. It conveyed, however, a real if not sufficient consolation to Eveena; the idea it implied being not wholly unfamiliar to a daughter of the Star. I was surprised that, almost shrinking from my last embrace, Eveena suddenly dropped her veil around her; till, turning, I saw that Ergimo was standing at the top of the ladder leading to the deck, and just in sight.

"I will send word," he said, addressing himself to me, but speaking for her ears, "of your safety at noon and at night. So far as my utmost efforts can ensure it you will be safe; an obligation higher, and enforced by sanctions graver, than even the Camptâ's command forbids me to lead a brother into peril, and fail to bring him out of it."

The significant word was spoken in so low a tone that it could not possibly reach the ears of our companions of the chase, who had mustered on shore within a few feet of the vessel. But Eveena evidently caught both the sound and the meaning, and I was glad that they should convey to her a confidence which seemed to myself no better founded than her alarms. To me its only value lay in the friendly relation it established with one I had begun greatly to like. I relied on my own strength and nerve for all that human exertion could do in such peril as we might encounter; and, in a case in which these might fail me, I doubted whether even the one tie that has binding force on Mars would avail me much.

Immediately outside the town were waiting, saddled but not bridled, some score of the extraordinary riding-birds Eveena had described. The seat of the rider is on the back, between the wings; but the saddle consists only of a sort of girth immediately in front, to which a pair of stirrups, resembling that of a lady's side-saddle, were attached. The creature that was to carry my unusual weight was the most powerful of all, but I felt some doubt whether even his strength might not break down. One of the hunters had charge of a carriage on which was fixed a cage containing two dozen birds

of a dark greenish grey, about the size of a crow, and with the slender form, piercing eyes, and powerful beak of the falcon. They were not intended, however, to strike the prey, but simply to do the part of dogs in tracing out the game, and driving it from the woods into the open ground.

Our birds, rising at once into the air, carried us some fifty feet above the tops of the trees. Here the chief huntsman took the guidance of the party, keeping in front of the line in which we were ranged, and watching through a pair of what might be called spectacles, save that a very short tube with double lenses was substituted for the single glass, the movement of the hawks, which had been released in the wood below us. These at first dispersed in every direction, extending at intervals from end to end of a line some three miles in length, and moving slowly forwards, followed by the hunters. A sharp call from one bird on the left gathered the rest around him, and in a few moments the rustling and rushing of an invisible flock through the glades of the forest apprised us that we had started, though we could not see, the prey. Ergimo, who kept close beside me, and who had often witnessed the sport before, kept me informed of what was proceeding underneath us, of which I could see but little. Glimpses here and there showed that we were pursuing a numerous flock of large white-plumed or white-haired creatures, standing at most some four feet in height; but what they were, even whether birds or quadrupeds, their movements left me in absolute uncertainty. Worried and frightened by the falcons, which, however, never ventured to close upon them, they were gradually driven in the direction intended by the huntsman towards the open plain, which bordered the forest at a distance of about six miles to the northward. In half-an-hour after the "find," the leader of the flock broke out of the wood two or three hundred yards ahead of us, and was closely followed by his companions. I then recognised in the objects of the chase the strange thernee described by Eveena, whose long soft down furnished the cloak she wore on our visit to the Astronaut. Their general form, and especially the length and graceful curve of the neck, led one instinctively to regard them as birds; but the fore-limbs, drawn up as they ran, but now and then outstretched with a sweep to strike at a falcon that ventured imprudently near, had, in the distance, much more resemblance to the arm

of a baboon than to the limb of any other creature, and bore no likeness whatever to the wing even of the bat. The object of the hunters was not to strike these creatures from a distance, but to run them down and capture them by sheer exhaustion. This the great wing-power of the caldectaa enabled us to do, though by the time we had driven the thernee to bay my own Pegasus was fairly tired. The hunters, separating and spreading out in the form of a semicircle, assisted the movements of the hawks, driving the prey gradually into a narrow defile among the hills bordering the plain to the north-eastward, whose steep upward slope greatly hindered and fatigued creatures whose natural habitat consists of level plains or seabord forests. At last, under a steep half-precipitous rock which defended them in rear, and between clumps of trees which guarded either flank—protected by both overhead—the flock, at the call of their leader, took up a position which displayed an instinctive strategy, whereof an Indian or African chief might have been proud. The caldectaa, however, well knew the vast superiority of their own strength and of their formidable beaks, and did not hesitate to carry us close to but somewhat above the thernee, as these stood ranged in line with extended fore-limbs and snouts; the latter armed with teeth about an inch and a half in length tapering singly to a sharp point, the former with spikes stronger, longer, and sharper than those of the porcupine; but, as I satisfied myself by a subsequent inspection, formed by rudimentary, or, more properly speaking, transformed or degenerated quills. The bite was easily avoided. It was not so easy to keep out of reach of the powerful fore-limb while endeavouring to strike a fatal blow at the neck with the long rapier-like cutting weapons carried by the hunters. My own shorter and sharp sword, to which I had trusted, preferring a familiar weapon to one, however suitable, to which I was not accustomed, left me no choice but to abandon the hope of active participation in the slaughter, or to venture dangerously near. Choosing the latter alternative, I received from the arm of the thernee I had singled out a blow which, caught upon my sword, very nearly smote it from my hand, and certainly would have disarmed at once any of my weaker companions. As it was, the stroke maimed the limb that delivered it; but with its remaining arm the creature maintained a fight so stubborn that, had both been available, the issue

could not have been in my favour. This conflict reminded me singularly of an encounter with the mounted swordsmen of Scindiah and the Peishwah; all my experience of sword-play being called into use, and my brute opponent using its natural weapon with an instinctive skill not unworthy of comparison with that of a trained horse-soldier; at the same time that it constantly endeavoured to seize with its formidable snout either my own arm or the wing or body of the caldecta, which, however, was very well able to take care of itself. In fact, the prey was secured at last not by my sword but by a blow from the caldecta's beak, which pierced and paralysed the slender neck of our antagonist. Some twenty thernee formed the booty of a chase certainly novel, and possessing perhaps as many elements of peril and excitement as that finest of Earthly sports which the affected cynicism of Anglo-Indian speech degrades by the name of "pig-sticking."

When the falcons had been collected and recaged, and the bodies of the thernee consigned to a carriage brought up for the purpose by a subordinate who had watched the hunters' course, our birds, from which we had dismounted, were somewhat rested; and Ergimo informed me that another and more formidable, as well as more valuable, prey was thought to be in sight a few miles off. Mounted on a fresh bird, and resolutely closing my ears to his urgent and reasonable dissuasion, I joined the smaller party which was detached for this purpose. As we were carried slowly at no great distance from the ground, managing our birds with ease by a touch on either side of the neck—they are spurred at need by a slight electric shock communicated from the hilt of the sword, and are checked by a forcible pressure on the wings—I asked Ergimo why the thernee were not rather shot than hunted, since utility, not sport, governs the method of capturing the wild beasts of Mars.

"We have," he replied, "two weapons adapted to strike at a distance. The asphyxiator is too heavy to be carried far or fast, and pieces of the shell inflict such injuries upon everything in the immediate neighbourhood of the explosion, as to render it useless where the value of the prey depends upon the condition of its skin. Our other and much more convenient, if less powerful, projective weapon has also its own disadvantage. It can be used

only at short distances; and at these it is apt to burn and tear a skin so soft and delicate as that of the thernee. Moreover, it so terrifies the caldecta as to render it unmanageable; and we are compelled to dismount before using it, as you may presently see. Four or five of our party are now armed with it, and I wish you had allowed me to furnish you with one."

"I prefer," I answered, "my own weapon, an air-gun which I can fire sixteen times without reloading, and which will kill at a hundred yards' distance.

With a weapon unknown to me I might not only fail altogether, but I might not improbably do serious injury, by my clumsiness and inexperience, to my companions."

"I wish, nevertheless," he said, "that you carried the mordyta. You will have need of an efficient weapon if you dismount to share the attack we are just about to make. But I entreat you not to do so. You can see it all in perfect safety, if only you will keep far enough away to avoid danger from the fright of your bird."

As he spoke, we had come into proximity to our new game, a large and very powerful animal, about four feet high at the shoulders, and about six feet from the head to the root of the tail. The latter carries, as that of the lion was fabled to do, a final claw, not to lash the creature into rage, but for the more practical purpose of striking down an enemy endeavouring to approach it in flank or rear. Its hide, covered with a long beautifully soft fur, is striped alternately with brown and yellow, the ground being a sort of silver-grey. The head resembles that of the lion, but without the mane, and is prolonged into a face and snout more like those of the wild boar. Its limbs are less unlike those of the feline genus than any other Earthly type, but have three claws and a hard pad in lieu of the soft cushion. The upper jaw is armed with two formidable tusks about twelve inches in length, and projecting directly forwards. A blow from the claw-furnished tail would plough up the thigh or rip open the abdomen of a man. A stroke from one of the paws would fracture his skull, while a wound from the tusk in almost any part of the body must prove certainly fatal. Fortunately, the kargynda has not the swiftness of movement belonging to nearly all our feline races, otherwise its skins, the most valuable prize of the Martial

hunter, would yearly be taken at a terrible cost of life. Two of these creatures were said to be reposing in a thick jungle of reeds bordering a narrow stream immediately in our front. The hunters, with Ergimo, now dismounted and advanced some two hundred yards in front of their birds, directing the latter to turn their heads in the opposite direction. I found some difficulty in making my wish to descend intelligible to the docile creature which carried me, and was still in the air when one of the enormous creatures we were hunting rushed out of its hiding-place. The nearest hunter, raising a shining metal staff about three and a half feet in length (having a crystal cylinder at the hinder end, about six inches in circumference, and occupying about one-third the entire length of the weapon), levelled it at the beast. A flash as of lightning darted through the air, and the creature rolled over. Another flash from a similar weapon in the hands of another hunter followed. By this time, however, my bird was entirely unmanageable, and what happened I learned afterwards from Ergimo. Neither of the two shots had wounded the creature, though the near passage of the first had for a moment stunned and overthrown him.

His rush among the party dispersed them all, but each being able to send forth from his piece a second flash of lightning, the monster was mortally wounded before they fairly started in pursuit of their scared birds, which—

their attention being called by the roar of the animal, by the crash accompanying each flash, and probably above all by the restlessness of my own caldecta in their midst—had flown off to some distance. My bird, floundering forwards, flung me to the ground about two hundred yards from the jungle, fortunately at a greater distance from the dying but not yet utterly disabled prey. Its companion now came forth and stood over the tortured creature, licking its sores till it expired. By this time I had recovered the consciousness I had lost with the shock of my fall, and had ascertained that my gun was safe. I had but time to prepare and level it when, leaving its dead companion, the brute turned and charged me almost as rapidly as an infuriated elephant. I fired several times and assured, if only from my skill as a marksman, that some of the shots had hit it, was surprised to see that at each it was only checked for a moment and then resumed its charge. It was so near now that I could aim with some

confidence at the eye; and if, as I suspected, the previous shots had failed to pierce the hide, no other aim was likely to avail. I levelled, therefore, as steadily as I could at its blazing eyeballs and fired three or four shots, still without doing more than arrest or rather slacken its charge, each shot provoking a fearful roar of rage and pain. I fired my last within about twenty yards, and then, before I could draw my sword, was dashed to the ground with a violence that utterly stunned me. When I recovered my senses Ergimo was kneeling beside me pouring down my throat the contents of a small phial; and as I lifted my head and looked around, I saw the enormous carcass from under which I had been dragged lying dead almost within reach of my hand. One eye was pierced through the very centre, the other seriously injured. But such is the creature's tenacity of life, that, though three balls were actually in its brain, it had driven home its charge, though far too unconscious to make more than convulsive and feeble use of any of its formidable weapons. When I fell it stood for perhaps a second, and then dropped senseless upon my lower limbs, which were not a little bruised by its weight. That no bone was broken or dislocated by the shock, deadened though it must have been by the repeated pauses in the kargynda's charge and by its final exhaustion, was more than I expected or could understand. Before I rose to my feet, Ergimo had peremptorily insisted on the abandonment of the further excursion we had intended, declaring that he could not answer to his Sovereign, after so severe a lesson, for my exposure to any future peril. The Camptâ had sent him to bring me into his presence for purposes which would not be fulfilled by producing a lifeless carcass, or a maimed and helpless invalid; and the discipline of the Court and central Administration allowed no excuse for disobedience to orders or failure in duty. My protest was very quickly silenced. On attempting to stand, I found myself so shaken, torn, and shattered that I could not again mount a caldecta or wield a weapon; and was carried back to Askinta on a sort of inclined litter placed upon the carriage which had conveyed our booty.

I was mortified, as we approached the place where our vessel lay, to observe a veiled female figure on the deck. Eveena's quick eye had noted our return some minutes before, and inferred from the early abandonment

of the chase some serious accident. Happily our party were so disposed that I had time to assume the usual position before she caught sight of me. I could not, however, deceive her by a desperate effort to walk steadily and unaided. She stood by quietly and calmly while the surgeon of the hunters dressed my hurts, observing exactly how the bandages and lotions were applied. Only when we were left alone did she in any degree give way to an agitation by which she feared to increase my evident pain and feverishness. It was impossible to satisfy her that black bruises and broad gashes meant no danger, and would be healed by a few days' rest. But when she saw that I could talk and smile as usual, she was unsparing in her attempts to coax from me a pledge that I would never again peril life or limb to gratify my curiosity regarding the very few pursuits in which, for the highest remuneration, Martialists can be induced to incur the probability of injury and the chance of that death they so abjectly dread.

Scarcely less reluctant to repeat the scolding she felt so acutely than to employ the methods of rebuke she deemed less severe, I had no little difficulty in evading her entreaties. Only a very decided request to drop the subject at once and for ever, enforced on her conscience by reminding her that it would be enforced no otherwise, at last obtained me peace without the sacrifice of liberty.

CHAPTER XVI - TROUBLED WATERS.

We were now in Martial N. latitude 57°, in a comparatively open part of the narrow sea which encloses the northern land-belt, and to the south-eastward lay the only channel by which this sea communicates with the main ocean of the southern hemisphere. Along this we took our course.

Rather against Ergimo's advice, I insisted on remaining on the surface, as the sea was tolerably calm. Eveena, with her usual self-suppression, professed to prefer the free air, the light of the long day, and such amusement as the sight of an occasional sea-monster or shoal of fishes afforded, to the fainter light and comparative monotony of submarine travelling. Ergimo, who had in his time commanded the hunters of the Arctic Sea, was almost as completely exempt as myself from sea-sickness; but I was surprised to find that the crew disliked, and, had they ventured, would have grumbled at, the change, being so little accustomed to any long superficial voyage as to suffer like landsmen from rough weather. The difference between sailing on and below the surface is so great, both in comfort and in the kind of skill and knowledge required, that the seamen of passenger and of mercantile vessels are classes much more distinct than those of the mercantile and national marine of England, or any other maritime Power on Earth. I consented readily that, except on the rare occasions when the heavens were visible, the short night, from the fall of the evening to the dissipation of the morning mists, should be passed under water. I have said that gales are comparatively rare and the tides insignificant; but the narrow and exceedingly long channels of the Martial seas, with the influence of a Solar movement from north to south more extensive though slower than that which takes place between our Winter and Summer Solstices, produce currents, atmospheric and oceanic, and sudden squalls that often give rise to that worst of all disturbances of the surface, known as a "chopping sea." When we crossed the tropic and came fairly into the channel separating the western coast of the continent on which the Astronaut had landed from the eastern seabord of that upon whose southern coast I was presently to disembark, this disturbance was even worse than, except on peculiarly disagreeable occasions, in the Straits of Dover. After enduring this for two or three hours, I observed that

Eveena had stolen from her seat beside me on the deck. Since we left Askinta her spirits had been unusually variable. She had been sometimes lively and almost excitable; more generally quiet, depressed, and silent even beyond her wont. Still, her manner and bearing were always so equable, gentle, and docile that, accustomed to the caprices of the sex on Earth, I had hardly noticed the change. I thought, however, that she was to-day nervous and somewhat pale; and as she did not return, after permitting the pilot to seek a calmer stratum at some five fathoms depth, I followed Eveena into our cabin or chamber. Standing with her back to the entrance and with a goblet to her lips, she did not hear me till I had approached within arm's length. She then started violently, so agitated that the colour faded at once from her countenance, leaving it white as in a swoon, then as suddenly returning, flushed her neck and face, from the emerald shoulder clasps to the silver snood, with a pink deeper than that of her robe.

"I am very sorry I startled you," I said. "You are certainly ill, or you would not be so easily upset."

I laid my hand as I spoke on her soft tresses, but she withdrew from the touch, sinking down among the cushions. Leaving her to recover her composure, I took up the half-empty cup she had dropped on the central table. Thirsty myself, I had almost drained without tasting it, when a little half-stifled cry of dismay checked me. The moment I removed the cup from my mouth I perceived its flavour—the unmistakable taste of the dravadoné ("courage cup"), so disagreeable to us both, which we had shared on our bridal evening. Wetting with one drop the test-stone attached to my watch-chain, it presented the local discoloration indicating the narcotic poison which is the chief ingredient of this compound.

"I don't think this is wise, child," I said, turning once more to Eveena. To my amazement, far from having recovered the effect of her surprise, she was yet more overcome than at first; crouching among the cushions with her head bent down over her knees, and covering her face with her hands.

Reclining in the soft pile, I held her in my arms, overcoming perforce what
seemed hysterical reluctance; but when I would have withdrawn the little hands, she threw herself on my knee, burying her face in the cushions.

"It is very wicked," she sobbed; "I cannot ask you to forgive me."

"Forgive what, my child? Eveena, you are certainly ill. Calm yourself, and don't try to talk just now."

"I am not ill, I assure you," she faltered, resisting the arm that sought to raise her; "but …"

In my hands, however, she was powerless as an infant; and I would hear nothing till I held her gathered within my arm and her two hands fast in my right. Now that I could look into the face she strove to avert, it was clear that she was neither hysterical nor simply ill; her agitation, however unreasonable and extravagant, was real.

"What troubles you, my own? I promise you not to say one word of reproach; I only want to understand with what you so bitterly reproach yourself."

"But you cannot help being angry," she urged, "if you understand what I have done. It is the charny, which I never tasted till that night, and never ought to have tasted again. I know you cannot forgive me; only take my fault for granted, and don't question me."

These incoherent words threw the first glimpse of light on the meaning of her distress and penitence. I doubt if the best woman in Christendom would so reproach and abase herself, if convicted of even a worse sin than the secret use of those stimulants for which the charny is a Martial equivalent. No Martialist would dream of poisoning his blood and besotting his brain with alcohol in any form. But their opiates affect a race addicted to physical repose, to sensuous enjoyment rather than to sensual excitement, and to lucid intellectual contemplation, with a sense of serene delight as supremely delicious to their temperament as the dreamy illusions of haschisch to the Turk, the fierce frenzy of bhang to the Malay, or the wild excitement of brandy or Geneva to the races of Northern Europe. But as with the luxury of intoxication in Europe, so in Mars indulgence in these drugs, freely permitted to the one sex, is strictly
forbidden by opinion and domestic rule to the other. A lady discovered in the use of charny is as deeply disgraced as an European matron detected in the secret enjoyment of spirits and cigars; and her lord and master takes care to render her sufficiently conscious of her fault.

And there was something stranger here than a violation of the artificial restraint of sex. Slightly and seldom as the Golden Circle touches the lines defining personal or social morality—carefully as the Founder has abstained from imposing an ethical code of his own, or attaching to his precepts any rule not directly derived from the fundamental tenets or necessary to the cohesion of the Order—he had expressed in strong terms his dread and horror of narcotism; the use for pleasure's sake, not to relieve pain or nervous excitement, of drugs which act, as he said, through the brain upon the soul. His judgment, expressed with unusual directness and severity and enforced by experience, has become with his followers a tradition not less imperative than the most binding of their laws. It was so held, above all, in that household in which Eveena and I had first learnt the

"lore of the Starlight." Esmo, indeed, regarded not merely as an unscientific superstition, but as blasphemous folly, the rejection of any means of restoring health or relieving pain which Providence has placed within human reach. But he abhorred the use for pleasure's sake of poisons affirmed to reduce the activity and in the long-run to impair the energies of the mind, and weaken the moral sense and the will, more intensely than the strictest follower of the

Arabian Prophet abhors the draughts which deprive man of the full use of the senses, intelligence, and conscience which Allah has bestowed, and degrade him below the brute, Esmo's children, moreover, were not more strictly compelled to respect the letter than carefully instructed in the principle of every command for which he claimed their obedience.

But in such measure as Eveena's distress became intelligible, the fault of which she accused herself became incredible. I could not believe that she could be wilfully disloyal to me—still less that she could have suddenly broken through the fixed ideas of her whole life, the principles engraved on her mind by education more stringently than the maxims of the Koran or

the Levitical Law on the children of Ishmael or of Israel; and this while the impressive rites of Initiation, the imprecation at which I myself had shuddered, were fresh in her memory—their impression infinitely deepened, moreover, by the awful mystery of that Vision of which even yet we were half afraid to speak to one another. While I hesitated to reply, gathering up as well as I could the thread of these thoughts as they passed in a few seconds through my mind, my left hand touched an object hidden in my bride's zone. I drew out a tiny crystal phial three parts full, taken, as I saw, from the medicine-chest Esmo had carefully stocked and as carefully fastened. As, holding this, I turned again to her, Eveena repeated: "Punish, but don't question me!"

"My own," I said, "you are far more punished already than you deserve or I can bear to see. How did you get this?"

Releasing her hands, she drew from the folds of her robe the electric keys, which, by a separate combination, would unlock each of my cases;—

without which it was impossible to open or force them.

"Yes, I remember; and you were surprised that I trusted them to you. And now you expect me to believe that you have abused that trust, deceived me, broken a rule which in your father's house and by all our Order is held sacred as the rings of the Signet, for a drug which twelve days ago you disliked as much as I?"

"It is true."

The words were spoken with downcast eyes, in the low faltering tone natural to a confession of disgrace.

"It is not true, Eveena; or if true in form, false in matter. If it were possible that you could wish to deceive me, you knew it could not be for long."

"I meant to be found out," she interrupted, "only not yet."

She had betrayed herself, stung by words that seemed to express the one doubt she could not nerve herself to endure—doubt of her loyalty to me.

Before I could speak, she looked up hastily, and began to retract. I stopped her.

"I see—when you had done with it. But, Eveena, why conceal it? Do you think I would not have given this or all the contents of the chest into your hands, and asked no question?"

"Do you mean it? Could you have so trusted me?"

"My child! is it difficult to trust where I know there is no temptation to wrong? Do you think that to-day I have doubted or suspected you, even while you have accused yourself? I cannot guess at your motive, but I am as sure as ever of your loyalty. Take these things,"—forcing back upon her the phial and the magnets,—"yes, and the test-stone." ... She burst into passionate tears.

"I cannot endure this. If I had dreamed your patience would have borne with me half so far, I would never have tried it so, even for your own sake.

I meant to be found out and accept the consequences in silence. But you trust me so, that I must tell you what I wanted to conceal. When you kept on the surface it made me so ill"—

"But, Eveena, if the remedy be not worse than the sickness, why not ask for it openly?"

"It was not that. Don't you understand? Of course, I would bear any suffering rather than have done this; but then you would have found me out at once. I wanted to conceal my suffering, not to escape it."

"My child! my child! how could you put us both to all this pain?"

"You know you would not have given me the draught; you would have left the surface at once; and I cannot bear to be always in the way, always hindering your pleasures, and even your discoveries. You came across a distance that makes a bigger world than this look less than that light, through solitude and dangers and horrors I cannot bear to think of, to see and examine this world of ours. And then you leave things unseen or half-seen, you spoil your work, because a girl is seasick! You ran great risk of death and got badly hurt to see what our hunting was like, and you will not let my head ache that you may find out what our sea-storms and currents are! How can I bear to be such a burden upon you? You trust me, and, I believe," (she added, colouring), "you love me, twelvefold more than

I deserve; yet you think me unwilling or unworthy to take ever so small an interest in your work, to bear a few hours' discomfort for it and for you.

And yet," she went on passionately, "I may sit trembling and heart-sick for a whole day alone that you may carry out your purpose. I may receive the only real sting your lips have given, because I could not bear that pain without crying. And so with everything. It is not that I must not suffer pain, but that the pain must not come from without. Your lips would punish a fault with words that shame and sting for a day, a summer, a year; your hand must never inflict a sting that may smart for ten minutes.

And it is not only that you do this, but you pride yourself on it. Why? It is not that you think the pain of the body so much worse than that of the spirit:—you that smiled at me when you were too badly bruised and torn to stand, yet could scarcely keep back your tears just now, when you thought that I had suffered half an hour of sorrow I did not quite deserve.

Why then? Do you think that women feel so differently? Have the women of your Earth hearts so much harder and skins so much softer than ours?"

She spoke with most unusual impetuosity, and with that absolute simplicity and sincerity which marked her every look and word, which gave them, for me at least, an unspeakable charm, and for all who heard her a characteristic individuality unlike the speech or manner of any other woman. As soon suspect an infant of elaborate sarcasm as Eveena of affectation, irony, or conscious paradox. Nay, while her voice was in my ears, I never could feel that her views were paradoxical. The direct straightforwardness and simple structure of the Martial language enhanced this peculiar effect of her speech; and much that seems infantine in translation was all but eloquent as she spoke it. Often, as on this occasion, I felt guilty of insincerity, of a verbal fencing unworthy of her unalloyed good faith and earnestness, as I endeavoured to parry thrusts that went to the very heart of all those instinctive doctrines which I could the less defend on the moment, because I had never before dreamed that they could be doubted.

"At any rate," I said at last, "your sex gain by my heresy, since they are as richly gifted in stinging words as we in physical force."

"So much the worse for them, surely," she answered simply, "if it be right that men should rule and women obey?"

"That is the received doctrine on Earth," I answered. "In practice, men command and women disobey them; men bully and women lie. But in truth, Eveena, having a wife only too loyal and too loving, I don't care to canvass the deserts of ordinary women or the discipline of other households. I own that it was wrong to scold you. Do not insist on making me say that it would have been a little less wrong to beat you!"

She laughed—her low, sweet, silvery laugh, the like of which I have hardly heard among Earthly women, even of the simpler, more child-like races of the East and South; a laugh still stranger in a world where childhood is seldom bright and womanhood mostly sad and fretful.

Of the very few satisfactory memories I bore away from that world, the sweetest is the recollection of that laugh, which I heard for the first time on the morrow of our bridals, and for the last time on the day before we parted. I cherish it as evidence that, despite many and bitter troubles, my bride's short married life was not wholly unhappy. By this time she had found out that we had left the surface, and began to remonstrate.

"Nay, I have seen all I care to see, my own. I confess the justice of your claim, as the partner of my life, to be the partner of its paramount purpose.

You are more precious to me than all the discoveries of which I ever dreamed, and I will not for any purpose whatsoever expose you to real peril or serious pain. But henceforth I will ask you to bear discomfort and inconvenience when the object is worth it, and to help me wherever your help can avail."

"I can help you?"

"Much, and in many ways, my Eveena. You will soon learn to understand what I wish to examine and the use of the instruments I employ; and then you will be the most useful of assistants, as you are the best and most welcome of companions."

As I spoke a soft colour suffused her face, and her eyes brightened with a joy and contentment such as no promise of pleasure or indulgence could

have inspired. To be the partner of adventure and hardship, the drudge in toil and sentinel in peril, was the boon she claimed, the best guerdon I could promise. If but the promise might have been better fulfilled!

It was not till in latitude 9° S. we emerged into the open ocean, and presently found ourselves free from the currents of the narrow waters, that, in order to see the remarkable island of which I had caught sight in my descent, I requested Ergimo to remain for some hours above the surface.

The island rises directly out of the sea, and is absolutely unascendible.

Balloons, however, render access possible, both to its summit and to its cave-pierced sides. It is the home of enormous flocks of white birds, which resemble in form the heron rather than the eider duck, but which, like the latter, line with down drawn from their own breasts the nests which, counted by millions, occupy every nook and cranny of the crystalline walls, about ten miles in circumference. Each of the nests is nearly as large as that of the stork. They are made of a jelly digested from the bones of the fish upon which the birds prey, and are almost as white in colour as the birds themselves. Freshly formed nest dissolved in hot water makes dishes as much to the taste of Martialists as the famous bird-nest soup to that of the Chinese. Both down and nests, therefore, are largely plundered; but the birds are never injured, and care is taken in robbing them to leave enough of the outer portion of the nest to constitute a bed for the eggs, and encourage the creatures to rebuild and reline it.

One harvest only is permitted, the second stripping of feathers and the rebuilt nest being left undisturbed. The caverns are lined with a white guano, now some feet thick, since it has ceased to be sought for manure; the Martialists having discovered means of saturating the soil with ammonia procured from the nitrogen of the atmosphere, which with the sewage and other similar materials enables them to dispense with this valuable bird manure. Whether the white colour of the island, perceptible even in a large Terrestrial telescope, is in any degree due to the whiteness of the birds, their nests, and leavings, or wholly to reflection from the bright spar-like surface of the rock itself, and especially of the flat table-like summit, I will not pretend to say.

From this point we held our course south-westward, and entered the northernmost of two extraordinary gulfs of exactly similar shape, separated by an isthmus and peninsula which assume on a map the form of a gigantic hammer. The strait by which each gulf is entered is about a hundred miles in length and ten in breadth. The gulf itself, if it should not rather be called an inland sea, occupies a total area of about 100,000 square miles. The isthmus, 500 miles in length by 50 in breadth, ends in a roughly square peninsula of about 10,000 square miles in extent, nearly the whole of which is a plateau 2000 feet above the sea-level. On the narrowest point of the isthmus, just where it joins the mainland, and where a sheltered bay runs up from either sea, is situated the great city of Amâkasfe, the natural centre of Martial life and commerce. At this point we found awaiting us the balloon which was to convey us to the Court of the Suzerain. A very light but strong metallic framework maintained the form of the "fish-shaped" or spindle-shaped balloon itself, which closely resembled that of our vessel, its dimensions being of necessity greater. Attached to this framework was the car of similar form, about twelve feet in length and six in depth, the upper third of the sides, however, being of open-work, so as not to interfere with the survey of the traveller. Eveena could not help shivering at the sight of the slight vehicle and the enormous machine of thin, bladder-like material by which it was to be upheld. She embarked, indeed, without a word, her alarm betraying itself by no voluntary sign, unless it were the tight clasp of my hand, resembling that of a child frightened, but ashamed to confess its fear. I noticed, however, that she so arranged her veil as to cover her eyes when the signal for the start was given. She was, therefore, wholly unconscious of the sudden spring, unattended by the slightest jolt or shake, which raised us at once 500 feet above the coast, and under whose influence, to my eyes, the ground appeared suddenly to fall from us. When I drew out the folds of her veil, it was with no little amazement that she saw the sky around her, the sea and the city far below.

An aerial current to the north-westward at our present level, which had been selected on that account, carried us at a rate of some twelve miles an hour; a rate much increased, however, by the sails at the stern of the car, sails of thin metal fixed on strong frames, and striking with a screw-like

motion. Their lack of expanse was compensated by a rapidity of motion such that they seemed to the eye not to move at all, presenting the appearance of an uniform disc reflecting the rays of the Sun, which was now almost immediately above us. Towards evening the Residence of the Camptâ became visible on the north-western horizon. It was built on a plateau about 400 feet above the sea-level, towards which the ground from all sides sloped up almost imperceptibly. Around it was a garden of great extent with a number of trees of every sort, some of them masses of the darkest green, others of bright yellow, contrasting similarly shaped masses of almost equal size clothed from base to top in a continuous sheet of pink, emerald, white or crimson flowers. The turf presented almost as great a variety of colours, arranged in. every conceivable pattern, above which rose innumerable flower-beds, uniform or varied, the smallest perhaps two, the largest more than 200 feet in diameter; each circle of bloom higher than that outside it, till in some cases the centre rose even ten feet above the general level. The building itself was low, having nowhere more than two stories. One wing, pointed out to me by Ergimo, was appropriated to the household of the Prince; the centre standing out in front and rear, divided by a court almost as wide as the wings; the further wing accommodating the attendants and officials of the Court. We landed, just before the evening mist began to gather, at the foot of an inclined way of a concrete resembling jasper, leading up to the main entrance of the Palace.

CHAPTER XVII - PRESENTED AT COURT.

Leading Eveena by the hand—for to hold my arm after the European fashion was always an inconvenience and fatigue to her—and preceded by Ergimo, I walked unnoticed to the closed gate of pink crystal, contrasting the emerald green of the outer walls. Along the front of this central portion of the residence was a species of verandah, supported by pillars overlaid with a bright red metal, and wrought in the form of smooth tree trunks closely clasped by creepers, the silver flowers of the latter contrasting the dense golden foliage and ruby-like stems. Under this, and in front of the gate itself, were two sentries armed with a spear, the shaft of which was about six feet in length, hollow, and almost as light as the cane or reed handle of an African assegai. The blade more resembled the triangular bayonet. Beside each, however, was the terrible asphyxiator, fixed on its stand, with a bore about as great as that of a nine-pounder, but incomparably lighter. These two weapons might at one discharge have annihilated a huge mob of insurgents threatening to storm the palace, were insurrections known in Mars, These men saluted us by dropping the points of their weapons and inclining the handle towards us; gazing upon me with surprise, and with something of soldierly admiration for physical superiority. The doors, wide enough to admit a dozen Martialists abreast, parted, and we entered a vaulted hall whose arched roof was supported not by pillars but by gigantic statues, each presenting the lustre of a different jewel, and all wrought with singular perfection of proportion and of beauty. Here we were met by two officers wearing the same dress as the sentries outside—a diaper of crimson and silver. The rank of those who now received us, however, was indicated by a silver ribbon passing over the left shoulder, and supporting what I should have called a staff, save that it was of metal and had a sharp point, rendering it almost as formidable a weapon as the rapier. Exchanging a word or two with Ergimo, these gentlemen ushered us into a small room on the right, where refreshments were placed before us. Eveena whispered me that she must not share our meal in presence of these strangers; an intimation which somewhat blunted the keen appetite I always derived from a journey through the Martial atmosphere. Checked as it was, however, that appetite

seemed a new astonishment to our attendants; the need of food among their race being proportionate to their inferior size and strength. When we rose, I asked Ergimo what was to become of Eveena, as the officers were evidently waiting to conduct me into the presence of their Sovereign, where it would not be appropriate for her to appear. He repeated my question to the principal official, and the latter, walking to a door in the farther corner of the room, sounded an electric signal; a few seconds after which the door opened, showing two veiled figures, the pink ground of whose robes indicated their matronhood, if I may apply such a term to the relation of his hundred temporary wives to the Camptâ. But this ground colour was almost hidden in the embroidery of crimson, gold, and white, which, as I soon found, were the favourite colours of the reigning Prince.

To these ladies I resigned Eveena, the officer saying, as I somewhat reluctantly parted from her, "What you entrust to the Camptâ's household you will find again in your own when your audience is over." Whether this avoidance of all direct mention of women were matter of delicacy or contempt I hardly knew, though I had observed it on former occasions.

When the door closed, I noticed that Ergimo had left us, and the officers indicated by gesture rather than by words that they were to lead me immediately into the presence. I had considered with some care how I was, on so critical an occasion, to conduct myself, and had resolved that the most politic course would probably be an assumption of courteous but absolute independence; to treat the Autocrat of this planet much as an English envoy would treat an Indian Prince. It was in accordance with this intention that I had assumed a dress somewhat more elaborate than is usually worn here, a white suit of a substance resembling velvet in texture, and moire in lustre, with collar and belt of silver. On my breast I wore my order of [illegible], and in my belt my one cherished Terrestrial possession—the sword, reputed the best in Asia, that had twice driven its point home within a finger's breadth of my life; and that clove the turban on my brow but a minute before it was surrendered—just in time to save its gallant owner and his score of surviving comrades. In its hilt I had set the emerald with which alone the Commander of the Faithful rewarded my services. The turban is not so unlike the masculine head-dress of Mars as to

attract any special attention. Re-entering the hall, I was conducted along a gallery and through another crystal door into the immediate presence of the Autocrat. The audience chamber was of no extraordinary size, perhaps one-quarter as large as the peristyle of Esmo's dwelling. Along the emerald walls ran a series of friezes wrought in gold, representing various scenes of peace and war, agricultural, judicial, and political; as well as incidents which, I afterwards learnt, preserved the memory of the long struggles wherein the Communists were finally overthrown. The lower half of the room was empty, the upper was occupied by a semicircle of seats forming part of the building itself and directly facing the entrance. These took up about one-third of the space, the central floor being divided from the upper portion of the room by a low wall of metal surmounted by arches supporting the roof and hung with drapery, which might be so lowered as to conceal the whole occupied part of the chamber. The seats rose in five tiers, one above the other. The semicircle, however, was broken exactly in the middle, that is, at the point farthest from the entrance, by a broad flight of steps, at the summit of which, and raised a very little above the seats of the highest tier, was the throne, supported by two of the royal brutes whose attack had been so nearly fatal to myself, wrought in silver, their erect heads forming the arms and front. About fifty persons were present, occupying only the seats nearest to the throne. On the upper tier were nine or ten who wore a scarlet sash, among whom I recognised a face I had not seen since the day of my memorable visit to the Astronaut; not precisely the face of a friend—Endo Zamptâ. Behind the throne were ranged a dozen guards, armed with the spear and with the lightning gun used in hunting.

That a single Martial battalion with its appropriate artillery could annihilate the best army of the Earth I could not but be aware; yet the first thought that occurred to me, as I looked on these formidably armed but diminutive soldiers, was that a score of my Arab horsemen would have cut a regiment of them to pieces. But by the time I had reached the foot of the steps my attention was concentrated on a single figure and face—the form and countenance of the Prince, who rose from his throne as I approached.

Those who remember that Louis XIV., a prince reputed to have possessed the most majestic and awe-inspiring presence of his age, was actually

beneath the ordinary height of Frenchmen, may be able to believe me when I say that the Autocrat of Mars, though scarcely five feet tall, was in outward appearance and bearing the most truly royal and imposing prince I have ever seen. His stature, rising nearly two inches over the tallest of those around him, perhaps added to the effect of a mien remarkable for dignity, composure, and self-confidence. The predominant and most immediately observable expression of his face was one of serene calm and command. A closer inspection and a longer experience explained why, notwithstanding, my first conception of his character (and it was a true one) ascribed to him quite as much of fire and spirit as of impassive grandeur. His voice, though its tone was gentle and almost strikingly quiet, had in it something of the ring peculiar to those which have sent the word of command along a line of battle. I felt as I heard it more impressed with the personal greatness, and even with the rank and power, of the Prince before me, than when I knelt to kiss the hand of the Most Christian King, or stood barefooted before the greatest modern successor of the conqueror of Stamboul.

"I am glad to receive you," he said. "It will be among the most memorable incidents of my reign that I welcome to my Court the first visitor from another world, or," he added, after a sudden pause, and with an inflection of unmistakable irony in his tone, "the first who has descended to our world from a height to which no balloon could reach and at which no balloonist could live."

"I am honoured, Prince," I replied, "in the notice of a greater potentate than the greatest of my own world."

These compliments exchanged, the Prince at once proceeded to more practical matters, aptly, however, connecting his next sentence with the formal phrases preceding it.

"Nevertheless, you have not shown excessive respect for my power in the person of one of my greatest officers. If you treated the princes of Earth as unceremoniously as the Regent of Elcavoo, I can understand that you found it convenient to place yourself beyond their reach."

I thought that this speech afforded me an opportunity of repairing my offence with the least possible loss of dignity.

"The proudest of Earthly princes," I replied, "would, I think, have pardoned the roughness which forgot the duty of a subject in the first obligations of humanity. No Sovereign whom I have served, but would have forgiven me more readily for rough words spoken at such a moment, than for any delay or slackness in saving the life of a woman in danger under his own eyes.

Permit me to take this opportunity of apologizing to the Regent in your presence, and assuring him that I was influenced by no disrespect to him, but only by overpowering terror for another."

"The lives of a dozen women," said the Camptâ, still with that covert irony or sarcasm in his tone, "would seem of less moment than threats and actual violence offered to the ruler of our largest and wealthiest dominion. The excuse which Endo Zamptâ must accept" (with a slight but perceptible emphasis on the imperative) "is the utter difference between our laws and ideas and your own."

The Regent, at this speech from his Sovereign, rose and made the usual gesture of assent, inclining his head and lifting his left hand to his mouth.

But the look on his face as he turned it on me, thus partly concealing it from the camptâ, boded no good should I ever fall into his power. The Prince then desired me to give an account of the motives which had induced my voyage and the adventures I had encountered. In reply, I gave him, as briefly and clearly as I could, a summary of all that is recorded in the earlier part of this narrative, carefully forbearing to afford any explanation of the manner in which the apergic force was generated. This omission the Prince noticed at once with remarkable quickness.

"You do not choose," he said, "to tell us your secret, and of course it is your property. Hereafter, however, I shall hope to purchase it from you."

"Prince," I answered, "if one of your subjects-found himself in the power of a race capable of conquering this world and destroying its inhabitants, would you forgive him if he furnished them with the means of reaching you?"

"I think," he replied, "my forgiveness would be of little consequence in that case. But go on with your story."

I finished my narration among looks of surprise and incredulity from no inconsiderable part of the audience, which, however, I noticed the less because the Prince himself listened with profound interest; putting in now and then a question which indicated his perfect comprehension of my account, of the conditions of such a journey and of the means I had employed to meet them.

"Before you were admitted," he said, "Endo Zamptâ had read to us his report upon your vessel and her machinery, an account which in every respect consists with and supports the truth of your relation. Indeed, were your story untrue, you have run a greater risk in telling it here than in the most daring adventure I have ever known or imagined. The Court is dismissed. Reclamomortâ will please me by remaining with me for the present."

When the assembly dispersed, I followed their Autocrat at his desire into his private apartments, where, resting among a pile of cushions and motioning me to take a place in immediate proximity to himself, he continued the conversation in a tone and manner so exactly the same as that he had employed in public as to show that the latter was not assumed for purposes of monarchical stage-play, but was the natural expression of his own character as developed under the influence of unlimited and uncontradicted power. He only exchanged, for unaffected interest and implied confidence, the tone of ironical doubt by which he had rendered it out of the question for his courtiers to charge him with a belief in that which public opinion might pronounce impossible, while making it apparent to me that he regarded the bigotry of scepticism with scarcely veiled contempt.

"I wish," he said, "I had half-a-dozen subjects capable of imagining such an enterprise and hardy enough to undertake it. But though we all profess to consider knowledge, and especially scientific knowledge, the one object for which it is worth while to live, none of us would risk his life in such an adventure for all the rewards that science and fame could give."

"I think, Prince," I replied, "that I am in presence of one inhabitant of this planet who would have dared at least as much as I have done."

"Possibly," he said. "Because, weary as most of us profess to be of existence, the weariest life in this world is that of him who rules it; living for ever under the silent criticism which he cannot answer, and bound to devote his time and thoughts to the welfare of a race whose utter extermination would be, on their own showing, the greatest boon he could confer upon them. Certainly I would rather be the discoverer of a world than its Sovereign."

He asked me numerous questions about the Earth, the races that inhabit it, their several systems of government, and their relations to one another; manifesting a keener interest, I thought, in the great wars which ended while I was yet a youth, than in any other subject. At last he permitted me to take leave. "You are," he said, "the most welcome guest I ever have or could have received; a guest distinguished above all others by a power independent of my own. But what honour I can pay to courage and enterprise, what welcome I can give such a guest, shall not be unworthy of him or of myself. Retire now to the home you will find prepared for you. I will only ask you to remember that I have chosen one near my own in order that I may see you often, and learn in private all that you can tell me."

At the entrance of the apartment I was met by the officer who had introduced me into the presence, and conducted at once to a door opening on the interior court or peristyle of the central portion of the Palace. This was itself a garden, but, unlike those of private houses, a garden open to the sky and traversed by roads in lieu of mere paths; not serving, as in private dwellings, the purposes of a common living room. Here a carriage awaited us, and my escort requested me to mount. I had some misgivings on Eveena's account, but felt it necessary to imitate the reserve and affected indifference on such subjects of those among whom I had been thrown, at least until I somewhat better understood their ways, and had established my own position. Traversing a vaulted passage underneath the rearward portion of the Palace, we emerged into the outer garden, and through this into a road lighted with a brilliancy almost equal to that of day. Our

journey occupied nearly half an hour, when we entered an enclosure apparently of great size, the avenue of which was so wide that, without dismounting, our carriage passed directly up to the door of a larger house than I had yet seen.

CHAPTER XVIII - A PRINCE'S PRESENT.

"This," said my escort, as we dismounted, "is the residence assigned to you by the Camptâ. Besides the grounds here enclosed, he has awarded you, by a deed which will presently be placed in your hands, an estate of some ten stoltau, which you can inspect at your leisure, and which will afford you a revenue as large as is enjoyed by any save by the twelve Regents. He has endeavoured to add to this testimony of his regard by rendering your household as complete as wealth and forethought could make it. What may be wanting to your own tastes and habits you will find no difficulty in adding."

We now entered that first and principal chamber of the mansion wherein it is customary to receive all visitors and transact all business. The hall was one of unusual size and magnificence. Here, at a table not far from the entrance, stood another official, not wearing the uniform of the Court, with several documents in his hand. As he turned to salute me, his face wore an expression of annoyance and discomfiture which not a little surprised me, till, by following his sidelong, uncomfortable glances, I perceived a veiled feminine figure, which could be no other than Eveena's. Misreading my surprise, the official said—

"It is no fault of mine, and I have not spoken except to remonstrate, as far as might be allowed, against so unusual a proceeding."

He must have been astonished and annoyed indeed to take such notice of a stranger's wife; and, above all, to take upon himself to comment on her conduct for good or ill. I thought it best to make no reply, and simply saluted him in form as I received the first paper handed to me, to which, by the absence of any blank space, I perceived that my signature was not required. This was indeed the document which bestowed on me the house and estate presented by the Sovereign. The next paper handed to me appeared to resemble the marriage-contract I had already signed, save that but one blank was left therein. Unable to decipher it, I was about to ask the official to read it aloud, when Eveena, who had stolen up to me unperceived, caught my arm and drew me a little way aside, indifferent to the wondering glances of the officials; who had probably never seen a

woman venture uncalled into the public apartments of her husband's house, still less interpose in any matter of business, and no doubt thought that she was taking outrageous advantage of my ignorance and inexperience.

"I will scold you presently, child," I said quickly and low. "What is it?"

"Sign at once," she whispered, "and ask no questions. Deal with me as you will afterwards. You must take what is given you now, without comment or objection, simply expressing your thanks."

"Must! Eveena?"

"It is not safe to refuse or slight gifts from such a quarter," she answered, in the same low tone. "Trust me so far; please do what I entreat of you now. I must bear your displeasure if I fail to satisfy you when we are alone."

Her manner was so agitated and so anxious that it recalled to me at once the advice of Esmo upon the same point, though the fears which had prompted so strange an intervention were wholly incomprehensible to me.

I knew her, however, by this time too well to refuse the trust she now for the first time claimed, and taking the documents one by one as if I had perfectly understood them, I wrote my name in the space left blank for it, and allowed the official to stamp the slips without a word. I then expressed briefly but earnestly my thanks both to the Autocrat and to the officials who had been the agents of his kindness. They retired, and I looked round for Eveena; but as soon as she saw that I was about to comply with her request, she had quitted the room. Alone in my own house, knowing nothing of its geography, having no notion how to summon the brute domestics—if, indeed, the dwelling were furnished with those useful creatures, without whom a Martial household would be signally incomplete—I could only look for the spring that opened the principal door. This should lead into the gallery which, as I judged, must divide the hall and the front apartments from those looking into the peristyle. Having found and pressed this spring, the door opened on a gallery longer, wider, and more elaborately ornamented than that of the only Martial mansions into which I had been hitherto admitted. Looking round in no little

perplexity, I observed a niche in which stood a statue of white relieved by a scarlet background; and beside this statue, crouching and half hidden, a slight pink object, looking at first like a bundle of drapery, but which in a moment sprang up, and, catching my hand, made me aware that Eveena had been waiting for me.

"I beg you," she said with an earnestness I could not understand, "I beg you to come this way," leading me to the right, for I had turned instinctively to the left in entering the gallery, perhaps because my room in Esmo's house had lain in that direction. Reaching the end of the gallery, she turned into one of the inner apartments; and as the door closed behind us, I felt that she was sinking to the ground, as if the agitation she had manifested in the hall, controlled till her object was accomplished, had now overpowered her. I caught and carried her to the usual pile of cushions in the corner. The room, according to universal custom in Martial houses after sunset, was brilliantly lighted by the electric lamp in the peristyle, and throwing back her veil, I saw that she was pale to ghastliness and almost fainting. In my ignorance of my own house, I could call for no help, and employ no other restoratives than fond words and caresses. Under this treatment, nevertheless, she recovered perhaps as quickly as under any which the faculty might have prescribed. She was, still, however, much more distressed than mere consciousness of the grave solecism she had committed could explain. But I had no other clue to her trouble, and could only hope that in repudiating this she would explain its real cause.

"Come, bambina!" I expostulated, "we understand one another too well by this time for you to wrong me by all this alarm. I know that you would not have broken through the customs of your people without good reason; and you know that, even if your reason were not sufficient, I should not be hard upon the error."

"I am sure you would not," she said. "But this time you have to consider others, and you cannot let it be supposed that you do not know a wife's duty, or will allow your authority to be set at naught in your own household."

"What matter? Do you suppose I listen in the roads?" [care for gossip], I rejoined. "Household rule is a matter of the veil, and no one—not even your autocratic Prince—will venture to lift it."

"You have not lifted it yourself yet," she answered. "You will understand me, when you have looked at the slips you were about to make them read aloud, had I not interrupted you."

"Read them yourself," I said, handing to her the papers I still held, and which, after her interposition, I had not attempted to decipher. She took them, but with a visible shudder of reluctance—not stronger than came over me before she had read three lines aloud. Had I known their purport, I doubt whether even Eveena's persuasion and the Autocrat's power together could have induced me to sign them. They were in very truth contracts of marriage—if marriage it can be called. The Sovereign had done me the unusual, but not wholly unprecedented, favour of selecting half a dozen of the fairest maidens of those waiting their fate in the Nurseries of his empire; had proffered on my behoof terms which satisfied their ambition, gratified their vanity, and would have induced them to accept any suitor so recommended, without the insignificant formality of a personal courtship. It had seemed to him only a gracious attention to complete my household; and he had furnished me with a bevy of wives, as I presently found he had selected a complete set of the most intelligent amlau, carvee, and tyree which he could procure. Without either the one or the other, the dwelling he had given me would have seemed equally empty or incomplete.

This mark of royal favour astounded and dismayed me more than Eveena herself. If she had entertained the wish, she would hardly have acknowledged to herself the hope, that she might remain permanently the sole partner of my home. But so sudden, speedy, and wholesale an intrusion thereon she certainly had not expected. Even in Mars, a first bride generally enjoys for some time a monopoly of her husband's society, if she cannot be said to enchain his affection. It was hard, indeed, before the thirtieth day after her marriage, to find herself but one in a numerous family—the harder that our union had from the first been close, intimate,

unrestrainedly confidential, as it can hardly be where neither expects that the tie can remain exclusive; and because she had learned to realise and rest upon such love as belongs to a life in which woman, never affecting the independence of coequal partnership, has never yet sunk by reaction into a mere slave and toy. It was hard, cruelly hard, on one who had given in the first hour of marriage, and never failed to give, a love whose devotion had no limit, no reserve or qualification; a submission that was less self-sacrifice or self-suppression than the absolute surrender of self—of will, feeling, and self-interest—to the judgment and pleasure of him she loved: hard on her who had neither thought nor care for herself as apart from me.

When I understood to what I had actually committed myself, I snatched the papers from her, and might have torn them to pieces but for the gentle restraining hand she laid upon mine.

"You cannot help it," she said, the tears falling from her eyes, but with a self-command of which I could not have supposed her capable. "It seems hard on me; but it is better so. It is not that you are not content with me, not that you love me less. I can bear it better when it comes from a stranger, and is forced upon you without, and even, I think, against your will."

The pressure of the arm that clasped her waist, and the hand that held her own, was a sufficient answer to any doubt that might be implied in her last words; and, lifting her eyes to mine, she said—

"I shall always remember this. I shall always think that you were sorry not to have at least a little while longer alone with me. It is selfish to feel glad that you are pained; but your sympathy, your sharing my own feeling, comforts me as I never could have been comforted when, as must have happened sooner or later, you had found for yourself another companion."

"Child, do you mean to say there is 'no portal to this passage;' and that, however much against my will, I am bound to women I have never seen, and never wish to see?"

"You have signed," replied Eveena gently. "The contracts are stamped, and are in the official's hands; and you could not attempt to break them without

giving mortal offence to the Prince, who has intended you a signal favour.

Besides, these girls themselves have done no wrong, and deserve no affront or unkindness from you."

I was silent for some minutes; at first simply astounded at the calm magnanimity which was mingled with her perfect simplicity, then, pondering the possibilities of the situation—

"Can we not escape?" I said at last, rather to myself than to her.

"Escape!" she repeated with surprise. "And from what? The favour shown you by our Sovereign, the wealth he has bestowed, the personal interest he has taken in perfecting every detail of one of the most splendid homes ever given save to a prince—every incident of your position—make you the most envied man in this world; and you would escape from them?"

Gazing for a few moments in my face, she added—

"These maidens were chosen as the loveliest in all the Nurseries of two continents; every one of them far more beautiful than I can be, even in your eyes. Pray do not, for my sake, be unkind to them or try to dislike them.

What is it you would escape?"

"Being false to you," I answered, "if nothing else."

"False!" she echoed, in unaffected wonder. "What did you promise me?"

Again I was silenced by the loyal simplicity with which she followed out ideas so strange to me that their consequences, however logical, I could never anticipate; and could hardly admit to be sound, even when so directly and distinctly deduced as now from the intolerable consistency of the premises.

"But," I answered at last, "how much did you promise, Eveena? and how much more have you given?"

"Nothing," she replied, "that I did not owe. You won your right to all the love I could give before you asked for it, and since."

"We 'drive along opposite lines,' Madonna; but we would both give and risk much to avoid what is before us. Let me ask your father whether it be

not yet possible to return to my vessel, and leave a world so uncongenial to both of us."

"You cannot!" she answered. "Try to escape—you insult the Prince; you put yourself and me, for whom you fear more, in the power of a malignant enemy. You cannot guide a balloon or a vessel, if you could get possession of one; and within a few hours after your departure was known, every road and every port would be closed to you."

"Can I not send to your father?" I said.

"Probably," she replied. "I think we shall find a telegraph in your office, if you will allow me to enter there, now there is no one to see; and it must be morning in Ecasfe."

Familiar with the construction and arrangement of a Martial house, Eveena immediately crossed the gallery to what she called the office—the front room on the right, where the head of the house carries on his work or study. Here, above a desk attached to the wall, was one of those instruments whose manipulation was simple enough for a novice like myself.

"But," I said, "I cannot write your stylic characters; and if I used the phonic letters, a message from me would be very likely to excite the curiosity of officials who would care about no other."

"May I," she suggested, "write your message for you, and put your purport in words that will be understood by my father alone?"

"Do," I rejoined, "but do it in my name, and I will sign it."

Under her direction, I took the stylus or pencil and the slip of tafroo she offered me, and wrote my name at the head. After eliciting the exact purport of the message I desired to send, and meditating for some moments, she wrote and read out to me words literally translated as follows:—

"The rich aviary my flower-bird thought over full. I would breathe home [air]. Health-speak." The sense of which, as I could already understand, was—

"A splendid mansion has been given us, but my flower-bird has found it too full. I wish for my native air. Prescribe."

The brevity of the message was very characteristic of the language. Equally characteristic of the stylography was the fact that the words occupied about an inch beyond the address. Following her pencil as she pointed to the ciphers, I said—

"Is not asny caré a false concord? And why have you used the past tense?"

This ill-timed pedantry, applying to Martial grammar the rules of that with which my boyhood had been painfully familiarised, provoked, amid all our trouble, Eveena's low silver-toned laugh.

"I meant it," she answered. "My father will look at his pupil's writing with both eyes."

"Well, you are out of reach even of the leveloo."

She laughed again.

"Asnyca-re," she said; the changed accentuation turning the former words into the well-remembered name of my landing-place, with the interrogative syllable annexed.

This message despatched, we could only await the reply. Nestling among the cushions at my knee, her head resting on my breast, Eveena said—

"And now, forgive my presumption in counselling you, and my reminding you of what is painful to both. But what to us is as the course of the clock, is strange as the stars to you. You must see—them, and must order all household arrangements; and" (glancing at a dial fixed in the wall) "the black is driving down the green."

"So much the better," I said. "I shall have less time to speak to them, and less chance of speaking or looking my mind. And as to arrangements, those, of course, you must make."

"I! forgive me," she answered, "that is impossible. It is for you to assign to each of us her part in the household, her chamber, her rank and duties. You forget that I hold exactly the same position with the youngest among them, and cannot presume even to suggest, much less to direct."

I was silent, and after a pause she went on—

"It is not for me to advise you; but"—

"Speak your thought, now and always, Eveena. Even if I did not stand in so much need of your guidance in a new world, I never yet refused to hear counsel; and it is a wife's right to offer it."

"Is it? We are not so taught," she answered. "I am afraid you have rougher ground to steer over than you are aware. Alone with you, I hope I should have done nay best, remembering the lesson of the leveloo, never to give you the pain of teaching a different one. But we shall no longer be alone; and you cannot hope to manage seven as you might manage one.

Moreover, these girls have neither had that first experience of your nature which made that lesson so impressive to me, nor the kindly and gentle training, under a mother's care and a father's mild authority, that I had enjoyed. They would not understand the control that is not enforced. They will obey when they must; and will feel that they must obey when they cannot deceive, and dare not rebel. Do not think hardly of them for this.

They have known no life but that of the strict clockwork routine of a great Nursery, where no personal affection and no rule but that of force is possible."

"I understand, Madonna. Your Prince's gift puts a man in charge of young ladies, hitherto brought up among women only, and, of course, petty, petulant, frivolous, as women left to themselves ever are! I wish you could see the ridiculous side of the matter which occurs to me, as I see the painful aspect which alone is plain to you. I can scarcely help laughing at the chance which has assigned to me the daily personal management of half-a-dozen school-girls; and school-girls who must also be wives! I don't think you need fear that I shall deal with them as with you: as a man of sense and feeling must deal with a woman whose own instincts, affection, and judgment are sufficient for her guidance. I never saw much of girls or children. I remember no home but the Western school and the Oriental camp. I never, as soldier or envoy, was acquainted with other men's homes.

While still beardless, I have ruled bearded soldiers by a discipline whose sanctions were the death-shot and the bastinado; and when I left the camp

and court, it was for colleges where a beardless face is never seen. I must look to you to teach me how discipline may be softened to suit feminine softness, and what milder sanction may replace the noose and the stick of the ferash" (Persian executioner).

"I cannot believe," Eveena answered, taking me, as usual, to the letter, "that you will ever draw the zone too tight. We say that 'anarchy is the worst tyranny.' Laxity which leaves us to quarrel and torment each other, tenderness which encourages disorder and disobedience till they must be put down perforce, is ultimate unkindness. I will not tell you that such indulgence will give you endless trouble, win you neither love nor respect, and probably teach its objects to laugh at you under the veil. You will care more for this—that you would find yourself forced at last to change 'velvet hand for leathern band.' Believe me, my—our comfort and happiness must depend on your grasping the helm at once and firmly; ruling us, and ruling with a strong hand. Otherwise your home will resemble the most miserable of all scenes of discomfort—an ungoverned school; and the most severe and arbitrary household rule is better by far than that. And—forgive me once more—but do not speak as if you would deal one measure with the left hand and another with the right. Surely you do not so misunderstand me as to think I counselled you to treat myself differently from others? 'Just rule only can be gentle.' If you show favouritism at first, you will find yourself driven step by step to do what you will feel to be cruel; what will pain yourself perhaps more than any one else. You may make envy and dislike bite (hold) their tongues, but you cannot prevent their stinging under the veil. Therefore, once more, you cannot let my interference pass as if none but you knew of it."

"Madonna, if I am to rule such a household, I will rule as absolutely as your autocratic Prince. I will tolerate no criticism and no questions."

"You surely forget," she urged, "that they know my offence, and do not know—must not know—what in your judgment excuses it. Let them once learn that it is possible so to force the springs [bolts] without a sting, it will take a salt-fountain [of tears] to blot the lesson from their memory."

"What would you have, Eveena? Am I to deal unjustly that I may seem just? That course steers straight to disaster. And, had you been in fault, could, I humble you in other eyes?"

"If I feel hurt by any mark of your displeasure, or humbled that it should be known to my equals in your own household," she replied, "it is time I were deprived of the privileges that have rendered me so overweening."

My answer was intercepted by the sound of an electric bell or miniature gong, and a slip of tafroo fell upon the desk. The first words were in that vocal character which I had mastered, and came from Esmo.

"Hysterical folly," he had said. "Mountain air might be fatal; and clear nights are dangerously cold for more than yourselves."

"What does he mean?" I asked, as I read out a formula more studiously occult than those of the Pharmacopoeia.

"That I am unpardonably silly, and that you must not dream of going back to your vessel. The last words, I suppose, warn you how carefully in such a household you need to guard the secrets of the Starlight."

"Well, and what is this in the stylic writing?"

Eveena glanced over it and coloured painfully, the tears gathering in her eyes.

"That," she said, pointing to the first cipher, "is my mother's signature."

"Then," I said, "it is meant for you, not for me."

"Nay," she answered. "Do you think I could take advantage of your not knowing the character?"—and she read words quite as incomprehensible to me as the writing itself.

"Can a star mislead the blind? I should veil myself in crimson if I have trained a bird to snatch sugar from full hands. Must even your womanhood reverse the clasps of your childhood?"

"It chimes midnight twice," I said—a Martial phrase meaning, 'I am as much in the dark as ever.' "Do not translate it, carissima. I can read in your face that it is unjust—reproachful where you deserve no reproach."

"Nay, when you so wrong my mother I must tell you exactly what she means:—'Can a child of the Star take advantage of one who relies on her to explain the customs of a world unknown to him? I blush to think that my child can abuse the tenderness of one who is too eager to indulge her fancies.'

"You see she is quite right. You do trust me so absolutely, you are so strangely over-kind to me, it is shameful I should vex you by fretting because you are forced to do what you might well have done at your own pleasure."

"My own, I was more than vexed; chiefly perhaps for your sake, but not by you. Where any other woman would have stung the sore by sending fresh sparks along the wire, you thought only to spare me the pain of seeing you pained. But what do the last words mean? No"—for I saw the colour deepen on her half-averted face—"better leave unread what we know to be written in error."

But the less agreeable a supposed duty, the more resolute was Eveena to fulfil it.

"They were meant to recall a saying familiar in every school and household," she said:—

"'Sandal loosed and well-clasped zone—
Childhood spares the woman grown.
Change the clasps, and woman yet
Pays with interest childhood's debt.'"

"This"—tightening and relaxing the clasp of her zone—"is the symbol of stricter or more indulgent household rule." Then bending so as to avert her face, she unclasped her embroidered sandal and gave it into my hand;—

"and this is what, I suppose, you would call its sanction."

"There is more to be said for the sandal than I supposed, bambina, if it have helped to make you what you are. But you may tell Zulve that its work and hers are done."

Kneeling before her, I kissed, with more studied reverence than the sacred stone of the Caaba, the tiny foot on which I replaced its covering.

"Baby as she thinks and I call you, Eveena, you are fast unteaching me the lesson which, before you were born and ever since, the women of the Earth have done their utmost to impress indelibly upon my mind—the lesson that woman is but a less lovable, more petulant, more deeply and incurably spoilt child. Your mother's reproach is an exact inversion of the truth. No one could have acted with more utter unselfishness, more devoted kindness, more exquisite delicacy than you have shown in this miserable matter. I could not have believed that even you could have put aside your own feelings so completely, could have recognised so promptly that I was not in fault, have thought so exclusively of what was best and safe for me in the first place, and next of what was kind and just and generous to your rivals. I never thought such reasonableness and justice possible to feminine nature; and if I cannot love you more dearly, you have taught me how deeply to admire and honour you. I accept the situation, since you will have it so; be as just and considerate henceforward as you have been to-night, and trust me that it shall bring no shadow between us—shall never make you less to me than you are now."

"But it must," she insisted. "I cannot now be other than one wife among many; and what place I hold among them is, remember, for you and you alone to fix. No rule, no custom, obliges you to give any preference in form or fact to one, merely because you chanced to marry her first."

"Such, nevertheless, did not seem to be the practice in your father's house. Your mother was as distinctly wife and mistress as if his sole companion."

"My father," she replied, "did not marry a second time till within my own memory; and it was natural and usual to give the first place to one so much older and more experienced. I have no such claim, and when you see my companions you may find good reason to think that I am the least fit of all to take the first place. Nor," she added, drawing me from the room, "do I wish it. If only you will keep in your mind one little place for the memory of our visit to your vessel and your promise respecting it, I shall be more than content."

Eveena's humble, unconscious self-abnegation was rendering the conversation intolerably painful, and even the embarrassing situation now at hand was a welcome interruption. Eveena paused before a door opening from the gallery into one of the rooms looking on the peristyle.

"You will find them there," she said, drawing back.

"Come with me, then," I answered; and as she shrank away, I tightened my clasp of her waist and drew her forward. The door opened, and we found ourselves in presence of six veiled ladies in pink and silver, all of them, with one exception, a little taller and less slight than my bride. Eveena, with the kindness which never failed under the most painful trial or the most powerful impulses of natural feeling, extricated herself gently from my hold, took the hand of the first, and brought her up to me. The girl was evidently startled at the first sight of her new possessor, and alarmed by a figure so much larger and more powerful than any she had ever seen, exceeding probably the picture drawn by her imagination.

"This," said Eveena gently and gravely, "is Eunané, the prettiest and most accomplished scholar in her Nursery."

As I was about to acknowledge the introduction with the same cold politeness with which I should have bowed to a strange guest on Earth, Eveena took my left hand in her own and laid it on the maiden's veil, recalling to me at once the proprieties of the occasion and the justice she had claimed for her unoffending and unintentional rivals; but at the same time bringing back in full force a remembrance she could not have forgotten, but whose effect upon myself the ideas to which she was habituated rendered her unable to anticipate. To accept in her presence a second bride, by the same ceremonial act which had so lately asserted my claim to herself, was intensely repugnant to my feelings, and only her own self-sacrificing influence could have overcome my reluctance. My hesitation was, I fear, perceptible to Eunané; for, as I removed her veil and head-dress, her expression and a colour somewhat brighter than that of mere maiden shyness indicated disappointment or mortified pride. She was certainly very beautiful, and perhaps, had I now seen them both for the first time, I might have acquiesced in the truth of Eveena's self-

depreciation. As it was, nothing could associate with the bright intelligent face, the clear grey eyes and light brown hair, the lithe active form instinct with nervous energy, that charm which from our first acquaintance their expression of gentle kindness, and, later, the devoted affection visible in every look, had given to Eveena's features.

It is, I suppose, hardly natural to man to feel actual unkindness towards a young and beautiful girl who has given no personal offence. Having once admitted, the justice of Eveena's plea, and feeling that she would be more pained by the omission than by the fulfilment of the forms which courtesy and common kindness imperatively demanded, I kissed Eunané's brow and spoke a few words to her, with as much of tenderness as I could feel or affect for Eveena's rival, after what had passed to endear Eveena more than ever. The latter waited a little, to allow me spontaneously to perform the same ceremony with the other girls; but seeing my hesitation, she came forward again and presented severally four others—Enva ("Snow") =

Blanche), Leenoo ("Rose"), Eiralé, Elfé, all more or less of the usual type of female beauty in Mars, with long full tresses varying in tinge from flax to deep gold or the lightest brown; each with features almost faultless, and with all the attraction (to me unfailing) possessed for men who have passed their youth by la beauté du Diable—the bloom of pure graceful girlhood.

Eivé, the sixth of the party, standing on the right of the others, and therefore last in place according to Martial usage, was smaller and slighter than Eveena herself, and made an individual impression on my attention by a manifest timidity and agitation greater than any of the rest had evinced. As I removed her veil I was struck by the total unlikeness which her face and form presented to those I had just saluted. Her hair was so dark as by contrast to seem black; her complexion less fair than those of her companions, though as fair as that of an average Greek beauty; her eyes of deepest brown; her limbs, and especially the hands and feet, marvellously perfect in shape and colour, but in the delicacy and minuteness of their form suggesting, as did all the proportions of her tiny figure, the peculiar grace of childhood; an image in miniature of faultless physical beauty. In Eivé alone of the bevy I felt a real interest; but the interest called forth by a singularly pretty child, in whose expression the first glance discerns a

character it will take long to read, rather than that commanded by the charms of earliest womanhood.

When I had completed the ceremonial round, there was a somewhat awkward silence, which Eveena at last broke by suggesting that Eunané should show us through the house, with which she had made the earliest acquaintance. This young girl readily took the lead thus assigned to her, and by some delicate manoeuvre, whose authorship I could not doubt, I found her hand in mine as we made our tour. The number of chambers was much greater than in Esmo's dwelling, the garden of the peristyle larger and more elaborately arranged, if not more beautiful. The ambau were more numerous than even the domestic service of so large a mansion appeared to require. The birds, whose duties lay outside, were by this time asleep on their perches, and we forbore to disturb them. The central chamber of the seraglio, if I may so call it, the largest and midmost of those in the rear of the garden, devoted as of course to the ladies of the household, was especially magnificent.

When we stood in its midst, shy looks askance from all the six betrayed their secret ambition; though Eivé's was but momentary, and so slight that I felt I might have unfairly suspected her of presumption. I left this room, however, in silence, and assigned to each, of my maiden brides, in order as they had been presented to me, the rooms on the left; and then, as we stood once more in the peristyle, having postponed all further arrangements, all distribution of household duties, to the morrow (assigning, however, to Eunané, whose native energy and forwardness had made early acquaintance with the dwelling and its dumb inhabitants, the charge of providing and preparing with their assistance our morning meal), I said, "I have let the business of the evening zyda actually encroach on midnight, and must detain you from your rest no longer. Eveena, you know, I still have need of you."

She was standing at a little distance, next to Eunané; and the latter, with a smile half malicious, half triumphant, whispered something in her ear.

There was a suppressed annoyance in Eveena's look which provoked me to interpose. On Earth I should never have been fool enough to meddle in a

woman's quarrel. The weakest can take her own part in the warfare of taunt and innuendo, better and more venomously than could dervish, priest, or politician. But Eveena could no more lower herself to the ordinary level of feminine malice than I could have borne to hear her do so; and it was intolerable that one whose sweet humility commanded respect from myself should submit to slight or sneer from the lips and eyes of petulant girls. Eunané started as I spoke, using that accent which gives its most peremptory force to the Martial imperative. "Repeat aloud what you have chosen to say to Eveena in my presence."

If the first to express the ill-will excited by Eveena's evident influence, though exerted in their own behalf, it was less that Eunané surpassed her companions in malice than that they fell short of her in audacity. Her school-mates had found her their most daring leader in mischief, the least reluctant scapegoat when mischief was to be atoned. But she was cowed, partly perhaps by her first collision with masculine authority, partly, I fear, by sheer dread of physical force visibly greater than she had ever known by repute. Perhaps she was too much frightened to obey. At any rate, it was from Eveena, despite her pleading looks, that I extorted an answer.

She yielded at last only to that formal imperative which her conscience would not permit her to disobey, and which for the first time I now employed in addressing her.

"Eunané only repeated," Eveena said, with a reluctance so manifest that one might have supposed her to be the offender, "a school-girl's proverb:—

"'Ware the wrath that stands to cool:
Then the sandal shows the rule.'"

The smile that had accompanied the whisper—though not so much suggestive of a woman's malignity as of a child's exultation in a companion's disgrace—gave point and sting to the taunt. It is on chance, I suppose, that the effect of such things depends. Had the saying been thrown at any of Eunané's equals, I should probably have been inclined to laugh, even if I felt it necessary to reprimand. But, angered at a hint which placed Eveena on their own level, I forgot how far the speaker's experience

and inexperience alike palliated the impertinence. That the insinuation shocked none of those around me was evident. Theirs were not the looks of women, however young and thoughtless, startled by an affront to their sex; but of children amazed at a child's folly in provoking capricious and irresponsible power. The angry quickness with which I turned to Eunané received a double, though doubly unintentional, rebuke, equally illustrative of Martial ideas and usages. The culprit cowered like a child expecting a brutal blow. A gentle pressure on my left arm evinced the same fear in a quarter from which its expression wounded me deeply. That pressure arrested not, as was intended, my hand, but my voice; and when I spoke the frightened girl looked up in surprise at its measured tones.

"Wrong, and wrong thrice over, Eunané. It is for me to teach you the bad taste of bringing into your new home the ideas and language of school.

Meanwhile, in no case would you learn more of my rule than concerned your own fault. Take in exchange for your proverb the kindliest I have learned in your language:—

"'Whispered warnings reach the heart;
Veil the blush and spare the smart.'

"But, happily for you, your taunt had not truth enough to sting; and I can tell the story about which you are unduly curious as frankly as you please.—Let me speak now, Eveena, that I may spare the need to speak again and in another tone.—That Eveena seemed to have put us both in a false position only convinced me that she had a motive she knew would satisfy me as fully as herself. When I learned what that motive was, I was greatly surprised at her unselfishness and courage. If you threw me your veil to save me from drowning, how would you feel if my first words to you were:—'No one must think I could not swim, therefore even the household must believe you, in unveiling, guilty of an unpardonable fault'?… Answer me, Eunané."

"I should let you sink next time," she replied, with a pretty half-dubious sauciness, showing that her worst fears at least were relieved.

"Quite right; but you are less generous than Eveena. To hide how I had acted on her advice, she would have had you suppose her guilty. That you might not laugh at my authority, and 'find a dragon in the esve's nest,' she would have had me treat her as guilty."

"But I deserved it. A girl has no right to break the seal in the master's absence," interposed Eveena, much more distressed than gratified by the vindication to which she was so well entitled.

"Let your tongue sleep, Eveena. So [with a kiss] I blot your first miscalculation, Eunané. Earth [the Evening Star of Mars] light your dreams."

It was with visible reluctance that Eveena followed me into the chamber we had last left; and she expostulated as earnestly as her obedience would permit against the fiat that assigned it to her.

"Choose what room you please, then," I said; "but understand that, so far as my will and my trust can make you, you are the mistress here."

"Well, then," she answered, "give me the little octagon beside your own:"—
the smallest and simplest, but to my taste the prettiest, room in the house.

"I should like to be near you still, if I may; but, believe me, I shall not be frozen (hurt) because you think another hand better able to steer the carriage, if mine may sometimes rest in yours."

Leading her into the room she had chosen, and having installed her among the cushions that were to form her couch, I silenced decisively her renewed protest.

"Let me answer you on this point, once and for ever, Eveena. To me this seems matter of right, not of favour or fitness. But favour and fitness here go with right. I could no more endure to place another before or beside you than I could break the special bond between us, and deny the hope of which the Serpent" (laying my hand on her shoulder-clasp, which, by mere accident, was shaped into a faint resemblance to the mystic coil) "is the emblem; the hope that alone can make such love as ours endurable, or even possible, to creatures that must die. She who knelt with me before the Emerald Throne, who took with me the vows so awfully sanctioned, shall
hold the first place in my home as in my heart till the Serpent's promise be fulfilled."

Both were silent for some time, for never could we refer to that Vision—
whether an objective fact, or an impression communicated from one spirit to the other by the occult force of intense sympathy—save by such allusion; and the remembrance never failed to affect us both with a feeling too deep for words. Eveena spoke again—

"I am sorry you have so bound yourself; perhaps only because you knew me first. And it shames me to receive fresh proof of your kindness to-night."

"And why, my own?"

"Do not make me feel," she said, "that—though the measured sentences you have taught me to call scolding seemed the sharpest of all penances—there is a heavier yet in the silence which withholds forgiveness."

"What have I yet to forgive, Madonna?"

But Eveena could read my feelings in spite of my words, and knew that the pain she had given was too recent to allow me to misconceive her penitence.

"I ought to say, my interference. It was your right to rule as you chose, and my meddling was a far worse offence than Eunané's malice. But it was not that you felt too deeply to reprove."

"True! Eunané hurt me a little; but I expected no such misjudgment from you. By the touch that proved your alarm I know that I gave no cause for it."

"How so?" she asked in surprise.

"You laid your hand instinctively on my left arm, the one your people use.

Had I made the slightest angry gesture, you would have held back my right. Had I deserved that Eveena should think so ill of me—think me capable of doing such dishonour to her presence and to my own roof, which should have protected an equal enemy from that which you feared for a helpless girl? For what you would have checked was such a blow as

men deal to men who can strike back; and the hand that had given it would have been unfit to clasp man's in friendship or woman's in love. You yourself must have shrunk from its touch."

She caught and held it fast to her lips.

"Can I forget that it saved my life? I don't understand you at all, but I see that I have frozen your heart. I did fancy for one moment you would strike, as passionate men and women often do strike provoking girls, perhaps forgetting your own strength; and I knew you would be miserable if you did hurt her—in that way. The next moment I was ashamed, more than you will believe, to have wronged you so. Like every man, from the head of a household to the Arch-Judge or the Camptâ, you must rule by fear. But your wrath will 'stand to cool;' and you will hate to make a girl cry as you would hate to send a criminal to the electric-rack, the lightning-stroke, or the vivisection-table. And, whatever you had done, do you fancy that I could shrink from you? I said, 'If you weary of your flower-bird you must strike with the hammer;' and if you could do so, do you think I should not feel for your hand to hold it to the last?"

"Hush, Eveena! how can I bear such words? You might forgive me for any outrage to you: I doubt your easily forgetting cruelty to another. I have not a heart like yours. As I never failed a friend, so I never yet forgave a foe.

Yet even I might pardon one of those girls an attempt to poison myself, and in some circumstances I might even learn to like her better afterwards. But I doubt if I could ever touch again the hand that had mixed the poison for another, though that other were my mortal enemy."

CHAPTER XIX - A COMPLETE ESTABLISHMENT.

Before I slept Eveena had convinced me, much to my own discomfiture, how very limited must be any authority that could be delegated to her. In such a household there could be no second head or deputy, and an attempt to devolve any effective charge on her would only involve her in trouble and odium. Even at the breakfast, spread as usual in the centre of the peristyle, she entreated that we should present ourselves separately.

Eunané appeared to have performed very dexterously the novel duty assigned to her. The ambau had obeyed her orders with well-trained promptitude, and the carvee, in bringing fruit, leaves, and roots from the outer garden, had more than verified all that on a former occasion Eveena had told me of their cleverness and quick comprehension of instructions.

Eunané's face brightened visibly as I acknowledged the neatness and the tempting appearance of the meal she had set forth. She was yet more gratified by receiving charge for the future of the same duty, and authority to send, as is usual, by an ambâ the order for that principal part of each day's food which is supplied by the confectioner. By reserving for Eveena the place among the cushions immediately on my left, I made to the assembled household the expected announcement that she was to be regarded as mistress of the house; feminine punctiliousness on points of domestic precedence strikingly contrasting the unceremonious character of intercourse among men out of doors. The very ambau recognise the mistress or the favourite, as dogs the master of their Earthly home.

The ladies were at first shy and silent, Eunané only giving me more than a monosyllabic answer to my remarks, and even Eunané never speaking save in reply to me. A trivial incident, however, broke through this reserve, and afforded me a first taste of the petty domestic vexations in store for me. The beverage most to my liking was always the carcarâ—juice flavoured with roasted kernels, something resembling coffee in taste. On this occasion the carcarâ and another favourite dish had a taste so peculiar that I pushed both aside almost untouched. On observing this, the rest—Enva, Leenoo, Elfé, and Eiralé—took occasion to criticise the articles in question with such remarks and grimaces as ill-bred children might venture for the annoyance

of an inexperienced sister. I hesitated to repress this outbreak as it deserved, till Eunané's bitter mortification was evident in her brightening colour and the doubtful, half-appealing glance of tearful eyes. Then a rebuke, such as might have been appropriately addressed yesterday to these rude school-girls by their governess, at once silenced them. As we rose, I asked Eveena, who, with more courtesy than the rest of us, had finished her portion—

"Is there any justice in these reproaches? I certainly don't like the carcarâ to-day, but it does not follow that Eunané is in fault."

The rest, Eunané included, looked their annoyance at this appeal; but Eveena's temper and kindness were proof against petulance.

"The carcarâ is in fault," she said; "but I don't think Eunané is. In learning cookery at school she had her materials supplied to her; this time the carve has probably given her an unripe or overripe fruit which has spoiled the whole."

"And do you not know ripe from unripe fruit?" I inquired, turning to Eunané.

"How should she?" interposed Eveena. "I doubt if she ever saw them growing."

"How so?" I asked of Eunané.

"It is true," she answered. "I never went beyond the walls of our playground till I came here; and though there were a few flower-beds in the inner gardens, there were none but shade trees among the turf and concrete yards to which we were confined."

"I should have known no better," observed Eveena; "but being brought up at home, I learned to know all the plants in my father's grounds, which were more various, I believe, than usual."

"Then," I said, "Eunané has a new life and a multitude of new pleasures before her. Has this peristyle given you your first sight of flowers beyond those in the beds of your Nursery? And have you never seen anything of the world about you?"

"Never," she said. "And Eveena's excuse for me is, I believe, perfectly true.
The carve must have been stupid, but I knew no better."

"Well," I rejoined, "you must forgive the bird, as we must excuse you for spoiling our breakfast. I will contrive that you shall know more of fruits and flowers before long. In the meantime, you will probably have a different if not a wider view from this roof than from that of your Nursery."

After all, Eunané's girlhood, typical of the whole life of many Martial women, had not, I suppose, been more dreary or confined than that of children in London, Canton, or Calcutta. But this incident, reminding me how dreary and limited that life was, served to excuse in my eyes the pettiness and poverty of the characters it had produced. A Martial woman's whole experience may well be confined within a few acres, and from the cradle to the grave she may see no more of the world than can be discerned from the roof of her school or her husband's home.

Eunané, with the assistance of the ambau, busied herself in removing the remains of the meal. The other five, putting on their veils, scampered up the inclined plane to the roof, much like children released from table or from tasks. Turning to Eveena, who still remained beside me, I said—

"Get your veil, and come out with me; I have not yet an idea where we are, and scarcely a notion what the grounds are like."

She followed me to my apartment, out of which, opened the one she had chosen, and as the window closed behind us she spoke in a tone of appeal—

"Do not insist on my accompanying you. As you bade me always speak my thought, I had much rather you would take one of the others."

"You professed," I said, "to take especial pleasure in a walk with me, and this time I will be careful that you are not overtired."

"Of course I should like it," she answered; "but it would not be just. Please let me this time remain to take my part of the household duties, and make myself acquainted with the house. Choose your companion among the others, whom you have scarcely noticed yet."

Preferring not only Eveena's company, but even my own, to that of any of the six, and feeling myself not a little dependent on her guidance and explanations, I remonstrated. But finding that her sense of justice and kindness would yield to nothing short of direct command, I gave way.

"You forget my pleasure," I said at last. "But if you will not go, you must at least tell me which I am to take. I will not pretend to have a choice in the matter."

"Well, then," she answered, "I should be glad to see you take Eunané. She is, I think, the eldest, apparently the most intelligent and companionable, and she has had one mortification already she hardly deserved."

"And is much the prettiest," I added maliciously. But Eveena was incapable of even understanding so direct an appeal to feminine jealousy.

"I think so," she said; "much the prettiest among us. But that will make no difference under her veil."

"And must she keep down her veil," I asked, "in our own grounds?"

Eveena laughed. "Wherever she might be seen by any man but yourself."

"Call her then," I answered.

Eveena hesitated. But having successfully carried her own way on the main question, she would not renew her remonstrances on a minor point; and finding her about to join the rest, she drew Eunané apart. Eunané came up to me alone, Eveena having busied herself in some other part of the house.

She approached slowly as if reluctant, and stood silent before me, her manner by no means expressive of satisfaction.

"Eveena thought," I said, "that you would like to accompany me; but if not, you may tell her so; and tell her in that case that she must come."

"But I shall be glad to go wherever you please," replied Eunané.

"Eveena did not tell me why you sent for me, and"——

"And you were afraid to be scolded for spoiling the breakfast? You have heard quite enough of that."

"You dropped a word last night," she answered, "which made me think you would keep your displeasure till you had me alone."

"Quite true," I said, "if I had any displeasure to keep. But you might spoil a dozen meals, and not vex me half as much as the others did."

"Why?" she asked in surprise. "Girls and women always spite one another if they have a chance, especially one who is in disfavour or disgrace with authority."

"So much the worse," I answered. "And now—you know as much or as little of the house as any of us; find the way into the grounds."

A narrow door, not of crystal as usual, but of metal painted to resemble the walls, led directly from one corner of the peristyle into the grounds outside. I had inferred on my arrival, by the distance from the road to the house, that their extent was considerable, but I was surprised alike by their size and arrangement. On two sides they were bounded by a wall about four hundred yards in length—that parting them from the road was about twice as long. They were laid out with few of the usual orchard plots and beds of different fruits and vegetables, but rather in the form of a small park, with trees of various sorts, among which the fruit trees were a minority. The surface was broken by natural rising grounds and artificial terraces; the soil was turfed in the manner I have previously described, with minute plants of different colours arranged in bands and patterns.

Here and there was a garden consisting of a variety of flower-beds and flowering shrubs; broad concrete paths winding throughout, and a beautiful silver stream meandering hither and thither, and filling several small ponds and fountains. That the grounds immediately appertaining to the house were not intended as usual for the purposes of a farm or kitchen-garden was evident. The reason became equally apparent when, looking towards the north, where no wall bounded them, I saw—over a gate in the middle of a dense hedge of flowering shrubs, which, with a ditch beyond it, formed the limit of the park in that direction—an extensive farm divided by the usual ditches into some twenty-five or thirty distinct fields, and more than a square mile in extent. This, as Eunané's native inquisitiveness and quickness had already learnt, formed part of the estate attached to the

mansion and bestowed upon me by the Camptâ. It was admirably cultivated, containing orchards, fields rich with various thriving crops, and pastures grazed by the Unicorn and other of the domestic birds and beasts kept to supply Martial tables with milk, eggs, and meat; producing nearly every commodity to which the climate was suited, and, as a very short observation assured me, capable of yielding a far greater income than would suffice to sustain in luxury and splendour a household larger than that enforced upon me. We walked in this direction, my companion talking fluently enough when once I had set her at ease, and seemingly free from the shyness and timidity which Eveena had at first displayed. She paused when we reached a bridge that spanned the ditch dividing the grounds from the farm, aware that, save on special invitation, she might not, even in my company, go beyond the former. I led her on, however, till soon after we had crossed the ditch I saw a man approaching us. On this, I desired Eunané to remain where she was, seating her at the foot of a fruit tree in one of the orchard plots, and proceeded to meet the stranger. After exchanging the usual salute, he came immediately to the point.

"I thought," he said, "that you would not care yourself to undertake the cultivation of so extensive an estate. Indeed, the mere superintendence would occupy the whole of one man's attention, and its proper cultivation would be the work of six or eight. I have had some little experience in agriculture, and determined to ask for this charge."

"And who has recommended you?" I said. "Or have you any sort of introduction or credentials to me?"

He made a sign which I immediately recognised. Caution, however, was imposed by the law to which that sign appealed.

"You can read," I said, "by starlight?"

"Better than by any other," he rejoined with a smile.

One or two more tokens interchanged left me no doubt that the claim was genuine, and, of course, irresistible.

"Enough," I replied. "You may take entire charge on the usual terms, which, doubtless, you know better than I."

"You trust me then, absolutely?" he said, in a tone of some little surprise.

"In trusting you," I replied, "I trust the Zinta. I am tolerably sure to be safe in hands recommended by them."

"You are right," he said, "and how right this will prove to you," and he placed in my hand a small cake upon which was stamped an impression of the signet that I had seen on Esmo's wrist. When he saw that I recognised it, he took it back, and, breaking it into fragments, chewed and swallowed it.

"This," he said, "was given me to avouch the following message:—Our Chiefs are informed that the Order is threatened with a novel danger.

Systematic persecution by open force or by law has been attempted and defeated ages ago, and will hardly be tried again. What seems to be intended now is the destruction of our Chiefs, individually, by secret means—means which it is supposed we shall not be able to trace to the instigators, even if we should detect their instruments."

"But," I remarked, "those who have warned you of the danger must know from whom it proceeds, and those who are employed in such an attack must run not only the ordinary risk of assassins, but the further risk entailed by the peculiar powers of those they assail."

"Those powers," he answered, "they do not understand or recognise. The instruments, I presume, will be encouraged by an assurance that the Courts are in their favour, and by a pledge in the last resort that they shall be protected. The exceptional customs of our Order, especially their refusal to send their children into the public Nurseries, mark out and identify them; and though our places of meeting are concealed and have never been invaded, the fact that we do meet and the persons of those who attend can hardly be concealed."

"But," I asked, "if a charge of assassination is once made and proved, how can the Courts refuse to do justice? Can the instigators protect the culprit without committing themselves?"

"They would appeal, I do not doubt, to a law, passed many ages ago with a special regard to ourselves, but which has not been applied for a score of

centuries, putting the members of a secret religious society beyond the pale of legal protection. That we shall ultimately find them out and avenge ourselves, you need not doubt. But in the meantime every known dissentient from the customs of the majority is in danger, and persons of note or prominence especially so. Next to Esmo and his son, the husband of his daughter is, perhaps, in as much peril as any one. No open attempt on your life will be adventured at present, while you retain the favour of the Camptâ. But you have made at least one mortal and powerful enemy, and you may possibly be the object of well-considered and persistent schemes of assassination. On the other hand, next to our Chief and his son, you have a paramount claim on the protection of the Order; and those who with me will take charge of your affairs have also charge to watch vigilantly over your life. If you will trust me beforehand with knowledge of all your movements, I think your chief peril will lie in the one sphere upon which we cannot intrude—your own household; and Clavelta directs your own special attention to this quarter. Immediate danger can scarcely threaten you as yet, save from a woman's hand."

"Poison?"

"Probably," he returned coolly. "But of the details of the plot our Council are, I believe, as absolutely ignorant as of the quarter from which it proceeds."

"And how," I inquired, "can it be that the witness who has informed you of the plot has withheld the names, without which his information is so imperfect, and serves rather to alarm than to protect us?"

"You know," he replied, "the kind of mysterious perception to which we can resort, and are probably aware how strangely lucid in some points, how strangely darkened in others, is the vision that does not depend on ordinary human senses?"

As we spoke we had passed Eunané once or twice, walking backwards and forwards along the path near which she sat. As my companion was about to continue, we were so certainly within her hearing that I checked him.

"Take care," I said; "I know nothing of her except the Camptâ's choice, and that she is not of us."

He visibly started.

"I thought," he said, "that the witness of our conversation was one at least as reliable as yourself. I forgot how it happened that you have diverged from the prudence which forbids our brethren to admit to their households aliens from the Order and possible spies on its secrets."

"Of whom do you speak as Clavelta?" I asked. "I was not even aware that the Order had a single head."

"The Signet," replied my friend in evident surprise, "should have distinguished the Arch-Enlightener to duller sight than yours."

We had not spoken, of course, till we were again beyond hearing; but my companion looked round carefully before he proceeded—

"You will understand the better, then, how strong is your own claim upon the care of your brethren, and how confidently you may rely upon their vigilance and fidelity."

"I should regret," I answered, "that their lives should be risked for mine. In dangers like those against which you could protect me, I have been accustomed from boyhood to trust my own right hand. But the fear of secret assassination has often unnerved the bravest men, and I will not say that it may not disturb me."

"For you," he answered, "personally we should care as for one of our brethren exposed to especial danger, For him who saved the descendant of our Founder, and who in her right, after her father and brother, would be the guardian, if not the head, of the only remaining family of his lineage, one and all of us are at need bound to die."

After a few more words we parted, and I rejoined Eunané, and led her back towards the house. I had learnt to consider taciturnity a matter of course, except where there was actual occasion for speech; but Eunané had chattered so fluently and frankly just before, that her absolute silence might have suggested to me the possibility that she had heard and was pondering

things not intended for her knowledge, had I been less preoccupied.

Enured to the perils of war, of the chase, of Eastern diplomacy, and of travel in the wildest parts of the Earth, I do not pretend indifference to the fear of assassination, and especially of poison. Cromwell, and other soldiers of equal nerve and clearer conscience, have found their iron courage sorely shaken by a peril against which no precautions were effective and from which they could not enjoy an hour's security. The incessant continuous strain on the nerves is, I suppose, the chief element in the peculiar dread with which brave men have regarded this kind of peril; as the best troops cannot endure to be under fire in their camp. Weighing, however, the probability that girls who had been selected by the Sovereign, and had left their Nursery only to pass directly into my house, could have been already bribed or seduced to become the instruments of murderous treachery, I found it but slight; and before we reached the house I had made up my mind to discard the apprehensions or precautions recommended to me on their account. Far better, if need be, to die by poison than to live in hourly terror of it. Better to be murdered than to suspect of secret treason those with whom I must maintain the most intimate relations, and whose sex and years made it intolerable to believe them criminal. I dismissed the thought, then; and believing that I had probably wronged them in allowing it to dwell for a moment in my mind, felt perhaps more tenderly than before towards them, and certainly indisposed to name to Eveena a suspicion of which I was myself ashamed.

Perhaps, too, youth and beauty weighed in my conclusion more than cool reason would have allowed. A Martial proverb says—

"Trust a foe, and you may rue it;
Trust a friend, and perish through it.
Trust a woman if you will;—

Thrice betrayed, you'll trust her still."

As to the general warning, I was wishful to consult Eveena, and unwilling to withhold from her any secret of my thoughts; but equally averse to

disturb her with alarms that were trying even to nerves seasoned by the varied experience of twenty years against every open peril.

CHAPTER XX - LIFE, SOCIAL AND DOMESTIC.

As we approached the house I caught sight of Eveena's figure among the party gathered on the roof. She had witnessed the interview, but her habitual and conscientious deference forbade her to ask a confidence not volunteered; and she seemed fully satisfied when, on the first occasion on which we were alone, I told her simply that the stranger belonged to the Zinta and had been recommended by her father himself to the charge of my estate. Though reluctant to disturb her mind with fears she could not shake off as I could, and which would make my every absence at least a season of terror, the sense of insecurity doubtless rendered me more anxious to enjoy whenever possible the only society in which it was permissible to be frank and off my guard. No man in his senses would voluntarily have accepted the position which had been forced upon me.

The Zveltau never introduce aliens into their households. Their leading ideas and fundamental principles so deeply affect the conduct of existence, the motives of action, the bases of all moral reasoning—so completely do the inferences drawn from them and the habits of thought to which they lead pervade and tinge the mind, conscience, and even language—that though it may be easy to "live in the light at home and walk with the blind abroad," yet in the familiar intercourse of household life even a cautious and reserved man (and I was neither) must betray to the keen instinctive perceptions of women whether he thought and felt like those around him, or was translating different thoughts into an alien language. This difficulty is little felt between unbelievers and Christians. The simple creed of the Zinta, however, like that of the Prophet, affects the thought and life as the complicated and subtle mysteries of more elaborate theologies, more refined philosophic systems rarely do.

One of Eveena's favourite quotations bore the unmistakable stamp of Zveltic mysticism:—
"Symbols that invert the sense
Form the Seal of Providence;
Contradiction gives the key,
Time unlocks the mystery."

The danger in which my relation to the Zinta and its chief involved me, and the presence of half a dozen rivals to Eveena—rivals also to that regard for the Star which at first I felt chiefly for her sake—likely as they seemed to impair the strength and sweetness of the tie between us, actually worked to consolidate and endear it. To enjoy, except on set occasions, without constant liability to interruption, Eveena's sole society was no easy matter.

To conceal our real secret, and the fact that there was a secret, was imperative. Avowedly exclusive confidence, conferences from which the rest of the household were directly shut out, would have suggested to their envious tempers that Eveena played the spy on them, or influenced and advised the exercise of my authority. To be alone with her, therefore, as naturally and necessarily I must often wish to be, required manoeuvres and arrangements as delicate and difficult, though as innocent, as those employed by engaged couples under the strict conventions of European household usage; and the comparative rarity of such interviews, and the manner in which they had often to be contrived beforehand, kept alive in its earliest freshness the love which, if not really diminished, generally loses somewhat of its first bloom and delicacy in the unrestrained intercourse of marriage. Absolutely and solely trusted, assured that her company was eagerly sought, and at least as deeply valued as ever—compelled by the ideas of her race to accept the situation as natural and right, and wholly incapable of the pettier and meaner forms of jealousy—

Eveena was fully content and happy in her relations with me. That, on the whole, she was not comfortable, or at least much less so than during our suddenly abbreviated honeymoon, was apparent; but her loss of brightness and cheerfulness was visible chiefly in her weary and downcast looks on any occasion when, after being absent for some hours from the house, I came upon her unawares. In my presence she was always calm and peaceful, kind, and seemingly at ease; and if she saw or heard me on my return, though she carefully avoided any appearance of eagerness to greet me sooner than others, or to claim especial attention, she ever met me with a smile of welcome as frank and bright as a young bride on Earth could

give to a husband returning to her sole society from a long day of labour for her sake.

In so far as compliance was possible I was compelled to admit the wisdom of Eveena's plea that no open distinction should be made in her favour.

Except in the simple fact of our affection, there was no assignable reason for making her my companion more frequently than Eunané or Eivé.

Except that I could trust her completely, there was no distinction of age, social rank, or domestic relation to afford a pretext for exempting her from restraints which, if at first I thought them senseless and severe, were soon justified by experience of the kind of domestic control which just emancipated school-girls expected and required. Nor would she accept the immunity tacitly allowed her. It was not that any established custom or right bounded the arbitrary power of domestic autocracy. The right of all but unbounded wrong, the liberty of limitless caprice, is unquestionably vested in the head of the household. But the very completeness of the despotism rendered its exercise impossible. Force cannot act where there is no resistance. The sword of the Plantagenet could cleave the helmet but not the quilt of down. I could do as I pleased without infringing any understanding or giving any right to complain.

"But," said Eveena, "you have a sense of justice which has nothing to do with law or usage. Even your language is not ours. You think of right and wrong, where we should speak only of what is or is not punishable. You can make a favourite if you will pay the price. Could you endure to be hated in your own home, or I to know that you deserved it? Or, if you could, could you bear to see me hated and my life made miserable?"

"They dare not!" I returned angrily fearing that they had dared, and that she had already felt the spite she was so careful not to provoke.

"Do you think that feminine malice cannot contrive to envenom a dozen stings that I could not explain if I would, and you could not deal with if I did?"

"But," I replied, "it seems admitted that there is no such thing as right or custom. As Enva said, I have bought and paid for them, and may do what I

please within the contract; and you agree that is just what any other man in this world would do."

"Yes," returned Eveena, "and I watched your face while Enva spoke. How did you like her doctrine? Of course you may do as you please—if you can please. You may silence discontent, you may suppress spiteful innuendos and even sulky looks, you may put down mutiny, by sheer terror. Can you? You may command me to go with you whenever you go out; you may take the same means to make me complain of unkindness as to make them conceal it; you may act like one of our own people, if you can stoop to the level of their minds. But we both know that you can do nothing of the kind. How could you bear to be driven into unsparing and undeserved severity, who can hardly bring yourself to enforce the discipline necessary to peace and comfort on those who will only be ruled by fear and would like you better if they feared you more? Did you hear the proverb Leenoo muttered, very unjustly, when she left your room yesterday, 'A favourite wears out many sandals'? No! You see the very phrase wounds and disgusts you. But you would find it a true one. Can you take vengeance for a fault you have yourself provoked? Can you decide without inquiry, condemn without evidence, punish without hearing? Men do these things, of course, and women expect them. But you—I do not say you would be ashamed so to act—you cannot do it, any more than you can breathe the air of our snow-mountains."

"At all events, Eveena, I no more dare do it in your presence than I dare forswear the Faith we hold in common."

But whatever Eveena might exact or I concede, the distinction between the wife who commanded as much respect as affection, and the girls who could at best be pets or playthings, was apparent against our will in every detail of daily life and domestic intercourse. It was alike impossible to treat Eveena as a child and to rule Enva or Eiralé as other than children. It was as unnatural to use the tone of command or rebuke to one for whom my unexpressed wishes were absolute law, as to observe the form of request or advice in directing or reproving those whose obedience depended on the consequences of rebellion. It only made matters worse that the distinction

corresponded but too accurately to their several deserts. No faults could have been so irritating to Eveena's companions as her undeniable faultlessness.

The ludicrous aspect of my relation to the rest of the household was even more striking than I had expected. That I should find myself in the absurd position of a man entrusted with the direct personal government of half-a-dozen young ladies was even "more truly spoke than meant." One at least among them might singly have made in time a not unlovable wife, and all, perhaps, might severally and separately have been reduced to conjugal complaisance. Collectively, they were, as Eveena had said, a set of school-girls, and school-girls used to stricter restraint and much sharper discipline than those of a French or Italian convent. They would have made life a burden to a vigorous English schoolmistress, and imperilled the soul of any Lady-Abbess whose list of permissible penances excluded the dark cell and the scourge. Fortunately for both parties, I had the advantage of governess and Superior in the natural awe which girls feel for the authority of manhood—till they have found out of what soft fibre men are made—and in the artificial fear inspired by domestic usage and tradition. For I was soon aware that even on its ridiculous side the relation was not to be trifled with. The simple indifference a man feels towards the escapades of girlhood was not applicable to women and wives, who yet lacked womanly sense and the feeling of conjugal duty. This serious aspect of their position soon contracted the indulgence naturally conceded to youth's heedlessness and animal spirits. These, displayed at first only in the energy and eagerness of their every movement within the narrow limits of conventional usage, broke all bounds when, after one or two half-timid, half-venturous experiments on my patience, they felt that they had, at least for the moment, exchanged the monotony, the mechanical routine, the stern repression of their life in the great Nurseries, not for the harsh household discipline to which they naturally looked forward, but for the

"loosened zone" which to them seemed to promise absolute liberty. When not immediately in my presence or Eveena's, their keen enjoyment of a life so new, the sudden development of the brighter side of their nature under circumstances that gave play to the vigorous vitality of youth, gave as

much pleasure to me as to themselves. But in contact with myself or Eveena they were women, and showed only the wrong side of the varied texture of womanhood. To the master they were slaves, each anxious to attract his notice, win his preference; before the favourite, spiteful, envious of her and of each other, bitter, malicious, and false. For Eveena's sake, it was impossible to look on with indolent indifference on freaks of temper which, childish in the form they assumed, were envenomed by the deliberate dislike and unscrupulous cunning of jealous women.

But even on the childish side of their character and conduct, they soon displayed a determination to test by actual experiment the utmost extent of the liberty allowed, and the nature and sufficiency of its limits. Eunané was always the most audacious trespasser and representative rebel. Fortunately for her, the daring which had bewildered and exasperated feminine guardians rather amused and interested me, giving some variety and relief to the monotonous absurdity of the situation. Nothing in her conduct was more remarkable or more characteristic than the simplicity and good temper with which she generally accepted as of course the less agreeable consequences of her outbreaks; unless it were the sort of natural dignity with which, when she so pleased, the game played out and its forfeit paid, the naughty child subsided into the lively but rational companion, and the woman simply ignored the scrapes of the school-girl.

As her character seemed to unfold, Eivé's individuality became as distinctly parted from the rest as Eunané's, though in an opposite direction.

Comparatively timid and indolent, without their fulness of life, she seemed to me little more than a child; and she fell with apparent willingness into that position, accepting naturally its privileges and exemptions. She alone was never in the way, never vexatious or exacting. Content with the notice that naturally fell to her share, she obtained the more. Never intruding between Eveena and myself, she alone was not wholly unwelcome to share our accidental privacy when, in the peristyle or the grounds, the others left us temporarily alone. On such occasions she would often draw near and crouch at my feet or by Eveena's side, curling herself like a kitten upon the turf or among the cushions, often resting her little head upon Eveena's knee

or mine; generally silent, but never so silent as to seem to be a spy upon our conversation, rather as a favourite child privileged, in consideration of her quietude and her supposed harmlessness and inattention, to remain when others are excluded, and to hear much to which she is supposed not to listen. Having no special duties of her own in the household, she would wait upon and assist Eveena whenever the latter would accept her attendance. When the whole party were assembled, it was her wont to choose her place not in the circle, still less at my side—Eveena's title to the post of honour on the left being uncontested, and Eunané generally occupying the cushions on my right. But Eivé, lying at our feet, would support herself on her arm between my knee and Eunané's, content to attract my hand to play with her curls or stroke her head. Under such encouragement she would creep on to my lap and rest there, but seldom took any part in conversation, satisfied with the attention one pays half-consciously to a child. A word that dropped from Enva, however, on one occasion, obliged me to observe that it was in Eveena's absence that Eivé always seemed most fully aware of her privileges and most lavish of her childlike caresses. The kind of notice and affection she obtained did not provoke the envy even of Leenoo or Eiralé. She no more affected to imitate Eveena's absolute devotion than she ventured on Eunané's reckless petulance. She kept my interest alive by the faults of a spoiled child. Her freaks were always such as to demand immediate repression without provoking serious displeasure, so that the temporary disgrace cost her little, and the subsequent reconciliation strengthened her hold on my heart.

But with Eveena, or in her presence, Eivé's waywardness was so suppressed or controlled that Eveena's perceptible coolness towards her—

it was never coldness or unkindness—somewhat surprised me.

Few Martialists, when wealthy enough to hand over the management of their property to others, care to interfere, or even to watch its cultivation.

This, however, to me was a subject of as much interest as any other of the many peculiarities of Martial society, commerce, and industry, which it concerned me to investigate and understand; and when not otherwise employed, I spent great part of my day in watching, and now and then directing, the work that went on during the whole of the sunlight, and not unfrequently during the night, upon my farm. Davilo, the superintendent, had engaged no fewer than eight subordinates, who, with the assistance of the ambau, the carvee, and the electric machines, kept every portion of the ground in the most perfect state of culture. The most valuable part of the produce consisted of those farinaceous fruits, growing on trees from twenty to eighty feet in height, which form the principal element of Martial food. Between the tropics these trees yield ripe fruit twice a year, during a total period of about three of our months—perhaps for a hundred days.

Various gourds, growing chiefly on canes, hanging from long flexile stalks that spring from the top of the stem at a height of from three to eight feet, yield juice which is employed partly in flavouring the various loaves and cakes into which the flour is made, partly in the numerous beverages (never allowed to ferment, and consequently requiring to be made fresh every day), of which the smallest Martial household has a greater variety than the most luxurious palace of the East. The best are made from hard-skinned fruits, whose whole pulp is liquified by piercing the rind before the fruit is fully ripe, and closing the orifice with a wax-like substance, almost exactly according to a practice common in different parts of Asia.

The drinks are made, of course, at home. The farinaceous fruits are sold to the confectioners, who take also a portion of the milk and all the meat supplied by the pastures. Many choice fruits grow on shrubs, ranging from the size of a large black currant tree to that of the smallest gooseberry bush.

Vines growing along the ground bear clustering nuts, whose kernels are sometimes as hard as that of a cocoa-nut, sometimes almost as soft as butter. The latter with the juicy fruits, are preserved if necessary for a whole year in storehouses dug in the ground and lined with concrete, in which, by chemical means, a temperature a little above the freezing-point is steadily maintained at very trivial cost. The number of dishes producible by the mixture of these various materials, with the occasional addition of meat, fish, and eggs, is enormous; and it is only when some particular compound is in special favour with the master of the house that it makes its appearance more than perhaps once in ten days upon the same table.

The invention of the confectioners is exquisite and inexhaustible; and every table is supplied with a variety of dainties sufficient for a feast in the most

hospitable and wealthy household of Europe. Many of the smaller fruit-trees and shrubs yield two crops in the year. The vegetables, crisper, and of much more varied taste than the best Terrestrial salads, sometimes possessing a flavour as piquant as that of cinnamon or nutmeg, are gathered continuously from one end of the year to the other.

The vines, tough and fibrous, supply the best and strongest cordage used in Mars. For this purpose they are dried, stripped, combed, and put through an elaborate process of manufacture, which, without weakening the fibres, renders them smooth, and removes the knots in which they naturally abound. The twisted cord of the nut-vine is almost as strong as a metallic wire rope of half its measurement. There is another purpose for which these fibres in their natural state are employed. Simply dried and twisted, they form a scourge as terrible as the Russian knout or African cowhide, though of a different character—a scourge which, even in its lightest form, reduces the wildest herd to instant order; and which, as employed on criminals, is hardly less dreaded than that electric rack whereby Martial science inflicts on every nerve a graduated torture such as even ecclesiastical malignity has not invented on Earth—such as I certainly will not place in the hands of Terrestrial rulers.

All these crops are raised with marvellously little human labour, the whole work of ploughing and sowing being done by machinery, that of weeding and harvesting chiefly by the carvee. The ambau climb the trees and pick the fruit from the ends of the branches, which they are also taught to pinch in, so that none grow so long as to break with the weight of these creatures, as clever and agile as the smaller monkeys, but almost as large as an ordinary baboon. It must always be remembered that, size for size, and cæteris paribus, all bodies, animate and inanimate, on Mars weigh less than half as much as they would on Earth.

Eunané's blunder about the carcarâ was not explained by any subsequent errors of the ambau or carvee, which always selected the ripe fruit with faultless skill, leaving the immature untouched, and throwing aside in small heaps to manure the ground the few that had been allowed to grow too ripe for use. The sums paid from time to time into my hands, received from the sales of produce, were far

greater than I could possibly spend in gratifying any taste of my own; and, as I presently found, the idea that the surplus might indulge those of the ladies never entered their minds.

Before we had been settled in our home for three days Eveena had made two requests which I was well pleased to grant. First, she entreated that I would teach her one at least of the languages with which I was familiar—a task of whose extreme difficulty she had little idea. Compared with her native tongue, the complication and irregularities of the simplest language spoken on Earth are far more arbitrary and provoking than seems the most difficult of ancient or Oriental tongues to a Frenchman or Italian. In order to fulfil my promise that she should assist me in recording my observations and writing out my notes, I chose Latin. Unhappily for her, I found myself as impatient and unsuccessful as I was inexperienced in teaching; and nothing but her exquisite gentleness and forbearance could have made the lessons otherwise than painful to us both. Well for me that the "right to govern wrong" was to her a simple truth—an inalienable marital privilege, to be met with that unqualified submission which must have shamed the worst temper into self-control. Eivé on one occasion made a similar request; but besides that I realised the convenience of a medium of communication understood by ourselves alone, I had no inclination to expose either my own temper or Eivé's to the trial. Eveena's second request came naturally from one whose favourite amusement had been the raising and modification of flowers. She asked to be entrusted with the charge of the seeds I had brought from Earth, and to be permitted to form a bed in the peristyle for the purpose of the experiment. Though this disfigured the perfect arrangement of the garden, I was delighted to have so important and interesting a problem worked out by hands so skilful and so careful. I should probably have failed to rear a single plant, even had I been familiar with those applications of electricity to the purpose which are so extensively employed in Mars. Eveena managed to produce specimens strangely altered, sometimes stunted, sometimes greatly improved, from about one-fourth of the seeds entrusted to her; and among those with which she was most brilliantly successful were some specimens of Turkish roses, the roses of the attar, which I had obtained at Stamboul. My

admiration of her patience and pleasure in her success deeply gratified her; and it was a full reward for all her trouble when I suggested that she should send to her sister Zevle a small packet of each of the seeds with which she had succeeded. It happened, however, that the few rose seeds had all been planted; and the flowers, though apparently perfect, produced no seed of their own, probably because they were not suited to the taste of the flower-birds, and Eveena somehow forgot or failed to employ the process of artificial fertilisation.

If anything could have fully reconciled my conscience to the household relations in which I was rather by weakness than by will inextricably entangled, it would have been the certainty that by the sacrifice Eveena had herself enforced on me, and which she persistently refused to recognise as such, she alone had suffered. True that I could not give, and could hardly affect for the wives bestowed on me by another's choice, even such love as the head of a Moslem household may distribute among as many inmates.

But to what I could call love they had never looked forward. But for the example daily presented before their own eyes they would no more have missed than they comprehended it. That they were happier than they had expected, far happier than they would have been in an ordinary home, happier certainly than in the schools they had quitted, I could not doubt, and they did not affect to deny. If my patience were not proof against vexations the more exasperating from their pettiness, and the sense of ridicule which constantly attached to them, I could read in the manner of most and understand from the words of Eunané, who seldom hesitated to speak her mind, whether its utterances, were flattering or wounding, that she and her companions found me not only far more indulgent, but incomparably more just than they had been taught to hope a man could be.

Of justice, indeed, as consisting in restraint on one's own temper and consideration for the temper of others, Martial manhood is incapable, or, at any rate, Martial womanhood never suspects its masters.

Moreover, though no longer blest with the spirits of youth, and finding little pleasure in what youth calls pleasure, I had escaped the kind of satiety that seems to attend lives more softly spent than mine had been;

and found a very real and unfading enjoyment in witnessing the keen enjoyment of these youthful natures in such liberty as could be accorded and such amusements as the life of this dull and practical world affords.

Among these, two at least are closely similar to the two favourite pleasures of European society. Music appears to have been carried, like most arts and sciences, to a point of mechanical perfection which, I should suppose, like much of the artificial accuracy and ease which civilisation has introduced, mars rather than enhances the natural gratification enjoyed by simpler ages and races. Almost deaf to music as distinguished from noise, I did not attempt to comprehend the construction of Martial instruments or the nature of the concords they emitted. One only struck me with especial surprise by a peculiarity which, if I could not understand, I could not mistake. A number of variously coloured flames are made to synchronise with or actually emit a number of corresponding notes, dancing to, or, more properly, weaving a series of strangely combined movements in accord with the music, whose vibrations were directly and inseparably connected with their motion. But all music is the work of professional musicians, never the occupation of woman's leisure, never made more charming to the ear by its association with the movement of beloved hands or the tones of a cherished voice. Electric wires, connected with the vast buildings wherein instruments produce what sounds like fine choral singing as well as musical notes, enable the householder to turn on at pleasure music equal, I suppose, to the finest operatic performances or the grandest oratorio, and listen to it at leisure from the cushions of his own peristyle. This was a great though not wholly new delight to Eunané and most of her companions. For their sake only would Eveena ever have resorted to it, for though herself appreciating music not less highly, and educated to understand it much more thoroughly, than they, she could derive little gratification from that which was clearly incomprehensible if not disagreeable to me—could hardly enjoy a pleasure I could not share.

The theatre was a more prized and less common indulgence. It is little frequented by the elder Martialists; and not enjoying it themselves, they seldom sacrifice their hours to the enjoyment of their women. But it forms

so important an aid to education, and tends so much to keep alive in the public memory impressions which policy will not permit to fade, that both from the State and from the younger portion of the community it receives an encouragement quite sufficient to reward the few who bestow their time and talent upon it. Great buildings, square or oblong in form, the stage placed at one end, the arched boxes or galleries from which the spectators look down thereon rising tier above and behind tier to the further extremity, are constantly filled. There are no actors, and Martial feeling would hardly allow the appearance of women as actresses. But an art, somewhat analogous to, but infinitely surpassing, that displayed in the manipulation of the most skilfully constructed and most complicated magic lanterns, enables the conductors of the theatre to present upon the stage a truly living and moving picture of any scene they desire to exhibit.

The figures appear perfectly real, move with perfect, freedom, and seem to speak the sounds which, in fact, are given out by a gigantic hidden phonograph, into which the several parts have long ago been carefully spoken by male and female voices, the best suited to each character; and which, by the reversal of its motion, can repeat the original words almost for ever, with the original tone, accent, and expression. The illusion is far more perfect than that obtained by all the resources of stage management and all the skill of the actor's art in the best theatres of France. After the first novelty, the first surprise and wonder were exhausted, I must confess that these representations simply bored me, the more from their length and character. But even Eveena enjoyed them thoroughly, and my other companions prized an evening or afternoon thus spent above all other indulgences. A passage running along at the back of each tier admits the spectator to boxes so completely private as to satisfy the strictest requirements of Martial seclusion.

The favourite scenes represent the most striking incidents of Martial history, or realise the life, usages, and manners of ages long gone by, before science and invention had created the perfect but monotonous civilisation that now prevails. One of the most interesting performances I witnessed commenced with the exhibition of a striking scene, in which the union of all the various States that had up to that time divided the planet's surface,

and occasionally waged war on one another, in the first Congress of the World, was realised in the exact reproduction of every detail which historic records have preserved. Afterwards was depicted the confusion, declining into barbarism and rapid degradation, of the Communistic revolution, the secession of the Zveltau and their merely political adherents, the construction of their cities, fleets, and artillery, the terrible battles, in which the numbers of the Communists were hurled back or annihilated by the asphyxiator and the lightning gun; and finally, the most remarkable scene in all Martial history, when the last representatives of the great Anarchy, squalid, miserable, degraded, and debased in form and features, as well as indicating by their dress and appearance the utter ruin of art and industry under their rule, came into the presence of the chief ruler of the rising State—surrounded by all the splendour which the "magic of property,"

stimulating invention and fostering science, had created—to entreat admission into the realm of restored civilisation, and a share in the blessings they had so deliberately forfeited and so long striven to deny to others.

CHAPTER XXI - PRIVATE AUDIENCES.

I spent my days between mist and mist, according to the Martial saying, not infrequently in excursions more or less extensive and adventurous, in which I could but seldom ask Eveena's company, and did not care for any other. Comparatively courageous as she had learned to be, and free from all affectation of pretty feminine fear, Eveena could never realise the practical immunity from ordinary danger which a strength virtually double that I had enjoyed on Earth, and thorough familiarity with the dangers of travel, of mountaineering, and of the chase, afforded me. When, therefore, I ventured among the hills alone, followed the fishermen and watched their operations, sometimes in terribly rough weather, from the little open surface-boat which I could manage myself, I preferred to give her no definite idea of my intentions. Davilo, however, protested against my exposure to a peril of which Eveena was happily as yet unaware.

"If your intentions are never known beforehand," he said, "still your habit of going forth alone in places to which your steps might easily be dogged, where you might be shot from an ambush or drowned by a sudden attack from a submarine vessel, will soon be pretty generally understood, if, as I fear, a regular watch is set upon your life. At least let me know what your intentions are before starting, and make your absences as irregular and sudden as possible. The less they are known beforehand, even in your own household, the better."

"Is it midnight still in the Council Chamber?" I asked.

"Very nearly so. She who has told so much can tell us no more. The clue that placed her in mental relations with the danger did not extend to its authorship. We have striven hard to find in every conceivable direction some material key to the plot, some object which, having been in contact with the persons of those we suspect, probably at the time when their plans were arranged, might serve as a link between her thoughts and theirs; but as yet unsuccessfully. Either her vision is darkened, or the connection we have sought to establish is wanting. But you know who is your unsparing personal enemy; and, after the Sovereign himself, no man in this world is so powerful; while the Sovereign himself is, owing to the restraints of his

position, less active, less familiar with others, less acquainted with what goes on out of his own sight. Again I say we can avenge; but against secret murder our powers only avail to deter. If we would save, it must be by the use of natural precautions."

What he said made me desirous of some conversation with Eveena before I started on a meditated visit to the Palace. If I could not tell her the whole truth, she knew something; and I thought it possible on this occasion so far to enlighten her as to consult with her how the secret of my intended journeys should in future be kept. But I found no chance of speaking to her until, shortly before my departure, I was called upon to decide one of the childish disputes which constantly disturbed my temper and comfort.

Mere fleabites they were; but fleas have often kept me awake a whole night in a Turkish caravanserai, and half-a-dozen mosquitos inside an Indian tent have broken up the sleep earned on a long day's march or a sharply contested battlefield. I need only say that I extorted at last from Eveena a clear statement of the trifle at issue, which flatly contradicted those of the four participants in the squabble. She began to suggest a means of proving the truth, and they broke into angry clamour. Silencing them all peremptorily, I drew Eveena into my own chamber, and, when assured that we were unheard, reproved her for proposing to support her own word by evidence.

"Do you think," I said, "that any possible proof would induce me to doubt you, or add anything to the assurance I derive from your word?"

"But," she urged, "that cannot be just to others. They must feel it very hard that your love for me makes you take all I say for truth." "Not my love, but my knowledge. 'Be not righteous overmuch.' Don't forget that they know the truth as well as you."

I would hear no more, and passed to the matter I had at heart....

Earnestly, and in a sense sincerely, as upon my second audience I had thanked the Camptâ for his munificent gifts, no day passed that I would not thankfully have renounced the wealth he had bestowed if I could at the same time have renounced what was, in intention and according to Martial

ideas, the most gracious and most remarkable of his favours. On the present occasion I thought for a moment that such renunciation might have been possible.

The Prince had, after our first interview, observed with regard to every point of my story on which I had been carefully silent a delicacy of reserve very unusual among Martialists, and quite unintelligible to his Court and officers. To-day the conversation in public turned again upon my voyage.

Endo and another studiously directed it to the method of steering, and the intentional diminution of speed in my descent, corresponding to its gradual increase at the commencement of the journey—points at which they hoped to find some opening to the mystery of the motive force. The Prince relieved me from some embarrassment by requesting me as usual to attend him to his private cabinet.

He said:—"I have not, as you must be aware, pressed you to disclose a secret which, for some reason or other, you are evidently anxious to preserve. Of course the exclusive possession of a motive power so marvellous as that employed in your voyage is of almost incalculable pecuniary value, and it is perfectly right that you should use your own discretion with regard to the time and the terms of its communication."

"Pardon me," I interposed, "if I interrupt you, Prince, to prevent any misconception. It is not with a view to profit that I have carefully avoided giving any clue whatever to my secret. Your munificence would render it most ungrateful and unjust in me to haggle over the price of any service I could render you; and I should be greedy indeed if I desired greater wealth than you have bestowed. If I may say so without offending, I earnestly wish that you would permit me, by resigning your gifts, to retain in my own eyes the right to keep my secret without seeming undutiful or unthankful."

"I have said," he replied, "that on that point you misconceive our respective positions. No one supposes that you are indebted to us for anything more than it was the duty of the Sovereign to give, as a mark of the universal admiration and respect, to our guest from another world; still less could any imagine that on such a trifle could be founded any claim to a secret so

invaluable. You will offend me much and only if you ever again speak of yourself as bound by personal obligation to me or mine. But as we are wishful to buy, so I cannot understand any reluctance on your part to sell your secret on your own terms."

"I think, Prince," I replied, "that I have already asked you what you would think of a subject of your own, who should put such a power into the hands of enemies as formidable to you as you would be to the races of the Earth."

"And I think," he rejoined with a smile, "that I reminded you how little my judgment would matter to one possessed of such a power. I have gathered from your conversation how easily we might conquer a world as far behind us in destructive powers as in general civilisation. But why should you object? You can make your own terms both for yourself and for any of your race for whom you feel an especial interest."

"A traitor is none the less a despicable and loathsome wretch because his Prince cannot punish him. I am bound by no direct tie of loyalty to any Terrestrial sovereign. I was born the subject of one of the greatest monarchs of the Earth; I left his country at an early age, and my youth was passed in the service of less powerful rulers, to one at least of whom I long owed the same military allegiance that binds your guards and officers to yourself.

But that obligation also is at an end. Nevertheless, I cannot but recognise that I owe a certain fealty to the race to which I belong, a duty to right and justice. Even if I thought, which I do not think, that the Earth would be better governed and its inhabitants happier under your rule, I should have no right to give them up to a conquest I know they would fiercely and righteously resist. If—pardon me for saying it—you, Prince, would commit no common crime in assailing and slaughtering those who neither have wronged nor can wrong you, one of themselves would be tenfold more guilty in sharing your enterprise."

"You shall ensure," he replied, "the good government of your own world as you will. You shall rule it with all the authority possessed by the Regents under me, and by the laws which you think best suited to races very different from our own. You shall be there as great and absolute as I am

here, paying only an obedience to me and my successors which, at so immense a distance, can be little more than formal."

"Is it to acquire a merely formal power that a Prince like yourself would risk the lives of your own people, and sacrifice those of millions of another race?"

"To tell you the truth," he replied, "I count on commanding the expedition myself; and perhaps I care more for the adventure than for its fruits. You will not expect me to be more chary of the lives of others than of my own?"

"I understand, and as a soldier could share, perhaps, a feeling natural to a great, a capable, and an ambitious Prince. But alike as soldier and subject it is my duty to resist, not to aid, such an ambition. My life is at your disposal, but even to save my life I could not betray the lives of hundreds of millions and the future of a whole world."

159

"I fail to understand you fully," he said, abandoning with a sigh a hope that had evidently been the object of long and eager day-dreams. "But in no case would I try to force from you what you will not give or sell; and if you speak sincerely—and I suppose you must do so, since I can see no motive but those you assign that could induce you to refuse my offer—I must believe in the existence of what I have heard of now and then but deemed incredible—men who are governed by care for other things than their own interests, who believe in right and wrong, and would rather suffer injustice than commit it."

"You may be sure, Prince," I replied, perhaps imprudently, "that there are such men in your own world, though they are perhaps among those who are least known and least likely to be seen at your Court."

"If you know them," he said, "you will render me no little service in bringing them to my knowledge."

"It is possible," I ventured to observe, "that their distinguishing excellences are connected with other distinctions which might render it a disservice to them to indicate their peculiar character, I will not say to yourself, but to those around you."

"I hardly understand you," he rejoined. "Take, however, my assurance that nothing you say here shall, without your own consent, be used elsewhere.

It is no light gratification, no trifling advantage to me, to find one man who has neither fear nor interest that can induce him to lie to me; to whom I can speak, not as sovereign to subject, but as man to man, and of whose private conversation my courtiers and officials are not yet suspicious or jealous.

You shall never repent any confidence you give to me."

My interest in and respect for the strange character so manifestly suited for, so intensely weary of, the grandest position that man could fill, increased with each successive interview. I never envied that greatness which seems to most men so enviable. The servitude of a constitutional King, so often a puppet in the hands of the worst and meanest of men—those who prostitute their powers as rulers of a State to their interests as chiefs of a faction—must seem pitiable to any rational manhood. But even the autocracy of the Sultan or the Czar seems ill to compensate the utter isolation of the throne; the lonely grandeur of one who can hardly have a friend, since he can never have an equal, among those around him. I do not wonder that a tinge of melancholo-mania is so often perceptible in the chiefs of that great House whose Oriental absolutism is only "tempered by assassination." But an Earthly sovereign may now and then meet his fellow-sovereigns, whether as friends or foes, on terms of frank hatred or loyal openness. His domestic relations, though never secure and simple as those of other men, may relieve him at times from the oppressive sense of his sublime solitude; and to his wife, at any rate, he may for a few minutes or hours be the husband and not the king. But the absolute Ruler of this lesser world had neither equal friends nor open foes, neither wife nor child.

How natural then his weariness of his own life; how inevitable his impatient scorn of those to whom that life was devoted! A despot not even accountable to God—a Prince who, till he conversed with me, never knew that the universe contained his equal or his like—it spoke much, both for the natural strength and soundness of his intellect and for the excellence of his education, that he was so sane a man, so earnest, active, and just a ruler.

His reign was signalised by a better police, a more even administration of justice, a greater efficiency, judgment, and energy in the execution of great

works of public utility, than his realm had known for a thousand years; and his duty was done as diligently and conscientiously as if he had known that conscience was the voice of a supreme Sovereign, and duty the law of an unerring and unescapable Lawgiver. Alone among a race of utterly egotistical cowards, he had the courage of a soldier, and the principles, or at least the instincts, worthy of a Child of the Star. With him alone could I have felt a moment's security from savage attempts to extort by terror or by torture the secret I refused to sell; and I believe that his generous abstinence from such an attempt was as exasperating as it was incomprehensible to his advisers, and chiefly contributed to involve him in the vengeance which baffled greed and humbled personal pride had leagued to wreak upon myself, as on those with whose welfare and safety my own were inextricably intertwined. It was a fortunate, if not a providential, combination of circumstances that compelled the enemies of the Star, primarily on my account, to interweave with their scheme of murderous persecution and private revenge an equally ruthless and atrocious treason against the throne and person of their Monarch.

My audience had detained me longer than I had expected, and the evening mist had fairly closed in before I returned. Entering, not as usual through the grounds and the peristyle, but by the vestibule and my own chamber, and hidden by my half-open window, I overheard an exceedingly characteristic discussion on the incident of the morning.

"Serve her right!" Leenoo was saying. "That she should for once get the worst of it, and be disbelieved to sharpen the sting!"

"How do you know?" asked Enva. "I don't feel so sure we have heard the last of it."

"Eveena did not seem to have liked her half-hour," answered Leenoo spitefully. "Besides, if he did not disbelieve her story, he would have let her prove it."

"Is that your reliance?" broke in Eunané. "Then you are swinging on a rotten branch. I would not believe my ears if, for all that all of us could
invent against her, I heard him so much as ask Eveena, 'Are you speaking the truth?'"

"It is very uneven measure," muttered Enva.

"Uneven!" cried Eunané. "Now, I think I have the best right to be jealous of her place; and it does sting me that, when he takes me for his companion out of doors, or makes most of me at home, it is so plain that he is taking trouble, as if he grudged a soft word or a kiss to another as something stolen from her. But he deals evenly, after all. If he were less tender of her we should have to draw our zones tighter. But he won't give us the chance to say, 'Teach the ambâ with stick and the esve with sugar.'"

"I do say it. She is never snubbed or silenced; and if she has had worse than what he calls 'advice' to-day, I believe it is the first time. She has never 'had cause to wear the veil before the household' [to hide blushes or tears], or found that his 'lips can give sharper sting than their kiss can heal,' like the rest of us."

"What for? If he wished to find her in fault he would have to watch her dreams. Do you expect him to be harder to her than to us? He don't 'look for stains with a microscope.' None of us can say that he 'drinks tears for taste.' None of us ever 'smarted because the sun scorched him.' Would you have him 'tie her hands for being white'?" [punish her for perfection].

"She is never at fault because he never believes us against her," returned Leenoo.

"How often would he have been right? I saw nothing of to-day's quarrel, but I know beforehand where the truth lay. I tell you this: he hates the sandal more than the sin, but, strange as it seems, he hates a falsehood worse still; and a falsehood against Eveena—If you want to feel 'how the spear-grass cuts when the sheath bursts,' let him find you out in an experiment like this! You congratulate yourself, Leenoo, that you have got her into trouble. Elnerve that you are!—if you have, you had better have poisoned his cup before his eyes. For every tear he sees her shed he will reckon with us at twelve years' usury."

"You have made her shed some," retorted Enva.

"Yes," said Eunané, "and if he knew it, I should like half a year's penance in the black sash" [as the black sheep or scapegoat of her Nursery] "better than my next half-hour alone with him. When I was silly enough to tie the veil over her mouth" [take the lead in sending her to Coventry] "the day after we came here, I expected to pay for it, and thought the fruit worth the scratches. But when he came in that evening, nodded and spoke kindly to us, but with his eyes seeking for her; when he saw her at last sitting yonder with her head down, I saw how his face darkened at the very idea that she was vexed, and I thought the flash was in the cloud. When she sprang up as he called her, and forced a smile before he looked into her face, I wished I

161

had been as ugly as Minn oo, that I might have belonged to the miseries, worst-tempered man living, rather than have so provoked the giant."

"But what did he do?"

"Well that he don't hear you!" returned Eunané. "But I can answer;—nothing. I shivered like a leveloo in the wind when he came into my room, but I heard nothing about Eveena. I told Eivé so next day—you remember Eivé would have no part with us? 'And you were called the cleverest girl in your Nursery!' she said; 'you have just tied your own hands and given your sandal into Eveena's. Whenever she tells him, you will drink the cup she chooses to mix for you, and very salt you will find it.'"

"Crach!" (tush or stuff), said Eiralé contemptuously. "We have 'filled her robe with pins' for half a year since then, and she has never been able to make him count them."

"Able!" returned Eunané sharply, "do you know no better? Well, I chose to fancy she was holding this over me to keep me in her power. One day she spoke—choosing her words so carefully—to warn me how I was sure to anger Clasfempta" (the master of the household) "by pushing my pranks so often to the verge of safety and no farther. I answered her with a taunt, and, of course, that evening I was more perverse than ever, till even he could stand it no longer. When he quoted—

"'More lightly treat whom haste or heat to headlong trespass urge; The heaviest sandals fit the feet that ever tread the verge'—

"I was well frightened. I saw that the bough had broken short of the end, and that for once Clasfempta could mean to hurt. But Eveena kept him awhile, and when he came to me, she had persuaded him that I was only mischievous, not malicious, teasing rather than trespassing. But his last words showed that he was not so sure of that. 'I have treated you this time as a child whose petulance is half play; but if you would not have your teasing returned with interest, keep it clipped; and—keep it for me.' I have often tormented her since then, but I could not for shame help you to spite her."

"Crach!" said Enva. "Eveena might think it wise to make friends with you; but would she bear to be slighted and persecuted a whole summer if she could help herself? You know that—

"Man's control in woman's hand
Sorest tries the household band.
Closer favourite's kisses cling,
Favourite's fingers sharper sting.'"

"Very likely," replied Eunané. "I cannot understand any more than you can why Eveena screens instead of punishing us; why she endures what a word to him would put down under her sandal; but she does. Does she cast no shadow because it never darkens his presence to us? And after all, her mind is not a deeper darkness to me than his. He enjoys life as no man here does; but what he enjoys most is a good chance of losing it; while those who find it so tedious guard it like watch-dragons. When the number of accidents made it difficult to fill up the Southern hunt at any price, the Camptâ's refusal to let him go so vexed him that Eveena was half afraid to show her sense of relief. You would think he liked pain—the scars of thekargynda are not his only or his deepest ones—if he did not catch at every excuse to spare it. And, again, why does he speak to Eveena as to the Camptâ, and to us as to children—'child' is his softest word for us? Then, he is patient where you expect no mercy, and severe where others would laugh. When Enva let the electric stove overheat the water, so that he was scalded horribly in his bath, we all counted that he would at least have
paid her back the pain twice over. But as soon as Eveena and Eivé had arranged the bandages, he sent for her. We could scarcely bring you to him, Enva; but he put out the only hand he could move to stroke your hair as he does Eivé's, and spoke for once with real tenderness, as if you were the person to be pitied! Any one else would have laughed heartily at

the figure her esve made with half her tail pulled out. But not all Eveena's pleading could obtain pardon for me."

"That was caprice, not even dealing," said Leenoo. "You were not half so bad as Enva."

"He made me own that I was," replied Eunané. "It never occurred to him to suppose or say that she did it on purpose. But I was cruel on purpose to the bird, if I were not spiteful to its mistress. 'Don't you feel,' he said, 'that intentional cruelty is what no ruler, whether of a household or of a kingdom, has a right to pass over? If not, you can hardly be fit for a charge that gives animals into your power.' I never liked him half so well; and I am sure I deserved a severer lesson. Since then, I cannot help liking them both; though it is mortifying to feel that one is nothing before her."

"It is intolerable," said Enva bitterly; "I detest her."

"Is it her fault?" asked Eunané with some warmth. "They are so like each other and so unlike us, that I could fancy she came from his own world. I went to her next day in her own room."

"Ay," interjected Leenoo with childish spite, "'kiss the foot and 'scape the sandal.'"

"Think so," returned Eunané quietly, "if you like. I thought I owed her some amends. Well, she had her bird in her lap, and I think she was crying over it. But as soon as she saw me she put it out of sight. I began to tell her how sorry I was about it, but she would not let me go on. She kissed me as no one ever kissed me since my school friend Ernie died three years ago; and she cried more over the trouble I had brought on myself than over her pet. And since then," Eunané went on with a softened voice, "she has showed me how pretty its ways are, how clever it is, how fond of her, and she tries to make it friends with me.... Sometimes I don't wonder she is so

much to him and he to her. She was brought up in the home where she was born. Her father is one of those strange people; and I fancy there is something between her and Clasfempta more than...."

I could not let this go on; and stepping back from the window as if I had but just returned, I called Eunané by name. She came at once, a little surprised at the summons, but suspecting nothing. But the first sight of my face startled her; and when, on the impulse of the moment, I took her hands and looked straight into her eyes, her quick intelligence perceived at once that I had heard at least part of the conversation.

"Ah," she said, flushing and hanging her head, "I am caught now, but"—in a tone half of relief—"I deserve it, and I won't pretend to think that you are angry only because Eveena is your favourite. You would not allow any of us to be spited if you could help it, and it is much worse to have spited her."

I led her by the hand across the peristyle into her own chamber, and when the window closed behind us, drew her to my side.

"So you would rather belong to the worst master of your own race than to me?"

"Not now," she answered. "That was my first thought when I saw how you felt for Eveena, and knew how angry you would be when you found how we—I mean how I—had used her, and I remembered how terribly strong you were. I know you better now. It is for women to strike with five fingers" (in unmeasured passion); "only, don't tell Eveena. Besides," she murmured, colouring, with drooping eyelids, "I had rather be beaten by you than caressed by another."

"Eunané, child, you might well say you don't understand me. I could not have listened to your talk if I had meant to use it against you; and with you I have no cause to be displeased. Nay" (as she looked up in surprise), "I know you have not used Eveena kindly, but I heard from yourself that you had repented. That she, who could never be coaxed or compelled to say what made her unhappy, or even to own that I had guessed it truly, has fully forgiven you, you don't need to be told."

"Indeed, I don't understand," the girl sobbed. "Eveena is always so strangely soft and gentle—she would rather suffer without reason than let us suffer who deserve it. But just because she is so kind, you must feel the more bitterly for her. Besides," she went on, "I was so jealous—as if you could compare me with her—even after I had felt her kindness. No! you cannot forgive for her, and you ought not."

"Child," I answered, sadly enough, for my conscience was as ill at ease as hers, with deeper cause, "I don't tell you that your jealousy was not foolish and your petulance culpable; but I do say that neither Eveena nor I have the heart—perhaps I have not even the right—to blame you. It is true that I love Eveena as I can love no other in this world or my own. How well she deserves that love none but I can know. So loving her, I would not willingly have brought any other woman into a relation which could make her dependent upon or desirous of such love as I cannot give. You know how this relation to you and the others was forced upon me. When I accepted it, I thought I could give you as much affection as you would find elsewhere. How far and why I wronged Eveena is between her and myself.

I did not think that I could be wronging you."

Very little of this was intelligible to Eunané. She felt a tenderness she had never before received; but she could not understand my doubt, and she replied only to my last words.

"Wrong us! How could you? Did we ask whether you had another wife, or who would be your favourite? Did you promise to like us, or even to be kind to us? You might have neglected us altogether, made one girl your sole companion, kept all indulgences, all favours, for her; and how would you have wronged us? If you had turned on us when she vexed you, humbled us to gratify her caprice, ill-used us to vent your temper, other men would have done the same. Who else would have treated us as you have done? Who would have been careful to give each of us her share in every pleasure, her turn in every holiday, her employment at home, her place in your company abroad? Who would have inquired into the truth of our complaints and the merits of our quarrels; would have made so many excuses for our faults, given us so many patient warnings?… Wronged us!

There may be some of us who don't like you; there is not one who could bear to be sent away, not one who would exchange this house for the palace of the camptâ though you pronounce him kingly in nature as in power."

She spoke as she believed, if she spoke in error. "If so, my child, why have you all been so bitter against Eveena? Why have you yourself been jealous of one who, as you admit, has been a favourite only in a love you did not expect?"

"But we saw it, and we envied her so much love, so much respect," she replied frankly. "And for myself,"—she coloured, faltered, and was silent.

"For yourself, my child?"

"I was a vain fool," she broke out impetuously. "They told me that I was beautiful, and clever, and companionable. I fancied I should be your favourite, and hold the first place; and when I saw her, I would not see her grace and gentleness, or observe her soft sweet voice, and the charms that put my figure and complexion to shame, and the quiet sense and truth that were worth twelvefold my quickness, my memory, and my handiness. I was disappointed and mortified that she should be preferred. Oh, how you must hate me, Clasfempta; for I hate myself while I tell you what I have been!"

According to European doctrine, my fealty to Eveena must then have been in peril. And yet, warmly as I felt for Eunané, the element in her passionate confession that touched me most was her recognition of Eveena's superiority; and as I soothed and comforted the half-childish penitent, I thought how much it would please Eveena that I had at last come to an understanding with the companion she avowedly liked the best.

"But, Eunané," I said at last, "do you remember what you were saying when I called you—called you on purpose to stop you? You said that there was something between Eveena and myself more than—-more than what?"

What did you mean? Speak frankly, child; I know that this time you were not going to scald me on purpose."

"I don't know quite what I meant," she replied simply. "But the first time you took me out, I heard the superintendent say some strange things; and then he checked himself when he found your companion was not Eveena.

Then Eivé—I mean—you use expressions sometimes in talking to Eveena that we never heard before. I think there is some secret between you."

"And if there be, Eunané, were you going to betray it—to set Enva and Leenoo on to find it out?"

"I did not think," she said. "I never do think before I get into trouble. I don't say, forgive me this time; but I will hold my tongue for the future."

By this time our evening meal was ready. As I led Eunané to her place, Eveena looked up with some little surprise. It was rarely that, especially on returning from absence, I had sought any other company than hers. But there was no tinge of jealousy or doubt in her look. On the contrary, as, with her entire comprehension of every expression of my face, and her quickness to read the looks of others, she saw in both countenances that we were on better terms than ever before, her own brightened at the thought.

As I placed myself beside her, she stole her hand unobserved into mine, and pressed it as she whispered—

"You have found her out at last. She is half a child as yet; but she has a heart—and perhaps the only one among them."

"The four," as I called them, looked up as we approached with eager malice:—bitterly disappointed, when they saw that Eunané had won something more than pardon. Whatever penance they had dreaded, their own escape ill compensated the loss of their expected pleasure in the pain and humiliation of a finer nature. Eunané's look, timidly appealing to her to ratify our full reconciliation, answered by Eveena's smile of tender, sisterly sympathy, enhanced and completed their discomfiture.

CHAPTER XXII - PECULIAR INSTITUTIONS.

A chief luxury and expense in which, when aware what my income was, I indulged myself freely was the purchase of Martial literature. Only ephemeral works are as a rule printed in the phonographic character, which alone I could read with ease. The Martialists have no newspapers. It does not seem to them worth while to record daily the accidents, the business incidents, the prices, the amusements, and the follies of the day; and politics they have none. In no case would a people so coldly wise, so thoroughly impressed by experience with a sense of the extreme folly of political agitation, legislative change, and democratic violence, have cursed themselves with anything like the press of Europe or America. But as it is, all they have to record is gathered each twelfth day at the telegraph offices, and from these communicated on a single sheet about four inches square to all who care to receive it. But each profession or occupation that boasts, as do most, an organisation and a centre of discussion and council, issues at intervals books containing collected facts, essays, reports of experiments, and lectures. Every man who cares to communicate his passing ideas to the public does so by means of the phonograph. When he has a graver work, which is, in his view at least, of permanent importance to publish, it is written in the stylographic character, and sold at the telegraphic centres.

The extreme complication and compression employed in this character had, as I have already said, rendered it very difficult to me; and though I had learnt to decipher it as a child spells out the words which a few years later it will read unconsciously by the eye, the only manner in which I could quickly gather the sense of such books was by desiring one or other of the ladies to read them aloud. Strangely enough, next to Eveena, Eivé was by far the best reader. Eunané understood infinitely better what she was perusing; but the art of reading aloud is useless, and therefore never taught, in schools whose every pupil learns to read with the usual facility a character which the practised eye can interpret incomparably faster than the voice could possibly utter it. This reading might have afforded many opportunities of private converse with Eveena, but that Eivé, whose knowledge was by no means proportionate to her intelligence, entreated

permission to listen to the books I selected; and Eveena, though not partial to her childish companion and admirer, persuaded me not to refuse.

The story of my voyage and reports of my first audience at Court were, of course, widely circulated and extensively canvassed. Though regarded with no favour, especially by the professed philosophers and scientists, my adventures and myself were naturally an object of great curiosity; and I was not surprised when a civil if cold request was preferred, on behalf of what I may call the Martial Academy, that I would deliver in their hall a series of lectures, or rather a connected oral account of the world from which I professed to have come, and of the manner in which my voyage had been accomplished. After consulting Eveena and Davilo, I accepted the invitation, and intended to take the former with me. She objected, however, that while she had heard much in her father's house and during our travels of what I had to tell, her companions, scarcely less interested, were comparatively ignorant. Indiscreetly, because somewhat provoked by these repeated sacrifices, as much of my inclination as her own, I mentioned my purpose at our evening meal, and bade her name those who should accompany me. I was a little surprised when, carefully evading the dictation to which she was invited, she suggested that Eunané and Eivé would probably most enjoy the opportunity. That she should be willing to get rid of the most wilful and petulant of the party seemed natural. The other selection confirmed the impression I had formed, but dared not express to one whom I had never blamed without finding myself in the wrong, that Eveena regarded Eivé with a feeling more nearly approaching to jealousy than her nature seemed capable of entertaining. I obeyed, however, without comment; and both the companions selected for me were delighted at the prospect.

The Academy is situated about half-way between Amacasfe and the Residence; the facilities of Martial travelling, and above all of telegraphic and telephonic communication, dispensing with all reason for placing great institutions in or near important cities. We travelled by balloon, as I was anxious to improve myself in the management of these machines. After frightening my companions so far as to provoke some outcry from Eivé,

and from Eunané some saucy remarks on my clumsiness, on which no one else would have ventured, I descended safely, if not very creditably, in front of the building which serves as a local centre of Martial philosophy.

The residences of some sixty of the most eminent professors of various sciences—elected by their colleagues as seats fall vacant, with the approval of the highest Court of Judicature and of the camptâ—cluster around a huge building in the form of a hexagon made up of a multitude of smaller hexagons, in the centre whereof is the great hall of the same shape. In the smaller chambers which surround it are telephones through which addresses delivered in a hundred different quarters are mechanically repeated; so that the residents or temporary visitors can here gather at once all the knowledge that is communicated by any man of note to any audience throughout the planet. On this account numbers of young men just emancipated from the colleges come here to complete their education; and above each of the auditory chambers is another divided into six small rooms, wherein these visitors are accommodated. A small house belonging to one of the members who happened to be absent was appropriated to me during my stay, and in its hall the philosophers gathered in the morning to converse with or to question me in detail respecting the world whose existence they would not formally admit, but whose life, physical, social, and political, and whose scientific and human history, they regarded with as much curiosity as if its reality were ascertained. Courtesy forbids evening visits unless on distinct and pressing invitation, it being supposed that the head of a household may care to spend that part of his time, and that alone, with his own family.

The Academists are provided by the State with incomes, of an amount very much larger than the modest allowances which the richest nations of the Earth almost grudge to the men whose names in future history will probably be remembered longer than those of eminent statesmen and warriors. Some of them have made considerable fortunes by turning to account in practical invention this or that scientific discovery. But as a rule, in Mars as on Earth, the gifts and the career of the discoverer, and the inventor are distinct. It is, however, from the purely theoretical labours of the men of science that the inventions useful in manufactures, in communication, in every department of life and business, are generally derived; and the prejudice or judgment of this strange people has laid it down that those who devote their lives to work in itself unremunerative, but indirectly most valuable to the public, should be at least as well off as the subordinate servants of the State. In society they are perhaps more honoured than any but the highest public authorities; and my audience was the most distinguished, according to the ideas of that world, that it could furnish.

At noon each day I entered the hall, which was crowded with benches rising on five sides from the centre to the walls, the sixth being occupied by a platform where the lecturer and the members of the Academy sat. After each lecture, which occupied some two hours, questions more or less perplexing were put by the latter. Only, however, on the first occasion, when I reserved, as before the Zinta and the Court, all information that could enable my hearers to divine the nature of the apergic force, was incredulity so plainly insinuated as to amount to absolute insult.

"If," I said, "you choose to disbelieve what I tell you, you are welcome to do so. But you are not at liberty to express your disbelief to me. To do so is to charge me with lying; and to that charge, whatever may be the customs of this world, there is in mine but one answer," and I laid my hand on the hilt of the sword I wore in deference to Davilo's warnings, but which he and others considered a Terrestrial ornament rather than a weapon.

The President of the Academy quietly replied—"Of all the strange things we have heard, this seems the strangest. I waive the probability of your statements, or the reasonableness of the doubts suggested. But I fail to understand how, here or in any other world, if the imputation of falsehood be considered so gross an offence—and here it is too common to be so regarded—it can be repelled by proving yourself more skilled in the use of weapons, or stronger or more daring than the person who has challenged your assertion."

The moral courage and self-possession of the President were as marked as his logic was irrefragable; but my outbreak, however illogical, served its purpose. No one was disposed to give mortal offence to one who showed

himself so ready to resent it, though probably the apprehension related less to my swordsmanship than the favour I was supposed to enjoy with the Suzerain.

Seriously impressed by the growing earnestness of Davilo's warnings, and feeling that I could no longer conceal the pressure of some anxiety on my mind, gradually, cautiously, and tenderly I broke to Eveena what I had learned, with but two reserves. I would not render her life miserable by the suggestion of possible treason in our own household. That she might not infer this for herself, I led her to believe that the existence and discovery of the conspiracy was of a date long subsequent to my acceptance of the Sovereign's unwelcome gift. She was deeply affected, and, as I had feared, exceedingly disturbed. But, very characteristically, the keenest impression made upon her mind concerned less the urgency of the peril than its origin, the fact that it was incurred through and for her. On this she insisted much more than seemed just or reasonable. It was for her sake, no doubt, that I had made the Regent of Elcavoo my bitter, irreconcilable foe. It was my marriage with her, the daughter of the most eminent among the chiefs of the Zinta, that had marked me out as one of the first and principal victims, and set on my head a value as high as on that of any of the Order save the Arch-Enlightener himself, whose personal character and social distinction would have indicated him as especially dangerous, even had his secret rank been altogether unsuspected. It was impossible to soothe Eveena's first outbreak of feeling, or reason with her illogical self-reproach.

Compelled at last to admit that the peril had been unconsciously incurred when she neither knew nor could have known it, she pleaded eagerly and earnestly for permission to repair by the sacrifice of herself the injury she had brought upon me. It was useless to tell her that the acceptance of such a sacrifice would be a thousand-fold worse than death. Even the depth and devotion of her own love could not persuade her to realise the passionate earnestness of mine. It was still more in vain to remind her that such a concession must entail the dishonour that man fears above all perils; would brand me with that indelible stain of abject personal cowardice which for ever degrades and ruins not only the fame but the nature of manhood, as the stain of wilful unchastity debases and ruins woman.

"Rescind our contract," she insisted, pleading, with the overpowering vehemence of a love absolutely unselfish, against love's deepest instincts and that egotism which is almost inseparable from it; giving passionate utterance to an affection such as men rarely feel for women, women perhaps never for men. "Divorce me; force the enemy to believe that you have broken with my father and with his Order; and, favoured as you are by the Sovereign, you will be safe. Give what reason you will; say that I have deserved it, that I have forced you to it. I know that contracts are revoked with the full approval of the Courts and of the public, though I hardly know why. I will agree; and if we are agreed, you can give or withhold reasons as you please. Nay, there can be no wrong to me in doing what I entreat you to do. I shall not suffer long—no, no, I will live, I will be happy"—her face white to the lips, her streaming tears were not needed to belie the words! "By your love for me, do not let me feel that you are to die—do not keep me in dread to hear that you have died—for me and through me."

If it had been in her power to leave me, if one-half of the promised period had not been yet to run, she might have enforced her purpose in despite of all that I could urge;—of reason, of entreaty, of the pleadings of a love in this at least as earnest as her own. Nay, she would probably have left me, in the hope of exhibiting to the world the appearance of an open quarrel, but for a peculiarity of Martial law. That law enforces, on the plea of either party, "specific performance" of the marriage contract. I could reclaim her, and call the force of the State to recover her. When even this warning at first failed to enforce her submission, I swore by all I held sacred in my own world and all she revered in hers—by the symbols never lightly invoked, and never, in the course of ages that cover thrice the span of Terrestrial history and tradition, invoked to sanction a lie; symbols more sacred in her eyes than, in those of mediæval Christendom, the gathered relics that appalled the heroic soul of Harold Godwinsson—that she should only defeat her own purpose; that I would reclaim my wife before the Order and before the law, thus asserting more clearly than ever the strength of the tie that bound me to her and to her house. The oath which it was impossible to break, perhaps yet more the cold and measured tone

with which I spoke, in striving to control the white heat of a passion as much stronger as it was more selfish than hers—a tone which sounded to myself unnatural and alien—at last compelled her to yield; and silenced her in the only moment in which the depths of that nature, so sweet and soft and gentle, were stirred by the violence of a moral tempest.... A marvellously perfect example of Martial art and science is furnished by the Observatory of the Astronomic Academy, on a mountain about twenty miles from the Residence. The hill selected stands about 4000 feet above the sea-level, and almost half that height above any neighbouring ground. It commands, therefore, a most perfect view of the horizon all around, even below the technical or theoretic horizon of its latitude. A volcano, like all Martial volcanoes very feeble, and never bursting into eruptions seriously dangerous to the dwellers in the neighbouring plains, existed at some miles' distance, and caused earthquakes, or perhaps I should more properly say disturbances of the surface, which threatened occasionally to perturb the observations. But the Martialists grudge no cost to render their scientific instruments, from the Observatory itself to the smallest lens or wheel it contains, as perfect as possible. Having decided that Eanelca was very superior to any other available site, they were not to be baffled or diverted by such a trifle as the opposition of Nature. Still less would they allow that the observers should be put out by a perceptible disturbance, or their observations falsified by one too slight to be realised by their senses. If Nature were impertinent enough to interfere with the arrangements of science, science must put down the mutiny of Nature. As seas had been bridged and continents cut through, so a volcano might and must be suppressed or extinguished. A tunnel thirty miles in length was cut from a great lake nearly a thousand feet higher than the base of the volcano; and through this for a quarter of a year, say some six Terrestrial months, water was steadily poured into the subterrene cavities wherein the eruptive forces were generated—the plutonic laboratory of the rebellious agency. Of course previous to the adoption of this measure, the crust in the neighbourhood had been carefully explored and tested by various wonderfully elaborate and perfect boring instruments, and a map or rather model of the strata for a mile below the surface, and for a distance around

the volcano which I dare not state on the faith of my recollection alone, had been constructed on a scale, as we should say, of twelve inches to the mile.

Except for minor purposes, for convenience of pocket carriage and the like, Martialists disdain so poor a representation as a flat map can give of a broken surface. On the small scale, they employ globes of spherical sections to represent extensive portions of their world; on the large scale (from two to twenty-four inches per mile), models of wonderfully accurate construction. Consequently, children understand and enjoy the geographical lesson which in European schools costs so many tears to so little purpose. A girl of six years knows more perfectly the whole area of the Martial globe than a German Professor that of the ancient Peloponnesus. Eivé, the dunce of our housed hold, won a Terrestrial picture-book on which she had set her fancy by tracing on a forty-inch globe, the first time she saw it, every detail of my journey from Ecasfe as she had heard me relate it; and Eunané, who had never left her Nursery, could describe beforehand any route I wished to take between the northern and southern ice-belts. Under the guidance afforded by the elaborate model abovementioned, all the hollows wherein the materials of eruption were stored, and wherein the chemical forces of Nature had been at work for ages, were thoroughly flooded. Of course convulsion after convulsion of the most violent nature followed. But in the course of about two hundred days, the internal combustion was overmastered for lack of fuel; the chemical combinations, which might have gone on for ages causing weak but incessant outbreaks, were completed and their power exhausted.

This source of disturbance extinguished in the reign of the twenty-fifth predecessor of my royal patron, the construction of the great Observatory on Eanelca was commenced. A very elaborate road, winding round and round the mountain at such an incline as to be easily ascended by the electric carriages, was built. But this was intended only as a subsidiary means of ascent. Right into the bowels of the mountain a vast tunnel fifty feet in height was driven. At its inner extremity was excavated a chamber whose dimensions are imperfectly recorded in my notes, but which was certainly much larger than the central cavern from which radiate the principal galleries of the Mammoth Cave. Around this were pierced a

dozen shafts, emerging at different heights, but all near the summit, and all so far outside the central plateau as to leave the solid foundation on which the Observatory was to rest, down to the very centre of the planet, wholly undisturbed. Through each of these, ascending and descending alternately, pass two cars, or rather movable chambers, worked by electricity, conveying passengers, instruments, or supplies to and from the most convenient points in the vast structure of the Observatory itself. The highest part of Ranelca was a rocky mass of some 1600 feet in circumference and about 200 in height. This was carved into a perfect octagon, in the sides of which were arranged a number of minor chambers—among them those wherein transit and other secondary observations were to be taken, and in which minor magnifying instruments were placed to scan their several portions of the heavens. Within these was excavated a circular central chamber, the dome of which was constructed of a crystal so clear that I verily believe the most exacting of Terrestrial astronomers would have been satisfied to make his observations through it. But an opening was made in this dome, as for the mounting of one of our equatorial telescopes, and machinery was provided which caused the roof to revolve with a touch, bringing the opening to bear on any desired part of the celestial vault. In the centre of the solid floor, levelled to the utmost perfection, was left a circular pillar supporting the polar axis of an instrument widely differing from our telescopes, especially in the fact that it had no opaque tube connecting the essential lenses which we call the eye-piece and the object-glass, names not applicable to their Martial substitutes. On my visit to the Observatory, however, I had not leisure to examine minutely the means by which the images of stars and planets were produced. I reserved this examination for a second opportunity, which, as it happened, never occurred.

On this occasion Eveena and Eunané were with me, and the astronomic pictures which were to be presented to us, and which they could enjoy and understand almost as fully as myself, sufficiently occupied our time.

Warned to stand at such a distance from the central machinery that in a whole revolution no part of it could by any possibility touch us, we were placed near an opening looking into a dark chamber, with our backs to the

objects of observation. In this chamber, not upon a screen but suspended in the air, presently appeared an image several thousand times larger than that of the crescent Moon as seen through a tube small enough to correct the exaggeration of visual instinct. It appeared, however, not flat, as does the Moon to the naked eye, but evidently as part of a sphere. At some distance was shown another crescent, belonging to a sphere whose diameter was a little more than one-fourth that of the former. The light reflected from their surfaces was of silver radiance, rather than the golden hue of the Moon or of Venus as seen through a small telescope. The smaller crescent I could recognise at once as belonging to our own satellite; the larger was, of course, the world I had quitted. So exactly is the clockwork or its substitute adapted to counteract both the rotation and revolution of Mars, that the two images underwent no other change of place than that caused by their own proper motion in space; a movement which, notwithstanding the immense magnifying power employed, was of course scarcely perceptible. But the rotation of the larger sphere was visible as we watched it. It so happened that the part which was at once lighted by the rays of the Sun and exposed to our observation was but little clouded. The atmosphere, of course, prevented its presenting the clear, sharply-defined outlines of lunar landscapes; but sea and land, ice and snow, were so clearly defined and easily distinguishable that my companions exclaimed with eagerness, as they observed features unmistakably resembling on the grand scale those with which they were themselves familiar. The Arctic ice was scarcely visible in the North. The vast steppes of Russia, the boundary line of the Ural mountains, the greyish-blue of the Euxine, Western Asia, Arabia, and the Red Sea joining the long water-line of the Southern Ocean, were defined by the slanting rays. The Antarctic ice-continent was almost equally clear, with its stupendous glacier masses radiating apparently from an elevated extensive land, chiefly consisting of a deeply scooped and scored plateau of rock, around the Pole itself. The terminator, or boundary between light and shade, was not, as in the Moon, pretty sharply defined, and broken only by the mountainous masses, rings, and sea-beds, if such they are, so characteristic of the latter. On the image of the Moon there intervened between bright light and utter darkness but the narrow belt to which only part of the Sun was as yet visible, and which, therefore, received comparatively few rays. The twilight to north and south extended on the image of the Earth deep into that part on which as yet the Sun was below the horizon, and consequently daylight faded into darkness all but imperceptibly, save between the tropics. We watched long and intently as league by league new portions of Europe and Africa, the Mediterranean, and even the Baltic, came into view; and I was able to point out to Eveena lands in which I had traveller, seas I had crossed, and even the isles of the Aegean, and bays in which my vessel had lain at anchor. This personal introduction to each part of the image, now presented to her for the first time, enabled her to realise more forcibly than a lengthened experience of astronomical observation might have done the likeness to her own world of that which was passing under her eyes; and at once intensified her wonder, heightened her pleasure, and sharpened her intellectual apprehension of the scene. When we had satiated our eyes with this spectacle, or rather when I remembered that we could spare no more time to this, the most interesting exhibition of the evening, a turn of the machinery brought Venus under view. Here, however, the cloud envelope baffled us altogether, and her close approach to the horizon soon obliged the director to turn his apparatus in another direction. Two or three of the Asteroids were in view. Pallas especially presented a very interesting spectacle. Not that the difference of distance would have rendered the definition much more perfect than from a Terrestrial standpoint, but that the marvellous perfection of Martial instruments, and in some measure also the rarity of the atmosphere at such a height, rendered possible the use of far higher magnifying powers than our astronomers can employ. I am inclined to agree, from what I saw on this occasion, with those who imagine the Asteroids to be—if not fragments of a broken planet which once existed as a whole—yet in another sense fragmentary spheres, less perfect and with surfaces of much greater proportionate irregularity than those of the larger planets. Next was presented to our view on a somewhat smaller scale, because the area of the chamber employed would not otherwise have given room for the system, the enormous disc and the four satellites of Jupiter.

The difference between 400 and 360 millions of miles' distance is, of course,

wholly unimportant; but the definition and enlargement were such that the image was perfect, and the details minute and distinct, beyond anything that Earthly observation had led me to conceive as possible. The satellites were no longer mere points or tiny discs, but distinct moons, with surfaces marked like that of our own satellite, though far less mountainous and broken, and, as it seemed to me, possessing a distinct atmosphere. I am not sure that there is not a visible difference of brightness among them, not due to their size but to some difference in the reflecting power of their surfaces, since the distance of all from the Sun is practically equal. That Jupiter gives out some light of his own, a portion of which they may possibly reflect in differing amount according to their varying distance, is believed by Martial astronomers; and I thought it not improbable. The brilliant and various colouring of the bands which, cross the face of the giant planet was wonderfully brought out; the bluish-grey around the poles, the clear yellowish-white light of the light bands, probably belts of white cloud, contrasted signally the hues—varying from deep orange-brown to what was almost crimson or rose-pink on the one hand and bright yellow on the other—of different zones of the so-called dark belts. On the latter, markings and streaks of strange variety suggested, if they failed-to prove, the existence of frequent spiral storms, disturbing, probably at an immense height above the surface, clouds which must be utterly unlike the clouds of Mars or the Earth in material as well as in form and mass. These markings enabled us to follow with clear ocular appreciation the rapid rotation of this planet. In the course of half-an-hour several distinct spots on different belts had moved in a direct line across a tenth of the face presented to us—

a distance, upon the scale of the gigantic image, so great that the motion required no painstaking observation, but forced itself upon the notice of the least attentive spectator. The belief of Martial astronomers is that Jupiter is not by any means so much less dense than the minor planets as his proportionately lesser weight would imply. They hold that his visible surface is that of an enormously deep atmosphere, within which lies, they suppose, a central ball, not merely hot but more than white hot, and probably, from its temperature, not yet possessing a solid crust. One writer argues that, since all worlds must by analogy be supposed to be inhabited,

and since the satellites of Jupiter more resemble worlds than the planet itself, which may be regarded as a kind of secondary sun, it is not improbable that the former are the scenes of life as varied as that of Mars itself; and that infinite ages hence, when these have become too cold for habitation, their giant primary may have gone through those processes which, according to the received theory, have fitted the interior planets to be the home of plants, animals, and, in two cases at least, of human beings.

It was near midnight before the manifest fatigue of the ladies overcame my selfish desire to prolong as much as possible this most interesting visit.

Meteorological science in Mars has been carried to high perfection; and the director warned me that but three or four equally favourable opportunities might offer in the course of the next half year.

CHAPTER XXIII - CHARACTERISTICS.

Time passed on, marked by no very important incident, while I made acquaintance with manners and with men around me, neither one nor the other worth further description. Nothing occurred to confirm the alarms Davilo constantly repeated.

I called the ladies one day into the outer grounds to see a new carriage, capable, according to its arrangement, of containing from two to eight persons, and a balloon of great size and new construction which Davilo had urgently counselled me to procure, as capable of sudden use in some of those daily thickening perils, of which I could see no other sign than occasional evidence that my steps were watched and dogged. Both vehicles enlisted the interest and curiosity of Eunané and her companions. Eveena, after examining with as much attention as was due to the trouble I took to explain it, the construction of the carriage, concentrated her interest and observation upon the balloon, the sight of which evidently impressed her.

When we had returned to the peristyle, and the rest had dispersed, I said—

"I see you apprehend some part of my reasons for purchasing the balloon. The carriage will take us to-morrow to Altasfe (a town some ten miles distant). 'Shopping' is an amusement so gratifying to all women on Earth, from the veiled favourites of an Eastern seraglio to the very unveiled dames of Western ballrooms, that I suppose the instinct must be native to the sex wherever women and trade co-exist. If you have a single feminine folly, you will enjoy this more than you will own. If you are, as they complain, absolutely faultless, you will enjoy with me the pleasure of the girls in plaguing one after another all the traders of Altasfe:" and with these words I placed in her hands a packet of the thin metallic plates constituting their currency. Her extreme and unaffected surprise was amusing to witness.

"What am I to do with this?" she inquired, counting carefully the uncounted pile, in a manner which at once dispelled my impression that her surprise was due to childish ignorance of its value.

"Whatever you please, Madonna; whatever can please you and the others."

"But," she remonstrated, "this is more than all our dowries for another year to come; and—forgive me for repeating what you seem purposely to forget—I cannot cast the shadow between my equals and the master.

Would you so mortify me as to make me take from Eunané's hand, for example, what should come from yours?"

"You are right, Madonna, now as always," I owned; wincing at the name she used, invariably employed by the others, but one I never endured from her. Her looks entreated pardon for the form of the implied reproof, as I resumed the larger part of the money she held out to me, forcing back the smaller into her reluctant hands. "But what has the amount of your dowries to do with the matter? The contracts are meant, I suppose, to secure the least to which a wife has a right, not to fix her natural share in her husband's wealth. You need not fear, Eveena; the Prince has made us rich enough to spend more than we shall care for."

"I don't understand you," she replied with her usual gentle frankness and simple logical consistency. "It pleases you to say 'we' and 'ours' whenever you can so seem to make me part of yourself; and I love to hear you, for it assures me each time that you still hold me tightly as I cling to you. But you know those are only words of kindness. Since you returned my father's gift, the dowry you then doubled is my only share of what is yours, and it is more than enough."

"Do you mean that women expect and receive no more: that they do not naturally share in a man's surplus wealth?"

While I spoke Enva had joined us, and, resting on the cushions at my feet, looked curiously at the metallic notes in Eveena's hand.

"You do not," returned the latter, "pay more foe what you have purchased because you have grown richer. You do not share your wealth even with those on whose care it chiefly depends."

"Yes, I do, Eveena. But I know what you mean. Their share is settled and is not increased. But you will not tell me that this affords any standard for household dealings; that a wife's share in her husband's fortune is really bounded by the terms of the marriage contract?"

"Will you let Enva answer you?" asked Eveena. "She looks more ready than I feel to reply."

This little incident was characteristic in more ways than one. Eveena's feelings, growing out of the realities of our relation, were at issue with and perplexed her convictions founded on the theory and practice of her world.

Not yet doubting the justice of the latter, she instinctively shrank from their application to ourselves. She was glad, therefore, to let Enva state plainly and directly a doctrine which, from her own lips, would have pained as well as startled me. On her side, Enva, though encouraged to bear her part in conversation, was too thoroughly imbued with the same ideas to interpose unbidden. As she would have said, a wife deserved the sandal for speaking without leave; nor—experience notwithstanding—would she think it safe to interrupt in my presence a favourite so pointedly honoured as Eveena. 'She waited, therefore, till my eyes gave the permission which hers had asked.

"Why should you buy anything twice over, Clasfempta, whether it be a wife or an ambâ? A girl sells her society for the best price her attractions will command. These attractions seldom increase. You cannot give her less because you care less for them; but how can she expect more?"

"I know, Enva, that the marriage contract here is an open bargain and sale, as among my race it is generally a veiled one. But, the bargain made, does it really govern the after relation? Do men really spend their wealth wholly on themselves, and take no pleasure in the pleasure of women?"

"Generally, I believe," Enva replied, "they fancy they have paid too much for their toy before they have possessed it long, and had rather buy a new one than make much of those they have. Wives seldom look on the increase of a man's wealth as a gain to themselves. Of course you like to see us prettily dressed, while you think us worth looking at in ourselves. But as a rule our own income provides for that; and we at any rate are better off than almost any women outside the Palace. The Prince did not care, and knew it would not matter to you, what he gave to make his gift worthy of him and agreeable to you. Perhaps," she added, "he wished to make it secure by offering terms too good to be thrown away by any foolish rebellion against a heavier hand or a worse temper than usual. You hardly understand yet half the advantages you possess."

The latent sarcasm of the last remark did not need the look of pretended fear that pointed it. If Enva professed to resent my inadequate appreciation of the splendid beauty bestowed on me by the royal favour more than any possible ill-usage for which she supposed herself compensated in advance, it was not for me to put her sincerity to proof.

"Once bought, then, wives are not worth pleasing? It is not worth while to purchase happy faces, bright smiles, and willing kisses now and then at a cost the giver can scarcely feel?"

Enva's look now was half malicious, half kindly, and wholly comical; but she answered gravely, with a slight imitation of my own tone—

"Can you not imagine, or make Eveena tell you, Clasfempta, why women once purchased think it best to give smiles and kisses freely to one who can command their tears? Or do you fancy that their smiles are more loyal and sincere when won by kindness than...."

"By fear? Sweeter, Enva, at any rate. Well, if I do not offend your feelings, I need not hesitate to disregard another of your customs."

She received her share willingly and gratefully enough, but her smile and kiss were so evidently given to order, that they only testified to the thorough literality of her statement. Leenoo, Eiralé, and Elfé followed her example with characteristic exactness. Equally characteristic was the conduct of the others. Eunané kept aloof till called, and then approached with an air of sullen reluctance, as if summoned to receive a reprimand rather than a favour. Not a little amused, I affected displeasure in my turn, till the window of her chamber closed behind us, and her ill-humour was forgotten in wondering alarm. Offered in private, the kiss and smile given and not demanded, the present was accepted with frank affectionate gratitude. Eivé took her share in pettish shyness, waiting the moment when she might mingle unobserved with her childlike caresses the childish reproach—

"If you can buy kisses, Clasfempta, you don't want mine. And if you fancy I sell them, you shall have no more."

I saw Davilo in the morning before we started. After some conversation on business, he said—

"And pardon a suggestion which I make, not as in charge of your affairs, but as responsible to our supreme authority for your safety. No correspondence should pass from your household unscrutinised; and if there be such correspondence, I must ask you to place in my hand, for the purpose of our quest, not any message, but some of the slips on which messages have been written. This may probably furnish precisely that tangible means of relation with some one acquainted with the conspiracy for which we have sought in vain."

My unwillingness to meddle with feminine correspondence was the less intelligible to him that, as the master alone commands the household telegraph, he knew that it must have passed through my hands. I yielded at last to his repeated urgency that a life more precious than mine was involved in any danger to myself, so far as to promise the slips required, to furnish a possible means of rapport between the clairvoyante and the enemy.

I returned to the house in grave thought. Eunané. corresponded by the telegraph with some schoolmates; Eivé, I fancied, with three or four of those ladies with whom, accompanying me on my visits, she had made acquaintance. But I hated the very thought of domestic suspicion, and, adhering to my original resolve, refused to entertain a distrust that seemed ill-founded and far-fetched. If there had been treachery, it would be impossible to obtain any letters that might have been preserved without resorting to a compulsion which, since both Eunané and Eivé had written in the knowledge that their letters passed unread, would seem like a breach of faith. I asked, however, simply, and giving no reason, for the production of any papers received and preserved by either. Eivé, with her usual air of simplicity, brought me the two or three which, she said, were all she had kept. Eunané replied with a petulance almost amounting to refusal, which to some might have suggested suspicion; but which to me seemed the very

last course that a culprit would have pursued. To give needless offence while conscious of guilt would have been the very wantonness of reckless temper.

"Bite your tongue, and keep your letters," I said sharply.

Turning to Eivé and looking at the addresses of hers, none of which bore the name of any one who could be suspected of the remotest connection with a political plot—

"Give me which of these you please," I said, taking from her hand that which she selected and marking it. "Now erase the writing yourself and give me the paper."

This incident gave Eunané leisure to recover her temper. She stood for a few moments ashamed perhaps, but, as usual, resolute to abide by the consequences of a fault. When she found that my last word was spoken, her mood changed at once.

"I did not quite like to give you Velna's letters. They are foolish, like mine; and besides—— But I never supposed you would let me refuse. What you won't make me do, I must do of my own accord."

Womanly reasoning, most unlike "woman's reasons!" She brought, with unaffected alacrity, a collection of tafroo-slips whose addresses bore out her account of their character. Taking the last from the bundle, I bade her erase its contents.

"No," she said, "that is the one I least liked to show. If you will not read it, please follow my hand as I read, and see for yourself how far I have misused your trust."

"I never doubted your good faith, Eunané"—But she had begun to read, pointing with her finger as she went on. At one sentence hand and voice wavered a little without apparent reason. "I shall," wrote her school-friend, some half year her junior, "make my appearance at the next inspection. I wish the Camptâ, had left you here till now; we might perhaps have contrived to pass into the same household."

"A very innocent wish, and very natural," I said, in answer to the look, half inquiring, half shy, with which Eunané watched the effect of her words. I could not now use the precaution in her case, which it had somehow seemed natural to adopt with Eivé, of marking the paper returned for erasure. On her part, Eunané thrust into my hand the whole bundle as they were, and I was forced myself to erase, by an electro-chemical process which leaves no trace of writing, the words of that selected. The absence of any mark on the second paper served sufficiently to distinguish the two when, of course without stating from whom I received them, I placed, them in Davilo's hands.

When we were ready to leave the peristyle for the carriage, I observed that Eunané alone was still unveiled, while the others wore their cloaks of down and the thick veils, without which no lady may present herself to the public eye.

"'Thieving time is woman's crime,'" I said, quoting a domestic proverb. "In another household you would; be left behind."

"Of course," she replied, such summary discipline seeming to her as appropriate as to an European child. "I don't like always to deserve the vine and receive the nuts."

"You must take which I like," I retorted, laughing. Satisfied or silenced, she hastened to dress, and enjoyed with unalloyed delight the unusual pleasure of inspecting dresses and jewellery, and making more purchases in a day than she had expected to be able to do in two years. But she and her companions acted with more consideration than ladies permitted to visit the shops of Europe show for their masculine escort. Eivé alone, on this as on other occasions, availed herself thoroughly of those privileges of childhood which I had always extended to her.

So quick are the proceedings and so excellent the arrangements of Martial commerce, even where ladies are concerned, that a couple of hours saw us on our way homeward, after having passed through the apartments of half the merchants in Altasfe. Purposely for my own pleasure, as well as for that of my companions, I took a circuitous route homeward, and in so doing came within sight of a principal feminine Nursery or girls' school. Recognising it, Eunané spoke with some eagerness—

"Ah! I spent nine years there, and not always unhappily."

Eveena, who sat beside me, pressed my hand, with an intention easily understood.

"And you would like to see it again?" I inquired in compliance with her silent hint.

"Not to go back," said Eunané. "But I should like to pay it a visit, if it were possible."

"Can we?" I asked Eveena.

"I think so," she answered. "I observe half a dozen people have gone in since we came in sight, and I fancy it is inspection day there."

"Inspection?" I asked.

"Yes," she replied in a tone of some little annoyance and discomfort. "The girls who have completed their tenth year, and who are thought to have as good a chance now as they would have later, are dressed for the first time in the white robe and veil of maidenhood, and presented in the public chamber to attract the choice of those who are looking for brides."

"Not a pleasant spectacle," I said, "to you or to myself; but it will hardly annoy the others, and Eunané shall have her wish."

We descended from our carriage at the gate, and entered the grounds of the Nursery. Studiously as the health, the diet, and the exercise of the inmates are cared for, nothing is done to render the appearance of the home where they pass so large and critical a portion of their lives cheerful or attractive in appearance. Utility alone is studied; how much beauty conduces to utility where the happiness and health of children are concerned, Martial science has yet to learn. The grounds contained no flowers and but few trees; the latter ruined in point of form and natural grace to render them convenient supports for gymnastic apparatus. A number of the younger girls, unveiled, but dressed in a dark plain garment reaching from the throat to the knees, with trousers giving free play to the

limbs, were exercising on the different swings and bars, flinging the light weights and balls, or handling the substitutes for dumb-bells, the use of which forms an important branch of their education. Others, relieved from this essential part of their tasks, were engaged in various sports. One of these I noticed especially. Perhaps a hundred young ladies on either side formed a sort of battalion, contending for the ground they occupied with light shields of closely woven wire and masks of the same material, and with spears consisting of a reed or grass about five feet in length, and exceedingly light. When perfectly ripened, these spears are exceeding formidable, their points being sharp enough to pierce the skin of any but a pachydermatous animal. Those employed in these games, however, are gathered while yet covered by a sheath, which, as they ripen, bursts and leaves the keen, hard point exposed. Considerable care is taken in their selection, since, if nearly ripe, or if they should ripen prematurely under the heat of the sun when severed from the stem, the sheath bursting in the middle of a game, very grave accidents might occur. The movements of the girls were so ordered that the game appeared almost as much a dance as a conflict; but though there was nothing of unseemly violence, the victory was evidently contested with real earnestness, and with a skill superior to that displayed in the movements of the actual soldiers who have long since exchanged the tasks of warfare for the duties of policemen, escorts, and sentries. I held Eveena's hand, the others followed us closely, venturing neither to break from our party without leave nor to ask permission, till, at Eveena's suggestion, it was spontaneously given. They then quitted us, hastening, Eunané to seek out her favourite companions of a former season, the others to mingle with the younger girls and share in their play.

We walked on slowly, stopping from time to time to watch the exercises and sports of the younger portion of a community numbering some fifteen hundred girls. When we entered the hall we were rejoined by Eunané, with one of her friends who still wore the ordinary school costume.

Conversation with or notice of a young lady so dressed was not only not expected but disallowed, and the pair seated themselves behind us and studiously out of hearing of any conversation conducted in a low tone.

The spectacle, as I had anticipated, was to me anything but pleasant. It reminded me of a slave-market of the East, however, rather than of the more revolting features of a slave auction in the United States. The maidens, most of them very graceful and more than pretty, their robes arranged and ornamented with an evident care to set off their persons to the best advantage, and with a skill much greater than they themselves could yet have acquired, were seated alone or by twos and threes in different parts of the hall, grouped so as to produce the most attractive general as well as individual effect. The picture, therefore, was a pretty one; and since the intending purchasers addressed the objects of their curiosity or admiration with courtesy and fairly decorous reserve, it was the known character rather than any visible incident of the scene that rendered it repugnant or revolting in my eyes. I need not say that, except Eveena, there was no one of either sex in the hall who shared my feeling.

After all, the purpose was but frankly avowed, and certainly carried out more safely and decorously than in the ball-rooms and drawing-rooms of London or Paris. Of the maidens, some seemed shy and backward, and most were silent save when addressed. But the majority received their suitors with a thoroughly business-like air, and listened to the terms offered them, or endeavoured to exact a higher price or a briefer period of assured slavery, with a self-possession more reasonable than agreeable to witness. One maiden seated in our immediate vicinity was, I perceived, the object of Eveena's especial interest, and, at first on this account alone, attracted my observation. Dressed with somewhat less ostentatious care and elegance than her companions, her veil and the skirt of her robe were so arranged as to show less of her personal attractions than they generally displayed. A first glance hardly did justice to a countenance which, if not signally pretty, and certainly marked by a beauty less striking than that of most of the others, was modest and pleasing; a figure slight and graceful, with hands and feet yet smaller than usual, even among a race the shape of whose limbs is, with few exceptions, admirable. Very few had addressed her, or even looked at her; and a certain resigned mortification was visible in her countenance.

"You are sorry for that child?" I said to Eveena.

"Yes," she answered. "It must be distressing to feel herself the least attractive, the least noticed among her companions, and on such an occasion. I cannot conceive how I could bear to form part of such a spectacle; but if I were in her place, I suppose I should be hurt and humbled at finding that nobody cared to look at me in the presence of others prettier and better dressed than myself."

"Well," I said, "of all the faces I see I like that the best. I suppose I must not speak to her?"

"Why not?" said Eveena in surprise. "You are not bound to purchase her, any more than we bought all we looked at to-day."

"It did not occur to me," I replied, "that I could be regarded as a possible suitor, nor do I think I could find courage to present myself to that young lady in a manner which must cause her to look upon me in that light. Ask Eunané if she knows her."

Here Eivé and the others joined us and took their places on my right.

Eveena, leaving her seat for a moment, spoke apart with Eunané.

"Will you speak to her?" she said, returning. "She is Eunané's friend and correspondent, Velna; and I think they are really fond of each other. It is a pity that if she is to undergo the mortification of remaining unchosen and going back to her tasks, at least till the next inspection, she will also be separated finally from the only person for whom she seems to have had anything like home affection."

"Well, if I am to talk to her," I replied, "you must be good enough to accompany me. I do not feel that I could venture on such an enterprise by myself."

Eveena's eyes, even through her veil, expressed at once amusement and surprise; but as she rose to accompany me this expression faded and a look of graver interest replaced it. Many turned to observe us as we crossed the short space that separated us from the isolated and neglected maiden. I had seen, if I had not noticed, that in no case were the men, as they made the tour of the room or went up to any lady who might have attracted their special notice, accompanied by the women of their households. A few of

these, however, sat watching the scene, their mortification, curiosity, jealousy, or whatever feeling it might excite, being of course concealed by the veils that hid every feature but the eyes, which now and then followed very closely the footsteps of their lords. The object of our attention showed marked surprise as we approached her, and yet more when, seeing that I was at a loss for words, Eveena herself spoke a kindly and gracious sentence. The girl's voice was soft and low, and her tone and words, as we gradually fell into a hesitating and broken conversation, confirmed the impression made by her appearance. When, after a few minutes, I moved to depart, there was in Eveena's reluctant steps and expressive upturned eyes a meaning I could not understand. As soon as we were out of hearing, moving so as partly to hide my countenance and entirely to conceal her own gesture from the object of her compassion, she checked my steps by a gentle pressure on my arm and looked up earnestly into my face.

"What is it?" I asked. "You seem to have some wish that I cannot conjecture; and you can trust by this time my anxiety to gratify every desire of yours, reasonable or not—if indeed you ever were unreasonable."

"She is so sad, so lonely," Eveena answered, "and she is so fond of Eunané."

"You don't mean that you want me to make her an offer!" I exclaimed in extreme amazement.

"Do not be angry," pleaded Eveena. "She would be glad to accept any offer you would be likely to make; and the money you gave me yesterday would have paid all she would cost you for many years. Besides, it would please Eunané, and it would make Velna so happy."

"You must know far better than I can what is likely to make her happy," I replied. "Strange to the ideas and customs of your world, I cannot conceive that a woman can wish to take the last place in a household like ours rather than the first or only one with the poorest of her people."

"She will hardly have the choice," Eveena answered. "Those whom you can call poor mostly wait till they can have their choice before they marry; and if taken by some one who could not afford a more expensive choice, she

would only be neglected, or dismissed ill provided for, as soon as he could purchase one more to his taste."

"If," I rejoined at last, "you think it a kindness to her, and are sure she will so think it; if you wish it, and will avouch her contentment with a place in the household of one who does not desire her, I will comply with this as with any wish of yours. But it is not to my mind to take a wife out of mere compassion, as I might readily adopt a child."

Once more, with all our mutual affection and appreciation of each other's character, Eveena and I were far as the Poles apart in thought if not in feeling. It was as impossible for her to emancipate herself utterly from the ideas and habits of her own world, as for me to reconcile myself to them. I led her back at last to her seat, and beckoned Eunané to my side.

"Eveena," I said, "has been urging me to offer your friend yonder a place in our household."

Though I could not see her face, the instant change in her attitude, the eager movement of her hands, and the elastic spring that suddenly braced her form, expressed her feeling plainly enough.

"It must be done, I suppose," I murmured rather to myself than to them, as Eunané timidly put out her hand and gratefully clasped Eveena's. "Well, it is to be done for you, and you must do it."

"How can I?" exclaimed Eunané in astonishment; and Eveena added, "It is for you; you only can name your terms, and it would be a strange slight to her to do so through us."

"I cannot help that. I will not 'act the lie' by affecting any personal desire to win her, and I could not tell her the truth. Offer her the same terms that contented the rest; nay, if she enters my household, she shall not feel herself in a secondary or inferior position."

This condition surprised even Eveena as much as my resolve to make her the bearer of the proposal that was in truth her own. But, however reluctant, she would as soon have refused obedience to my request as have withheld a kindness because it cost her an unexpected trial. Taking Eunané with her, she approached and addressed the girl. Whatever my own doubt

as to her probable reception, however absurd in my own estimation the thing I was induced to do, there was no corresponding consciousness, no feeling but one of surprise and gratification, in the face on which I turned my eyes. There was a short and earnest debate; but, as I afterwards learned, it arose simply from the girl's astonishment at terms which, extravagant even for the beauties of the day, were thrice as liberal as she had ventured to dream of. Eveena and Eunané were as well aware of this as herself; the right of beauty to a special price seemed to them as obvious as in Western Europe seems the right of rank to exorbitant settlements; but they felt it as impossible to argue the point as a solicitor would find it unsafe to expound to a gentleman the different cost of honouring Mademoiselle with his hand and being honoured with that of Milady. Velna's remonstrances were suppressed; she rose, and, accompanied by Eveena and Eunané, approached a desk in one corner of the room, occupied by a lady past middle life. The latter, like all those of her sex who have adopted masculine independence and a professional career, wore no veil over her face, and in lieu of the feminine head-dress a band of metal around the head, depending from which a short fall of silken texture drawn back behind the ears covered the neck and upper edge of the dark robe. This lady took from a heap by her side a slip containing the usual form of marriage contract, and filled in the blanks. At a sign from Eveena, I had by this time approached close enough to hear the language of half-envious, half-supercilious wonder in which the schoolmistress congratulated her pupil on her signal conquest, and the terms she had obtained, as well as the maiden's unaffected acknowledgment of her own surprise and conscious unworthiness. I could feel, despite the concealment of her form and face, Eveena's silent expression of pained disgust with the one, and earnest womanly sympathy with the other. The document was executed in the usual triplicate.

The girl retired for a few minutes, and reappeared in a cloak and veil like those of her new companions, but of comparatively cheap materials. As we passed the threshold, Eveena gently and tacitly but decisively assigned to her protégée her own place beside me, and put her right hand in my left.

The agitation with which it manifestly trembled, though neither strange

nor unpleasing, added to the extreme embarrassment I felt; and I had placed her next to Eunané in the carriage and taken my seat beside Eveena, whom I never permitted to resign her own, before a single spoken word had passed in this extraordinary courtship, or sanctioned the brief and practical ceremony of marriage.

I was alone in my own room that evening when a gentle scratching on the window-crystal entreated admission. I answered without looking up, assuming that Eveena alone would seek me there. But hers were not the lips that were earnestly pressed on my hand, nor hers the voice that spoke, trembling and hesitating with stronger feeling than it could utter in words—

"I do thank you from my heart. I little thought you would wish to make me so happy. I shrank from showing you the letter lest you should think I dared to hope…. It is not only Velna; it is such strange joy and comfort to be held fast by one who cares—to feel safe in hands as kind as they are strong. You said you could love none save Eveena; but, Clasfempta, your way of not loving is something better, gentler, more considerate than any love I ever hoped or heard of."

I could read only profound sincerity and passionate gratitude in the clear bright eyes, softened by half-suppressed tears, that looked up from where she knelt beside me. But the exaggeration was painfully suggestive, confirming the ugly view Enva had given yesterday of the life that seemed natural and reasonable to her race, and made ordinary human kindness appear something strange and romantic by contrast.

"Surely, Eunané, every man wishes those around him happy, if it do not cost too much to make them so?"

"No, indeed! Oftener the master finds pleasure in punishing and humiliating, the favourite in witnessing her companions' tears and terror.

They like to see the household grateful for an hour's amusement, crouching to caprice, incredulously thankful for barest justice. One book much read in our schools says that 'cruelty is a stronger, earlier, and more tenacious human instinct than sympathy;' and another that 'half the pleasure of

power lies in giving pain, and half the remainder in being praised for sparing it.' ... But that was not all: Eveena was as eager to be kind as you were."

"Much more so, Eunané."

"Perhaps. What seemed natural to her was strange to you. But it was your thought to put Velna on equal terms with us; taking her out of mere kindness, to give her the dowry of a Prince's favourite. That surprised Eveena, and it puzzled me. But I think I half understand you now, and if I do.... When Eveena told us how you saved her and defied the Regent, and Eivé asked you about it, you said so quietly, 'There are some things a man cannot do.' Is buying a girl cheap, because she is not a beauty, one of those things?"

"To take any advantage of her misfortune—to make her feel it in my conduct—to give her a place in my household on other terms than her equals—to show her less consideration or courtesy than one would give to a girl as beautiful as yourself—yes, Eunané! To my eyes, your friend is pleasant and pretty; but if not, would you have liked to feel that she was of less account here than yourself, because she has not such splendid beauty as yours?"

Eunané was too frank to conceal her gratification in this first acknowledgment of her charms, as she had shown her mortification while it was withheld—not, certainly, because undeserved. Her eyes brightened and her colour deepened in manifest pleasure. But she was equally frank in her answer to the implied compliment to her generosity, of whose justice she was not so well assured.

"I am afraid I should half have liked it, a year ago. Now, after I have lived so long with you and Eveena, I should be shamed by it! But, Clasfempta, the things 'a man cannot do' are the things men do every day;—and women every hour!"

CHAPTER XXIV - WINTER.

Hitherto I had experienced only the tropical climate of Mars, with the exception of the short time spent in the northern temperate zone about the height of its summer. I was anxious, of course, to see something also of its winter, and an opportunity presented itself. No institution was more obviously worth a visit than the great University or principal place of highest education in this world, and I was invited thither in the middle of the local winter. To this University many of the most promising youths, especially those intended for any of the Martial professions—architects, artists, rulers, lawyers, physicians, and so forth—are often sent directly from the schools, or after a short period of training in the higher colleges. It is situate far within the north temperate zone on the shore of one of the longest and narrowest of the great Martial gulfs, which extends from north-eastward to south-west, and stretches from 43° N. to 10° S. latitude. The University in question is situate nearly at the extremity of the northern branch of this gulf, which splits into two about 300 miles from its end, a canal of course connecting it with the nearest sea-belt. I chose to perform this journey by land, following the line of the great road from Amacasfe to Qualveskinta for about 800 miles, and then turning directly northward. I did not suppose that I should find a willing companion on this journey, and was myself wishful to be alone, since I dared not, in her present state of health, expose Eveena to the fatigue and hardship of prolonged winter travelling by land. To my surprise, however, all the rest, when aware that I had declined to take her, were eager to accompany me. Chiefly to take her out of the way, and certainly with no idea of finding pleasure in her society, I selected Enva; next to Leenoo the most malicious of the party, and gifted with sufficient intelligence to render her malice more effective than Leenoo's stupidity could be. Enva, moreover, with the vigorous youthful vitality-so often found on Earth in women of her light Northern complexion, seemed less likely to suffer from the severity of the weather or the fatigue of a land journey than most of her companions. When I spoke of my intention to Davilo, I was surprised to find that he considered even feminine company a protection.

"Any attempt upon you," he said, "must either involve your companion, for which there can be no legal excuse preferred, or else expose the assailant to the risk of being identified through her evidence."

I started accordingly a few days before the winter solstice of the North, reaching the great road a few miles from the point at which it crosses another of the great gulfs running due north and south, at its narrowest point in latitude 3° S. At this point the inlet is no more than twenty miles wide, and its banks about a hundred feet in height. At this level and across this vast space was carried a bridge, supported by arches, and resting on pillars deeply imbedded in the submarine rock at a depth about equal to the height of the land on either side. The Martial seas are for the most part shallow, the landlocked gulfs being seldom 100 fathoms, and the deepest ocean soundings giving less than 1000. The vast and solid structure looked as light and airy as any suspension bridge across an Alpine ravine. This gigantic viaduct, about 500 Martial years old, is still the most magnificent achievement of engineering in this department. The main roads, connecting important cities or forming the principal routes of commerce in the absence of convenient river or sea carriage, are carried over gulfs, streams, ravines, and valleys, and through hills, as Terrestrial engineers have recently promised to carry railways over the minor inequalities of ground. That which we were following is an especially magnificent road, and signalised by several grand exhibitions of engineering daring and genius. It runs from Amacasfe for a thousand miles in one straight line direct as that of a Roman road, and with but half-a-dozen changes of level in the whole distance. It crossed in the space of a few miles a valley, or rather dell, 200

feet in depth, and with semi-perpendicular sides, and a stream wider than the Mississippi above the junction of the Ohio. Next it traversed the precipitous side of a hill for a distance of three or four miles, where Nature had not afforded foothold for a rabbit or a squirrel. The stupendous bridges and the magnificent open road cut in the side of the rock, its roof supported on the inside by the hill itself, on the outside by pillars left at regular intervals when the stone was cut, formed from one point a single splendid view. Pointing it out to Enva, I was a little surprised to find her capable, under the guidance of a few remarks from myself, of appreciating

and taking pride in the marvellous work of her race. In another place, a tunnel pierced directly an intervening range of hills for about eight miles, interrupted only in two points by short deep open cuttings. This passage, unlike those on the river previously mentioned, was constantly and brilliantly lighted. The whole road indeed was lit up from the fall of the evening to the dispersion of the morning mist with a brilliancy nearly equal to that of daylight. As I dared not travel at a greater rate than twenty-five miles per hour—my experience, though it enabled me to manage the carriage with sufficient skill, not giving me confidence to push it to its greatest speed—the journey must occupy several days. We had, therefore, to rest at the stations provided by public authority for travellers undertaking such long land journeys. These are built like ordinary Martial houses, save that in lieu of peristyle or interior garden is an open square planted with shrubs and merely large enough to afford light to the inner rooms. The chambers also are very much smaller than those of good private houses. As these stations are nearly always placed in towns or villages, or in well-peopled country neighbourhoods, food is supplied by the nearest confectioner to each traveller individually, and a single person, assisted by the ambau, is able to manage the largest of them.

The last two or three days of our journey were bitterly cold, and not a little trying. My own undergarment of thick soft leather kept me warmer than the warmest greatcoat or cloak could have done, though I wore a large cloak of the kargynda's fur in addition—the prize of the hunt that had so nearly cost me dear, a personal and very gracious present from the Camptâ. My companion, who had not the former advantage, though wrapped in as many outer garments and quilts as I had thought necessary, felt the cold severely, and felt still more the dense chill mist which both by night and day covered the greater part of the country. This was not infrequently so thick as to render travelling almost perilous; and but that an electric light, required by law, was placed at each end of the carriage, collisions would have been inevitable. These hardships afforded another illustration of the subjection of the sex resulting from the rule of theoretical equality. More than a year's experience of natural kindness and consideration had not given Enva courage to make a single complaint; and

at first she did her best to conceal the weeping which was the only, but almost continuous, expression of her suffering. She was almost as much surprised as gratified by my expressions of sympathy, and the trouble I took to obtain, at the first considerable town we reached, an apparatus by which the heat generated by motion itself was made to supply a certain warmth through the tubular open-work of the carriage to the persons of its occupants. The cold was as severe as that of a Swedish winter, though we never approached within seventeen degrees of the Arctic circle, a distance from the Pole equivalent to that of Northern France. The Martial thermometer, in form more like a watch-barometer, which I carried in my belt, marked a cold equivalent to 12° below zero C. in the middle of the day; and when left in the carriage for the night it had registered no less than 22° below zero.

One of the Professors of the University received us as his guests, assigning to us, as is usual when a lady is of the party, rooms looking on the peristyle, but whose windows remained closed. Enva, of course, spent her time chiefly with the ladies of the family. When alone with me she talked freely, though needing some encouragement to express her own ideas, or report what she had heard; but she had no intention of concealment, perhaps no notion that I was interested in her accounts of the prevalent feeling respecting the heretics of whom she heard much, except of course that Eveena's father was among them. Through her I learned that much pains had been taken to intensify and excite into active hostility the dislike and distrust with which they had always been regarded by the public at large, and especially by the scientific guilds, whose members control all educational establishments. That some attempt against them was meditated appeared to be generally reported. Its nature and the movers in the matter were not known, so far as I could gather, even to men so influential as the chief Professors of the University. It was not merely that the women had heard nothing on this point, but that their lords had dropped expressions of surprise at the strictness with which the secret was kept.

As their parents pay, when first the children are admitted to the public Nurseries, the price of an average education, this special instruction is given in the first instance at the cost of the State to those who, on account of their taste and talent, are selected by the teachers of the Colleges. But before they leave the University a bond is taken for the amount of this outlay, which has to be repaid within three years. It is fair to say that the tax is trivial in comparison with the ordinary gains of their professions; the more so that no such preference as, in our world, is almost universally given to a reputation which can only be acquired by age, excludes the youth of Mars from full and profitable employment.

The youths were delighted to receive a lecture on the forms of Terrestrial government, and the outlines of their history; a topic I selected because they were already acquainted with the substance of the addresses elsewhere delivered. This afforded me an opportunity of making the personal acquaintance of some of the more distinguished pupils. The clearness of their intellect, the thoroughness of their knowledge in their several studies, and the distinctness of their acquaintance with the outlines and principles of Martial learning generally,—an acquaintance as free from smattering and superficiality as necessarily unembarrassed by detail,—

testified emphatically to the excellence of the training they had received, as well as to the hereditary development of their brains. What was, however, not less striking was the utter absence at once of what I was accustomed to regard as moral principle, and of the generous impulses which in youth sometimes supply the place of principle. They avowed the most absolute selfishness, the most abject fear of death and pain, with a frankness that would have amazed the Cynics and disgusted the felons of almost any Earthly nation. There were partial exceptions, but these were to be found exclusively among those in training for what we should call public life, for administrative or judicial duties. These, though professing no devotion to the interest of others, and little that could be called public spirit, did nevertheless understand that in return for the high rank, the great power, and the liberal remuneration they would enjoy, they were bound to consider primarily the public interest in the performance of their functions—the right of society to just or at least to carefully legal judgment,

and diligent efficient administration. Their feeling, however, was rather professional than personal, the pride of students in the perfection of their art rather than the earnestness of men conscious of grave human responsibilities.

In conversing with the chief of this Faculty, I learned some peculiarities of the system of government with which I was not yet acquainted. Promotion never depends on those with whom a public servant comes into personal contact, but on those one or two steps above the latter. The judges, for instance, of the lower rank are selected by the principal judge of each dominion; these and their immediate assistants, by the Chief of the highest Court. The officers around and under the Governor of a province are named by the Regent of the dominion; those surrounding the Regent, as the Regent himself, by the Sovereign. Every officer, however, can be removed by his immediate superior; but it depends on the chief with whom his appointment rests, whether he shall be transferred to a similar post elsewhere or simply dismissed. Thus, while no man can be compelled to work with instruments he dislikes, no subordinate is at the mercy of personal caprice or antipathy.

Promotion, judicial and administrative, ends below the highest point. The judges of the Supreme Court are named by the Sovereign—with the advice of a Council, including the Regents, the judges of that Court, and the heads of the Philosophic and Educational Institutes—from among the advocates and students of law, or from among the ablest administrators who seem to possess judicial faculties. The code is written and simple. Every dubious point that arises in the course of litigation is referred, by appeal or directly by the judge who decides it, to the Chief Court, and all points of interpretation thus referred, are finally settled by an addition to the code at its periodical revision. The Sovereign can erase or add at pleasure to this code. But he can do so only in full Council, and must hear, though he need not regard, the opinions of his advisers. He can, however, suspend immediately till the next meeting of the Council the enforcement of any article.

The Regents are never named from among subordinate officials, nor is a Regent ever promoted to the throne. It is held that the qualities required in an absolute Sovereign are not such as are demanded from or likely to be developed in the subordinate ruler of a dominion however important, and that functions like those of a Regent, at least as important as those of the Viceroy of India, ought not to be entrusted to men trained in subaltern administrative duties. Among the youths of greatest promise, in their eighth year, a certain small number are selected by the chiefs of the University, who visit for this purpose all the Nurseries of the kingdom.

With what purpose these youths are separated from their fellows is not explained to them. They are carefully educated for the highest public duties. Year by year those deemed fitter for less important offices are drafted off. There remain at last the very few who are thought competent to the functions of Regent or Camptâ, and from among these the Sovereign himself selects at pleasure his own successor and the occupant of any vacant Regency. The latter, however, holds his post at first on probation, and can, of course, be removed at any time by the Sovereign. If the latter should not before his death have named his own successor, the Council by a process of elimination is reduced to three, and these cast lots which shall name the new Autocrat from among the youths deemed worthy of the throne, of whom six are seldom living at the same time. No Prince is ever appointed under the age of fourteen (twenty-seven) or over that of sixteen (thirty). No Camptâ, has ever abdicated; but they seldom live to fall into that sort of inert indolence which may be called the dotage of their race.

The nature of their functions seems to preserve their mental activity longer than that of others; and probably they are not permitted to live when they have become manifestly unfit or incapable to reign.

When first invited to visit the University, I had hoped to make it only a stage and stepping-stone to something yet more interesting—to visit the Arctic hunters once more, and join them in the most exciting of their pursuits; a chase by the electric light of the great Amphibia of the frozen sea-belt immediately surrounding the permanent ice-cap of the Northern Pole. For this, however, the royal licence was required; and, as when I made a similar request during the fur-chase of the Southern season, I met

with a peremptory refusal. "There are two men in this world," said the Prince, "who would entertain such a wish. I dare not avow it; and if there were a third, he would assuredly be convicted of incurable lunacy, though on all other points he were as cold-blooded as the President of the Academy or the Vivisector-General." I did not tell Eveena of my request till it had been refused; and if anything could have lessened my vexation at the loss of this third opportunity, it would have been the expression of her countenance at that moment. Indeed, I was then satisfied that I could not have left her in the fever of alarm and anxiety that any suspicion of my purpose would have caused.

I seized, however, the opportunity of a winter voyage in a small vessel, manned by four or five ocean-hunters, less timid and susceptible to surface disturbances than ordinary seamen. On such an excursion, Enva, though a far less pleasant companion, was a less anxious charge than Eveena. We made for the Northern coast, and ran for some hundred miles, along a seabord not unlike that of Norway, but on a miniature scale. Though in some former age this hemisphere, like Europe, has been subject to glacial action much more general and intense than at present, its ice-seas and ice-rivers must always have been comparatively shallow and feeble. Beaching at last a break in the long line of cliff-guarded capes and fiords, where the sea, half covered with low islands, eats a broad and deep ingress into the landbelt, I disembarked, and made a day's land journey to the northward.

The ground was covered with a sheet of hard-frozen snow about eighteen inches deep, with an upper surface of pure ice. For the ordinary carriage, here useless, was substituted a sledge, driven from behind by an instrument something between a paddle-wheel and a screw, worked, of course, by the usual electric machinery. The cold was far more intense than I had ever before known it; and the mist that fell at the close of the very short zyda of daylight rendered it all but intolerable. The Arctic circular thermometer fell to within a few points from its minimum of—50°

Centigrade [?]. No flesh could endure exposure to such an atmosphere; and were not the inner mask and clothing of soft leather pervaded by a constant feeble current of electricity….

As we made our way back to the open sea, the temptation to disobey the royal order was all but irresistible. No fewer than three kargyndau were within shot at one and the same time; plunging from the shore of an icy island to emerge with their prey—a fish somewhat resembling the salmon in form and flavour. My companions, however, were terrified at the thought of disobedience to the law; and as we had but one mordyta (lightning-gun) among the party, and the uncertainty of the air-gun had been before proven to my cost, there was some force in their supplementary argument that, if I did not kill the kargynda, it was probable that the kargynda might board us; in which event our case would be summarily disposed of, without troubling the Courts or allowing time to apply, even by telegraph, for the royal pardon. I was suggesting, more to the alarm than amusement of the crew, that we might close the hatches, and either carry the regal beast away captive, or, at worst, dive and drown him—for he cannot swim very far—when their objections were enforced in an unexpected manner. We were drifting beyond shot of the nearest brute, when the three suddenly plunged at once, and as if by concert, and when they rose, were all evidently making for the vessel, and within some eighty yards. I then learnt a new advantage of the electric machinery, as compared with the most powerful steam-engine. A pressure upon a button, and a few seconds sufficed to exchange a speed of four for one of twenty miles an hour; while, instead of sinking the vessel below the surface, the master directed the engine to pump out all the liquid ballast she contained. The waterspout thus sent forth half-drowned the enemy which had already come within a few yards of our starboard quarter, and effectually-scared the others. It was just as well that Enva, who heartily hated the bitter cold, was snugly ensconced in the warm cushions of the cabin, and had not, therefore, the opportunity of giving to Eveena, on our return, her version of an adventure whose alarming aspect would have impressed them both more than its ludicrous side, For half a minute I thought that I had, in sheer folly, exposed half a dozen lives to a peril none the less real and none the more satisfactory that, if five had been killed, the survivor could not have so told the story as to avoid laughing—or being laughed at.

Sweet and serene as was Eveena's smile of welcome, it could not conceal the traces of more than mere depression on her countenance. Heartily willing to administer an effective lesson to her tormentors, I seized the occasion of the sunset meal to notice the weary and harassed look she had failed wholly to banish.

"You look worse each time I return, Madonna. This time it is not merely my absence, if it ever were so. I will know who or what has driven and hunted you so."

Taken thus by surprise, every face but one bore witness to the truth: Eveena's distress, Eunané's mixed relief and dismay, shared in yet greater degree by Velna, who knew less of me, the sheer terror and confusion of the rest, were equally significant. The Martial judge who said that "the best evidence was lost because colour could not be tested or blushes analysed," would have passed sentence at once. But if Eivé's air of innocent unconsciousness and childish indifference were not sincere, it merited the proverbial praise of consummate affectation, "more golden than the sun and whiter than snow." Eveena's momentary glance at once drew mine upon this "pet child," but neither disturbed her. Nor did she overact her part. "Eivé," said Enva one day, "never salts her tears or paints her blushes."

As soon as she caught my look of doubt—

"Have I done wrong?" she said, in a tone half of confidence, half of reproach. "Punish me, then, Clasfempta, as you please—with Eveena's sandal."

The repartee delighted those who had reason to desire any diversion. The appeal to Eveena disarmed my unwilling and momentary distrust. Eveena, however, answered by neither word nor look, and the party presently broke up. Eivé crept close to claim some silent atonement for unspoken suspicion, and a few minutes had elapsed before, to the evident alarm of several conscious culprits, I sought Eveena in her own chamber.

In spite of all deprecation, I insisted on the explanation she had evaded in public. "I guess," I said, "as much as you can tell me about 'the four.' I have borne too long with those who have made your life that of a hunted therne,

and rendered myself anxious and restless every day and hour that I have left you alone. Unless you will deny that they have done so—— Well, then, I will have peace for you and for myself. I cannot leave you to their mercy, nor can I remain at home for the next twelve dozen days, like a chained watch-dragon. Pass them over!" (as she strove to remonstrate); "there is something new this time. You have been harassed and frightened as well as unhappy."

"Yes," she admitted, "but I can give nothing like a reason. I dare not entreat you not to ask, and yet I am only like a child, that wakes screaming by night, and cannot say of what she is afraid. Ought she not to be whipped?"

"I can't say, bambina; but I should not advise Eivé to startle you in that way! But, seriously, I suppose fear is most painful when it has no cause that can be removed. I have seen brave soldiers panic-stricken in the dark, without well knowing why."

I watched her face as I spoke, and noted that while the pet name I had used in the first days of our marriage, now recalled by her image, elicited a faint smile, the mention of Eivé clouded it again. She was so unwilling to speak, that I caught at the clue afforded by her silence.

"It is Eivé then? The little hypocrite! She shall find your sandal heavier than mine."

"No, no!" she pleaded eagerly. "You have seen what Eivé is in your presence; and to me she is always the same. If she were not, could I complain of her?"

"And why not, Eveena? Do you think I should hesitate between you?"

"No!" she answered, with unusual decision of tone. "I will tell you exactly what you would do. You would take my word implicitly; you would have made up your mind before you heard her; you would deal harder measure to Eivé than to any one, because she is your pet; you would think for once not of sparing the culprit, but of satisfying me; and afterwards"——

She paused, and I saw that she would not conclude in words a sentence I could perhaps have finished for myself.

"I see," I replied, "that Eivé is the source of your trouble, but not what the trouble is. For her sake, do not force me to extort the truth from her."

"I doubt whether she has guessed my misgiving," Eveena answered. "It may be that you are right—that it is because she was so long the only one you were fond of, that I cannot like and trust her as you do. But ... you leave the telegraph in my charge, understanding, of course, that it will be used as when you are at home. So, after Davilo's warning, I have written their messages for Eunané and the others, but I could not refuse Eivé's request to write her own, and, like you, I have never read them."

"Why?" I asked. "Surely it is strange to give her, of all, a special privilege and confidence?"

Eveena was silent. She could in no case have reproached me in words, and even the reproach of silence was so unusual that I could not but feel it keenly. I saw at that moment that for whatever had happened or might happen I might thank myself; might thank the doubt I would not avow to my own mind, but could not conceal from her, that Eveena had condescended to something like jealousy of one whose childish simplicity, real or affected, had strangely won my heart, as children do win hearts hardened by experience of life's roughness and evil.

"I know nothing," Eveena said at last: "yet somehow, and wholly without any reason I can explain, I fear. Eivé, you may remember, has, as your companion, made acquaintance with many households whose heads you do not believe friends to you or the Zinta. She is a diligent correspondent.

She never affects to conceal anything, and yet no one of us has lately seen the contents of a note sent or received by her."

There was nothing tangible in Eveena's suspicion. It was most repugnant to my own feelings, and yet it implanted, whether by force of sympathy or of instinct, a misgiving that never left me again.

"My own," I answered, "I would trust your judgment, your observation or feminine instinct and insight into character, far sooner than my own conclusions upon solid facts. But instincts and presentiments, though we are not scientifically ignorant enough to disregard them, are not evidence on which we can act or even inquire."

"No," she said. "And yet it is hard to feel, as I cannot help feeling, that the thunder-cloud is forming, that the bolt is almost ready to strike, and that you are risking life, and perhaps more than life, out of a delicacy no other man would show towards a child—since child you will have her—who, I feel sure, deserves all she might receive from the hands of one who would have the truth at any cost."

"You feel," I answered, "for me as I should feel for you. But is death so terrible to us? It means leaving you—I wish we knew that it does not mean losing for ever, after so brief an enjoyment, all that is perishable in love like ours—or it would not be worth fearing. I don't think I ever did fear it till you made my life so sweet. But life is not worth an unkindness or injustice.

Better die trusting to the last than live in the misery and shame of suspecting one I love, or dreading treacherous malice from any hand under my own roof."

When I met Davilo the next morning, the grave and anxious expression of his face—usually calm and serene even in deepest thought, as are those of the experienced members of an Order confident in the consciousness of irresistible secret power—not a little disturbed me. As Eveena had said, the thunder-cloud was forming; and a chill went to my heart which in facing measurable and open peril it had never felt.

"I bring you," he said; "a message that will not, I am afraid, be welcome. He whose guest you were at Serocasfe invites you to pay him an immediate visit; and the invitation must be accepted at once."

I drew myself up with no little indignation at the imperative tone, but feeling at least equal awe at the stern calmness with which the mandate was spoken.

"And what compels me to such haste, or to compliance without consideration?"

"That power," he returned, "which none can resist, and to which you may not demur."

Seeing that I still hesitated—in truth, the summons had turned my vague misgiving into intense though equally vague alarm and even terror, which as unmanly and unworthy I strove to repress, but which asserted its domination in a manner as unwonted as unwelcome—he drew aside a fold of his robe, and showed within the silver Star of the Order, supported by the golden sash, that marked a rank second only to that of the wearer of the Signet itself. I understood too well by this time, through conversations with him and other communications of which it has been needless to speak, the significance of this revelation. I knew the impossibility of questioning the authority to which I had pledged obedience. I realised with great amazement the fact that a secondary position on my own estate, and a personal charge of my own safety, had been accepted by a Chief of the Zinta.

"There is, of course," I replied at last, "no answer to a mandate so enforced. But, Chief, reluctant as I am to say it, I fear—fear as I have never done before; and yet fear I cannot say, I cannot guess what."

"There is no cause for alarm," he said somewhat contemptuously. "In this journey, sudden, speedy, and made under our guard as on our summons, there is little or none of that peril which has beset you so long."

"You forget, Chief," I rejoined, "that you speak to a soldier, whose chosen trade was to risk life at the word of a superior; to one whose youth thought no smile so bright as that of naked steel, and had often 'kissed the lips of the lightning' ere the down darkened his own. At any rate, you have told me daily for more than a year that I am living under constant peril of assassination; have I seemed to quail thereat? If, then, I am now terrified for the first time, that which I dread, without knowing or dreaming what it is, is assuredly a peril worse than any I have known, the shadow of a calamity against which I have neither weapon nor courage. It cannot be for myself that I am thus appalled," I continued, the thought flashing into my mind as I spoke it, "and there is but one whose life is so closely bound with mine that danger to her should bring such terror as this. I go at your bidding, but I will not go alone."

He paused for some time, apparently in perplexity, certainly in deep thought, before he replied.

"As you will. One thing more. The slips of tafroo with which you furnished me have been under the eyes of which you have heard. This" (handing me the one that bore no mark) "has passed, so far as the highest powers of the sense that is not of the body can perceive, through none but innocent hands. The hand from which you received this" (the marked slip) "is spotted with treason, and may to-morrow be red."

I was less impressed by this declaration than probably would have been any other member of the Order. I had seen on Earth the most marvellous perceptions of a perfectly lucid vision succeeded, sometimes within the space of the same day, by dreams or hallucinations the most absolutely deceptive. I felt, therefore, more satisfaction in the acquittal of Eunané, whom I had never doubted, than trouble at the grave suspicion suggested against Eivé—a suspicion I still refused to entertain.

"You should enter your balloon as soon as the sunset mist will conceal it,"

said Davilo. "By mid-day you may reach the deep bay on the mid sea-belt of the North, where a swift vessel will meet you and convey you in two or three days by a direct course through the canal and gulf you have traversed already, to the port from which you commenced your first submarine voyage."

"You had better," I said, "make your instruction a little more particular, or I shall hardly know how to direct my course."

"Do not dream," he answered, "that you will be permitted to undertake such a journey but under the safest guidance. At the time I have named all will be ready for your departure, and you have simply to sleep or read or meditate as you will, till you reach your destination."

Eveena was not a little startled when I informed her of the sudden journey before me, and my determination that she should be my companion. It was unquestionably a trying effort for her, especially the balloon voyage, which would expose her to the cold of the mists and of the night, and I feared to the intenser cold of the upper air. But I dared not leave her, and she was

pleased by a peremptory decision which made her the companion of my absence, without leaving room for discussion or question. The time for our departure was drawing near when, followed by Eunané, she came into my chamber.

"If we are to be long away," she said, "you must say on whom my charges are to devolve."

"As you please," I answered, sure of her choice, and well content to see her hand over her cares to Eunané, who, if she lacked the wisdom and forbearance of Eveena, could certainly hold the reins with a stronger hand.

"Eivé," she said, "has asked the charge of my flowerbed; but I had promised it, and"——

"And you would rather give it," I answered, "to Eunané? Naturally; and I should not care to allow Eivé the chance of spoiling your work. I think we may now trust whatever is yours in those once troublesome hands,"

looking at Eunané, "with perfect assurance that they will do their best."

I had never before parted even from Eunané with any feeling of regret; but on this occasion an impulse I could not account for, but have ever since been glad to remember, made me turn at the last moment and add to Eveena's earnest embrace a few words of affection and confidence, which evidently cheered and encouraged her deputy. The car that awaited us was of the light tubular construction common here, formed of the silvery metal zorinta. About eighteen feet in length and half that breadth, it was divided into two compartments; each, with the aid of canopy and curtains, forming at will a closed tent, and securing almost as much privacy as an Arab family enjoys, or opening to the sky. In that with which the sails and machinery were connected were Davilo and two of his attendants. The other had been carefully lined and covered with furs and wrappings, indicating an attention to my companion which indeed is rarely shown to women by their own lords, and which none but the daughter of Esmo would have received even among the brethren of the Order. Ere we departed I had arranged her cushions and wrapped her closely in the warmest coverings; and flinging over her at last the kargynda skin received

from the Camptâ, I bade her sleep if possible during our aerial voyage.

There was need to provide as carefully as possible for her comfort. The balloon shot up at once above the evening mists to a height at which the cold was intense, but at which our voyage could be guided by the stars, invisible from below, and at which we escaped the more dangerously chilling damp. The wind that blew right in our teeth, caused by no atmospheric current but by our own rapid passage, would in a few moments have frozen my face, perhaps fatally, had not thick skins been arranged to screen us. Even through these it blew with intense severity, and I was glad indeed to cover myself from head to foot and lie down beside Eveena. Her hand as she laid it on mine was painfully cold; but the shivering I could hardly suppress made her anxious to part in my favour with some at least of the many coverings that could hardly screen herself from the searching blast. Not at the greatest height I reached among the Himalayas, nor on the Steppes of Tartary, had I experienced a cold severer than this. The Sun had just turned westward when we reached the port at which we were to embark. Despite the cold, Eveena had slept during the latter part of our voyage, and was still sleeping when I placed her on the cushions in our cabin. The sudden and most welcome change from bitter cold to comfortable warmth awakened her, as it at last allowed me to sleep.

Our journey was continued below the surface at a rate of more than twelve hundred miles in the day, a speed which made observation through the thick but perfectly transparent side windows of our cabin impossible. I was indisposed for meditation, which could have been directed to no other subject than the mysterious purpose of our journey, and had not provided myself with books. But in Eveena's company it was impossible that the time should pass slowly or wearily.

In this balloon journey I had a specially advantageous opportunity of observing the two moons—velnaa, as they are called. Cavelna, or Caulna, the nearer, in diameter about 8' or a little more than one-fourth that of our Moon, is a tolerably brilliant object, about 5000 miles from the surface.

Moving, like all planets and satellites, from west to east, it completes its stellar revolution and its phases in less than seven and a half hours; the contrary revolution of the skies prolongs its circuit around the planet to a

period of ten hours. Zeelna (Zevelna) returns to the same celestial meridian in thirty hours; but as in this time the starry vault has completed about a rotation and a quarter in the opposite direction, it takes nearly five days to reappear on the same horizon. It is about 3' in diameter, and about 12,000

miles from the surface. The result of the combined motions is that the two moons, to the eye, seem to move in opposite directions. When we rose above the mists, Caulna was visible as a very fine crescent in the west; Zeelna was rising in the east, and almost full; but hardly a more brilliant object than Venus when seen to most advantage from Earth. Both moved so rapidly among the stars that their celestial change of place was apparent from minute to minute. But, as regarded our own position, the appearance was as opposite as their direction. Zeelna, traversing in twelve hours only one-fifth of the visible hemisphere, while crossing in the same time 144° on the zodiac—twelve degrees per hour, or our Moon's diameter in two minutes and a half—was left behind by the stars; and fixing what I may call the ocular attention on her, she seemed to stand still while they slowly passed her; thus making their revolution perceptible to sense as it never is on Earth, for lack of a similar standard. Caulna, rising in the west and moving eastwards, crossed the visible sky in five hours, and passed through the stars at the rate of 48° per hour, so that she seemed to sail past them like a golden cloudlet or celestial vessel driven by a slow wind. It happened this night that she passed over the star Fomalhaut—an occultation which I watched with great interest through an excellent field-glass, but which lasted only for about half a minute. About an hour before midnight the two moons passed each other in the Eastern sky; both gibbous at the moment, like our Moon in her last quarter. The difference in size and motion was then most striking; Caulna seeming to rush past her companion, and the latter looking like a stationary star in the slowly moving sky.

CHAPTER XXV - APOSTACY.

We were received on landing by our former host and conducted to his house. On this occasion, however, I was not detained in the hall, but permitted at once to enter the chamber allotted to us. Eveena, who had exacted from me all that I knew, and much that I meant to conceal, respecting the occasion of our journey, was much agitated and not a little alarmed. My own humble rank in the Zinta rendered so sudden and imperative a summons the more difficult to understand, and though by this time well versed in the learning, neither of us was familiar with the administration of the Brotherhood. I was glad therefore on her account, even more than on my own, when, a scratch at the door having obtained admission for an ambâ, it placed before me a message from Esmo requesting a private conference. Her father's presence set Eveena's mind at rest; since she had learned, strangely enough from myself, what she had never known before, the rank he held among the brethren.

"I have summoned you," he said as soon as I joined him, "for more than one reason. There is but one, however, that I need now explain. Important questions, are as a rule either settled by the Chiefs alone in Council, or submitted to a general meeting of the Order. In this case neither course can be adopted. It would not have occurred to myself that, under present circumstances, you could render material service in either of the two directions in which it may be required. But those by whom the cause has been prepared have asked that you should be one of the Convent, and such a request is never refused. Indeed, its refusal would imply either such injustice as would render the whole proceeding utterly incompatible with the first principles of our cohesion, or such distrust of the person summoned as is never felt for a member of the Brotherhood. I would rather say no more on the subject now. Your nerve and judgment will be sufficiently tried to-night; and it is a valuable maxim of our science that, in the hours immediately preceding either an important decision or a severe trial, the spirit should be left as far as possible calm and unvexed by vague shadows of that which is to come."

The maxim thus expressed, if rendered into the language of material medicine, is among those which every man of experience holds and practically acts upon. I turned the conversation, then, by inviting Esmo into my own apartment; and I was touched indeed by the eager delight, even stronger than I had expected, with which Eveena welcomed her father, and inquired into the minutest details of the home life from which she had been, as it seemed to her, so long separated. What was, however, specially characteristic was the delicate care with which, even in this first meeting with one of her own family, she contrived still to give the paramount place in her attention to her husband, and never for a moment to let him feel excluded from a conversation with whose topics he was imperfectly acquainted, and in which he might have been supposed uninterested. The hours thus passed pleasantly away; and, except when Kevimâ, joined us at the evening meal, adding a new and unexpected pleasure to Eveena's natural delight in this sudden reunion, we remained undisturbed until a very low electric signal, sounding apparently through several chambers at once, recalled Esmo's mind to the duties before him.

"You will not," he said, "return till late, and I wish you would induce Eveena to ensure, by composing herself to sleep before your return, that you shall not be asked to converse until the morning."

He withdrew with Kevimâ, and, as instructed, I proceeded to change my dress for one of pure white adapted to the occasion, with only a band of crimson around the waist and throat, and to invest myself in the badge of the Order. The turban which I wore, without attracting attention, in the Asiatic rather than in the Martial form, was of white mingled with red; a novelty which seemed to Eveena's eyes painfully ominous. In Martial language, as in Zveltic symbolism, crimson generally takes the place of black as the emblem of guilt and peril. When Esmo re-entered our chamber for a moment to summon me, he was invested, as in the Shrine itself, in the full attire of his office, and I was recalled to a recollection of the reverence due to the head of the Brotherhood by the sudden change in Eveena's manner. To her father, though a most respectful, she was a fearlessly affectionate child. For Clavelta she had only the reverence, deeply

intermingled with awe, with which a devout Catholic convert from the East may approach for the first time some more than usually imposing occupant of the Chair of St. Peter. Before the arm that bore the Signet, and the sash of gold, we bent knee and head in the deference prescribed by our rules—a homage which the youngest child in the public Nurseries would not dream of offering to the Camptâ himself. At a sign from his hand I followed Esmo, hoping rather than expecting that Eveena would obey the counsel indirectly addressed to her. Traversing the same passages as before, save that a slight turn avoided the symbolic bridge, and formally challenged at each point as usual by the sentries, who saluted with profoundest reverence the Signet of the Order, we passed at last into the Hall of Initiation.

But on this occasion its aspect was completely changed. A space immediately in front of what I may call the veil of the Shrine was closed in by drapery of white bordered with crimson. The Chiefs occupied, as before, their seats on the platform. Some fifty members of the Order sat to right and left immediately below; but Esmo, on this occasion, seated himself on the second leftward step of the Throne, which, with the silver light and the other mystic emblems, was unveiled in the same strange manner as before at his approach. Near the lower end of the small chamber thus formed, crossing the passage between the seats on either hand, was a barrier of the bright red metal I have more than once mentioned, and behind it a seat of some sable material. Behind this, to right and left, stood silent and erect two sentries robed in green, and armed with the usual spear. A deep intense absolute silence prevailed, from the moment when the last of the party had taken his place, for the space of some ten minutes. In the faces of the Chiefs and of some of the elder Initiates, who were probably aware of the nature of the scene to follow, was an expression of calm but deep pain and regret; crossed now and then by a shade of anxiety, such as rarely appeared in that abode of assured peace and profound security. On no countenance was visible the slightest shadow of restlessness or curiosity. In the changed aspect of the place, the changed tone of its associations and of the feelings habitual to its frequenters, there was something which impressed and overawed the petulance of youth, and even the indifference

of an experience like my own. At last, stretching forth the ivory-like staff of mingled white and red, which on this occasion each of the Chiefs had substituted for their usual crystal wand, Esmo spoke, not raising his voice a single semitone above its usual pitch, but with even unwonted gravity—

"Come forward, Asco Zvelta!" he said.

The sight I now witnessed, no description could represent to one who had not seen the same. Parting the drapery at the lower end, there came forward a figure in which the most absolutely inexperienced eye could not fail to recognise a culprit called to trial. "Came forward," I have said, because I can use no other words. But such was not the term which would have occurred to any one who witnessed the movement. "Was dragged forward," I should say, did I attempt to convey the impression produced;—

save that no compulsion, no physical force was used, nor were there any to use it. And yet the miserable man approached slowly, reluctantly, shrinking back as one who strives with superior corporeal power exerted to force him onward, as if physically dragged on step by step by invisible bonds held by hands unseen. So with white face and shaking form he reached the barrier, and knelt as Esmo rose from his place, honouring instinctively, though his eyes seemed incapable of discerning them, the symbols of supreme authority. Then, at a silent gesture, he rose and fell back into the chair placed for him, apparently unable to stand and scarcely able to sustain himself on his seat.

"Brother," said the junior of the Chiefs, or he who occupied the place farthest to the right;—and now I noticed that eleven were present, the last seat on the right of him who spoke being vacant—"you have unveiled to strangers the secrets of the Shrine."

He paused for an answer; and, in a tone strangely unnatural and expressionless, came from the scarcely parted lips of the culprit the reply—
"

"It is true."

"You have," said the next of the Chiefs, "accepted reward to place the lives of your brethren at the mercy of their enemies."

"It is true."

"You have," said he who occupied the lowest seat upon the left, "forsworn in heart and deed, if not in word, the vows by which you willingly bound yourself, and the law whose boons you had accepted."

Again the same confession, forced evidently by some overwhelming power from one who would, if he could, have denied or remained silent.

"And to whom," said Esmo, interposing for the first time, "have you thus betrayed us?"

"I know not," was the reply.

"Explain," said the Chief immediately to the left of the Throne, who, if there were a difference in the expression of the calm sad faces, seemed to entertain more of compassion and less of disgust and repulsion towards the offender than any other.

"Those with whom I spoke," replied the culprit, in the same strange tone,

"were not known to me, but gave token of authority next to that of the Camptâ. They told me that the existence of the Order had long been known, that many of its members were clearly indicated by their household practices, that their destruction was determined; that I was known as a member of the Order, and might choose between perishing first of their victims and receiving reward such as I should name myself for the information I could give."

"What have you told?" asked another of the Chiefs.

"I have not named one of the symbols. I have not betrayed the Shrine or the passwords. I have told that the Zinta is. I have told the meaning of the Serpent, the Circle, and the Star, though I have not named them."

"And," said he on the left of the Throne, "naming the hope that is more than all hope, recalling the power that is above all power, could you dare to renounce the one and draw on your own head the justice of the other?

What reward could induce a child of the Light to turn back into darkness?

What authority could protect the traitor from the fate he imprecated and accepted when he first knelt before the Throne?" "The hope was distant and the light was dim," the offender answered. "I was threatened and I was tempted. I knew that death, speedy and painless, was the penalty of treason to the Order, that a death of prolonged torture might be the vengeance of the power that menaced me. I hoped little in the far and dim future of the Serpent's promise, and I hoped and feared much in the life on this side of death."

"Do you know," asked the last inquirer again, "no name, and nothing that can enable us to trace those with whom you spoke or those who employed them?"

"Only this," was the answer, "that one of them has an especial hatred to one Initiate present," pointing to myself; "and seeks his life, not only as a child of the Star, not only as husband of the daughter of Clavelta, but for a reason that is not known to me."

"And," asked another Chief, "do you know what instrument that enemy seeks to use?"

"One who has over her intended victim such influence as few of her sex ever have over their lords; one of whom his love will learn no distrust, against whom his heart has no guard and his manhood no wisdom."

A shiver of horror passed over the forms of the Chiefs and of many who sat near them, incomprehensible to me till a sudden light was afforded by the indignant interruption of Kevimâ, who sat not far from myself.

"It cannot be," he cried, "or you can name her whom you accuse."

"Be silent!" Esmo said, in the cold, grave tone of a president rebuking disorder, mingled with the deeper displeasure of a priest repressing irreverence in the midst of the most solemn religious rite. "None may speak here till the Chiefs have ceased to speak."

None of the latter, however, seemed disposed to ask another question. The guilt of the accused was confessed. All that he could tell to guide their further inquiries had been told. To doubt that what was forced from him was to the best of his knowledge true, was to them, who understood the mysterious power that had compelled the spirit and the lips to an unwilling confession, impossible. And if it had seemed that further

information might have been extracted relative to my own personal danger, a stronger tie, a deeper obligation, bound them to the supposed object of the last obscure imputation, and none was willing to elicit further charges or clearer evidence. Probably also they anticipated that, when the word was extended to the Initiates, I should take up my own cause.

"Would any brother speak?" asked Esmo, when the silence of the Chiefs had lasted for a few moments.

But his rebuke had silenced Kevimâ, and no one else cared to interpose.

The eyes of the assembly turned upon me so generally and so pointedly, that at last I felt myself forced, though against my own judgment, to rise.

"I have no question to ask the accused," I said.

"Then," replied Esmo calmly, "you have nothing now to say. Give to the brother accused before us the cup of rest."

A small goblet was handed by one of the sentries to the miserable creature, now half-insensible, who awaited our judgment. In a very few moments he had sunk into a slumber in which his face was comparatively calm, and his limbs had ceased to tremble. His fate was to be debated in the presence indeed of his body, but in the absence of consciousness and knowledge.

"Has any elder brother," inquired Esmo, "counsel to afford?"

No word was spoken.

"Has any brother counsel to afford?"

Again all were silent, till the glance which the Chief cast in order along the ranks of the assembly fell upon myself.

"One word," I said. "I claim permission to speak, because the matter touches closely and cruelly my own honour."

There was that inaudible, invisible, motionless "movement," as some French reporters call it, of surprise throughout the assembly which communicates itself instinctively to a speaker.

"My own honour," I continued, "in the honour dearer and nearer to me even than my own. What the accused has spoken may or may not be true."

"It is true," interposed a Chief, probably pitying my ignorance.

"May be true," I continued, "though I will not believe it, to whomsoever his words may apply. That no such treason as they have suggested ever for one moment entered, or could enter, the heart of her who knelt with me, in presence of many now here, before that Throne, I will vouch by all the symbols we revere in common, and with the life which it seems is alone threatened by the feminine domestic treason alleged, from whomsoever that treason may proceed. I will accuse none, as I suspect none; but I will say that the charge might be true to the letter, and yet not touch, as I know it does not justly touch, the daughter of our Chief."

A deep relief was visible in the faces which had so lately been clouded by a suspicion terrible to all. Esmo's alone remained impassive throughout my vindication, as throughout the apparent accusation and silent condemnation of his daughter.

"Has any brother," he said, "counsel to speak respecting the question actually before us?"

One and all were silent, till Esmo again put the formal question:—

"Has he who was our brother betrayed the brotherhood?"

From every member of the assembly came a clear unmistakable assent.

"Is he outcast?"

Silence rather than any distinct sign answered in the affirmative.

"Is it needful that his lips be sealed for ever?"

One or two of the Chiefs expressed in a single sentence an affirmative conviction, which was evidently shared by all present except myself.

Appealing by a look to Esmo, and encouraged by his eye, I spoke—

"The outcast has confessed treason worthy of death. That I cannot deny.

But he has sinned from fear rather than from greed or malice; and to fear, courage should be indulgent. The coward is but what Allah has made him, and to punish cowardice is to punish the child for the heritage his parents have inflicted. Moreover, no example of punishment will make cowards

brave. It seems to me, then, that there is neither justice nor wisdom in taking vengeance upon the crime of weakness."

In but two faces, those of Esmo and of his next colleague on the left, could I see the slightest sign of approval. One of the other chiefs answered briefly and decisively my plea for mercy.

"If," he said, "treason proceed from fear, the more cause that a greater fear should prevent the treason of cowardice for the future. The same motives that have led the offender to betray so much would assuredly lead him to betray more were he released; and to attempt lifelong confinement is to make the lives of all dependent on a chance in order to spare one unworthy life. The excuse which our brother has pleaded may, we hope, avail with a tribunal which can regard the conscience apart from the consequences. It ought not to avail with us."

But the law of the Zinta, as I now learned, will not allow sentence of death to be passed save by an absolutely unanimous vote. It is held that if one judge educated in the ideas of the Order, appreciating to the full the priceless importance of its teaching and the guilt of treason against it, is unpersuaded that there exists sufficient cause for the supreme penalty, the doubt is such as should preclude the infliction of that penalty. It is, however, permitted and expected that the dissentients, if few in number, much more a single dissentient, shall listen attentively and give the most respectful and impartial consideration to the arguments of brethren, and especially of seniors. If a single mind remains unmoved, its dissent is decisive. But it would be the gravest dereliction of duty to persist from wilfulness, obstinacy, or pride, in adhesion to a view perhaps hastily expressed in opposition to authority and argument. The debate to which my speech gave rise lasted for two hours. Each speaker spoke but a few terse expressive sentences; and after each speech came a pause allowing full time for the consideration of its reasoning. Two points were very soon made clear to all. The offender had justly forfeited his life; and if his death were necessary or greatly conducive to the safety of the rest, the mercy which for his sake imperilled worthier men and sacred truths would have been no less than a crime. The thought, however, that weighed most with

me against my natural feeling was an experience to which none present could appeal. I had sat on many courts-martial where cowardice was the only charge imputed; and in every case in which that charge was proved, sentence of death had been passed and carried out on a ground I could not refuse to consider sufficient:—namely, that the infection of terror can best be repressed by an example inspiring deeper terror than that to which the prisoner has yielded. Compelled by these precedents, though with intense reluctance, I submitted at last to the universal judgment. Esmo having collected the will, I cannot say the voices, of the assembly, paused for a minute in silence.

"The Present has pronounced," he said at last. "Are the voices of the Past assentient?"

He looked around as if to see whether, under real or supposed inspiration, any of those before him would give in another name a judgment opposite to that in which all had concurred. Instinctively I glanced towards the Throne, but it remained vacant as ever. Then, fixing his eyes for a few moments upon the culprit, who started and woke to full consciousness under his gaze—and receiving from the Chief nearest to him on the left a chain of small golden circles similar to that of the canopy, represented also on the Signet, while he on the right held a small roll, on the golden surface of which a long list of names was inscribed—our Superior pronounced, amid deepest stillness, in a low clear tone, the form of excommunication; breaking at the appropriate moment one link from the chain, and, at a later point, drawing a broad crimson bar through one cipher on the roll:—

"Conscience-convict, tried in truth,
Judged in justice, doomed in ruth;
Ours no more—once ours in vain—
Falls the Veil and snaps the Chain,
Drops the link and lies alone:—
Traitor to the Emerald Throne,
Alien from the troth we plight,
 Kature native to the night;
Trained in Light the Light to scorn,
Soul apostate and forsworn,
False to symbol, sense, and sign,
To the Serpent's pledge divine,
To the Wings that reach afar,
To the Circle and the Star;
Recreant to the mystic rule,
Outlaw from the sacred school—
Backward is the Threshold crossed;
Lost the Light, the Life is lost.
Go; the golden page we blot:
Go; forgetting and forgot!
Go—by final sentence shriven,
Be thy crime absolved in Heaven!"

Once more the Throne and the Emblems behind and above it had been veiled in impenetrable darkness. Instinctively, as it seemed, every one present had risen to his feet, and stood with bent head and downcast eyes as the Condemned, rising mechanically, turned without a word and passed away.

CHAPTER XXVI - TWILIGHT.

I was, perhaps, the only member of the assembly to whom the doomed man was not personally known, and to all of us the tie which had been severed was one at least as close as that of natural brotherhood on Earth.

How long the pause lasted—how, or why, or when we resumed our seats, even I knew not. The Shrine was unveiled, and Esmo's next colleague spoke again—

"A seat among the elders has been three days vacant by the departure of one well known and dear to all. His colleagues have considered how best it may be filled. The member they have selected is of the youngest in experience here; but from the first moment of his initiation it was evident to us that more than half the learning of the Starlight had been his before.

Nothing could so deeply confirm our joy and confidence in that lore, as to find that in another world the truths we hold dearest are held with equal faith, that many of our deepest secrets have there been sought and discovered by societies not unlike our own. For that reason, and because of that House, whereof now but two members are left us, he is by wedlock and adoption the third, the elder brethren have unanimously resolved to recommend to Clavelta, and to the Children of the Star, that this seat," and he pointed to the vacant place, "shall be filled by him who has but now expressed, with a warmth seldom shown in this place, his love and trust for the daughter of our Chief, the descendant of our Founder."

Certainly not on my own account, but from the earnest attachment and devotion they felt for Esmo, both personally as a long-tried and deservedly revered Chief, and as almost the last representative of a lineage so profoundly loved and honoured, the approval of all present was expressed with a sudden and eager warmth which deeply affected me; the more that it expressed an hereditary regard and esteem, not for myself but for Eveena, rarely or never, even among the Zveltau, paid to a woman. Esmo bent his head in assent, and then, addressing me by name, called me to the foot of the platform.

He held in his hand the golden sash and rose-coloured wand which marked the rank about to be bestowed on me. I felt very deeply my own
incompetence and ignorance; and even had I valued more the proffered honour, I should have been bound to decline it. But at the third word I spoke, I was silenced with a stern though perfectly calm severity. Flinging back the fold of his robe that covered his left arm, with a gesture that placed the Signet full before my eyes, he said—

"You have sworn obedience."

A soldier's instinct or habit, the mesmeric command of Esmo's glance, and the awe, due less to my own feeling than to the infectious reverence of others, which the symbols and the oaths of the Order extorted, left me no further will to resist. At the foot of the Throne I received the investiture of my new rank; and as I rose and faced my brethren, every hand was lifted to the lips, every head bent in salutation of their new leader. Then, as I passed to the extreme place on the right, they came forward to grasp my hand and utter a few words of sympathy and kindness, in which a frank spirit of affectionate comradeship, that reminded me forcibly of the mess-tent and the bivouac fire, was mingled with the sense of a deeper and more sacred tie.

Scarcely had we resumed our places than a startling incident gave a new turn to the scene. Approaching the barrier, a woman, veiled, but wearing the sash and star, knelt for a moment to the presence of the Arch-Teacher, and then, as the barrier was thrown open by the sentries, came up to the dais.

"She," said the new-comer, "has a message for you, Clavelta, for your Council, and particularly for the last of its members."

"It is well," he answered.

The messenger took her seat among the Initiates, and Esmo dismissed the assembly in the solemn form employed on the former occasion. Then, followed by the twelve, and guided by the messenger (the gloved fingers of whose left hand, as I observed, he very slightly touched with his own right), he passed by another door out of the Hall, and along one of the many passages of the subterrene Temple, into a chamber resembling in every respect an apartment in an ordinary residence. Here, with her veil, as

is permitted only to maidenhood, drawn back from her face, but covering almost entirely her neck and bosom, and clad in the vestal white, reclined with eyes nearly closed a young girl, in whose countenance a beauty almost spiritual was enhanced rather than marred by signs of physical ill-health painfully unmistakable. Warning us back with a slight movement of his hand, Esmo approached her. Our presence had at first seemed to cast her into almost convulsive agitation; but under his steady gaze and the movement of his hands, she lapsed almost instantly into what appeared to be profound slumber.

The practical information that concerned the present peril menacing the Order delivered, and when it was plain that no further revelation or counsel was to be expected on this all-important topic, Esmo beckoned to me, taking my hand in his own and placing it very gently and carefully in that of the unconscious sybil. The effect, however, was startling. Without unclosing her eyes, she sprang into a sitting posture and clasped my hand almost convulsively with her own long, thin all but transparent fingers.

Turning her face to mine, and seeming, though her eyes were closed, as if she looked intently into it, she murmured words at first unintelligible, but which seemed by degrees to bear clearer and clearer reference to some of the stormy scenes of my youth in another world. Then—as one looking upon pictures but partially intelligible to her, and commenting on them as a girl who had never seen or known the passions and the mutual enmity of men—she startled me by breaking into the kind of chant in which the peculiar verse of her language is commonly delivered. My own thought of the moment was not her guide. The Moslem battle-cry had rung too often in my ears ever to be forgotten; but up to that moment I had never recalled to memory the words in which on my last field I retorted upon my Arab comrades, when flinching from a third charge against those terrible "sons of Eblis," whose stubborn courage had already twice hurled us back in confusion and disgrace with a hundred empty saddles. At first her tone was one of simple amaze and horror. It softened afterwards into wonder and perplexity, and the oft-repeated rebuke or curse was on its last recurrence spoken with more of pitying tenderness and regret than of severity:—

"What! those are human bosoms whereon the brute hath trod!

What! through the storm of slaughter rings the appeal to God!

Through the smoke and flash of battle a single form is shown; O'er clang and crash and rattle peals out one trumpet-tone—

'Strike, for Allah and the Prophet! let Eblis take his own!'

"Strange! the soul that, fresh from carnage, quailed not alone to face The unfathomed depths of Darkness, the solitudes of Space!

Strange! the smile of scorn, while nerveless dropped the sword-arm from the sting,

On the death that scowled at distance, on the closing murder-ring.

Strange! no crimson stain on conscience from the hand in gore imbrued!

But Death haunts the death-dealer; blood taints the life of blood!

"Strange! the arm that smote and spared not in the tempest of the strife, Quivers with pitying terror—clings, for a maiden's life!

Strange! the heart steel-hard to death-shrieks by girlish tears subdued; The falcon's sheathless talons among the esve's brood!

But Death haunts the death-dealer; blood taints the life of blood.

"The breast for woman's peril that dared the despot's ire, Shall dauntless front, and scathless, the closing curve of fire.

The heart, by household treason stung home, that can forgive, Shall brave a woman's hatred, a woman's wiles, and live.

"A woman's well-won fealty shall give the life he gave, Love shall redeem the loving, and Sacrifice shall save.

But—God heal the tortured spirit, God calm the maddened mood; For Death haunts the death-dealer; blood taints the life of blood!"

Relaxing but not releasing her grasp of my own hand, she felt about with her left till Esmo gently placed his own therein. Then, in a tone at first of deep and passionate anxiety and eagerness, passing into one of regretful admiration, and varying with the purport of each utterance, she broke into another chant, in which were repeated over and again phrases familiar in the traditions and prophetic or symbolic formularies of the Zinta:—

"Ever on deadliest peril shines the Star with steadiest ray; Ever quail the fiercest hunters when Kargynda turns at bay.

Close, Children of the Starlight! close, for the Emerald Throne!

Close round the life that closeth your life within the zone!

Rests the Golden Circle's glory, rests the silver gleam on her Who shall rein Kargynda's fury with a thread of gossamer.

He metes not mortal measure, He pays not human price,

Who crowns that life's devotion with the death of sacrifice!

Woe worth the moment's panic; woe worth the victory won!

But the Night is near the breaking when the Stranger claims his own.

"Ever on deadliest peril shines the Star with steadiest ray; Ever quail the fiercest hunters when Kargynda turns at bay.

No life is worth the living that counts each fleeting breath; No eyes from God averted can meet the eyes of Death.

Vague fear and spectral terrors haunt the soul that dwells in shade, Nor e'er can crimson conscience confront the crimson blade.

From a cloud of shame and sorrow breaks the Light that shines afar, And cold and dark the household spark that lit the Silver Star.

The triumph is a death-march; the victor's voice a moan:—But the Powers of Night are broken when the Stranger wins his own!

"Ever in blackest midnight shines the Star with brightest ray;

Woe to them that hunt the theme if Kargynda cross the way!

In the Home of Peace, Clavelta, can our fears thy spirit move?

Look down! whence comes the rescue to the household of thy love?

As the All-Commander's lightning falls the Vengeance from above!

A shriek from thousand voices; a thunder crash; a groan; A thousand homes in mourning—a thousand deaths in one!

Woe to the Sons of Darkness, for the Stranger wields his own!

Oh, hide that scene of horror in the deepest shades of night!

Look upward to the welkin, where the Vessel fades from sight ...

But the Veil is rent for ever by the Hand that veiled the Shrine; And, on a peace of ages, the Star of Peace shall shine!"

Esmo listened with the anxious attention of one who believed that her every word had a real and literal meaning; and his face was overclouded with a calm but deep sadness, which testified to the nature of the impression made on his mind by language that hardly conveyed to my own more than a dim and general prediction of victory, won through scenes of trial and trouble. But when she had closed, a quiet satisfaction in what seemed to be the final promise of triumph to the Star, at whatever cost to the noblest of its adherents, was all that I could trace in his countenance.

The sibyl fell back as the last word passed her lips, with a sigh of relief, into what was evidently a profound and insensible sleep. Those around me must have witnessed such scenes at least as often as I; but it was plain that the impression made, even on the experienced Chiefs of the Order, was far deeper than had affected myself. I should hardly have been able to remember the words of the prophecy, but for subsequent conversation thereon with Eveena, when one part had been fulfilled and the rest was on the eve of a too terribly truthful fulfilment; but for the events that fixed their prediction in my mind—it may be in terms a little more precise than

those actually employed, though I have endeavoured to record these with conscientious accuracy.

Led by Esmo, we passed along another gallery into the small chamber where met the secret Council of the Order, and long and anxious were the debates wherein the revelations of the dreamer were treated as conveying the most certain and unquestionable warning. The first rays of morning were stealing through the mists into the peristyle of our host's dwelling before I re-entered Eveena's chamber. She was slumbering, but restlessly, and so lightly that she sprang up at once on my entrance. For a few moments all other thought was lost in the delight of my return after an absence whose very length had alarmed her, despite her father's previous assurance. But as at last she drew back sufficiently to look into my face, its expression seemed to startle and sadden her. The questions that sprang to her lips died there, as she probably saw in my eyes a look not only of weariness and perplexity, but of profound reluctance to speak of what had passed. Expressing her sympathy only by look and touch, she began to unclasp my robe at the throat, aware that my only wish was for rest, and content to postpone her own anxiety and natural curiosity. Then, as the golden sash which I had not removed met her sight, she looked up for a moment with a glance of natural pride and fondness, intensely gratified by the highly-prized honour paid to her husband; then bent low and kissed my hand with the gesture wherewith the presence of a superior is acknowledged by the members of the Order. "Used as my earlier life was, Eveena, to the Eastern prostrations of my own world, I hate all that recals them; and if I must accept, as I fulfil, these forms in the Halls of the Zinta, let me never be reminded of them by you."

CHAPTER XXVII - THE VALLEY OF THE SHADOW.

If I could have endured to describe to Eveena the terrible trial scene, that which occurred before she had the chance to question me would have certainly sealed my lips. The past night had told upon me as no fatigue, no anxiety, no disaster of my life on Earth had ever done. I awoke faint and exhausted as a nervous valetudinarian, and I suppose my feeling must have been plainly visible in my face, for Eveena would not allow me to rise from the cushions till she had summoned an ambâ and procured the material of a morning meal, though the hour was noon. Far too considerate to question me then, she was perhaps a little disappointed that, almost before I had dressed, a message from her father summoned me to his presence.

"It is right," he said quietly, and with no show of feeling, though his face was somewhat pale, "that you should be acquainted with the fulfilment of the sentence you assisted to pass. The outcast was found this morning dead in his own chamber. Nay, you need not start! We need no deathsman; alike by sudden disease, by suicide, by accident, our doom executes itself. But enough of this. I accepted the vote which invested you with the second rank in our Order, less because I think you will render service to it here than that I desired you to possess that entire knowledge of its powers and secrets which might enable you to plant a branch or offshoot where none but you could carry it ... That you will soon leave this world seemed to me probable, before the anticipations of practical prudence were confirmed by the voice of prophecy. Your Astronaut shall be stored with all of which I know you have need, and with any materials whose use I do not know that you may point out. To remove it from Asnyea would now be too dangerous. If you receive tidings that shall bring you again into its neighbourhood, do not lose the opportunity of re-entering it.... And now let me take leave of you, as of a dear friend I may not meet again."

"Do you know," I said, more touched by the tone than by the words, "that Eveena asked and I gave a promise that when I do re-enter it she shall be my companion?"

"I did not know it, but I took for granted that she would desire it, and I should have been grieved to doubt that you would assent. I cannot disturb her peace by saying to her what I have just said to you, and must part from her as on any ordinary occasion."

That parting, happily, I did not witness. Before evening we re-entered our vessel, and returned home without any incident worthy of mention.

To my surprise, my return plunged me at once into the kind of vexation which Eveena had so anxiously endeavoured to spare me, and which I had hoped Eunané's greater decision and less exaggerated tenderness would have avoided. She seemed excited and almost fretful, and before we had been half an hour at home had greeted me with a string of complaints which, on her own showing, seemed frivolous, and argued as much temper on her part as customary petulance on that of others. On one point, however, her report confirmed the suggestions of Eveena's previous experience. She had wrested at once from Eivé's hand the pencil that had hitherto been used in absolute secrecy, and the consequent quarrel had been sharp enough to suggest, if not to prove, that the privilege was of practical as well as sentimental moment. Though aggravated by no rebuke, my tacit depreciation of her grievances irritated Eunané to an extreme of petulance unusual with her of late; which I bore so long as it was directed against myself, but which, turned at last on Eveena, wholly exhausted my patience. But no sooner had I dismissed the offender than Eveena herself interposed, with even more than her usual tenderness for Eunané.

"Do not blame my presumption," she said; "do not think that I am merely soft or weak, if I entreat you to take no further notice of Eunané's mood. I cannot but think that, if you do, you will very soon repent it."

She could not or would not give a reason for her intercession; but some little symptoms I might have seen without observing, some perception of the exceptional character of Eunané's outbreak, or some unacknowledged misgiving accordant with her own, made me more than willing to accept Eveena's wish as a sufficient cause for forbearance. When we assembled at the morning meal Eunané appeared to be conscious of error; at all events, her manner and temper were changed. Watching her closely, I thought that neither shame for an outbreak of unwonted extravagance nor fear of my displeasure would account for her languor and depression. But illness is so rare among a race educated for countless generations on principles scientifically sound and sanitary, inheriting no seeds of disease from their ancestry, and safe from the infection of epidemics long extirpated, that no apprehension of serious physical cause for her changes of temper and complexion entered into my mind. To spare her when she deserved no indulgence was the surest way to call forth Eunané's best impulses; and I was not surprised to find her, soon after the party had dispersed, in Eveena's chamber. That all the amends I could desire had been made and accepted was sufficiently evident. But Eunané's agitation was so violent and persistent, despite all Eveena's soothing, that I was at last seriously apprehensive of its effect upon the latter. The moment we were alone Eveena said—

"I have never seen illness, but if Eunané is not ill, and very ill, all I have gathered in my father's household from such books as he has allowed me, and from his own conversation, deceives me wholly; and yet no illness of which I have ever heard in the slightest degree resembles this."

"I take it to be," I said, "what on Earth women call hysteria and men temper."

To this opinion, however, I could not adhere when, watching her closely, I noticed the evident lack of spirit and strength with which the most active and energetic member of the household went about her usual pursuits. A terrible suspicion at first entered my mind, but was wholly discountenanced by Eveena, who insisted that there was no conceivable motive for an attempt to injure Eunané; while the idea that mischief designed for others had unintentionally fallen on her was excluded by the certainty that, whatever the nature of her illness, if it were such, it had commenced before our return. Long before evening I had communicated with Esmo, and received from him a reply which, though exceedingly unsatisfactory, rather confirmed Eveena's impression. The latter had taken upon herself the care of the evening meal; but, before we could meet there, my own observation had suggested an alarm I dared not communicate to

her—one which a wider experience than hers could neither verify nor dispel. Among symptoms wholly alien, there were one or two which sent a thrill of terror to my heart;—which reminded me of the most awful and destructive of the scourges wherewith my Eastern life had rendered me but too familiar. It was not unnatural that, if carried to a new world, that fearful disease should assume a new form; but how could it have been conveyed? how, if conveyed, could its incubation in some unknown vehicle have been so long? and how had it reached one, and one only, of my household—one, moreover, who had no access to such few relics of my own world as I had retained, of which Eveena had the exclusive charge?

All Esmo's knowledge, even were he within reach, could hardly help me here. I dared, of course, suggest my apprehension to no one, least of all to the patient herself. As, towards evening, her languor was again exchanged for the feverish excitement of the previous night, I seized on some petulant word as an excuse to confine her to her room, and, selfishly enough, resolved to invoke the help of the only member of the family who should, and perhaps would, be willing to run personal risk for the sake of aiding Eunané in need and protecting Eveena. I had seen as yet very little of Velna, Eunané's school companion; but now, calling her apart, I told her frankly that I feared some illness of my own Earth had by some means been communicated to her friend.

"You have here," I said, "for ages had no such diseases as those which we on Earth most dread; those which, communicated through water, air, or solid particles, spread from one person to another, endangering especially those who come nearest to the sufferers. Whoever approaches Eunané risks all that I fear for her, and that 'all' means very probably speedy death. To leave her alone is impossible; and if I cannot report that she is fully cared for in other hands, no command, nothing short of actual compulsion, will keep Eveena away from her."

The girl looked up with a steady frank courage and unaffected readiness I had not expected.

"I owe you much, Clasfempta, and still more perhaps to Eveena. My life is not so precious that I should not be ready to give it at need for either of

you; and if I should lose Eunané, I would prefer not to live to remember my loss."

The last words reminded me that to her who spoke death meant annihilation; a fact which has deprived the men of her race of nearly every vestige of the calm courage now displayed by this young girl, indebted as little as any human being could be to the insensible influences of home affection, or the direct moral teaching which is sometimes supposed to be a sufficient substitute. I led her at once into her friend's chamber, and a single glance satisfied me that my apprehensions were but too well-founded. Remaining long enough to assure the sufferer that the displeasure I had affected had wholly passed away, and to suggest the only measures of relief rather than of remedy that occurred to me, I endeavoured for a few moments to collect my thoughts and recover the control of my nerves in solitude. In my own chamber Eveena would assuredly have sought me, and I chose therefore one of those as yet unoccupied. It did not take long to convince me that no ordinary resources at my command, no medical experience of my own, no professional science existing among a race who probably never knew the disease in question, and had not for ages known anything like it, could avail me. My later studies in the occult science of Eastern schools had not furnished me with any antidote in which I believed on Earth, and if they had, it was not here available. Despair rather than hope suggested an appeal to those which the analogous secrets of the Starlight might afford.

Anxiety, agitation, personal interest so powerful as now disturbed me, are generally fatal to the exercise of the powers recently placed at my command; so recently that, but for Terrestrial experience, I should hardly have known how to use them. But the arts which assist in and facilitate that tremendous all-absorbing concentration of will on which the exertion of those powers depends, are far more fully developed in the Zveltic science than in its Earthly analogues. A desperate effort, aided by those arts, at last controlled my thoughts, and turned them from the sick-room to that distant chamber in which I had so lately stood.

* * * * *

I seemed to stand beside her, and at once to be aware that my thought was visible to the closed eyes. From lips paler than ever, words—so generally resembling those I had previously heard that some readers may think them the mere recollection thereof—appeared to reach my sense or my mind as from a great distance, spoken in a tone of mingled pity, promise, and reproof:—

"What is youth or sex or beauty in the All-Commander's sight?
For the arm that smote and spared not, shall His wisdom spare to smite?
Yet, love redeems the loving; yet in thy need avail
The Soul whose light surrounds thee, the faith that will not fail.
Thy lips shall soothe the terror, call to yon couch afar The solace of the Serpent, the shadow of the Star!
Strength shall sustain the strengthless, nor the soft hand loose its grasp
Of the hand it trusts and clings to—till another meet its clasp....
—Steel-hard to man's last anguish, wax-soft to woman's mood!—
Death quits not the death-dealer; blood haunts the life of blood!"

Returning to the peristyle, I encountered Eveena, who had been seeking me anxiously. Much alarmed for her, I bade her return at once to her room. She obeyed as of course, equally of course surprised and a little mortified; while I, marvelling by what conceivable means the plague of Cairo or Constantinople could have been conveyed across forty million miles of space and some two years of Earthly time, paced the peristyle for a few minutes. As I did so, my eye fell on the roses which grew just where chance arrested my steps. If they do not afford an explanation which scientific medicine will admit, I can suggest no other. But, if it were so, how fearfully true the warning!—by what a mysterious fate did death dog my footsteps, and "blood haunt the life of blood!"

The reader may not remember that the central chamber of the women's apartments, next to which was Eunané's, had been left vacant. This I determined to occupy myself, and bade the girls remove at once to those on its right, as yet unallotted. I closed the room, threw off my dress, and endeavoured by means of the perfumed shower-bath to drive from my person what traces of the infection might cling to it; for Eveena had the keys of all my cases and of the medicine-chest, and I could not make up my mind to reclaim them by a simple unexplained message sent by an ambâ, or, still worse, by the hands of Enva or Eivé. I laid the clothes I had worn on one of the shelves of the wall, closing over them the crystal doors of the sunken cupboard; and, having obtained through the amban a dress which I had not worn since my return, and which therefore could hardly have about it any trace of infection, I sought Eveena in her own room.

That something had gone wrong, and gravely wrong, she could not but know; and I found her silent and calm, indeed, but weeping bitterly, whether for the apprehension of danger to me, or for what seemed want of trust in her. I asked her for the keys, and she gave them; but with a mute appeal that made the concealment I desired, however necessary, no longer possible. Gently, cautiously as I could, but softening, not hiding, any part of the truth, I gave her the full confidence to which she was entitled, and which, once forced out of the silence preserved for her sake, it was an infinite relief to give. If I could not observe equal gentleness of word and manner in absolutely forbidding her to approach, either Eunané's chamber or my own, it was because, the moment she conceived what I was about to say, her almost indignant revolt from the command was apparent. For the first and last time she distinctly and firmly refused compliance, not merely with the kindly though very decided request at first spoken, but with the formal and peremptory command by which I endeavoured to enforce it.

"You command me to neglect a sister in peril and suffering," she said. "It is not kind; it is hardly worthy of you; but my first duty is to you, and you have the right, if you will, to insist that I shall reserve my life for your sake.

But you command me also to forsake you in danger and in sorrow; and nothing but the absolute force you may of course employ shall compel me to obey you in that."

"I understand you, Eveena; and you, in your turn, must think and feel that I intend to express neither displeasure nor pain; that I mean no harshness to you, no less respect as well as love than I have always shown you, when I say that obey you shall; that the same sense of duty which impels you to refuse obliges me to enforce my command. At no time would I have allowed you to risk your life where others might be available. But if you were the only one who could help, I should, under other circumstances, have felt that the same paramount duty that attaches to me attached in a lighter degree to yourself. Now, as you well know, the case is different; and even were Eunané not quite safe in my hands and in Velna's, you must not run a risk that can be avoided. You will promise me to remain on this side the peristyle or in the further half of it, or I must confine you perforce; and it is not kind or right in this hour of trouble to impose upon me so painful a task."

With every tone, look, and caress that could express affection and sympathy, Eveena answered—

"Do what seems your duty, and do not think that I misunderstand your motive or feel the shadow of humiliation or unkindness. Make me obey if you can, punish me if I disobey; but obey you, when you tell me, for my own life's sake or for any other, to desert you in the hour of need, of danger, and of sorrow, I neither will nor can." I cut short the scene, bidding her a passionate farewell in view of the probability that we should not meet again. I closed the door behind me, having called her whom at this moment and in this case I could best trust, because her worse as well as her better qualities were alike guarantees for her obedience.

"Enva," I said, "you will keep this room till I release you; and you will answer it to me, as the worst fault you can commit, if Eveena passes this threshold, under whatever circumstances, until I give her permission, or until, if it be beyond my power to give it, her father takes the responsibilities of my home upon himself."

I procured the sedatives which might relieve the suffering I could not hope to cure. I wrote to Esmo, stating briefly but fully the position as I conceived it; and, on a suggestion from Eivé, I despatched another message to a

female physician of some repute—one of those few women in Mars who lead the life and do the work of men, and for whose attendance, as I remembered, Eunané had expressed a strong theoretical preference.

From that time I scarcely left her chamber save for a few minutes, and Velna remained constantly at her friend's side, save when, to give her at least a chance of escape, I sent her to her room to bathe, change her dress, and seek the fresh air for the half hour during which alone I could persuade her to leave the sufferer. The daftare (man-woman) physician came, but on learning the nature of the disease, expressed intense indignation that she had been summoned to a position of so much danger to herself.

I answered by a contemptuous inquiry regarding the price for which she would run so much risk as to remain in the peristyle so long as I might have need of her presence; and, for a fee which would ensure her a life-income as large as that secured to Eveena herself, she consented to remain within speaking distance for the few hours in which the question must be decided. Eunané was seldom insensible or even delirious, and her quick intelligence caught very speedily the meaning of my close attendance, and of the distress which neither Velna nor I could wholly conceal. She asked and extracted from me what I knew of the origin of her illness, and answered, with a far stronger feeling than I should have expected even from her—

"If I am to die, I am glad it should be through trying to serve and please Eveena.... It may seem strange, Clasfempta," she went on presently,

"scarcely possible perhaps; but my love for her is not only greater than the love I bear you, but is so bound up with it that I always think of you together, and love you the better that I love her, and that you love her so much better than me.... But," she resumed later, "it is hard to die, and die so young. I had never known what happiness meant till I came here.... I have been so happy here, and I was happier each day in feeling that I no longer made Eveena or you less happy. Ah! let me thank you and Eveena while I can for everything, and above all for Velna.... But," after another long pause, "it is terrible and horrible—never to wake, to move, to hear

your voices, to see you, to look upon the sunlight, to think, or even to dream again! Once, to remove a tooth and straighten the rest, they made me senseless; and that sinking into senselessness, though I knew I should waken in a minute, was horrible; and—to sink into senselessness from which I shall never waken!"

She was sinking fast indeed, and this terror of death, so seldom seen in the dying, grew apparently deeper and more intense as death drew near. I could not bear it, and at last took my resolve and dismissed Velna, forbidding her to return till summoned.

"Ah!" said Eunané, "you send her away that she may not see the last.

Is it so near?"

"No, darling!" I replied (she, like Eveena, had learnt the meaning of one or two expressions of human affection in my own tongue), "but I have that to say which I would not willingly say in her presence. You dread death not as a short terrible pain, and for you it will not be so, not as a short sleep, but as eternal senselessness and nothingness. Has it never seemed to you strange that, loving Eveena as I do, I do not fear to die? Though you did not know it, I have lived almost since first you knew me under the threat of death; and death sudden, secret, without warning, menacing me every day and every hour. And yet, though death meant leaving her and leaving her to a fate I could not foresee, I have been able to look on it steadily. Kneeling here, I know that I am very probably giving my life to the same end as yours. I do not fear. That may not seem strange to you; but Eveena knows all I know, and I could scarcely keep Eveena away. So loving each other, we do not fear to die, because we believe, we know, that that in us which thinks, and feels, and loves will live; that in death we lay aside the body as we lay aside our worn-out clothing. If I thought otherwise, Eunané, I could not bear this parting."

She clasped my hands, almost as much surprised and touched, I thought, for the moment by the expression of an affection of which till that hour neither of us were fully aware, as by the marvellous and incredible assurance she had heard.

"Ah!" she said, "I have heard her people are strange, and they dream such things. No, Clasfempta, it is a fancy, or you say it to comfort me, not because it is true."

The expression of terror that again came over her face was too painful for endurance. To calm that terror I would have broken every oath, have risked every penalty. But in truth I could never have paused to ask what in such a case oath or law permitted, "Listen, Eunané," I said, "and be calm.

Not only Eveena, not only I, but hundreds, thousands, of the best and kindliest men and women of your world hold this faith as fast as we do.

You feel what Eveena is. What she is and what others are not, she owes to this trust:—to the assurance of a Power unseen, that rules our lives and fortunes and watches our conduct, that will exact an account thereof, that holds us as His children, and will never part with us. Do you think it is a lie that has made Eveena what she is?"

"But you think, you do not know."

"Yes, I know; I have seen." Here a touch, breaking suddenly upon that intense concentration of mind and soul on a single thought, violently startled me, gentle as it was; and to my horror I saw that Eveena was kneeling with me by the couch.

"Remember," she said, in the lowest, saddest whisper, "'the Veil that guards the Shrine.'"

"No matter, Eveena," I answered in the same tone, the pain at my heart suppressing even the impulse of indignation, not with her, but with the law that could put such a thought into her heart. "Neither penalty nor oath should silence me now. Whether I break our law I know not; but I would forfeit life here—I would forfeit life hereafter, rather than fail a soul that rests on mine at such a moment."

The clasp of her hand showed how thoroughly, despite the momentary doubt, she felt with me; and I could not now recur to that secondary selfishness which had so imperiously repelled her from the sick-chamber.

"I have seen," I repeated, as Eunané still looked earnestly into my face, "and Eveena has seen at the same moment, one long ages since departed this

world—the Teacher of this belief, the Founder of that Society which holds it, the ancestor of her own house—in bodily form before us."

"It is true," said Eveena, in answer to Eunané's appealing look.

"And I," I added, "have seen more than once in my own world the forms of those I have known in life recalled, according to promise, to human eyes."

The testimony, or the contagion of the strong undoubting confidence we felt therein, if they did not convince the intellect, changed the tone of thought and feeling of the dying girl. Too weak now to reason, or to resist the impression enforced upon her mind by minds always far more powerful than her own in its brightest hours, she turned instinctively from the thought of blackness, senselessness eternal, to that of a Father whose hand could uphold, of the wings that can leap the grave. Her left hand clasped in mine, her right in Eveena's,— looking most in my face, because weakness leant on strength even more than love appealed to love—Eunané spent the remaining hours of that night in calm contentment and peace.

Perhaps they were among the most perfectly peaceful and happy she had known. To strong, warm, sheltering affection she had never been used save in her new home; and in the love she received and returned there was much too strange and self-contradicting to be satisfactory. But no shadow of jealousy, doubt, or contradictory emotion troubled her now: assured of Eveena's sisterly love as of my own hardly and lately won trust and tenderness.

The light had been long subdued, and the chamber was dim as dimmest twilight, when suddenly, with a smile, Eunané cried—

"It is morning already! and there,—why, there is Erme."

She stretched out her arms as if to greet the one creature she had loved—

perhaps more dearly than she loved those now beside her. The hands dropped; and Eveena's closed for ever on the sights of this world the eyes whose last vision had been of another.

CHAPTER XXVIII - DARKER YET.

Leading Eveena from the room, I hastily dictated every precaution that could diminish the danger to her and others. Velna had run risks that could not well be increased, and on her and on myself must devolve what remained to be done. I sent an ambâ to summon Davilo, gathered the garments that Eveena had thrown off, and removed them to the death-chamber. When the first arrangements were made, and I had paid the fee of Astona, the woman-physician, I passed out into the garden, and Davilo met me at the door of the peristyle. A few words explained all that was necessary. It was still almost dark; and as we stood close by the door, speaking in the low tone partly of sadness, partly of precaution, two figures were dimly discernible just inside, and we caught a few broken words.

"You have heard," said a harsh voice, which seemed to be Astona's, "there is no doubt now. You have your part to play, and can do it quickly and safely."

I paid little attention to words whose dangerous significance would at another moment have been plain to me. But Davilo, greatly alarmed, laid his hand upon my arm. As he did so, another voice thrilled me with intensest pain and amazement.

"Be quick to bear your message," Eivé said, in rapid guarded tones. "They have means of vengeance certain and prompt, and they never spare."

Astona departed without seeing us. Eivé closed the door, and Davilo and I, hastily and unperceived, followed the spy to the gate of the enclosure.

Some one waited for her there. What passed we could not hear; but, as we saw Astona and another depart, Davilo spoke imprudently aloud—

"She has the secret, and she must die. Nay (as I would have expostulated), she is spy, traitress, and assassin, and merits her doom most richly."

"Hist!" said I, "your words may have fallen into other ears;" for I thought that beyond the wall I discerned a crouching figure. If that of a man, however, it was too far off, and dressed in colours too dark, to be clearly seen; and in another instant it had certainly vanished.

"Remember," he urged, "you have heard that one quite as dangerous is under your own roof; and, once more, it is not only your life that is at stake.

What you call courage, what seems to us sheer folly, may cost you and others what you value far more than your life. An error of softness now may make your future existence one long and useless remorse."

Half-an-hour later, having warned the women to their rooms—ordering a variety of disinfecting measures in which Martial science excelled while they were needed there—I opened the door of the death chamber to those who carried in a coffer hollowed out of a dark, exceedingly dense natural stone, and half-filled with a liquid of enormous destructive power. Then I lifted tenderly the lifeless form, laid it on cushions arranged therein, kissed the lips, and closed the coffer. Two of Davilo's attendants had meantime adjusted the electric machinery. We carried the coffer into the apartment where this worked to heat the stove, to keep the lights burning, to raise, warm, and diffuse the water through the house, and perform many other important household services. Two strong bars of conducting metal were attached to the apparatus, and fitted into two hollows of the coffer. A flash, a certain hissing sound, followed. After a few moments the coffer was opened, and Davilo, carefully gathering a few handfuls of solid white material, something resembling pumice stone in appearance, placed them in a golden chest about twelve inches cube, which was then soldered down by the heat derived from the electric power. Then all infected clothes and the contents of the death chamber were carried out for destruction; while, with a tool adjusted to the machinery, one of the attendants engraved a few characters upon the chest. Whatever the risk, I could not part with every relic of her we had lost; and, after passing them through such chemical purification as Martial science suggested, I took the three long chestnut locks I had preserved. Velna's quick fingers wove them into plaits, one of which I left with her, one bound around my own neck, and one reserved for Eveena. As soon as the sun had risen, I had despatched a message to the Prince, explaining the danger of infection to which I had been subjected, and asking permission notwithstanding to wait upon him. The emergency was so pressing that neither sorrow nor peril would allow me to neglect an embassy on which the lives of hundreds, and perhaps the safety of his

kingdom, might depend. Passing Eivé as I turned towards Eveena's room, and fevered with intense thirst, I bade her bring me thither a cup of the carcarâ. I need not dwell on the terribly painful moments in which I bound round Eveena's arm a bracelet prized above all the choicest ornaments she possessed. To calm her agitation and my own by means of the charny, I sought the keys. They were not at my belt, and I asked, "Have I returned them to you?"

"Certainly not," said Eveena, startled. "Can you not find them?"

At this moment Eivé entered the room and presented me with the cup for which I had asked. It struck me with surprise, even at that moment, that Eveena took it from my hand and carried it first to her own lips. Eivé had turned to leave the room; but before she had reached the threshold Eveena had sprung up, placed her foot upon the spring that closed the door, and snatching the test-stone from my watch chain dipped it into the cup. Her face turned white as death, while she held up to my eyes the discoloured disc which proved the presence of the deadliest Martial poison.

"Be calm," she said, as a cry of horror burst from my lips. "The keys!"

"You have them," Eivé said with a gasp, her face still averted.

"I took them from Eveena myself," I answered sternly. "Stand back into that corner, Eivé," as I opened the door and called sharply the other members of the household. When they entered, unable to stand, I had fallen back upon a chair, and called Eivé to my side. As I laid my hand on her arm she threw herself on the floor, screaming and writhing like a terrified child rather than a woman detected in a crime, the conception and execution of which must have required an evil courage and determination happily seldom possessed by women.

"Stand up!" I said. "Lift her, then, Enva and Eiralé. Unfasten the shoulder-clasps and zone."

As her outer robe dropped, Eivé snatched at an object in its folds, but too late; and the electric keys, which gave access to all my cases, papers, and to the medicine-chest above all, lay glittering on the ground.

"That cup Eivé brought to me. Which of you saw her?"

"I did," said Enva quietly, all feelings of malice and curiosity alike awed into silence by the evidence of some terrible, though as yet to them unknown, secret. "She mixed it and brought it hither herself."

"And," I said, "it contains a poison against which, had I drunk one-half the draught, no antidote could have availed—a poison to which these keys only could have given access."

Again the test-stone was applied, and again the discoloration testified to the truth of the charge.

"You have seen?" I said.

"We have seen," answered Enva, in the same tone of horror, too deep to be other than quiet.

We all left the room, closing the door upon the prisoner. Dismissing the girls to their own chambers, with strict injunctions not to quit them unpermitted, I was left alone with Eveena. We were silent for some minutes, my own heart oppressed with mingled emotions, all intensely painful, but so confused that, while conscious of acute suffering, I scarcely realised anything that had occurred. Eveena, who knelt beside me, though deeply horror-struck, was less surprised and was far less agitated than I. At last, leaning forward with her arms on my knee and looking up in my face, she was about to speak. But the touch and look seemed to break a spell, and, shuddering from head to foot, I burst into tears like those of an hysterical girl. When, with the strongest effort that shame and necessity could prompt, aided by her silent soothing, I had somewhat regained my self-command, Eveena spoke, in the same attitude and with the same look:—

"You said once that you could pardon such an attempt. That you should ever forgive at heart cannot be. That punishment should not follow so terrible a crime, even I cannot desire. But for my sake, do not give her up to the doom she has deserved. Do you know" (as I was silent) "what that doom is?"

"Death, I suppose."

"Yes!" she said, shuddering, "but death with torture—death on the vivisection-table. Will you, whatever the danger—can you, give up to such a fate, to such hands, one whom your hand has caressed, whose head has rested on your heart?"

"It needs not that, Eveena," I answered; "enough that she is woman. I would face that death myself rather than, for whatever crime, send a woman, above all a young girl, to such an end. I would rather by far slay my worst enemy with my own hand than consign him to a death of torture.

But, more than that, my conscience would not permit me to call on the law to punish a household treason, where household authority is so strong and so arbitrary as here. Assassination is the weapon of the oppressed and helpless; and it is not for me so to be judge in my own cause as to pronounce that Eivé has had no provocation."

"Shame upon her!" said Eveena indignantly. "No one under your roof ever had or could have reason to raise a hand, I do not say against your life, but to give you a moment's pain. I do not ask, I do not wish you to spare her; only I am glad to think you will deal with her yourself—remember she has herself removed all limit to your power—and not by the shameless and merciless hands to which the law would give her."

We returned to Eveena's chamber. The scene that followed I cannot bear to recall. Enough that Eivé knew as well as Eveena the law she had broken and the penalty she had incurred; and, petted darling as she had been, she utterly lacked all faith in the tenderness she had known so well, or even in the mercy to which Eveena had confidently appealed. Understanding at last that she was safe from the law, the expression of her gratitude was as vehement as her terror had been intense. But the new phase of passion was not the less repugnant. Not that there was anything strange in the violent revulsion of feeling. Born and trained among a race who fear to forgive, Eivé was familiar by report at least with the merciless vengeance of cowards. Whatever they might have done later, few would have promised mercy in the very moment of escape to an ordinary assassin; and if Eivé understood any aspect of my character, that she could best appreciate was the outraged tenderness which forbade me to look on hers as ordinary

guilt. Acutely sensitive to pain and fear, she had both known the better to what terror might prompt the injured, and was the more appalled by the prospect. Her eagerness to accept by anticipation whatever degradation and pain domestic power could inflict, when released by the terrible alternative of legal prosecution from its usual limits, breathed more of doubt and terror than of shame or penitence. But at first it keenly affected me. It was with something akin to a bodily pang that I heard this fragile girl, so easily subdued by such rebuke or menace as her companions would scarcely have affected to fear, now pleading for punishment such as would have quelled the pride and courage of the most high-spirited of her sex. I felt the deepest pity, not so much for the fear with which she still trembled as for the agony of terror she must have previously endured. Eveena averted from her abject supplications a face in which I read much pain, but more of what would have been disgust in a less intensely sympathetic nature. And ere long I saw or felt in Eivé's manner that which caused me suddenly to dismiss Eveena from the room, as from a presence unfit for her spotless purity and exquisite delicacy. Finding in me no sign of passionate anger, no readiness, but reluctance to visit treason with physical pain, Eivé's own expression changed. Unable to conceive the feeling that rendered the course she had at first expected simply impossible to me, a nature I had utterly misconceived caught at an idea few women, not experienced in the worst of life's lessons, would have entertained. The tiny fragile form, the slight limbs whose delicate proportions seemed to me almost those of infancy, their irrepressible quivering plainly revealed by the absence of robe and veil, no man worthy of the name could have beheld without intense compassion. But such a feeling she could not realise. As her features lost the sincerity of overwhelming fear, as the drooping lids failed for one moment to conceal a look of almost assured exultation in the dark eyes, my soul was suddenly and thoroughly revolted. I had forgiven the hand aimed at a heart that never throbbed with a pulse unkind to her. I might have forgotten the treason that requited tenderness and trust by seeking my life; but I could never forget, never recover, that moment's insight into thoughts that so outraged an affection which, if my conscience belied me not, was absolutely stainless and unselfish.

It cost a strong persistent effort of self-control to address her again. But a confession full and complete my duty to others compelled me to enforce.

The story of the next hour I never told or can tell. To one only did I give a confidence that would have rendered explanation natural; and that one was the last to whom I could have spoken on this subject. Enough that the charming infantine simplicity had disguised an elaborate treachery of which I reluctantly learned that human nature is capable. The caressed and caressing child had sold my life, if not her own soul, for the promise of wealth that could purchase nothing I denied her, and of the first place among the women of her world. That promise I soon found had not been warranted, directly or indirectly, by him who alone could at present fulfil it. Needless to relate the details either of the confession or its extortion.

Enough that Eivé learnt at last perforce that though I had, as it seemed to her, been fool enough to spare her the vengeance of the law, and to spare her still as far as possible, her power to fool me further was gone for ever.

Needless to speak of the lies repeated and sustained, till truth was wrung from quivering lips and sobbing voice; of the looks that appealed long and incredulously to a love as utterly forfeited as misunderstood. To the last Eivé could not comprehend the nature that, having spared her so much, would not spare wholly; the mercy felt for the weakness, not for the charms of youth and sex. Shamed, grieved, wounded to the quick, I quitted the presence of one who, I fear, was as little worth the anguish I then endured for her, as the tenderness she had so long betrayed; and left the late darling of my house a prisoner under strict guard, necessary for the safety of others than ourselves.

Finding a message awaiting me, I sought at once the interview which the Sovereign fearlessly granted.

"I see," said the Prince with much feeling, as he received my salute, "that you have gone through deeper pain than such domestic losses can well cause to us. I am sorry that you are grieved. I can say no more, and perhaps the less I say the less pain I shall give. Only permit me this remark. Since I have known you, it has seemed to me that the utter distinction between our character and yours, showing as it does at so many points, springs from some single root-difference. We, so careful of our own life and comfort, care little for those of others. We, so afraid of pain, are indifferent to its infliction, unless we have to witness it, and only some of us flinch from the sight. The softness of heart you show in this trouble seems in some strange way associated with the strength of heart which you have proved in dangers, the least of which none of us would have encountered willingly, and which, forced on us, would have unnerved us all. I am glad to prove to you that to some extent I depart from my national character and approach, however, distantly, to yours. I can feel for a friend's sorrow, and I can face what you seem to consider a real danger. But you had a purpose in asking this audience. My ears are open—your lips are unsealed."

"Prince," I replied, "what you have said opens the way to that I wished to ask. You say truly that courage and tenderness have a common root, as have the unmanly softness and equally unmanly hardness common among your subjects. Those for whom death ends all utterly and for ever will of necessity, at least as soon as the training of years and of generations has rendered their thought consistent, dread death with intensest fear, and love to brighten and sweeten life with every possible enjoyment. Animal enjoyment becomes the most precious, since it is the keenest. Higher pleasures lose half their value, when the distinction between the two is reduced to the distinction between the sensations of higher and lower nerve centres. Thus men care too much for themselves to care for others; and after all, strong deep affection, entwined with the heartstrings, can only torture and tear the hearts for which death is a final parting. Such love as I have felt for woman—even such love as I felt for her, your gift, whom I have lost—would be pain intolerable if the thought were ever present that one day we must, and any day we might, part for ever. I put the knife against my breast, my life in your hand, when I say this, and I ask of you no secrecy, no favour for myself; but that, as I trust you, you will guard the life that is dearest to me if you take from me the power to guard it.... There are those among your subjects who are not the cowards you find around your throne, who are not brutal in their households, not incapable of tenderness and sacrifice for others."

As I spoke I carefully watched the Prince's face, on which no shade of displeasure was visible; rather the sentiment of one who is somewhat gratified to hear a perplexing problem solved in a manner agreeable to his wishes.

"And the reason is," I continued, "that these men and women believe or know that they are answerable to an eternal Sovereign mightier than yourself, and that they will reap, not perhaps here, but after death as they shall have sown; that if they do not forfeit the promise by their own deed, they shall rejoin hereafter those dearest to them here."

"There are such?" he said. "I would they were known to me. I had not dreamed that there were in my realm men who would screen the heart of another with their own palm."

"Prince," I replied earnestly, "I as their ambassador as one of their leaders, appeal to you to know and to protect them. They can defend themselves at need, and, it may be, might prevail though matched one against a thousand. For their weapons are those against which no distance, no defences, no numbers afford protection. But in such a strife many of their lives must be lost, and infinite suffering and havoc wrought on foes they would willingly spare. They are threatened with extermination by secret spite or open force; but open force will be the last resort of enemies well aware that those who strike at the Star have ever been smitten by the lightning."

A slight change in his countenance satisfied me that the Emblem was not unknown to him.

"You say," he replied, "that there is an organised scheme to destroy these people by force or fraud?"

"The scheme, Prince, was confessed in my own hearing by one of its instruments; and in proof thereof, my own life, as a Chief of the Order, was attempted this morning."

The Prince sprang to his feet in all the passion of a man who for the first time receives a personal insult; of an Autocrat stung to the quick by an unprecedented outrage to his authority and dignity.

"Who has dared?" he said. "Who has taken on himself to make law, or form plans for carrying out old law, without my leave? Who has dared to strike at the life over which I have cast the shadow of my throne? Give me their names, my guest, and, before the evening mist closes in to-morrow, pronounce their doom."

"I cannot obey your royal command. I have no proof against the only man who, to my knowledge, can desire my death. Those who actually and immediately aimed at my life are shielded by the inviolable weakness of sex from the revenge and even the justice of manhood."

"Each man," returned the Prince, but partially conceiving my meaning, "is master at home. I wish I were satisfied that your heart will let you deal justly and wisely with the most hateful offspring of the most hateful of living races—a woman who betrays the life of her lord. But those who planned a general scheme of destruction—a purpose of public policy—

without my knowledge, must aim also at my life and throne; for even were their purpose such as I approved, attempted without my permission, they know I would never pardon the presumption. I do not sit in Council with dull ears, or silent lips, or empty hands; and it is not for the highest more than for the lowest under me to snatch my sceptre for a moment."

"Guard then your own," I said. "Without your leave and in your lifetime, open force will scarcely be used against us; and if against secret murder or outrage we appeal to the law, you will see that the law does justice?"

"I will," he replied; "and I pardon your advice to guard my own, because you judge me by my people. But a Prince's life is the charge of his guards; the lives of his people are his care."

He was silent for a few minutes, evidently in deep reflection.

"I thank you," he said at last, "and I give you one warning in partial return for yours. There is a law which can be used against the members of a secret society with terrible effect. Not only are they exposed to death if detected, but those who strike them are legally exempt from punishment. I will care that that law shall not menace you long. Whilst it remains guard yourselves; I am powerless to break it."

As I quitted the Palace, Ergimo joined me and mounted my carriage.

Seizing a moment when none were within sight or hearing, he said—

"Astona was found two hours ago dead, as an enemy or a traitor dies. She was seen to fall from the roof of her house, and none was near her when she fell. But Davilo has already been arrested as her murderer, on the ground that he was heard before sunrise this morning to say that she must die."

"Who heard that must have heard more. Let this news be quickly known to whom it concerns."

I checked the carriage instantly, and turned into a road that conducted us in ten minutes to a public telegraph office.

"Come with me," I said, "quickly. As an officer of the Camptâ your presence may ensure the delivery of letters which might otherwise be stopped."

He seized the hint at once, and as we approached a vacant desk he said to the nearest officer, "In the Camptâ's name;" a form which ensured that the most audacious and curious spy, backed by the highest authority save that invoked, dared neither stop nor search into a message so warranted. Before I left the desk every Chief of the Zinta at his several post had received, through that strange symbolic language of which I have already given samples, from me advice of what had occurred and from Esmo warning to meet at an appointed place and time.

The day at whose close we should meet was that of Davilo's trial. I mingled with the crowd around the Court doors, a crowd manifesting bitter hostility to the prisoner and to the Order, of whose secrets a revelation was eagerly expected. Easily forcing my way through the mass, I felt on a sudden a touch, a sign; and turning my eyes saw a face I had surely never looked on before. Yet the sign could only have been given by a colleague.

That which followed implied the presence of the Signet itself.

"I told you," whispered a voice I knew well, "how completely we can change even countenance at will."

It was so; but though acquainted with the process, I had never believed that the change could be so absolute. By help of my strength and height, still more perhaps by the subtle influence of his own powerful will acting none the less imperiously on minds unconscious of its influence, Esmo made his way with me into the Court.

Around five sides of the hexagon were seats, tier above tier, appropriated to the public who wish to see as well as hear. The phonograph reported every word uttered to hundreds of distant offices. Against the sixth side were placed the seats of the seven judges; in front, at an equal elevation, the chair of the prisoner, the seats of the advocates on right and left, and the place from which each witness must deliver his testimony in full view and within easy hearing both of the bench, the bar, and the audience.

Davilo sat in his chair unguarded, but in an attitude strangely constrained and motionless. Only his bright eyes moved freely, and his head turned a little from side to side. He recognised us instantly, and his look expressed no trace of fear.

"The quârry" whispered Esmo, observing my perplexity.

"It paralyses the nerves of motion, leaving those of sensation active; and is administered to a prisoner on the instant of his arrest, so as to keep him absolutely helpless till his sentence is executed, or till on his acquittal an antidote is administered."

The counsel for the prosecution stated in the briefest possible words the story of Astona, from the moment when she left my house to that at which she was found dead, and the method of her death; related Davilo's words, and then proceeded to call his witnesses. Of course the one vital question was whether by possibility Davilo, who had never left my premises since the words were uttered, could have brought about a death, evidently accidental in its immediate cause, at a distance of many miles. His words were attested by one whom I recognised as an officer of Endo Zamptâ, and I was called to confirm or contradict them. The presiding judge, as I took my place, read a brief telling terrible menace, expounding the legal penalties of perjury.

"You will speak the truth," he said, "or you know the consequences."

As he spoke, he encountered Esmo's eyes, and quailed under the gaze, sinking back into his seat motionless as the bird under the alleged fascination of the serpent. I admitted that the words in question had been addressed to me; and I proved that Davilo had been busily engaged with me from that moment until an hour later than that of the fatal accident.

There being thus no dispute as to the facts, a keen contest of argument proceeded between the advocates on either side. The defenders of the prisoner ridiculed with an affectation of scientific contempt—none the less effective because the chief pleader was himself an experienced member of our Order—the idea that the actions or fate of a person at a distance could be affected by the mere will of another; and related, as absurd and incredible traditions of old to this purport, some anecdotes which had been communicated to me as among the best attested and most striking examples of the historical exercise of the mystic powers. The able and bigoted sceptics, who prosecuted this day in the interests of science, insisted, with equal inconsistency and equal skill, on the innumerable recorded and attested instances of some diabolical power possessed by certain supposed members of a detested and malignant sect. A year ago the judges would probably have sided unanimously with the former. But the feeling that animated the conspiracy, if it should be so called, against the Zinta, had penetrated all Martial society; and in order to destroy the votaries of religion, Science, in the persons of her most distinguished students, was this day ready to abjure her character, and forswear her most cherished tenets. As has often happened in Mars, and may one day happen on Earth as the new ideas come into greater force, proven fact was deliberately set against logical impossibility; and for once—what probably had not happened in Mars for ten thousand years—proven fact and common sense carried the day against science and "universal experience;"

but, unhappily, against the prisoner. After retiring separately for about an hour, the Judges returned. Their brief and very confused decisions were read by the Secretary. The reasons were seldom intelligible, each contradicting himself and all his colleagues, and not one among the judgments having even the appearance of cohesion and consistency. But,

by six to one, they doomed the prisoner to the vivisection-table. As he was carried forth his eyes met ours, and the perfect calm and steadiness of their glance astounded me not a little.

My natural thought prompted, of course, an appeal to the mercy of the Throne. In every State a power of giving effect in the law's despite to public policy, or of commanding that, in certain strange and unforeseen circumstances, common sense and practical justice shall override a sentence which no court bound by the letter of the law can withhold, must rest with the Sovereign. But in Mars the prerogative of mercy, in the proper sense of the word—judicial rather than political mercy—is exercised less by the Prince himself than by a small council of judges advising him and pronouncing their decision in his name. Even if we could have relied on the Camptâ with absolute confidence, there were many reasons against an appeal which would, in fact, have asked him to declare himself on our side.

While such a declaration might, in the existing state of public feeling, have caused revolt or riot, it would have put on their guard, perhaps driven to a premature attempt which he was not prepared to meet, the traitors whose scheme against his life the Prince felt confident that he should speedily detect and punish.

All these considerations were brought before our Council, whose debate was brief but not hurried or excited. The supreme calm of Esmo's demeanour communicated itself to all the eleven, in not one of whom could I recognise till they spoke my colleagues of our last Council. The order went forth that a party should attend Esmo's orders at a point about half a mile distant from the studio in which, for the benefit of a great medical school, my unhappy friend was to be put to torture indescribable.

"Happily," said Esmo, "the first portion of the experiment will be made by the Vivisector-General alone, and will commence at midnight. Half an hour before that time our party will be assembled."

I had insisted on being one of the band, and Esmo had very reluctantly yielded to the unanimous approval of colleagues who thought that on this occasion physical strength might render essential service at some unforeseen crisis. Moreover, the place lying within my geographical

province, several of those engaged looked up to me as their immediate chief, and it was thought well to place me on such an occasion at their head.

The night was, as had been predicted, absolutely dark, but the roads were brilliantly lighted. Suddenly, however, as we drew towards the point of meeting, the lights went out, an accident unprecedented in Martial administration.

"But they will be relighted!" said one of my companions.

"Can human skill relight the lamps that the power of the Star has extinguished?" was the reply of another.

We fell in military order, with perfect discipline and steadiness, under the influence of Esmo's silent will and scarcely discernible gestures. The wing of the college in which the dissection was to take place was guarded by some forty sentinels, armed with the spear and lightning gun. But as we came close to them, I observed that each stood motionless as a statue, with eyes open, but utterly devoid of sight.

"I have been here before you," murmured Esmo. "To the left."

The door gave way at once before the touch of some electric instrument or immaterial power wielded by his hand. We passed in, guided by him, through one or two chambers, and along a passage, at the end of which a light shone through a crystal door. Here proof of Esmo's superior judgment was afforded. He would fain have had the party much smaller than it was, and composed exclusively of the very few old and experienced members of the Zinta within reach at the moment. We were nearly a score in number, some even more inexperienced than myself, half the party my own immediate followers; and I remembered far better the feelings of a friend and a soldier than the lessons of the college or the Shrine. As the door opened, and we caught sight of our friend stretched on the vivisection table, the younger of the company, hurried on by my own example, lost their heads and got, so to speak, out of hand. We rushed tumultuously forward and fell on the Vivisector and two assistants, who stood motionless and perhaps unconscious, but with glittering knives just ready

for their fiendish work. Before Esmo could interpose, these executioners were cut down with the "crimson blade" (cold steel); and we bore off our friend with more of eagerness and triumph than at all befitted our own consciousness of power, or suited the temper of our Chief.

Never did Esmo speak so sharply or severely as in the brief reprimand he gave us when we reassembled; the justice of which. I instinctively acknowledged, as he ceased, by the salute I had given so often at the close of less impressive and less richly deserved reprimands on the parade ground or the march. Uninjured, and speedily relieved from the effects of thequârry, Davilo was carried off to a place of temporary concealment, and we dispersed.

Eveena heard my story with more annoyance than interest, mortified not a little by the reproof I had drawn upon myself and my followers; and, despite her reluctance to seem to acknowledge a fault in me, apparently afraid that a similar ebullition of feeling might on some future occasion lead to serious disaster.

CHAPTER XXIX - AZRAEL.

To detain as a captive and a culprit, thus converting my own house into a prison, my would-be murderess and former plaything, was intolerably painful. To leave her at large was to incur danger such as I had no right to bring on others. To dismiss her was less perilous than the one course, less painful than the other, but combined peril and pain in a degree which rendered both Eveena and myself most reluctant to adopt it. From words of Esmo's, and from other sources, I gathered that the usual course under such circumstances would have been to keep the culprit under no other restraint than that confinement to the house which is too common to be remarkable, trusting to the terror which punishment inflicted and menaced by domestic authority would inspire. But Eivé now understood the limits which conscience or feeling imposed on the use of an otherwise unlimited power. She knew very nearly how much she could have to fear; and, timid as she was, would not be cowed or controlled by apprehensions so defined and bounded. Eveena herself naturally resented the peril, and was revolted by the treason even more intensely than myself; and was for once hardly content that so heinous a crime should be so lightly visited. In interposing

"between the culprit and the horrors of the law, she had taken for granted the strenuous exertion of a domestic jurisdiction almost as absolute under the circumstances as that of ancient Rome.

"What suggested to you," I asked one day of Eveena, "the suspicion that so narrowly saved my life?"

"The carefully steadied hand—you have teased her so often for spilling everything it carried—and the unsteady eyes. But," she added reluctantly,

"I never liked to watch her—no, not lest you should notice it—but because she did not seem true in her ways with you; and I should have missed those signs but for a strange warning." ... She paused.

"I would not be warned," I answered with a bitter sigh. "Tell me, Madonna."

"It was when you left me in this room alone," she said, her exquisite delicacy rendering her averse to recal, not the coercion she had suffered, but the pain she knew I felt in so coercing her. "Dearest," she added with a

sudden effort, "let me speak frankly, and dispel the pain you feel while you think over it in silence."

I kissed the hand that clasped my own, and she went on, speaking with intentional levity.

"Had a Chief forgotten?" tracing the outline of a star upon her bosom. "Or did you think Clavelta's daughter had no share in the hereditary gifts of her family?"

"But how did you unlock the springs?"

"Ah! those might have baffled me if you had trusted to them. You made a double mistake when you left Enva on guard.... You don't think I tempted her to disobey? Eager as I was for release, I could not have been so doubly false. She did it unconsciously. It is time to put her out of pain."

"Does she know me so little as to think I could mean to torture her by suspense? Besides, even she must have seen that you had secured her pardon."

"Or my own punishment," Eveena answered.

"Spare me such words, Eveena, unless you mean to make me yet more ashamed of the compulsion I did employ. I never spoke, I never thought"—

"Forgive me, dearest. Will it vex you to find how clearly your flower-bird has learned to read your will through your eyes? When I refused to obey, and you felt yourself obliged to compel, your first momentary thought was to threaten, your next that I should not believe you. When you laid your hand upon my shoulder, thus, it was no gesture of anger or menace. You thought of the only promise I must believe, and you dropped the thought as quickly as your hand. You would not speak the word you might have to keep. Nay, dearest, what pains you so? You gave me no pain, even when you called another to enforce your command. Yet surely you know that that must have tried my spirit far more than anything else you could do.

You did well. Do you think that I did not appreciate your imperious anxiety for me; that I did not respect your resolution to do what you thought right, or feel how much it cost you? If anything in the ways of love

like yours could pain me, it would be the sort of reserved tenderness that never treats me as frankly and simply as" ... "There was no need to name either of those so dearly loved, so lately—and, alas! so differently—lost.

Trusting the loyalty of my love so absolutely in all else, can you not trust it to accept willingly the enforcement of your will ... as you have enforced it on all others you have ruled, from the soldiers of your own world to the rest of your household? Ah! the light breaks through the mist. Before you gave Enva her charge you said to me in her presence, 'Forgive me what you force upon me;' as if I, above all, were not your own to deal with as you will. Dearest, do you so wrong her who loves you, and is honoured by your love, as to fancy that any exertion of your authority could make her feel humbled in your eyes or her own?"

It was impossible to answer. Nothing would have more deeply wounded her simple humility, so free from self-consciousness, as the plain truth; that as her character unfolded, the infinite superiority of her nature almost awed me as something—save for the intense and occasionally passionate tenderness of her love—less like a woman than an angel.

"I was absorbed," she continued, "in the effort that had thrown Enva into the slumber of obedience. I did not know or feel where I was or what I had next to do. My thought, still concentrated, had forgotten its accomplished purpose, and was bent on your danger. Somehow on the cushioned pile I seemed to see a figure, strange to me, but which I shall never forget. It was a young girl, very slight, pale, sickly, with dark circles round the closed eyes, slumbering like Enva, but in everything else Enva's very opposite. I suppose I was myself entranced or dreaming, conscious only of my anxiety for you, so that it seemed natural that everything should concern you. I remember nothing of my dream but the words which, when I came to myself in the peristyle, alone, were as clear in my memory as they are now:—

"'Watch the hand and read the eyes;
On his breast the danger lies—
Strength is weak and childhood wise.
 "'Fail the bowl, and—'ware the knife!
Rests on him the Sovereign's life,
Rests the husband's on the wife.
"'They that would his power command
Know who holds his heart in hand:
Silken tress is surest band.
"'Well they judge Kargynda's mood,
Steel to peril, pain, and blood,
Surely through his mate subdued.
"'Love can make the strong a slave,
Fool the wise and quell the brave ...

Love by sacrifice can save.'"

"She again!" I exclaimed involuntarily.

"You hear," murmured Eveena. "In kindness to me heed my warning, if you have neglected all others. Do not break my heart in your mercy to another. Eivé"——

"Eivé!—The prophetess knows me better than you do! The warning means that they now desire my secret before my life, and scheme to make your safety the price of my dishonour. It is the Devil's thought—or the Regent's!"

As I could not decide to send Eivé forth without home, protection, or control, and Eveena could suggest no other course, the days wore on under a domestic thunder-cloud which rendered the least sensitive among us uncomfortable and unhappy, and deprived three at least of the party of appetite, of ease, and almost of sleep, till two alarming incidents broke the painful stagnation.

I had just left Eivé's prison one morning when Eveena, who was habitually entrusted with the charge of these communications, put into my hands two slips of tafroo. The one had been given her by an ambâ, and came from Davilo's substitute on the estate. It said simply: "You and you alone were

recognised among the rescuers of your friend. Before two days have passed an attempt will be made to arrest you." The other came from Esmo, and Eveena had brought it to me unread, as was indeed her practice. I could not bear to look at her, though I held her closely, as I read aloud the brief message which announced the death, by the sting of two dragons (evidently launched by some assassin's hand, but under circumstances that rendered detection by ordinary means hopeless for the moment), of her brother and Esmo's son, Kevimâ; and invited us to a funeral ceremony peculiar to the Zinta. I need not speak of the painful minutes that followed, during which Eveena strove to suppress for my sake at once her tears for her loss and her renewed and intensified terror on my own account. It was suddenly announced by the usual signs of the mute messenger that a visitor awaited me in the hall. Ergimo brought a message from the Camptâ, which ran as follows:—

"Aware that their treachery is suspected, the enemy now seek your secret first, and then your life. Guard both for a very short time. Your fate, your friends', and my own are staked on the issue. The same Council that sends the traitors to the rack will see the law repealed."

I questioned Ergimo as to his knowledge of the situation.

"The enemy," he said, "must have changed their plan. One among them, at least, is probably aware that his treason is suspected both by his Sovereign and by the Order. This will drive him desperate; and if he can capture you and extort your secret, he will think he can use it to effect his purpose, or at least to ensure his escape. He may think open rebellion, desperate as it is, safer than waiting for the first blow to come from the Zinta or from the Palace."

My resolve was speedily taken. At the same moment came the necessity for escape, and the opportunity and excuse. I sought out the writer of the first message, who entirely concurred with me in the propriety of the step I was about to take; only recommending me to apply personally for a passport from the Camptâ, such as would override any attempt to detain me even by legal warrant. He undertook to care for those I left behind; to release and provide for Eivé, and to see, in case I should not return, that full justice

was done to the interests of the others, as well as to their claim to release from contracts which my departure from their world ought, like death itself, to cancel. The royal passport came ere I was ready to depart, expressed in the fullest, clearest language, and such as none, but an officer prepared instantly to rebel against the authority which gave it, dared defy.

During the last preparations, Velna and Eveena were closeted together in the chamber of the former; nor did I care to interrupt a parting the most painful, save one, of those that had this day to be undergone. I went myself to Eivé.

"I leave you," I said, "a prisoner, not, I hope, for long. If I return in safety, I will then consider in what manner the termination of your confinement can be reconciled with what is due to myself and others. If not, you will be yet more certainly and more speedily released. And now, child whom I once loved, to whom I thought I had been especially gentle and indulgent, was the miserable reward offered you the sole motive that raised your hand against my life? Poison, I have always said, is the protection of the household slave against the domestic tyrant. If I had ever been harsh or unjust to you, if I had made your life unhappy by caprice or by severity, I could understand. But you of all have had least reason to complain. Not Enva's jealous temper, not Leenoo's spite, ever suggested to them the idea which came so easily and was so long and deliberately cherished in your breast."

She rose and faced me, and there was something of contempt in the eyes that answered mine for this once with the old fearless frankness.

"I had no reason to hate you? Not certainly for the kind of injury which commonly provokes women to risk the lives their masters have made intolerable. That your discipline was the lightest ever known in a household, I need not tell you. That it fell more lightly, if somewhat oftener, on me than on others, you know as well as I. Put all the correction or reproof I ever received from you into one, and repeat it daily, and never should I have complained, much less dreamed of revenge. You think Enva or Leenoo might less unnaturally, less unreasonably, have turned upon you, because your measure to their faults was somewhat harder and your heart colder to them! You did not scruple to make a favourite of me after a fashion, as you would never have done even of Eunané. You could pet and play with me, check and punish me, as a child who would not 'sicken at the sweets, or be humbled by the sandal.' You forbore longer, you dealt more sternly with them, because, forsooth, they were women and I a baby. I, who was not less clever than Eunané, not less capable of love, perhaps of devotion to you, than Eveena, I might rest my head on your knee when she was by, I might listen to your talk when others were sent away; I was too much the child, too little the woman, to excite your distrust or her jealousy.

Do you suppose I think better of you, or feel the more kindly towards you, that you have not taken vengeance? No! still you have dealt with me as a child; so untaught yet by that last lesson, that even a woman's revenge cannot make you treat me as a woman! Clasfempta! you bear, I believe, outside, the fame of a wise and a firm man; but in these little hands you have been as weak a fool as the veriest dotard might have been;—and may be yet."

"As you will," I answered, stung into an anger which at any rate quelled the worst pain I had felt when I entered the room. "Fool or sage, Eivé, I was your fellow-creature, your protector, and your friend. When bitter trouble befals you in life, or when, alone, you find yourself face to face with death, you may think of what has passed to-day. Then remember, for your comfort, my last words—I forgive you, and I wish you happy."

To Velna I could not speak. Sure that Eveena had told her all she could wish to know or all it was safe to tell, a long embrace spoke my farewell to her who had shared with me the first part of the long watch of the death-chamber. Enva and her companions had gathered, not from words, that this journey was more than an ordinary absence. Some instinct or presentiment suggested to them that it might, possibly at least, be a final parting; and I was touched as much as surprised by the tears and broken words with which they assured me that, greatly as they had vexed my home life, conscious as they were that they had contributed to it no element but bitterness and trouble, they felt that they had been treated with

unfailing justice and almost unfailing kindness. Then, turning to Eveena, Enva spoke for the rest—

"We should have treated you less ill if we could at all have understood you.

We understand you just as little now. Clasfempta is man after all, bridling his own temper as a strong man rules a large household of women or a herd of ambau. But you are not woman like other women; and yet, in so far as women are or think they are softer or gentler than men, so far, twelvefold twelve times told, are you softer, tenderer, gentler than woman."

Eveena struggled hard so far to suppress her sobs as to give an answer.

But, abandoning the effort, she only kissed warmly the lips, and clasped long and tenderly the hands, that had never spoken a kind word or done a kind act for her. At the very last moment she faltered out a few words which were not for them.

"Tell Eivé," she said, "I wish her well; and wishing her well, I cannot wish her happy—yet."

We embarked in the balloon, attended as on our last journey by two of the brethren in my employment, both, I noticed, armed with the lightning gun.

I myself trusted as usual to the sword, strong, straight, heavy, with two edges sharp as razors, that had enabled my hand so often to guard my head; and the air-gun that reminded me of so many days of sport, the more enjoyed for the peril that attended it. Screened from observation, both reclining in our own compartment of the car, Eveena and I spent the long undisturbed hours of the first three days and nights of our journey in silent interchange of thought and feeling that seldom needed or was interrupted by words. Her family affections were very strong. Her brother had deserved and won her love; but conscious so long of a peril surrounding myself, fearfully impressed by the incident which showed how close that peril had come, her thought and feeling were absorbed in me. So, could they have known the present and foreseen the future, even those who loved her best and most prized her love for them would have wished it to be. As we crossed, at the height of a thousand feet, the river dividing that continent between east and west which marks the frontier of Elcavoo, a

slight marked movement of agitation, a few eager whispers of consultation, in the other compartment called my attention. As I parted the screen, the elder of the attendant brethren addressed me—

"There is danger," he said in a low tone, not low enough to escape Eveena's quick ear when my safety was in question. "Another balloon is steering right across our path, and one in it bears, as we see through the pavlo (the spectacle-like double field-glass of Mars), the sash of a Regent, while his attendants wear the uniform of scarlet and grey" (that of Endo Zamptâ).

"Take, I beg you, this lightning-piece. Will you take command, or shall we act for you?"

Parting slightly the fold of the mantle I wore, for at that height, save immediately under the rays of the sun, the atmosphere is cold, I answered by showing the golden sash of my rank. We went on steadily, taking no note whatever of the hostile vessel till it came within hailing distance.

"Keep your guns steadily pointed," I said, "happen what may. If you have to fire, fire one at any who is ready to fire at us, the other at the balloon itself."

A little below but beside us Endo Zamptâ hailed. "I arrest you," he said, addressing me by name, "on behalf of the Arch-Court and by their warrant.

Drop your weapons or we fire."

"And I," I said, "by virtue of the Camptâ's sign and signet attached to this,"

and Eveena held forth the paper, while my weapon covered the Regent,

"forbid you to interrupt or delay my voyage for a moment."

I allowed the hostile vessel to close so nearly that Endo could read through his glass the characters—purposely, I thought, made unusually large—of his Sovereign's peremptory passport. To do so he had dropped his weapon, and his men, naturally expecting a peaceable termination to the interview, had laid down theirs. Mine had obeyed my order, and we were masters of the situation, when, with a sudden turn of the screw, throwing his vessel into an almost horizontal position, Endo brought his car into collision with ours and endeavoured to seize Eveena's person, as she leaned over with the paper in her hand. She was too quick for him, and I called out at once,

"Down, or we fire." His men, about to grasp their pieces, saw that one of ours was levelled at the balloon, and that before they could fire, a single shot from us must send them earthwards, to be crushed into one shapeless mass by the fall. Endo saw that he had no choice but to obey or affect obedience, and, turning the tap that let out the gas by a pipe passing through the car, sent his vessel rapidly downward, as with a formal salute he affected to accept the command of his Prince. Instantly grasping, not the lightning gun, which, if it struck their balloon, must destroy their whole party in an instant, but my air-gun, which, by making a small hole in the vast surface, would allow them to descend alive though with unpleasant and perilous rapidity, I fired, and by so doing prevented the use of an asphyxiator concealed in the car, which the treacherous Regent was rapidly arranging for use.

The success of these manoeuvres delighted my attendants, and gave them a confidence they had not yet felt in my appreciation of Martial perils and resources. We reached Ecasfe and Esmo's house without further molestation, and a party of the Zinta watched the balloon while Eveena and I passed into the dwelling.

Preserved from corruption by the cold which Martial chemistry applies at pleasure, the corpse of Kevimâ looked as the living man looked in sleep, but calmer and with features more perfectly composed. Quietly, gravely, with streaming tears, but with self-command which dispelled my fear of evil consequences to her, Eveena kissed the lips that were so soon to exist no longer. From the actual process by which the body is destroyed, the taste and feeling of the Zinta exclude the immediate relatives of the dead; and not till the golden chest with its inscription was placed in Esmo's hands did we take further part in the proceeding. Then the symbolic confession of faith, by which the brethren attest and proclaim their confidence in the universal all-pervading rule of the Giver of life and in the permanence of His gift, was chanted. A Chief of the Order pronounced a brief but touching eulogy on the deceased. Another expressed on behalf of all their sympathy with the bereaved father and family. Consigned to their care, the case that contained all that now remained to us of the last male heir of the Founder's house was removed for conveyance to the mortuary chamber of the subterrene Temple. But ere those so charged had turned to leave the chamber in which the ceremony had passed, a flash so bright as at noonday to light up the entire peristyle and the chambers opening on it, startled us all; and a sentinel, entering in haste and consternation, announced the destruction of our balloon by a lightning flash from the weapon of some concealed enemy. Esmo, at this alarming incident, displayed his usual calm resolve. He ordered that carriages sufficient to convey some twenty-four of the brethren should be instantly collected, and announced his resolve to escort us at once to the Astronaut. Before five minutes had elapsed from the destruction of the balloon, Zulve and the rest of the family had taken leave of Eveena and myself. Attended by the party mustered, occupying a carriage in the centre of the procession, we left the gate of the enclosure. I observed, what seemed to escape even Esmo's attention, that angry looks were bent upon us from many a roof, and that here and there groups were gathered in the enclosures and on the road, among whom I saw not a few weapons. I was glad to remember that a party of the Zveltau still awaited Esmo's return at his own residence. We drove as fast as the electric speed would carry us along the road I had traversed once before in the company of her who was now my wife—to be, I hoped, for the future my sole wife—and of him who had been ever since our mortal enemy. Where the carriages could proceed no further we dismounted, and Esmo mustered the party in order. All were armed with the spear and lightning gun. Placing Eveena in the centre of a solid square, Esmo directed me to take my place beside her. I expostulated—

"Clavelta, it is impossible for me to take the place of safety, when others who owe me nothing may be about to risk life on my behalf. Eveena, as woman and as descendant of the Founder, may well claim their protection.

It is for me to share in her defence, not in her safety."

He raised the arm that bore the Signet, and looked at me with the calm commanding glance that never failed to enforce his will. "Take your place,"

he said; and recalled to the instincts of the camp, I raised my hand in the military salute so long disused, and obeyed in silence.

"Strike promptly, strike hard, and strike home," said Esmo to his little party. "The danger that may threaten us is not from the law or from the State, but from an attempt at murder through a perversion of the law and in the name of the Sovereign. Those who threaten us aim also at the Camptâ's life, and those we may meet are his foes as well as ours.

Conquered here, they can hardly assail us again. Victorious, they will destroy us, not leave us an appeal to the law or to the throne."

Placing himself a little in front of the troop, our Chief gave the signal to advance, and we moved forward. It seemed to me a fatal error that no scout preceded us, no flanking party was thrown out. This neglect reminded me that, my comrades and commander were devoid of military experience, and I was about to remonstrate when, suddenly wheeling on the rocky platform on which I had first paused in my descent from the summit, and facing towards the latter, we encountered a force outnumbering our own as two to one and wearing the colours of the Regent. The front ranks quailed, as men always quailed under Esmo's steady gaze, and lost nerve and order as they fell back to right and left; a movement intended to give play to the asphyxiator they had brought with them. Their strategy was no less ridiculous than our own. Devoid for ages of all experience in conflict, both leaders might have learned better from the conduct of the theme at bay. The enemy were drawn up so near the turn that there was no room for the use of their most destructive engine; and, had we been better prepared, neither this nor their lightning guns would have been quick enough to anticipate a charge that would have brought us hand to hand. Even had they been steady and prompt, the suffocating shell would probably have annihilated both parties, and the discharge would certainly have been as dangerous to them as to us. In another instant a flash from several of our weapons, simultaneously levelled, shattered the instrument to fragments. We advanced at a run, and the enemy would have given way at once but that their retreat lay up so steep an incline, and neither to right nor left could they well disperse, being hemmed in by a rocky wall on one side and a precipitous descent on the other. From our right rear, however, where the ground would have concealed a numerous ambush, I apprehended an attack which must have

been fatal; but even so simple and decisive a measure had never occurred to the Regent's military ignorance.

At this critical moment a flash from a thicket revealed the weapon of some hidden enemy, who thus escaped facing the gaze that none could encounter; and Esmo fell, struck dead at once by the lightning-shot. The assassin sprang up, and I recognised the features of Endo Zamptâ.

Confounded and amazed, the Zveltau broke and fell backward, hurrying Eveena away with them. Enabled by size and strength to extricate myself at once, I stood at bay with my back against the rocks on our left, a projection rising as high as my knee assisting to hinder the enemy from entirely and closely surrounding me. I had thrown aside at the moment of the attack the mantle that concealed my sash and star; and I observed that another Chief had done the same. It was he who, occupying at the trial the seat on Esmo's left, had shown the strongest disposition to mercy, and now displayed the coolest courage amid confusion and danger.

"Rally them," I cried to him, "and trust the crimson blade [cold steel]. These hounds will never face that."

The enemy had rushed forward as our men fell back, and I was almost in their midst, thus protected to a considerable extent from the lightning projectile, against which alone I had no defence. Hand to hand I was a match for more than one or two of my assailants, though on this occasion I wore no defensive armour, and they were clad in shirts of woven wire almost absolutely proof against the spear in hands like theirs.

To die thus, to die for her under her eyes, leaving to her widowed life a living token of our love—what more could Allah grant, what better could a lover and a soldier desire? There was no honour, and little to satisfy even the passion of vengeance, in the sword-strokes that clove one enemy from the shoulder to the waist, smote half through the neck of a second, and laid two or three more dead or dying at my feet. If the weight of the sword were lighter here than on Earth, the arm that wielded it had been trained in very different warfare, and possessed a strength which made the combat so unequal that, had no other life hung on my blows, I should have been ashamed to strike. As I paused for a moment under this feeling, I noted

that, outside the space half cleared by slaughter and by terror, the bearers of the lightning gun were forming a sort of semicircle, embarrassed by the comrades driven back upon them, but drawing momentarily nearer, and seeking to enclose before firing the object of their aim. They would have shattered my heart and head in another instant but that—springing on the projecting stone of which I have spoken, which raised her to my level—

Eveena had flung her arms around me, and sheltered my person with her own. This, and the confusion, disconcerted the aim of most of the assailants. The roar and flash half stunned me for a moment;—then, as I caught her in my left arm, I became aware that it was but her lifeless form that I clasped to my breast. Giving her life for mine, she had made mine worse than worthless. My sword fell for a moment from my hand, retained only by the wrist-knot, as I placed her gently and tenderly on the ground, resting against the stone which had enabled her to effect the sacrifice I as little desired as deserved. Then, grasping my weapon again, and shouting instinctively the war-cry of another world, I sprang into the midst of the enemy. At the same moment, "Ent ân Clazinta" (To me the Zinta), cried the Chief behind; and having rallied the broken ranks, even before the sight of Eveena's fall had inspired reckless fury in the place of panic confusion, he led on the Zveltau, the spear in hand elevated over their heads, and pointed at the unprotected faces of the enemy. Exposed to the cold steel or its Martial equivalent, the latter, as I had predicted, broke at once. My sword did its part in the fray. They scarcely fought, neither did they fling down their weapons. But in that moment neither force nor surrender would have availed them. We gave no quarter to wounded or unwounded foe. When, for lack of objects, I dropped the point of my streaming sword, I saw Endo Zamptâ alive and unwounded in the hands of the victors.

"Coward, scoundrel, murderer!" I cried. "You shall die a more terrible death than that which your own savage law prescribes for crimes like yours. Bind him; he shall hang from my vessel in the air till I see fit to let him fall! For the rest, see that none are left alive to boast what they have done this day."

Struggling and screaming, the Regent was dragged to the summit, and hung by the waist, as I had threatened, from the entrance window of the Astronaut. Esmo's body and those of the other slain among the Zveltau had been raised, and our comrades were about to carry them to the carriages and remove them homeward. From the wardrobe of the Astronaut, furnished anew for our voyage, I brought a long soft therne-cloak, intended for Eveena's comfort; and wrapped in it all that was left to us of the loveliest form and the noblest heart that in two worlds ever belonged to woman. I shred one long soft tress of mingled gold and brown from those with which my hand had played; I kissed for the last time the lips that had so often counselled, pleaded, soothed, and never spoken a word that had better been left unsaid. Then, veiling face and form in the soft down, I called around me again the brethren who had fallen back out of sight of my last farewell, and gave the corpse into their charge. Turning with restless eagerness from the agony, which even the sudden shock that rendered me half insensible could not deaden into endurable pain, to the passion of revenge, I led two or three of our party to the foot of the ladder beneath the entrance window of my vessel, and was about in their presence to explain his fate more fully to the struggling, howling victim, half mad with protracted terror. But at that moment my purpose was arrested. I had often repeated to Eveena passages from those Terrestrial works whose purport most resembled that of the mystic lessons she so deeply prized; and words, on which in life she had especially dwelt, seemed now to be whispered in my ear or my heart by the voice which with bodily sense I could never hear again:— "Vengeance is Mine; I will repay." The absolute control of my will and conscience, won by her perfect purity and unfailing rectitude, outlasted Eveena's life. Turning to her murderer—

"You shall die," I said, "but you shall die not by revenge but by the law; and not by your own law, but by that which, forbidding that torture shall add to the sting of death, commands that 'Whoso sheddeth man's blood, by man shall his blood be shed.' Yet I cannot give you a soldier's death," as my men levelled their weapons. Cutting the cord that bound him, and grasping him from behind, I flung the wretch forth from the summit far into the air; well assured that he would never feel the blow that would

dismiss his soul to its last account, before that Tribunal to whose judgment his victim had appealed. Then I entered the vessel, waved my hand in farewell to my comrades, and, putting the machinery in action, rose from the surface and prepared to quit a world which now held nothing that could detain or recal me.

CHAPTER XXX - FAREWELL!

My task was not quite done. It was well for me in the first moments of this new solitude, of this maddening agony, that there was instant work imperatively demanding the attention of the mind as well as the exercise of the body. I had first, by means of the air pump, to fill the vessel with an atmosphere as dense as that in which I had been born and lived so long; then to close the entrance window and seal it hermetically, and then to arrange the steering gear. To complete the first task more easily, I arrested the motion of the vessel till she rose only a few feet per minute. Whilst employed on the air pump, I became suddenly aware, by that instinct by which most men have been at one time or another warned of the unexpected proximity of friend or foe, that I was not alone. Turning and looking in the direction of the entrance, I saw, or thought I saw, once more the Presence beheld in the Hall of the Zinta. But commanding, enthralling as were those eyes, they could not now retain my attention; for beside that figure appeared one whose presence in life or death left me no thought for aught beside. I sprang forward, seemed to touch her hand, to clasp her form, to reach the lips I bent my head to meet:—and then, in the midst of the bright sunlight, a momentary darkness veiled all from my eyes. Lifting my head, however, my glance fell, through the window to which the Vision had drawn me, directly upon Ecasfe and upon the home from which I had taken her whose remains were now being carried back thither.

Snatching up my field-glass, I scanned the scene of which I had thus caught a momentary and confused glimpse. The roof was occupied by a score of men armed with the lightning weapon, and among them glanced the familiar badge—the band and silver star. Clambering over the walls of the wide enclosure, and threatening to storm the house, were a mob perhaps a thousand in number, many of them similarly armed, the rest with staves, spears, or such rude weapons as chance might afford. Two minutes brought me immediately over them. In another, I was descending more rapidly than prudence would have suggested. The strife seemed for a moment to cease, as one of the crowd pointed, not to the impending destruction overhead, but to some object apparently at an equal elevation to westward. A shout of welcome from the remaining defenders of the

house called right upward the eyes of their assailants. For an instant they felt the bitterness of death; a cry of agony and terror that pierced even the thick walls and windows of the Astronaut reached my ears. Then a violent shock threw me from my feet. Springing up, I knew what wholesale slaughter had avenged Eveena and her father, preserved her family, and given a last victory to the Symbol she so revered. In another instant I was on the roof, and my hands clasped in Zulve's.

"We know," she said. "Our darling's esve brought us a line that told all; and what is left of those who were all to me, of her who was so much to you, will now be returned to us almost at once."

We were interrupted. A cry drew my eyes to the right, where, springing from a balloon to the car of which was attached a huge flag emblazoned with the crimson and silver colours of the Suzerain, Ergimo stood before us.

"I am too late," he said, "to save life; in time only to put an end to rebellion and avert murder. The Prince has fulfilled his promise to you; has repealed the law that was to be a weapon in the hands that aimed at his life and throne, as at the Star and its children. The traitors, save one, the worst, have met by this time their just doom. That one I am here to arrest. But where is our Chief? And," noticing for the first time the group of women, who in the violence of alarm and agony of sorrow had burst for once unconsciously the restraints of a lifetime—"where ... Are you alone?"

"Alone for ever," I said; and as I spoke the procession that with bare and bent heads carried two veiled forms into the peristyle below told all he sought to know. I need not dwell on the scene that followed. I scarcely remember anything, till a chest of gold, bearing the cipher which though seldom seen I knew so well, was placed in my hands. I turned to Zulve, and to Ergimo, who stood beside her.

"Have you need of me?" I said. "If I can serve her house I will remain willingly, and as long as I can help or comfort."

"No," replied Ergimo; for Zulve could not speak. "The household of Clavelta are safe and honoured henceforth as no other in the land.

Something we must ask of him who is, at any rate for the present, the head of this household, and the representative of the Founder's lineage. It may be," he whispered, "that another" (and his eyes fell on the veiled forms whose pink robes covered with dark crimson gauze indicated the younger matrons of the family) "may yet give to the Children of the Star that natural heir to the Signet we had hoped from your own household. But the Order cannot remain headless."

Here Zulve, approaching, gave into my hand the Signet unclasped from her husband's arm ere the coffer was closed upon his form. I understood her meaning; and, as for the time the sole male representative of the house, I clasped it on the arm of the Chief who succeeded to Esmo's rank, and to whom I felt the care of Esmo's house might be safely left. The due honour paid to his new office, I turned to depart. Then for the first time my eyes fell on the unveiled countenance and drooping form of one unlike, yet so like Eveena—her favourite and nearest sister, Zevle. I held out my hand; but, emotion overcoming the habits of reserve, she threw herself into my arms, and her tears fell on my bosom, hardly faster than my own as I stooped and kissed her brow. I had no voice to speak my farewell. But as the Astronaut rose for the last time from the ground, the voices of my brethren chanted in adieu the last few lines of the familiar formula—

"Peace be yours no force can break,
Peace not Death hath power to shake;"
"Peace from peril, fear, and pain;
Peace—until we meet again!
Not before the sculptured stone,
But the All-Commander's Throne."

Printed in Great Britain
by Amazon